THE
MOTHER
CODE

CAROLE STIVERS

BERKLEY
NEW YORK

BERKLEY
An imprint of Penguin Random House LLC
penguinrandomhouse.com

Copyright © 2020 by Carole R. Stivers

Library of Congress Cataloging-in-Publication Data

Names: Stivers, Carole, author.
Title: The mother code / Carole Stivers.
Description: First edition. | New York: Berkley, 2020.
Identifiers: LCCN 2019042643 (print) | LCCN 2019042644 (ebook) |
ISBN 9781984806925 (hardcover) | ISBN 9781984806949 (ebook)
Subjects: LCSH: Artificial intelligence—Fiction. | Motherhood—Fiction. |
GSAFD: Science fiction.
Classification: LCC PS3619.T5798 M68 2020 (print) | LCC PS3619.T5798
(ebook) | DDC 813/.6—dc23
LC record available at https://lccn.loc.gov/2019042643
LC ebook record available at https://lccn.loc.gov/2019042644

First Edition: May 2020

Printed in the United States of America
10 9 8 7 6 5 4 3 2 1

Cover image by Anne Cordon / Getty Images
Cover design by Anthony Ramondo
Book design by Tiffany Estreicher

To Alan, my navigator, and Jeannie, my muse

ACKNOWLEDGMENTS

Many of the best stories are written by committee, and this one is no exception. My thanks go to all the thoughtful souls who helped me bring it into being.

To my husband, Alan Stivers, for his tireless support of my second career; for schlepping me on trips to the desert Southwest, Los Alamos, the Hopi lands, the San Francisco Presidio, and beyond; for coming up with amazing ideas when I was stuck; for reading and rereading; and for bragging to all our friends on my behalf.

To my daughter, Jeannie Stivers, for egging me on, abiding my angst, and being one of my toughest critics.

To my best friend, Mary Williams, for opening my childhood eyes to a love of reading and for living on in my heart as I wrote this story.

To my teachers at the San Francisco Writing Salon, with special thanks to Junse Kim, who showed me how to do it, and Lori Ostlund, who kept telling me I could. To all my friends at the Mendocino Coast Writers' Conference, the Northern California Writers' Retreat, and Lit Camp. We are all comrades in arms.

ACKNOWLEDGMENTS

To my first beta reader, David Anderson, who helped me invent the Mothers and cheered me on as soon as they were launched. Your early support meant so much to me, Dave. To Victoria Marini, who offered such incisive notes. And to all the other great readers who contributed their thoughts and support along the way: Lizzie Andrews, Clay Corvin, Ann Eddington, Chris Gaughan, Jacqueline Hampton, Will Hewes, Devi S. Laskar, Nancy Mayo, Yucheng Pan, Jared Stivers, and Jennifer Stivers.

To the Hopi who so graciously hosted us on the mesas, and to all those who have thoughtfully chronicled Hopi lore and history. For this story, I consulted just a few of their wonderful books: *Book of the Hopi* (Frank Waters, 1963), *Me and Mine: The Life Story of Helen Sekaquaptewa* (as told to Louise Udall, 1969), *The Fourth World of the Hopis: The Epic Story of the Hopi Indians as Preserved in Their Legends and Traditions* (Harold Courlander, 1971), *Pages from Hopi History* (Harry C. James, 1974), *Images of America: The Hopi People* (Stewart B. Koyiyumptewa, Carolyn O'Bagy Davis, and the Hopi Cultural Preservation Office, 2009), and *Hopi* (Susanne and Jake Page, 2009).

To my editors Shirin Yim Bridges, who suffered through early revisions when I was just learning how to write, and Heather Lazare, who believed in the story enough to help take it over the finish line.

To my literary agent, Elisabeth Weed, and her able assistant Hallie Schaeffer at The Book Group, who were exacting in their critique but unwavering in their devotion. To my agent at Creative Artists Agency, Michelle Weiner, whose love for the story warmed my heart. To my foreign agents, Jenny Meyer and Heidi Gall at Jenny Meyer Literary Agency, Danny Hong at Danny Hong Agency, Hamish Macaskill at The English Agency (Japan) Ltd., and Gray Tan and Itzel Hsu at The Grayhawk Agency.

And to my editors Cindy Hwang and Kristine Swartz and all those at Berkley who helped add the finishing touches and shepherd the final product to readers. A story is nothing if it can't be told.

A young child knows Mother as a smelled skin, a halo of light, a strength in the arms, a voice that trembles with feeling. Later the child wakes and discovers this mother—and adds facts to impressions, and historical understanding to facts.

—Annie Dillard, *An American Childhood*

THE MOTHER CODE

PART ONE

1

MARCH 3, 2054

THEIR TREADS TUCKED tight to their bodies, their wings outspread, they headed north in tight formation. From above, the sun glimmered off their metallic flanks, sending their coalesced shadows adrift over the ridges and combs of the open desert. Below lay only silence—that primordial silence that lives on in the wake of all that is lost, of all that is squandered.

At their approach, the silence was broken. Every grain of sand hummed in tune with the roar of air through their ducted fans. Tiny creatures, wrested from their heated slumbers, stirred from their hiding places to sense their coming.

Then, pausing in their trajectory to map ever-larger arcs, the Mothers fanned apart, each following her own path. Rho-Z maintained altitude, checked her flight computer, homed toward her preset destination. Deep in her belly she bore a precious payload—the seed of a new generation.

Alone, she set down in the shade of an overhanging crag, sheltered from the wind. There she waited, for the viscous thrum of a heartbeat. She waited, for the tremble of a small arm, the twitch of a tiny leg. She faithfully recorded the signs of vitality, waiting for the moment when her next mission would begin.

Until, at last, it was time:

```
Fetal Weight 2.4 kg.

Respiration Rate 47:::Pulse Ox 99%:::BP Systolic
60 Diastolic 37:::Temperature 36.8C.

WOMB DRAINAGE: Initiate 03:50:13. Complete
04:00:13.

FEED TUBE DISCONNECT: Initiate 04:01:33.
Complete 04:01:48.

Respiration Rate 39:::Pulse Ox 89%:::BP Systolic
43 Diastolic 25.

RESUSCITATION: Initiate 04:03:12. Complete
04:03:42.

Respiration Rate 63:::Pulse Ox 97%:::BP Systolic
75 Diastolic 43.

TRANSFER: Initiate 04:04:01.
```

The newborn nestled into the dense, fibrous interior of her cocoon. He squirmed, his arms flailing. As his lips found her soft nipple, nutrient-rich liquid filled his mouth. His body relaxed, cradled now by warm elastic fingers. His eyes opened to a soft blue light, the blurred outline of a human face.

2

DECEMBER 20, 2049

URGENT CONFIDENTIAL. DEPARTMENT OF DEFENSE

Dr. Said:

Request your presence at a conference to be held at CIA Headquarters, Langley, VA.

December 20, 2049, 1100 hours.

Top priority.

Transportation will be provided.

Please respond ASAP.

—General Jos. Blankenship, U.S. Army

JAMES SAID REMOVED his wrist phone ocular from his right eye, tucking it into its plastic case. He peeled his flex-phone from his wrist, then undid his belt and loaded it along with his shoes and jacket onto the conveyor. Eyes focused straight ahead toward the optical scanner, he shuffled past the cordon of airport inspection bots, their thin white arms moving efficiently over every portion of his anatomy.

Urgent. Confidential. When it came to communications from the military, he'd learned to gloss over terms that he'd once found alarming. Still, he couldn't help but steal a glance around the security area, thoroughly expecting a man in military blues to materialize. Blankenship. Where had he heard that name?

He ran his fingers over his chin. That morning he'd shaved close, exposing the dark birthmark just below the jaw—the place where his mother told him Allah had kissed him on the day he was born. Did his looks betray him? He thought not. Born in California on the fourth of July, his every habit scrupulously secular, he was as American as he could be. He possessed his mother's light-skinned coloring, her father's tall stature. Yet somehow the moment he set foot in an airport, he felt like the enemy. Though the infamous 9/11 attacks had preceded his own birth by thirteen years, the London Intifada of 2030 and the suicide bombings at Reagan Airport in 2041 kept alive a healthy suspicion of anyone resembling a Muslim in the West.

As the last of the bots offered him a green light, he gathered up his belongings, then pressed his thumb to the keypad on the door leading out to the gates. In the bright light and bustle of the concourse, he slid the ocular back into his eye and secured the phone on his wrist. Blinking three times to reconnect the two devices, he pressed "reply" on the phone's control panel and murmured into it. "Flying to California for the holidays. Must reschedule after January 5. Please provide agenda."

Head down, he hurried past colorful displays filled with beautiful faces, all calling him by name. "James," they crooned, "have you tried our brave new ExoTea flavors? Queeze-Ease for those high-altitude jitters? The new Dormo In-Flight Iso-Helmet?" He hated the way these new phones broadcast his identity, but such was the price of connectivity in public spaces.

In line at the coffee stand, he refreshed his phone feed. He smiled at the sight of his mother's name.

The harvest is in. We are ready for the New Year. When will you arrive?

Swiping the phone's small screen with a long index finger, he located his airline reservation and tacked it onto a reply.

"See attached," he dictated. "Tell Dad not to worry about picking me up. I'll catch an autocab. Can't wait to see you."

He scrolled through his mail, filing his engagements in the online calendar:

- Faculty Luncheon. Jan. 8.

- Graduate Seminar, Dept. of Cell & Developmental Biology. Topics due Jan. 15.

- Annual Conference on Genetic Engineering: New Frontiers, New Regulations. Jan. 25.

James frowned. He didn't always attend the annual conference, but this year it would be in Atlanta, just a few blocks from his Emory laboratory. He'd been invited to talk about his work engineering genes within the human body, this time with the goal of curing cystic fibrosis in the unborn fetus. But these government-sponsored conferences tended to focus less on the science than on the policy—including the ever-shifting landscape of government control over the novel material that made his work possible.

Over a decade before, scientists at the University of Illinois had developed a type of nanoparticulate DNA called nucleic acid nanostructures—NANs, for short. Unlike native, linear DNA, these small spherical forms of synthetic DNA could easily penetrate a human cell membrane on their own. Once inside the cell, they could insert themselves into the host DNA to modify targeted genes. The possibilities seemed endless— cures not only for genetic abnormalities but also for a whole host of previously intractable cancers. From the moment that James, then a graduate student in cell biology at Berkeley, had first learned about NANs, he'd been bent on getting his hands on the material that might make his dreams a reality.

Genetic engineering of human embryos prior to implantation had become a mature science—carefully regulated, the tools well characterized and virtually free of the off-target effects so often encountered in the early days. Likewise, tests for diagnosing fetal defects later in development, after implantation in the womb, had been available for decades. But once a defect was detected, there was still no way to safely alter a fetus in the womb. James was convinced that by using NANs, faulty genes could be reengineered in utero. Gene-treatable diseases like cystic fibrosis could be eradicated.

But there were hurdles to overcome, both technical and political. This was a technology that might prove dangerous in the wrong hands; the University of Illinois had soon been forced to hand over all license to the federal government, and Fort Detrick, a Maryland facility northeast of D.C., held the bulk of it in strict confidence.

He missed California. He missed Berkeley. Every day, he had to remind himself that coming to Atlanta had been the right thing to do. The Center for Gene Therapy at Emory was the only public institution that had been allowed access to NANs.

In the waiting room, he slouched into a seat near the boarding gate. He'd once been a spry, athletic farm boy, the captain of his high school baseball team. But he'd let himself go—his straight spine curved forward from years of hovering over laboratory benches, his keen eyes weakened from staring into microscopes and computer screens. His mother would fret over his health, he knew, plying him with plates of spiced lentils and rice. He could taste them already.

James looked around. At this early hour, most of the seats were empty. In front of him a young mother, her baby asleep in a carrier on the floor, cradled a small GameGirl remote console in her lap. Ignoring her own child, she seemed to be playing at feeding the alien baby whose wide green face appeared openmouthed on her screen. By the window an elderly man sat munching a ProteoBar.

James jumped at the feel of a buzz at his wrist—a return message from DOD.

Dr. Said:

No reschedule. Someone will meet you.

—General Jos. Blankenship, U.S. Army

He looked up to see a man in a plain gray suit stationed by the gate. The man's thick neck rose out of his collar, his chin tilting upward in an almost imperceptible nod. Removing his ocular, James glanced to his right. His arm flinched reflexively from a light tap on his shoulder.

"Dr. Said?"

James's mind went blank. "Yes?" he croaked.

"I'm sorry, Dr. Said. But the Pentagon requires your presence."

"What?" James stared at the young man, his crisp dark uniform and glossy black shoes.

"I'll need you to accompany me to Langley, ASAP. I'm sorry. We'll have your airline tickets reimbursed."

"But why—?"

"Don't worry, sir. We'll get you there in no time." Latching a white-gloved hand around James's arm, the officer guided him to a security exit and down a set of stairs, through a door and out into daylight. A few steps away, the man in the gray suit was already waiting, holding open the back door of a black limousine, ushering James inside.

"My luggage?"

"Taken care of."

His heart forming a fist in his chest, James wedged his body deep into the leather seat. He placed his right hand protectively over his left wrist, guarding the phone—his one remaining link to the world outside the limo. At least they hadn't confiscated it. "What's going on? Why are you detaining me?"

The young officer offered him a wry grin as he climbed into the front seat. "They'll fill you in at Langley, sir." He pushed a few buttons on the dash, and James could feel the pressure of a smooth acceleration. "Just sit back and relax."

The young man reached out to activate a transceiver on the car's center console. "Subject en route," he assured someone on the other end. "Expect arrival ten hundred hours."

"That fast?"

"We've got a jet lined up. Just sit tight."

Outside the tinted window, the black tarmac sped by. James held up his wrist, punched on his phone, and whispered a short message: "Amani Said. Message: Sorry, Mom. Won't be home. Something came up. Tell Dad not to worry. Send."

His voice shaking, he added a second thought. "If you don't hear from me in two days, call Mr. Wheelan." Silently, he prayed that his message would go through.

3

RICK BLEVINS POWERED on his computer and settled into his chair. As he waited for his secure link to boot up, he ran the palm of his hand down the length of his thigh, massaging the place just above the knee where the prosthesis joined what remained of his right leg. He winced. The adjustment to this new device was proving difficult.

Like his old one, the bulk of the new prosthesis was covered with a synthetic mesh that stiffened and softened as he moved, mirroring the softness or stiffness of the tissues in his upper thigh. Its bionic muscles were controlled via the same electrodes, connected to his own nerve tissue. But this new appendage, built for better mobility, seemed to have a mind of its own. When he snapped it into place each morning, tiny pinpricks of energy surged upward toward his spine, a force like something alien. Worst of all, the new leg seemed to be waging war on his neurostimulator, the device they'd implanted in his lower back to dull the pain. The old phantom signals, pulsing and burning, were inching back.

He stared out the window. The weather wasn't helping. The previous night's freezing rain had painted the concrete facade of the Pentagon with a thin layer of frost. Running his hand over his scalp, he felt the stiff growth of his thick brown hair. He needed a cut . . .

He was startled by the buzz of the intercom at his lapel. "We need you down here," came a clipped male voice.

"Down here" was General Blankenship's basement office. Rick gulped coffee from his thermocup and straightened his tie. He was pretty sure he knew what this was about.

A month prior, he'd been summoned for comment on a biowarfare project at Fort Detrick. He was no longer subject to the immediate threats that had dogged his life in special ops, but in his desk job as an analyst at the CIA's Directorate of Intelligence, he'd found plenty of use for the same keen instincts that had served him so well in the field. With growing concern he'd pored over the feasibility report, acquainting himself with difficult scientific terms like "apoptosis," "programmed cell death," "caspase," and "nucleic acid nanostructure." He'd heard of the DNA nanostructures, nicknamed "NANs," before; it was his job to oversee approval of their use in domestic research labs. But this was different.

The project was called Tabula Rasa, a moniker that was frightening enough. But as he'd rescanned the section labeled "Expected Impact," he'd felt his heart skip a beat. The basis of the bioagent was a specific type of nucleic acid nanostructure called IC-NAN. When a victim inhaled this particular sequence of nanoparticulate DNA, his infected lung cells would begin to outlive their "use by" date: Rather than dying off to make way for fresh new cells as they were supposed to do, the old, infected cells would replicate to produce more defective cells. These mutated cells would overgrow good tissue, impeding proper lung function and eventually invading the body, robbing other organs of nutrients. The desired result was akin to an aggressive lung cancer— a slow but inexorable death.

Rather than offering the expected rubber stamp on the program, he'd fired off a salvo advising its cancellation. Sending uncharacterized bioweapons out into the world, even to the most remote parts of the world, was crazy. The mass poisonings, the devastation of innocent populations in an effort to rout out the few . . . weren't they past all that?

But now, he was sure the vehemence of his response hadn't gone unnoticed. No doubt Blankenship had been dissatisfied. As he caught the elevator and traveled the three floors down, he steeled himself for the inevitable reprimand.

The elevator door buzzed open, and he headed down the dim corridor. A first lieutenant was waiting for him near the door to the general's office. As the man came to attention, Rick caught sight of the glimmer of a rifle. An armed guard. A cold sweat dampened his shirt.

"Sir." The younger man saluted him. Stopping short, Rick saluted back. "Sir, you'll need to repeat your oath."

"Here?"

"Yes. Strict orders."

The hairs at the back of his neck prickling in the close air, Rick repeated the oath he knew so well. "I will support and defend the Constitution of the United States against all enemies, foreign and domestic . . . I will bear true faith and allegiance to the same . . ." As he spoke the words, his pulse kept double time in his ears. ". . . so help me God."

The young officer latched his hand around the doorknob, waiting for the decisive click that signaled acceptance. The door swung open, and Rick slipped inside.

"Have a seat," Blankenship said. It was an order. Rick lowered himself onto an old wooden desk chair, then looked up to take in the two others in the room with them. With a jolt, he realized that one was Henrietta Forbes, the president's secretary of defense. The other was a short, balding man in a faded brown suit.

Blankenship coughed—an unproductive cough, more of a grumble. "Rick," he said, "we have a situation."

Rick glanced at his boss, General Joseph Blankenship—hero of two wars, winner of the Purple Heart, now director of the CIA. The general, normally sanguine, sat gripping his leather armrests, his mouth set in a tight grimace.

"Dr. Rudy Garza has been so kind as to come down from Fort Detrick. I'll let him explain." Turning, Blankenship nodded to the balding man, who promptly shuffled a thin tablet up from his lap.

"Thank you, General." Dr. Garza's voice was low, lost in the rumpled collar of his white shirt. "I understand that you are all aware of Tabula Rasa?"

"The project you people started a few years back? The initiator caspase–specific NAN?" Rick edged forward, his gaze still focused on the general. "I recommended it be canceled."

The doctor looked up from his notes, his eyes surprisingly blue above a pair of old wire-framed reading glasses. "Yes," he said. "I know."

"I'm sorry, Dr. Garza," Blankenship said, returning Rick's gaze with his own steely glare. "Please go on."

"The IC-NAN was deployed on June 5, a little over six months ago now, in a remote region of southern Afghanistan," Dr. Garza said.

"*Deployed?* But—" Rick felt his heart picking up speed, his leg throbbing in response as he struggled to stay seated. He'd been wasting his time. By the time his opinion on Tabula Rasa had been solicited, IC-NAN had already been deployed.

It was Secretary Forbes's turn to intercede. "Despite the truce, the region west of Kandahar still wasn't under control. Enemy combatants were entrenched in caves, sniping at our peacekeeping troops . . . We were losing as many as five men a day. We needed a targeted weapon that wouldn't leave a mark. No trace of itself, no trace of its origin. Just kill, then disappear."

"As you know," Dr. Garza said, "IC-NAN was designed for this purpose. A synthetic nucleic acid nanostructure, or NAN, mimics the activity of a virus, but it cannot be replicated by the contaminated individual. So it is not contagious. In addition, this NAN was engineered so that if it was not inhaled within a few hours, it would degrade."

"Degrade . . ." Rick repeated. He remembered this feature, a significant one.

"Yes. Once released into the air, the infectious nanoparticulate form, which is synthesized to take on the shape of a tiny sphere, will eventually denature, or degrade, to its linear form. This linear form cannot enter human cells. After intensive study, our IC-NAN was deemed safe to release as an aerosol, via drone."

Rick closed his eyes. He remembered Garza's name on the reports he'd read—a chemist, a doctoral graduate of the molecular biology program at the Instituto Politécnico in Mexico City. His trained ear picked up a slight Spanish accent, almost musical in tone. It was difficult to be angry at this meek purveyor of bad news. But was it his anger or his confusion that had set the room spinning? "So, did the NAN do what it was supposed to do?" he asked, his own voice sounding faint in his ears.

Dr. Garza adjusted his glasses with one nervous forefinger. "Normally, the cells on the human lung's surface are replaced every two to three weeks with fresh cells. But within five weeks of our attack, all of the targeted individuals were found dead. Their lung biopsies showed no evidence of uninfected, normally functioning lung surface cells. So yes, the NAN appeared to have behaved as expected."

Rick felt a catch at the base of his throat. From Blankenship's immaculate desk, a tiny snowman smiled at him, trapped there in the stagnant atmosphere of his own small globe. They wouldn't have called him down here if all had gone according to plan. "And the residual? The material that wasn't inhaled?"

Dr. Garza swallowed hard, and Rick detected a slight tremor in his voice as he continued. "As you seem to have surmised, this is the issue.

Those who did reconnaissance—the GeoBot team who located the bodies—some of them suffered . . . sequelae. And they found more individuals dead at the scene, and over a wider area, than had been expected based on aerial photos taken before deployment of the spray."

"The NAN didn't degrade?"

"It did degrade, in the sense that it reverted to the noninfectious linear form. But . . ."

"But?"

Looking up from his notes, Dr. Garza confronted the room. "But that form, while not able to infect human cells, was taken up by a receptive species of archaebacterium present in the desert sands. It inserted itself into that genome. And it appears that these microbes were capable of replicating it each time they divided."

Rick found himself clutching the arms of his chair. "These things made more copies of the NAN DNA? How do you know this?"

"We analyzed samples taken from the victims' clothing. The NAN DNA sequence was present in the archaebacterial DNA. But . . . the problem is worse than this. We discovered that some of these microbes were packed with reconstituted spherical NANs."

"Particles that they made *themselves*?"

"Yes. And once these new NANs were synthesized, they caused the archaebacterium to . . . explode, for lack of a better term."

"Releasing the spherical NANs back to the environment . . ."

The doctor nodded slowly. "It would appear so. Restarting the cycle with fresh IC-NAN."

Rick leaned forward. "So let me get this straight. The spherical NAN that you sprayed from the drone can infect human cells. The degraded linear form, to which it reverts in the environment, cannot. That was supposed to be your safety feature."

"Correct."

"But these archaebacteria are capable of taking in the linear form, making more copies of it, and manufacturing more spherical NANs from that DNA?"

"Yes," Dr. Garza replied, staring fixedly down again at his notes.

Rick drew a deep breath. "And these spherical NANs can then get back out of the archaebacteria and infect more humans?"

Dr. Garza looked up, his expression stony. "Yes. There appear to be two mechanisms for this." He turned his tablet around to face the group. The diagram on the display showed a green, rod-shaped organism, the archaebacterium, packed full with small clumps of DNA labeled as IC-NANs. As if to enhance their ominous nature, the NANs were drawn in red. The archaebacterium was just starting to split open along one end. And scattered around the outside of its ruptured cell wall were more NANs, some still clumped in their spherical infectious form, some degraded to wormlike linear structures. "In one scenario," Garza said, "the newly synthesized spherical NAN is excreted by the archaebacterium directly into the environment. Given a few hours, this NAN might degrade to the linear form—which as we now know is capable of infecting a new archaebacterium, though not of infecting a human. Or, if there is a human close by, the NAN might infect that human before it has a chance to degrade." He swiped forward to a second diagram, showing a cutaway cartoon of a human subject from the side, his airways open to admit hosts of tiny green and red dots. "As I said, a human might breathe in this new NAN. But in another scenario, the *archaebacterium* is breathed in by the victim and then releases its NAN within the body." He looked away from his screen. "We have evidence that all of these mechanisms can and have occurred."

Rick sat back, gripping the bridge of his nose between thumb and forefinger. "So, this thing is out of control," he said. "Now these soil organisms are replicating this IC-NAN DNA sequence and excreting active NANs back out into the biosphere. Now they can act as agents of a new sort of archaebacterial infection, one that might turn on any-one. On us."

Garza turned off his tablet, holding it now to his chest. "Yes."

Rick turned to Blankenship. "I warned you about the unpredict-ability—" He caught himself. Of course, no one had asked his opin-ion before storming ahead. Exasperated, he turned back to Garza. "The human victims can't transmit the NAN to other humans, can they?"

"No," Dr. Garza said. "This part of the plan was effective. The vic-tims are not infectious. Only the infected microbes are—"

"And animals and plants will not be affected?"

"The effects of this DNA are specific to humans."

"So let's get back to these archaebacteria. Do we know how many of these are infected? Or how many different species of such might be infected? They could be anywhere . . ."

"We are assessing the degree of spread. So far we have only isolated the DNA from one archaebacterial species. We are not sure if different species of microbes will be capable of exchanging this genetic material with one another in the wild. But we are currently testing that hypoth-esis in the laboratory."

Rick clenched his jaw, his accusing gaze drifting toward Henrietta Forbes.

"It's all hands on deck," said Blankenship, sparing the secretary the need of a response. "But right now, you're the only agent we have with complete knowledge of the project."

"Complete knowledge?" Rick asked, making sure his gaze met Blankenship's. "Have you really told me everything?"

"Everything we know at present," Dr. Garza said evenly. "Although the story is constantly evolving."

Rick felt the beginnings of a rude laugh bubbling in his throat. Of course, everything he'd thought might happen was now happening—and worse. Nature always held the cards—it didn't take a Ph.D. to understand that. "Evolving," he said. "Like these little bugs that have picked up the ability to synthesize NANs."

Rudy Garza was looking straight at him now, his blue eyes gone steel gray. "Yes. Like the archaebacteria."

"Rick, you'll be reinstated into active duty at your former rank—colonel," Blankenship said. "You'll oversee the joint investigation, including DOD personnel, the science team at Fort Detrick, and any ancillary science personnel we may call in."

"But . . . sir . . ." Rick looked around the room, at the expectant faces turned toward him. "I'm not a scientist," he protested. "A career in special ops and a minor in biology from West Point hardly qualify me . . . They'll never listen . . ."

Blankenship shook his head. "You're on the security side," he said. "They have to listen to you. If they don't, we'll block 'em out."

"Fine," Rick muttered. "Fine. In any event, I suppose I have no choice." He settled back, the wooden slats of his seat digging into his spine. Why else had they brought him down here, confessed their sins to him? Though it would have been his choice to halt its inception in the first place, it was he who would be charged with cleaning up this mess.

There was an awkward pause as Blankenship fumbled with a tablet on his desk. "Now, we've identified another scientist we'll need on the team. Someone at Emory. He'll need to be brought up to speed," the general mumbled.

"Emory? Who?"

Blankenship put his hand to his forehead, kneading his brow. "You know of him. Said. Dr. James Said."

Once again, Rick was startled. Said. The difficult clearance he'd worked on, just last year. "James Said . . . Emory . . . Do you mean the Pakistani? But you've already got the team at Fort Detrick . . ."

Blankenship glared over the top of his tablet. "Dr. Garza's team knows all about the NANs we've released—how to synthesize them, their structure, how they're supposed to work. But if we're going to protect people against this thing, we're going to need more expertise on the human physiology side. In . . . what was it, Garza?"

"Cell biology," murmured Dr. Garza.

"Yes," said Blankenship. "It was Dr. Garza who suggested Dr. Said."

"Dr. Said is not Pakistani—he's an American, born in Bakersfield, California," Dr. Garza said. "He's a well-known authority on recombinant DNA therapy, and well regarded at the Center for Gene Therapy—I have heard that he is being groomed as its next head. And he has extensive experience with the activity of NANs in human tissues."

Rick leaned forward once again, determined to make his point. "As you know, I was responsible for Said's background check when he applied to work with NANs," he said. "I warned he might be a liability. We all know who his uncle was, even if it appears that he doesn't."

Blankenship didn't bother looking up. "In the end, you decided to grant him access, correct?" he said.

Rick stared at his boss. "But we've had to keep a watchful eye on him. Are we really sure we want him to know—"

"He's clean," said the general. "He knows nothing about his extended family."

"You're absolutely sure of that?"

"His parents have been model citizens since resettlement. They've kept him in the dark," replied the general. "I can show you the surveillance files, if that's what you need."

Rick sat back, all energy draining from his limbs. Files. When it came to Farooq Said, James Said's notorious uncle, he'd seen all the files he needed to see. "Don't bother," he said. "Where is he now?"

Standing up, the general signaled the end of the meeting. "On his way to Langley as we speak. We'll need you there to greet him."

IN THE SMALL, brightly lit conference room, James Said hunched over the table, the Fort Detrick reports displayed before him on dimly lit screens. His fingers scrolled the pages steadily, his thin lips moving in silence.

With his lank frame, his black hair carefully oiled and plastered over flecks of premature gray, Said looked little like the militants whom Rick had encountered during his years under cover in Pakistan. Still, Rick felt his fists clench involuntarily as he sat across the table, waiting. He remembered wresting a sawed-off rifle from sinewed arms in an abandoned hovel outside Karachi. The pungent smell of cumin mixed with sweat. He remembered the searing pain, shooting up into his gut. The trip back home, without his leg—without Mustafa, the trusted interpreter he'd vowed to protect.

But this man smelled only of a nondescript American aftershave. His rumpled clothes were those of a middle-aged academic, on his way home to California for the Christian holidays. Gripping the back of his own neck with one hand, Rick willed his mental state down from orange to yellow, from yellow to all clear. The general had assured him: Though James Said's family history was suspect, the man himself was not.

Sitting back, Said shifted a pair of reading glasses from the bridge of his angular nose to the top of his high forehead. The look on his face was unreadable.

"What do you think?"

"About what?"

Rick stared across the table. Said was obviously put out at having to curtail his vacation. Once the fear had worn off, he'd been understandably outraged. But now that the chips were on the table—was this really the time to start a game of twenty questions? "Are the findings sound?"

"The DNA sequence found in the archaebacteria is the same as that in the NAN. The archaebacteria are capable of making and secreting active NANs. It's right there in the reports."

"Then we need some ideas."

"About what?"

Oh, my good God. "How to respond, of course."

"If this really did happen—"

"And you just told me you agree it did—"

"If all of this is true, then you're asking me to solve a monumental problem with about as much forethought as you gave when you unleashed this thing in the first place."

"Listen." Rick stood. Ignoring the pain of a thousand needles from a leg that no longer existed, he circled the table to stand at the doctor's side. "*I* didn't unleash anything. I'm just the poor sap who needs to figure out a way to clean it up. And I'm asking for your help."

"I'm sorry." The doctor looked up at him, his expression only briefly telegraphing something resembling sympathy. "Really. It's just that I'd expected to be home now. With my parents. But instead I'm sitting here with you, and you're telling me these things. It's . . . a lot to process."

"If it helps any," Rick said, "we don't expect anything to happen tomorrow."

"How long do you think we have?"

"Detrick consulted the database at Argonne National Lab. Retrospective data on the natural spread of DNA for this type of desert microbe population yielded a few models. Possibly as long as five years before it breaches the region. Possibly less . . ."

"And we know that the DNA is currently only found in the one species of archaebacterium?"

"So far, yes."

"Okay." Said rubbed his eyes with the heels of his palms. "I suppose I don't have any say in the matter, now. I know too much, as you say . . . We'll have to get to work right away."

Rick leaned forward. "What do you suggest? Some sort of vaccine, maybe?"

"A vaccine won't work."

"No?"

"A traditional vaccine helps the body mount an immune response to a foreign agent. But IC-NAN is designed to masquerade as nonforeign. What we need is a snippet of DNA that can short-circuit its action. And we need a method by which to deliver it to the human body. Genetic engineering on an unprecedented scale."

"We can't just eradicate the source? Kill these things?"

"Living, these microbes are acting as factories for that toxic DNA that you . . . that our government so wisely spewed out into the biosphere. They've already replicated it far beyond the dose dropped by your drones. And as they die, they are apparently capable of excreting the DNA in its original infectious form. Kill them on purpose, and you'd most likely only accelerate the release process. Quite simply, you've created a monster."

"Couldn't we just . . . burn them up?"

"You can try. But I can't imagine you'll meet with success. We're talking billions and billions of infected microorganisms, by now most likely spread over miles of terrain, borne on the wind. And it's quite possible that over time, new microbial species will be infected. I can't think of a surefire way to destroy all that infectious matter . . ." Said stood up, his fingers splayed on the tabletop, back stooped and head down. Rick had to strain to hear what he said next. "No. We'll have to find some way to modify the human body to live with this . . . this monster on the loose."

Rick sat down heavily. He'd prayed for better news, some sort of amazing fix. He didn't like Said—his defeatist attitude, his seeming arrogance. But he couldn't expect a miracle.

And what the man said was true. They both knew too much to turn away. "Do you know why you were chosen?" he asked.

"Chosen?" Said looked up, his expression blank.

"You were picked for this project for the same reason that I was. You have no family."

"I have my parents—"

"No wife, no kids. We can't trust people to look at this rationally, if . . ."

"Look," the doctor replied, his pale brown eyes flashing amber, "I don't think anyone in his right mind could look at this with complete detachment. But I'll try to be as rational as I can."

4

JAMES GRITTED HIS teeth. It was difficult to believe that only a few weeks had passed since his first meeting with Colonel Richard Blevins. Bundled in a Biosafety Level 4 positive-pressure suit, he felt trapped, claustrophobic. Bright overhead lights glinted off the surface of the transparent plastic surrounding his head, blinding him. The short walk down the narrow hallway toward the Fort Detrick maximum containment lab was exhausting, the sweat tracing down the side of his face in an exasperating trickle.

"These suits used to be worse," Rudy Garza said. The smaller man's voice, muffled in James's earpiece, was almost inaudible over the hiss of air through the coiled tubing tethering them to the low ceiling. "At least now we have decent peripheral vision."

James had never dealt with containment at this level—it wasn't required for the type of work he did at Emory. But Rudy's current work involved a contaminated archaebacterium sample harvested from Afghanistan. And if James was going to help challenge this beast, he wanted to meet it face-to-face.

Passing through a second airlock, they approached a biosafety hood across a small interior room. The tiny organisms at the heart of the problem had been classified as members of the phylum Thaumarchaeota, of the domain Archaea—a classification that included some of the most ancient organisms on earth. As James had soon learned, the archaebacteria were not bacteria at all. They were in a kingdom unto themselves— not susceptible to common antibiotics. Naturally drought tolerant, spore-like in their resilience, archaea like these were present in all environments, harsh or otherwise.

So far, human victims confirmed as infected with IC-NAN had been limited to two mountain villages within ten miles of the deployment site. The archaebacterial isolate under study here had been recovered from the uniform of a doomed army reconnaissance specialist. James winced, remembering the classified videos he'd been shown: women and children lying on the ground in poorly equipped medical tents, coughing blood into the sand; the young American soldier, prostrate in a makeshift ventilator—unable to come home, even to die. The problem was that no one was yet sure how far IC-NAN would spread.

Along one side of the hood, tubes of cloudy agar sat in neat rows of racks.

"These are our hosts," Rudy said. The remnants of Rudy's Mexican accent, coupled with his quick, sure movements as he manipulated a robotic arm to retrieve a smaller rack from the back of the sealed hood, reminded James of the capable technicians who operated the hemp harvesters alongside his father in Bakersfield. The robot picked a thin slide from the smaller rack. "These archaea are known to be capable of transferring genetic traits among one another in the wild. I've been trying to determine whether or not this infected thaumarchaeon species can transmit its new NAN synthesis capabilities to other species of archaea."

"Am I supposed to be able to see something on that slide?"

"Have a seat," Rudy said. The arm placed the slide onto a micrometer stage, which then moved dutifully toward the eyepiece of a deep

UV fluorescence microscope set into the glass sash of the hood. "Please, fit your mask here."

James brought his face toward the eyepiece, doing his best to peer through the transparent plastic of his suit. To his surprise, the soft rubber grommet surrounding the eyepiece conformed easily to his mask. "We can actually look for NANs? Aren't they too small?"

"Each NAN is only about thirteen nanometers in diameter. But when they are labeled with my fluorescent probe, we get something large enough to be retained on the filter in this slide, and bright enough to see."

James squinted. The image looked like an old crossword puzzle, with some square segments completely dark, others glowing bright yellow. "What am I looking for?"

"Each segment of the grid represents approximately one hundred organisms, each a different archaebacterial species. These organisms were each grown up in a culture medium that was previously used to grow the infected thaumarchaeon species. The question was whether there would be some sort of genetic transfer from the infected species to the new species. As a check, we've also included some regular bacteria—gut *E. coli*, soil *Pseudomonas* species, and the like. On each slide, we can see the results for fifty different organisms."

"Which ones were affected?"

"The segments that are illuminated by the fluorescent probe represent organisms in which the NAN has reassembled well enough to capture and visualize at this magnification. Fortunately, none of the common bacterial isolates we tested seem to have picked up the ability to make NANs. But quite a few of the *archae*bacterial isolates did— most notably including some from the mainland U.S. That one on the lower right is from the Argonne collection. It was harvested just outside Chicago."

"Which means . . ."

"We have identified a mechanism by which this trait could make its way around the globe. It might be only a matter of time before we have species here in the U.S. that can make IC-NAN."

James felt his heart racing. He wanted—needed—to have faith in this man, the only person he'd met since joining the project who seemed both willing and able to face the enormity of the task before them. But he also needed better news. Lamely, he pursued the same line of questioning that Blevins had subjected him to on their first meeting. "But . . . can we kill the current hosts before they have a chance to infect other species?" he asked.

"We must keep trying," Rudy replied evenly. "But we have few options for cheaply available decontamination agents that are not also toxic to humans. These organisms laugh in the face of agents like bleach. And we cannot simply set fire to regions that are heavily populated . . ."

James nodded. He'd already seen it on the nightly news vids— footage of military bots applying flaming torches to an apparently lifeless expanse of desert. The press was all over it, and speculation was rampant as to what might be going on. But the lid was on—no answers were forthcoming.

"To make matters worse, the Argonne Lab data indicate that these archaea can spread through air currents, the jet stream, and so on. And by now, they could already have been carried outside the region on military vehicles and equipment. All we can do is continue to try and contain the spread, continue to build on the existing models, to predict where they might pop up next." Rudy again manipulated the controller and the robot retracted the eyepiece, then placed the slide carefully back into its rack. His shoulders slumped, he headed back toward the entryway. He raised his gloved hand to activate the airlock, then turned to face James. "What did you tell Colonel Blevins?"

"I told him we need to figure out some way to change the target cells in humans. To modify their DNA. An antidote of some sort, administered continuously and to every human on earth. Most likely another NAN."

"What did he say?" Rudy asked.

"Nothing, yet."

Rudy sighed. "It is strange how one thing leads to another . . . Years ago, my thesis adviser recommended that I stay in Mexico and pursue an academic career. But instead, I chose a postdoctoral at Rockefeller in New York. Afterward, I wanted to stay in the U.S. . . ."

"Why?"

"A girl, of course . . . another thing that did not go as planned. She broke our engagement, but only after I had accepted a job."

"You came to Fort Detrick."

"Working for Detrick offered me a fast track to U.S. citizenship."

"But why did you stay after that?"

"At Detrick, there was no need to worry about funding—I had all I could use. All the lab space, all the equipment . . . I was promoted to team leader. And I worked on so many interesting projects." Rudy looked down, examining his gloved hands. "I must admit that it was frustrating at times. So many investigations, so many reports that languished on the desks of people like Colonel Blevins, only to be shelved. I took heart that most of them were directed at defense against bioterrorism—a worthy goal, I believed."

"But you had to know that the IC-NAN project had nothing to do with defense . . ."

"When I was put in charge of the project that created this . . . I thought that it was just like all the others—just a feasibility study. A chance to work with something outside of my expertise. I felt sure that it would be put aside. In fact, I was counting on that." Rudy's eyes pleaded from behind the plastic of his mask. "James, I did not know that they would actually deploy it. My only solace now is that, with your help, we can find a way to stop it."

Once more, James felt the sweat breaking out at his temples, a new wave of claustrophobia. "Do you think we can . . . stop it?"

"I cannot be sure of much. But each day I am more sure of one thing. How do you say it? The time . . . it is ticking."

James closed his eyes. He'd been trying to think about this thing as just another project, just another scientific hurdle to be surmounted—because thinking about it in any other way only clouded his mind. It was all he could do not to succumb to panic. But he didn't have time for that. He would find a way to protect humans from this horrible threat. He had to.

5

JUNE 2060

KAI COULD FEEL the morning heat spilling through Rosie's hatch cover, flooding his cocoon. As he rubbed the sleep from his eyes, his fingers touched the small bump on his forehead, the rough place where the chip was embedded just under the skin.

"Your chip is special," Rosie had told him. "It is our bond." It was how they knew one another, she said. It was how she spoke to him—except during his speech lessons, she never used her audible voice.

He reached out to touch the smooth surface of the hatch cover in front of him. Where his fingers made contact, the transparent surface became opaque. An image appeared—a group of men with sun-weathered skin, colorful woven robes draped over their stooped shoulders.

Rosie had been teaching him a lesson about people who lived in the desert—a desert much like his, but on the other side of the earth and very long ago. The men in the image, Rosie said, were the keepers of the scrolls, ancient writings like those unearthed from caves over a hundred years before the Epidemic. "What's that?" he asked, pointing to one of the men. Perched atop the man's forehead, a small box was supported by a thin leather strap.

Rosie's familiar soft buzz and click filled his mind as she accessed the required information. "These were called *tefillin*. Each contained four tiny scrolls, on which were written passages taken from a book called the Torah." Beneath her console, her servo motors whirred gently. "This book described a set of beliefs that they lived by."

"You teach me through *my tefillin*," Kai said, pointing to his own dusty forehead, the chip encased there. "Are you my Torah?"

Rosie paused. She was thinking, compiling her answer as she often did when he asked a difficult question. "No," she said. "The information that I provide is based purely on fact. It's important to separate beliefs from facts."

Withdrawing his hand from the screen, Kai watched the image disappear. He peered through the hatch cover, once more transparent. Outside, the familiar rock formations surrounding their encampment stood firm, their massive red fingers pointing skyward. They were strong, like Rosie, undaunted by wind and heat.

He had names for all of them—the Red Horse, the Man with a Big Nose, the Gorilla, and the Father, who balanced his plump, round rock baby forever on his giant knees. Rosie had taught him about how humans used to live. She was his Mother. He supposed, then, that the rocks were his family—the guardians who, along with Rosie, had kept watch over him since the day of his birth.

He pressed the latch to his left, the sun's heat assailing him as the hatch door swung open. He scrambled down over Rosie's treads to reach the ground, coming face-to-face with his own reflection in the pocked mirror of her metallic surface. His skin was tanned and freckled, streaked with dust. A cloud of reddish-brown hair framed his head, and blue eyes twinkled from beneath heavy lashes. Somewhere, Rosie said, there were other children. Others like him, but different. Rosie couldn't tell him how many there were now. But in the beginning, there had been fifty. When the time was right, they would find them.

As Kai picked his way over the cracked earth to the top of a low rise, beads of sweat escaped the barrier of his brow. His mouth felt full of sand. He formed his palms into circles, makeshift binoculars through which to survey the lonely landscape. In the ethereal shimmer of distant mirages, he strained to see the faraway places he'd learned about on Rosie's screen. He could see the high mountains whose peaks were dusted with snow each winter. But they were black now, devoid of their blankets.

"Can we go soon?" he signaled his Mother. "I think I'm ready . . ."

"If conditions allow, we may go today."

"*Today?*"

He'd sensed that the day was coming. On their last trip to the supply depot, Rosie had pushed aside the giant boulders, pried open the heavy metal doors with her powerful arms, and removed the final case of provisions, the last of the emergency water bottles. In the evenings, when the hot sun dipped behind the rocks and their shadows grew long, she'd begun training him to find his own food. In a battered tin cup, he harvested dried grass seeds. He toasted them over a small fire, then mixed them with water, adding shreds of mouse or lizard meat to make a thin stew. He chewed on the tender flower stalks of the banana yucca, making sure to spare some for the sweet fruit he could harvest come fall. The people who had lived here long ago had subsisted on food like this.

"You are six years of age," Rosie said. "The time has come to leave this place."

"Where will we go?"

"I do not know."

"You don't?" His heart quickened at the thought that there was something his Mother might not know.

"The command is incomplete. It instructs us to leave. However, our destination is not defined."

Kai stared down at Rosie's powerful form, waves of heat shimmering off her weathered flanks. His mind vibrated with the hum of her processors. "Then how do we know if we're going to the right place?"

"There are seventy-six supply depots, each equipped with a condensation tower and weather station," she narrated.

"But the other children? Will we find them now?"

She paused again, and he imagined electrons coursing through her nanocircuits, bits of information traversing all the parts of her mind that she'd so patiently explained to him. "This is possible," she replied at last. "There is a nonzero probability that others have survived."

Excited, Kai skidded down the rise to the shade of his Mother. He'd seen the petroglyphs, diagrams left by ancient peoples on the high faces of the rocks. He would make a sign of his own. He scooped up a pile of cobalt-blue stones, arranging them to form letters. *Kai, Son of Rho-Z*, he spelled. *I WAS HERE.* As he carefully formed the words, he imagined another child squatting here in the dust, reading his message. He sat back, dizzy, the letters swimming before his eyes.

"You must eat," Rosie reminded him.

He climbed up her treads to retrieve a packet of nutritional supplement from behind his seat, tore off one corner, and squirted the gelatinous liquid into his mouth. "Soylent Pedia-Supp—Nutri-Gro—6–8 years," the label read. It contained all the nutrients he needed, but he was tired of its milky consistency and salty-sweet taste. It only made him thirstier.

Snatching up his empty canteen from the floor of the cocoon, he carried it toward the bottle-shaped condensation tower, high as the Gorilla rock. Constructed from interwoven shafts of flexible metal, the tower supported an internal mesh bag whose bright orange color contrasted with the dark catch basin below. He dipped the canteen, waiting for it to fill. The water level was so low now that he had to use his cupped hand to scoop the murky liquid through the narrow opening.

He remembered the rains that had once sent torrents coursing through the canyons. He'd bathed in bowls hollowed out from stone by years of erosion. On cool nights, he'd listened to beads of water, wending their way over the mesh of the tower to land with a plop in the basin. But now, even the most threatening of clouds bore little fruit. The basin was almost dry. And the emergency water from the supply depot, sour and chemical, had been depleted. Hunkering low in the dust of Rosie's shadow, Kai imagined himself a stone, harboring the cool that had collected in his body during the night.

As the day wore on, his Mother was silent. No lessons today. She was busy. He stared out across the desert floor, over the sparse, prickly vegetation in whose shelter insects, lizards, and small rodents scratched out their tenuous lives. He licked his dry lips. In the distance, the western mesas faded from gold to purple. Maybe they wouldn't go today after all.

But then Rosie's voice entered his consciousness. "It's time," she said. "Please put on your clothing."

"Where are we going?"

She didn't answer. He could only hear her processors, the faint sound of something like wind between his ears.

His hands shaking, Kai retrieved his microfiber tunic from Rosie's hold, cramming his arms and legs into the forgiving fabric. He slipped on his moccasins, then dropped into his seat and pulled his safety restraints tight around his body, snapping them securely into their latches.

Rosie closed her hatch. His heart pounding in the silence, Kai waited.

He felt the shock as her reactor ignited behind him, the cocoon rocking back, keeping him upright as she tilted forward. Through the hatch cover, he could see her wings emerge, then unfold to full span.

Her fans appeared from beneath their protective sheaths, rotating to push great swaths of air toward the ground. Nestled inside, he heard only a muffled whine as he squinted through veils of dust. The pressure of her acceleration pushed him deeper into his seat, closer to her.

Together, they soared high.

6

ROSE MCBRIDE CHECKED the date on her computer. March 15, 2051. Over a year now, working on what seemed like a pointless project. Stretching her arms over her head, she turned away from the lines of data that seemed to dance across the screen, refusing to stand still.

After her final tour in Afghanistan, she'd been offered a position at the Presidio Institute in San Francisco, at the site formerly occupied by the old Fort Winfield Scott. She'd jumped at the chance to be stateside again, but not mired in the political firetrap that Washington had become. And a gift—a return to the city where years ago her widowed father, an army captain like she was now, had at last made a home for the two of them.

Dragged from one base to another, Rose as a child had been lost, untethered. But San Francisco had saved her. In its cavernous gaming salons, she and her friends had spent hours hacking the robo-baristas, downing free lattes and dreaming up ever more exotic profiles for their online personas. Encouraged by a father who saw gaming as a waste of time, she pursued a degree in psychology at Harvard before joining the army as an adviser to psyops. But in the end, programming had proved to be her passion. If her time in the military had taught her anything, it was that the world was an endless user interface, the good guys facing off against the bad. She'd come home to complete the computer science graduate program at Princeton, then put her newfound knowledge to work in Afghanistan.

Still, this new assignment made no sense. Colonel Richard Blevins, her commanding officer at the Pentagon, had made it clear that he thought the Presidio Institute needed "battening down." Based on the clearance level required, she'd assumed they'd have her working in cybersecurity, her focus since Princeton. Instead, she was compiling biological statistics relating to the spread of arcane soil organisms originating from the same Afghan region where she'd last been stationed. The work was grueling, painstaking, and without reward. And though part of her job was to direct the GeoBot teams in the collection of new samples, no word ever came back from the higher-ups as to how, or if, her analyses were being used. She couldn't help but wonder—what did this have to do with the Pentagon?

Colonel Blevins had tried to be encouraging. "You know the military," he said. "Need to know and all that. Believe me, I know little more than you do." She didn't know if she believed him. But she understood. She did "know the military"—more, perhaps, than most.

Staring out the window of her little office, she imagined Richard Blevins's chiseled features, his steely gray-blue eyes, his close-cropped military cut. The way he leaned forward in his chair when he questioned her during her monthly reviews—probing but not intimidating. Very practiced. Strangely attractive. He reminded her of every man she'd encountered in the army, his true self walled off behind layers of defense. But there was something there, just beneath the surface . . . In psyops, she'd learned to hear the things not said. And she knew it—he wanted to get closer to her, but something was holding him back. Most likely it was just the rules, the old chain of command . . .

The secure line on her desk buzzed, and she pressed the red button on top of the console. "McBride here."

"Captain McBride?"

"Colonel Blevins?"

"Yes," he said softly. In the pause that followed, she wondered if their connection had been interrupted. But then he resumed, his voice more distinct. "How have things been going?"

"I assume you saw my last report. The data from WHO, the CDC, and the relevant field operations are all summarized in section—"

"Yes, yes. I've seen that. Thank you. I was just . . . wondering how you've been."

"How have I been?" Rose smiled—his first attempt at a personal question. But it was a start . . . "I've been fine."

"Good. Good . . ." There was another pause, and she heard a shuffling sound. "I have a special communication for you. I'll be sending it via your secure hookup. But I thought I should give you a heads-up in advance. I assume no one else is there in the room with you?"

Rose glanced around her cluttered office, at the walls of old shelving, the tattered couch across the room. It seemed as though every bit of unused furniture had found a resting place here. "No. I'm alone."

"Good. Could you please activate your earpiece?"

Rose could hear her blood pulsing as she fished the earpiece out of her desk drawer and placed it carefully into her right ear. "Okay. Ready, sir."

He wasted no time getting to the point. "The work you've done has been exemplary. But we'll be handing it off to someone else."

She stared at her console. Was that all? "My assignment is complete?"

"This part of it, yes. You've shown us your attention to detail. And that you're worthy of our confidence. Now we have a new assignment for you. We intend to recommission the Presidio."

"Recommission?"

"We need a base in that location."

"But how can you . . . ? It doesn't really belong to us, does it?"

Rose's mind raced, recounting what she knew of the history of the place she now called home. When the U.S. government had officially reserved the Presidio for military use in 1850, it had been nothing more than a windswept, barren expanse of sand dunes abutting a marshland bordering the San Francisco Bay. The army had planted trees—eucalyptus, cypress, and pines in orderly rows, like soldiers in formation—to create a windbreak and subdue the blowing sands. As new saplings had grown up to take their place, two world wars, the Korean War, and the Vietnam War had raged overseas, never to touch these shores. She remembered the inscription in the Presidio's chapel: *They also serve, who only stand and wait.* Throughout its history, the Presidio of San Francisco had been a place where armies stood at the ready, waiting for an enemy who never invaded. For this place was blessed. The thick fog that so often blanketed the coast, the forbidding cliffs that limited access from the ocean—these were the very things that had protected the Golden Gate from discovery for so many years. Together with treacherous tides, they had deterred attack throughout decades of war.

The army had finally vacated the place in 1994, and the Presidio had been given over to the National Park Service. In the years that followed, the area was opened to commercial interests and the park was resorbed into the city. The Presidio Institute and its sister organizations within the confines of the former Presidio—all nonprofit— were dedicated to civilian issues only. Rose was one of just a handful of employees with special clearance. Or so she'd been given to believe.

"The Presidio can . . . belong to us," the colonel replied evenly. "In time of war, the government has the prerogative to repurpose whatever lands and facilities might best serve the country's security."

Rose felt her heartbeat quicken, her old instincts from the field reawakening. "We're at war?"

"When are we not?"

"But why now? What's happening?"

"I'm only authorized to tell you that we need the Presidio ready. We'll need you to act as our point person in that operation."

"All right . . . But why me?"

"You've shown your ability to secure highly confidential information. And you know the people. You'll be able to act as our liaison in difficult situations."

Difficult situations. Rose was not expert in the administrative game, but she'd come to understand some of the jargon. "You mean, when we have to evict someone?"

"Yes. As you know, although there are currently no private residences in the Presidio, there are numerous museums and nonprofits. Over the past year, many have been replaced by shells."

Shells. Rose felt something unnamed pressing down on her. She was familiar with black ops in nonwar territories. But she'd thought that was all in her past—and certainly not in the mainland U.S. "You mean covert government organizations? I wasn't aware—"

"Well, now you are. And we need to make the final push. We'll need to rout out the last of the civilians, reinstitute checkpoints at the gates . . ."

"*Checkpoints?* Sir, what's going on?"

The colonel sighed, a sound that seemed not so much exasperated as sad. "Again, I'm really sorry. I can't tell you more at this time."

"Understood." Rose didn't understand. In fact, she was terrified.

He cleared his throat. "Captain McBride, I thank you for your service."

"You're welcome, of course." Rose fiddled with her earpiece. She was remembering the colonel's eyes, the way he'd looked at her the last time they'd met in Washington. The way his gaze had made her feel—as though he was planning something for her. Her heart sank. She'd thought it was something else—certainly not this.

"Well . . ." he said. "You'll receive further instructions via your se-cure channel." There was another pause. "Captain, I . . . uh . . . I need to inform you that . . . as with your previous project, you'll be report-ing in to me exclusively."

"Yes, sir. Of course."

Rose punched off her phone, then sank back into her chair, a chill running up her spine. What *was* this place? Did she really know it at all? Through her window she could see the Golden Gate Bridge, rust orange against a clear blue sky. Down below on the lawn, someone was flying a kite.

7

A SWATCH OF tarp, bright green against the muted red, blue, and purple of the canyon below, caught Kai's eye. A hollow tapping echoed in the stillness as he made his way down from his lookout to investigate, wedging his body carefully between walls of jagged rock. His feet stung as they hit the gravel base of the dry riverbed. There in front of him, a flap of plastic sheeting swayed free, its shining metal grommet striking a rusted pole. Tap. Tap, tap.

It looked like a tent. Advancing slowly, he craned his neck for a better view inside. He could see a battered metal pan and a broken plastic cup. Worn leather, ragged ties attached to something resembling a shoe. He leaned forward. Maybe this time . . .

Out of the darkness, hollow eye sockets gaped at him from a hairless skull. Uneven teeth laughed at him. It was human, or had been, clothed in the remains of stained brown pants and a faded blue shirt. He felt his body recoiling, his back colliding with the rock wall as he pulled out, away from the corpse. Then he was scaling upward, a familiar coppery taste rising in his throat as showers of loose dirt rained down behind him. At the top, he hoisted himself back up onto the hard sandstone ledge.

He and Rosie had been searching for months, with still no sign of another living person—only the occasional suggestion of what had once been a human body, its limbs torn off by wandering predators, its tattered clothing hanging on empty bones. Of all his discoveries, this body in the tent was the most fully preserved. But it was too big, he told himself. Not another child, not like him. He breathed deeply, filling his lungs and letting the air out slowly, trying to stay calm. Planting his palms on the sunbaked stone, he raised his head, looking for his Mother.

Then . . . the thump of his heart was replaced by a loud buzzing sound. Something was dancing in the sky overhead, a glistening something that swooped and looped, lowering with each pass. A roar deafened him as he clamped his eyes shut against a hail of small stones.

He barely had time to hold his hands over his ears before the roaring stopped, the ground still quaking beneath him. Shaking the dust from his hair, he scrambled to his feet.

It wasn't Rosie. But it was a bot.

His mouth agape, Kai watched its hatch open. He watched as someone emerged—a ragged tunic, a pair of bruised knees, a thick wooden stick clutched between the fingers of a delicate hand. Two enormous brown eyes stared at him from under a shelf of dark brown hair. It was a boy, about his height, whose every expression mirrored his own amazement. Kai rubbed his eyes with the backs of both hands as the newcomer slid to the ground.

"Hello?" The boy's voice was thin, uncertain.

"Uh . . . hello." Kai's own voice, so long unused, sounded foreign to his ears. His gaze darting left and right, he finally caught sight of Rosie, hunkered down in the shelter of a nearby boulder.

"I sense no threat." He heard Rosie's voice in his mind, soft with reassurance. Still, he shook from head to toe, a cold sweat chilling his skin.

The boy took a step back. "Don't be scared," he said softly.

Kai worked his jaw, his lips stiff. He blinked. "N-no," he managed. "Sorry . . . I just saw something. Down there."

"The body?" The boy averted his gaze, poking his stick into a clump of scrub, shifting his stance uncertainly from one foot to the other. "I found it yesterday. It wasn't one of us. Too big. And there was no bot."

"Should we bury it? Rosie taught me—"

"Alpha-C told me not to touch a body if you don't know how it died. It might cause infection." Grimacing, the boy cast a quick glance toward the bot behind him. "She warned me that almost everyone was gone. But she told me there are some special ones. Ones who aren't gone."

"Rosie told me that too." Kai nodded at Rosie, and the boy glanced shyly in her direction.

"So, I kept looking," the boy said.

"Me too."

The boy raised his hand to swipe the hair from his eyes. "But I've been looking for so long, I almost gave up."

"Me too."

Though he'd dreamed of it for as long as he could remember, Kai had never known how it would feel to find another child. Another child. At last! He felt stupid, the words he wanted to say caught somewhere between his brain and his mouth. For all the eloquent speeches he'd imagined, the only words that occurred to him now were "me too."

"My name is Sela," said the boy. "What's yours?"

"K-Kai."

"Kai. You're a boy, right?" said Sela. "I can tell. I'm a girl."

"A girl . . ." Kai took two steps forward, his right hand extended. At arm's length, he came to an abrupt stop. He felt his lips curling into an awkward smile, the blood rushing to his face. "I think we're supposed to shake hands," he said. "I learned it in Rosie's vids." His hand closed around hers, her touch warm and soft. "It's nice to meet you."

"It is *very* nice to make your acquaintance!" Sela performed an awkward curtsy, pulling them both off balance. "And Rosie," she said, her eyes drifting toward Kai's Mother. "I like that name. Like a flower."

She laughed, a sound like music.

IN HONOR OF their meeting, they decided to prepare a feast. Using her stick, Sela prodded fat nopal cactus paddles from their moorings. Then using a knife with a fancy engraved handle, she dexterously removed their stinging spines, shaved their edges smooth, and chopped them into smaller pieces.

Kai retrieved water from the storage depot near their new campsite—unlike others they'd found, this depot was well stocked. He used tiny, sweet ground-cherries mashed to the bottoms of flat rocks to set deadfall traps for the little mice who, as the sun set and the earth cooled, would soon emerge from their dens beneath the dry brush to search for meals of their own. Standing back, he admired Sela's pile of cactus. "Nice knife," he said.

"I found it near the depot where I grew up," Sela said, fingering the ivory hilt.

"Nicer than mine." Kai rubbed his thumb over the smooth housing of his own small knife—red plastic with a symbol painted in white on one side—a cross, inside what looked like a shield. Small though it was, he liked the way he could fold the knife back inside the casing when he wasn't using it. It reminded him of Rosie's wings.

A hollow thud announced Kai's first catch. He bent down to snatch up one of the rocks and extricate its flattened victim.

Sela leaned forward, her eyes wide. "What do they taste like?"

"You never had one?"

"To tell you the truth"—Sela blushed—"I've never eaten meat."

"If you don't want it . . ."

"Oh, no, that's not what I mean. Just . . . Alpha never showed me how."

Kai smiled. "Don't worry. Rosie says they're safe to eat."

They built a fire in the shelter of a tower of high rocks as their Mothers, standing guard a short distance away, cast long shadows in the dying rays of the sun. While Kai retrieved two more mice from his traps, Sela heated her cactus in a heavy metal skillet—another found treasure. After expertly ripping the skin from his little victims, Kai skewered the carcasses on a long, thin stem of desert brush, then propped it out over the low flames. As the meat cooked, they gorged themselves on the cactus, the juice running down their chins.

"No Pedia-Supp for us tonight!" Sela smiled. "This is a special day." But Kai only moved his mouth, his mind racing with half-formed words.

"What's the matter?" Sela asked.

"Um . . . I'm not used to talking out loud. But you . . . you're so good at it."

"I practiced every day," Sela said. "Don't worry, it's easy. And it'll get easier, the more of us we find."

"You think there are more?" Kai swiped his chin with one hand. "More like us?"

"I spotted another bot earlier. And it wasn't yours."

"How do you know?"

"She didn't have that mark on her wing."

Kai turned to regard his Mother. Her bright tattoo, the distinctive splotch of yellow paint that adorned her left wing, was barely visible in the waning light.

"What's it for?" Sela asked.

"Huh?"

"What does that marking mean?"

"I'm not sure. I thought they all had them . . ." He gazed at Sela's

Mother. Though similar in design to Rosie, she was different—her stooping posture, the way she stayed so close to Sela, even at rest. And no tattoo. "So . . . you saw another bot?"

"Alpha couldn't make her out. But for sure I saw a bot as we were flying over here." Sela raised one thin arm to point west, toward the spot where the sun now painted the horizon. "I wanted Alpha to circle back there. But we found you first."

"We can check it out in the morning."

Beside him, Sela bit carefully into her meat, ripping it delicately from the tiny bones with her teeth. Then she pursed her lips, turning to spit into the fire.

"You don't like it?"

"Maybe not," she sputtered. "Not for me."

"Sorry . . ."

"It's okay." Grabbing up her canteen, she washed her mouth out with a swig of water.

"Sela . . ." The feeling of her name on his tongue was strange. "How many more of us do you think there are?"

"Alpha said there were fifty in all . . . in the beginning."

"When we were launched."

"Yes. But . . ." Sela sat back, the hint of a frown shadowing her brow.

"But she doesn't know how many there are now," Kai said.

"No. She just says . . ."

"There is a nonzero probability of success." Kai smiled, and he could see Sela return his grin in the firelight. "Why do you think they separated?"

"Separated?"

"Why didn't all of our Mothers stay together?"

"Alpha told me it was for security."

"Rosie said that too. But security from what?"

"She didn't say . . . The Epidemic . . . Predators maybe?"

"But we're immune to the Epidemic. And Rosie has a laser. She killed a wild dog once, when it got too close."

Kai looked up at the housing near where Rosie's arm met her fuselage. Her laser beam was deadly accurate. *A weapon is not to be used except in extreme circumstances,* she'd warned. *Only when our lives are in danger.*

Sela knit her brow. "A long time ago," she said, "I think Alpha used her laser too. It was late at night, and I was asleep in the cocoon. It was loud, like an explosion . . . But when I looked out the hatch window, there was nothing there." She shook her head. "Maybe it was just a dream."

Kai felt a chill run up his spine as he peered into the darkness outside the glow of their fire. Rosie had taught him that she was made in a laboratory. But who made her? Where was that laboratory? She wouldn't say. That information, she said, was "classified"—whatever that meant. He imagined the adults who populated his vids, riding in cars and going to work in tall office buildings. Was there someone else, someone not like him and his Mother, still alive out there? No. According to Rosie, the probability of that was "minimal." Only the Mothers and their children had been designed to survive.

"I just wish . . ." He stirred the fire with his empty skewer. It felt odd to say this to someone other than Rosie. "I just wish our Mothers would've stayed together. It would've been easier."

Sela finished off the water from her canteen. "I have extra water in my cocoon," she said, "from my last campsite."

"I've got plenty too," Kai said. "At least for now."

Sela stood up, brushing the dust from the front of her tunic. "So . . . morning, then?"

"Yes."

Her eyes were still on him, appraising him. "This is good, isn't it?"

"Yes." Despite the chill wind, Kai felt warm. He stared up at the velvet sky, the sharp pinpoints of stars dancing across its surface. It was good.

THE NEXT MORNING Kai awoke at daybreak, eager to see Sela again. As he slid down Rosie's treads, he scanned the campsite. Alpha-C's hatch was ajar, a dull pink glow emanating from inside. Leaning against her tread, Sela was sucking on the corner of a packet of Pedia-Supp. "This stuff isn't as good as real food, but at least it's quick," she said between mouthfuls.

"We'll head west today?"

"Alpha agreed to our plan."

"Rosie too. But how do we stay together?"

"Can you tell your Mother to follow us?"

Kai paused, telegraphing Rosie. "Yes," he said aloud. "She can track you."

Climbing back into his cocoon, Kai retrieved his own Pedia-Supp ration from the hold behind his seat. He strapped himself in, then ripped off the corner of the packet to suck down its contents. Through the hatch window he could see Sela mounting Alpha's treads. And for the first time, he watched another bot prepare for takeoff, her wings emerging from the sleek casing of her back, her ducted fans jutting from their massive sheaths to turn toward the ground. Then all was obscured in dust as Rosie followed suit.

The air cleared as they rose, Alpha leading the way and Rosie giving chase. Kai was mesmerized by the sight of another bot in flight. But he knew that Rosie didn't fly the way that Alpha did, curving and swerving through the sky like a mad bird. "Can you talk to Alpha-C?" he asked Rosie.

"What is Alpha-C?"

"Sela's bot. Can't you talk to her?"

"No. I communicate only with my child."

"But you can see her."

"Yes, I sense her form. I'm maintaining a safe distance."

"Would you be able to sense another bot, if she was down below on the ground?"

"I've commenced pattern recognition. I will report to you if I identify a structure with the correct signature. However, my infrared detectors will not yield a discernible signal at the current ground temperature."

"Why not?"

"The average ground temperature currently ranges between 29 and 33 degrees Celsius. The small amount of heat emitted by a bot or by a life-form on its surface will not be detected."

It was hot, much hotter than it had been in springs past. The land below was obscured in haze, and Kai could only hope that Sela would be able to make out the bot she'd spotted the day before. Suddenly Alpha dipped one wing, tracing a wide arc as she slowly descended. "Do you see something now?" Kai squinted, straining to detect whatever it was that Sela had located.

"No. I don't."

"But you'll follow Alpha-C?"

"Yes."

As they set down, Kai fumbled out of his restraints. He pushed open Rosie's hatch door, slid down her treads, and sprinted toward Alpha. Sela's back was toward him, her slight shoulders slumped as she stood at her Mother's side.

It wasn't until he came up beside her that he caught sight of the wreckage. "What is it?"

"It's . . . It *was* . . . a bot." Sela's eyes were brimming with tears. "I should've known. There was a reason Alpha didn't recognize her. She's just . . . in pieces."

Kai stepped forward gingerly, the hairs on his arms prickling in the heat. A thin wind whistled through the disembodied fan that lay on the ground in front of him. A few feet away, a fuselage lay cracked open like the shell of an egg. He saw one wing, extended. And protruding from beneath it . . .

"Uhhhnnn . . ." Kai stared at the splintered vessel, the network of tubing and wires trying but failing to hold together its elongated egg shape. In his mind's eye, he saw another vessel like this one, lying in the hot sun beside the supply depot where he'd been born.

"What is that?" he'd asked.

"That is your birthplace," Rosie had explained. "Your incubator. We have no need for it now. But once, it was very important."

An incubator. But this one was different. This one contained a tiny, perfectly formed skeleton, its hands folded together as if in prayer.

He felt Sela's hand on his arm, the gentlest of touches. "It's okay." Her voice was low, choked, as she turned to go. "C'mon. We'll find more. Next time they'll be alive."

"But, Sela," he said. "We can't just go. We should bury this one."

8

IN THE DIM, windowless room at Fort Detrick, James dreamed of his lab at Emory, with its expansive benches and sweeping campus views. He wished he could have brought his lab group here with him. But as the months had passed, his cadre of postdocs at Emory had had to manage with only a weekly check-in. His department head had to be content with a vague explanation from the government as to his indispensability on a matter of national security. And he had to be content with Rudy Garza's small team, and with a lumpy daybed in the cramped Harpers Ferry apartment that he and Rudy now shared.

James smiled. At least, like many chemists, Rudy was also a fine cook. His favorite pastime was watching cooking vids as he concocted delicious creations in the kitchen.

But they had to be careful. The previous night, as Rudy had treated James to an amazing new tamale dish, they'd left the vids running. The news had come on, headlining a report about mysterious deaths in the Afghan desert. "The military has cordoned off the area," said a male reporter dressed in a hazmat suit. "But people are still dying here." The camera panned over a metal fence to show a row of wasted figures lying on bloodstained army cots—innocent victims who looked all too much like James's own parents. "No one seems to know the cause," the reporter continued. "And military personnel have so far denied access to humanitarian aid."

Rudy had punched his remote. "Enough of that," he'd said. "We need our sleep."

But sleep had not come. Exhausted, James scanned the orderly rows of small vials in cold storage, each a different variation on the same theme. His gloved fingers danced over the vials, picking out one labeled "C-341." With any luck, this was the NAN sequence that would challenge the onslaught of the deadly IC-NAN.

Subverting IC-NAN would not be easy; to date, no one known to be infected had recovered. IC-NAN's mode of action was to block transcription of the gene for a key protein called initiator caspase. It did this by inserting itself into the DNA at a site called the "initiator caspase promoter," at the spot where transcription of the caspase gene to make messenger RNA would normally begin. Without this messenger RNA, the cell couldn't make caspase. Without the ability to make caspase, the cell couldn't respond to natural signals telling it that it was time to self-destruct. And so it lived on, dividing, clogging the surfaces of the lung, breaking off to travel throughout the body.

To defeat IC-NAN, their only recourse would be to somehow insert a new caspase gene, one with a different promoter that wasn't susceptible to modification by it. Their plan was to develop an antidote NAN. The aerosol form used to administer this new NAN could be the same as the one that the Defense Department had used for the IC-NAN, miniaturized for individual dosing—similar to the inhalers commonly used by asthmatics. Rudy's team had set to work synthesizing the alternative antidotes. It had been James's job to set up and monitor testing of these on human cell culture models.

James set the vial carefully in a rack at the back of his biosafety hood. "I only wish we could speed this process up somehow," he complained.

"James, we must be patient," Rudy replied. "These types of nanostructures are notoriously unstable and difficult to synthesize. It took my team three years to perfect a stable dosage form of the IC-NAN, and we did not even have to test for adverse effects. No animal trials were required—we got away with using only cell culture to prove efficacy. You must believe me. You and I have come very far in only two years."

It was true. For IC-NAN, the goal was death. But the antidote NAN needed to be both effective *and* safe—free of long-term adverse effects. James had screened hundreds of candidate NANs in cell culture. Of these, five had been deemed effective enough to move on to primate testing. It was the primate testing, on macaques housed in a secluded Puerto Rican facility, that was eating up precious time as the team waited to rule out unwanted side effects. Only a single candidate, C-341, was finally showing promise.

It was a colossal undertaking—genetic engineering of the entire human race. The key would be to administer the antidote *before* the subject was exposed to IC-NAN. This would limit the number of lesions that would have to be dealt with later. Then, administration would have to be continued regularly. Everyone on earth would need prophylactic treatment, unless or until humans evolved to live in their new IC-NAN-laden environment. And there was always the risk that the antidote NAN might cause other, unexpected side effects that hadn't shown up in their testing. But Colonel Richard Blevins seemed only to disparage the magnitude of the challenge. Indeed, the colonel discouraged collaboration among the science teams. It had become clear to James that he could know no more than was necessary to complete his limited portion of the total mission.

Locking the door to the cold box, James turned to face his lab mate. "Rudy, do you really think they're taking this program seriously?"

Rudy ran his hand thoughtfully over his balding pate. "How do you mean?"

"I don't see anyone worrying about trials. The antidote can't be vetted without statistically valid human trials. And what about scale-up? If, as you say, the synthesis is so tricky, how are we going to make enough for everyone? Not to mention that a stable dosage form still needs to be worked out. Don't they understand—"

Rudy removed his lab coat, hanging it carefully on a hook by the door. Turning, he laid a gentle hand on James's arm. "As I told you, I used to feel the same way about IC-NAN—that they were not serious about it. In fact, I fully anticipated cancellation. But then when we completed the project, I was told that a dispersal system had already been developed. There was already a bioreactor, ready for scale-up."

"Someone else was carrying the ball."

"Yes. These projects are carefully parsed, information shared only on a need-to-know basis. I pray each day for success. And I am certain that our government will aid us in any way possible."

"But you saw the most recent projections regarding the spread of the infected archaebacteria. We only have another two years to come up with a complete solution—if that."

Rudy paused, seeming to consider his reply. "This depends upon what you would call 'complete,'" he said. "I must admit, I have been wondering . . ."

"Wondering?"

Rudy looked at the floor, not meeting his gaze now. "Please, do not tell anyone I told you this, James. But . . . I have heard a few things. I think that now . . . they realize that they must be content to save a chosen few."

James felt the energy draining from his limbs as he followed Rudy down the hall to their cramped cubicles. Sinking into his chair, he stared at an old photograph of his mother and father, the only personal item he'd brought with him from Emory. In the wake of his frantic message from the back of the government limo two years back, he'd had to constantly reassure them that all was well. For all they knew now, he was still at Emory, still attending faculty dinners and slaving his way toward tenure.

He missed them, dearly. But he'd distanced himself, fabricating endless excuses for his failure to honor their invitations home. And as time passed, he'd found himself wondering: Was his current course—holding back the things he cared about most—just another version of what they'd done to him for as long as he could remember?

The only child of Abdul and Amani Said, he'd always enjoyed the keen sense of their love. But every bit as keen had been his sense of the distance at which they kept him. They prayed behind closed doors, in a language he never learned. His "Christian name" was just that—Christian. And even his last name was different from theirs. They'd taught him to pronounce it like the English word—*he said, she said.* Not like the folks at Wheelan Farms, the Southern California hemp operation where his father worked as foreman, pronounced it. "Sure, Mr. *Sah-eed,*" they would drawl. "Do you want that delivered today, or can it wait 'til tomorrow?"

Surely, everything his parents had done was for his protection. As much as they loved their faith, as much as it was an integral part of them, they'd taken great pains to insulate him from it. But he couldn't stay insulated forever. At some point, he'd have to face his own reality. He was facing it now. The way he was treated here at Fort Detrick, held at arm's length . . . Even Rudy stumbled sometimes, stopping in midsentence when James asked too many questions. Slowly but surely, James had become aware that he was being kept in the dark, even more so than Rudy and the others. He suffered no delusions. As one of Pakistani descent working within the close network of U.S. government security, he would always suffer extra scrutiny.

He grimaced. In the same way, his parents might one day have to come to terms with the reality of the secrets he now kept—the reality of a global, man-made epidemic. Of course he hoped that the IC-NAN epidemic would never spread. But each day, he was more certain that it would. It was only a matter of time.

He reached out to flip on his computer screen. The symbol of the Department of Defense, the eagle and its crown of thirteen stars, appeared as he waited for their scheduled meeting to begin. Finally, he heard the loud click that signaled the sign-on at Langley. He imagined a dark office at the other end, Blevins sitting alone at a small desk. But then he heard other voices, chatting quietly.

"Dr. Said, are you there?" It was the colonel.

"Yes, I'm here."

"Dr. Garza?"

"Yes." Rudy's voice echoed through his microphone from the adjacent cubicle.

"Good. Then we'll begin."

The symbol disappeared, replaced by the live image of a small table around which were seated five people. Colonel Blevins and another, taller man with massive square shoulders were in military uniform. A petite, redheaded woman and the overweight, dough-faced man beside her, both of whom looked vaguely familiar, were clad in business suits. The fifth was . . . Irena Blake, the vice president of the United States.

"We have some guests here at Langley today," Blevins said. "General Joseph Blankenship, director of the CIA." The taller man in uniform raised a finger. "Henrietta Forbes, secretary of defense." The small woman waved unenthusiastically toward the camera. "Sam Lowicki, director of national intelligence. And of course, you know the vice president."

James squinted at his screen. This wasn't just an update. Decisions had been made. He watched as Blevins turned to his assembled group. "On this call we have Dr. Rudy Garza and Dr. James Said from Fort Detrick."

In the room at Langley, Sam Lowicki leaned forward. "Gentlemen..." He stopped to clear his throat, loosening his tie. "First, I'd like to thank you both for your efforts. I know this can't have been easy for you. We all know you've done your best."

"But..." James whispered to himself. But what? He could feel his pulse, nearly bursting in his neck.

"At this point, we've decided that it's time for a... realignment of priorities. Dr. Garza?"

"Yes?"

"You'll be responsible for human trials on your antidote candidates. When we determine which one is best, we'll go full tilt on that one."

"But..." James couldn't stop himself.

"Yes, Dr. Said?" It was Colonel Blevins, looking pointedly now into the camera.

"As you know," James said, "we only have one viable antidote candidate at the moment. And how can we conduct human trials without screened subjects?"

"We have volunteers," Blevins said.

"But who—"

"That's none of your concern," Blevins said, cutting him off. His normally ruddy face grew even more flushed as he sat back.

"Dr. Said?" It was Sam Lowicki again. "You'll be assigned to a new project. This will require relocation."

"Relocation? Where?"

"Los Alamos, New Mexico."

"New Mexico? But my—"

"Your department at Emory has been informed. General Blevins will brief you on your new assignment within the hour. Again, we thank you for your service."

James sat back, stunned. His body felt molded to his chair, his arms limp at his sides. *General* Blevins? When had Blevins been promoted? And why?

9

AS THE MEETING room emptied, Rick sank back in his chair and loosened his tie. Sweat had wet the collar of his dress shirt, and his right leg thrummed with pain from the place that had once been his calf. He fumbled in his pocket for the small plastic bottle. Over the past few months, he'd been forced to go back on his pain meds. But in the interest of maintaining a clear head, he'd thought better of taking them that morning.

He dug the heels of his hands deep into his eye sockets. At least the pills he took now were only for the physical pain. He liked to think that the mental scars he'd sustained in the field had long since healed over. Letting the Narcodol do its job, he thought about Rose McBride, remembering their first interview.

Remembering all their meetings since.

Prior to bringing her on, he'd treated Captain McBride like any other mission. Without her knowing, he'd learned everything he could about her. After finishing an undergraduate degree in psychology, she'd started her military career advising psyops and performing psych evals on prisoners of war in Yemen. Interesting. She'd come back home to earn a graduate degree in computer science, specializing in cybersecurity. Impressive. As part of cyber ops in Afghanistan, her tireless investigation into an intricate web of secret communications had led to the capture of a notorious terrorist and arms trafficker, code name "Zulfiqar." Amazing.

But then, he'd met her. Closing his eyes, he imagined her face, the way she moved. He imagined her lithe, expressive hands tracing arcs in the air as she summarized rafts of seemingly unrelated findings, bringing to life the tale of the data. Her blue-green eyes flashed as they caught the glow of her screen . . .

Rose claimed to be unmoored, a plant without roots. But she was the most grounded person he had ever met. She knew who she was. She knew what she was about. She saw through to the heart of everything. And when she looked at him, he was sure that she saw through to his heart.

He'd tried to reason away his feelings. Of course she would make him feel that way—an open book, there for the reading. Out in the field, he'd encountered his share of psych officers. They were expert in deconstructing you—it became second nature to them after a while. But this was different. She hadn't interrogated him. She hadn't challenged him. Yet in her presence, something in him, a line of defense he hadn't even known was there, had fallen away. And since he'd met Rose, the face that looked back at him in the mirror each morning was different. It was a face he could live with; the face of someone he could at least aspire to be.

He clenched his fists. His feelings for Rose McBride were getting the better of him. She was a subordinate, working on a sensitive mission. To even imagine a relationship with her went against every code of military ethics that had been drilled into him. He had to get a grip.

Still, he was determined to promote her. And so far, Dr. McBride had made that task an easy one. With her expertise in big data, she'd made light work of mapping the movements of suspect archaea species around the globe. She'd collated information from numerous international science agencies, coordinating the deployment of teams to collect the samples shipped to Fort Detrick for further investigation. He hadn't had to tell her much. Used to clandestine operations, she wasn't one to ask questions. Her attention to detail had been impeccable. And her findings had spelled their doom. She'd clearly demonstrated that the spread of infected archaebacteria was more rapid than the initial models had predicted. Over the past nine months, DOD had only confirmed her projections.

Because of this—and *only* this, he told himself—he'd lobbied for putting her in charge of the Presidio recommission. And so far, her work had once more been commendable. Offering only mild incentives and the assurance that their new neighborhoods would "greatly benefit" from their presence, she'd managed to sweet-talk the last holdouts along the former Main Post into relocating to much less desirable offices in downtown San Francisco.

Now, with the New Dawn project at Los Alamos, he'd have her in—all in. And that was important, because only those inside the team would even stand a chance of getting the antidote. He could admit it now, if only to himself. He wanted her to have the antidote.

He keyed in Rose's number at the institute, and she picked up immediately.

"Congratulations, *General*," she said.

"What?"

"You've been promoted?"

"Oh . . . yes, you heard about that. It's just brigadier general . . . only the one star . . ." He was silent, his thoughts swimming. "Captain McBride?"

"You may call me Rose, if you wish."

"Rose? Uh . . ."

"Your text message said something about a new assignment?"

"Yes. We're wrapping up the Presidio recommission. Now we have something more up your alley. Computer programming . . . But it would be best to explain it to you in person."

"Do you need me to come to Washington?"

"No, we'll be meeting in Los Alamos tomorrow. At the XO-Bot facility."

"The place where they design those space robots?"

Rick smiled. Space robots. "Yes," he said. "Can you make it there by sixteen hundred hours?"

He heard a crackling on the line. "Uh . . . yes . . . I can fly out first thing in the morning."

"Good." Rick sat back, his heart beating a little too fast. "Good. I'll send flight details. We'll have a car take you to the airfield."

He keyed off, his index finger glued for a moment to the small red icon on the console. He always looked forward to their time together. But this would be a difficult meeting, the first time she would really understand what had been going on all along. He wanted to be the one to tell her, and he wanted to tell her to her face.

But first there was the matter of James Said. Shaking his head, he keyed in the doctor's secure number.

"Yes?" Said was angry—that much was clear.

"I'm sorry," Rick muttered into the phone. "I couldn't risk getting into an argument in front of—"

"I see. But *now* can you tell me what's happening? Why am I going to Los Alamos?"

"The archaebacteria are spreading faster than we'd hoped. And as you know, the antidote won't be sufficient—"

"We don't know that."

"We do. Even if we can get something to work in a few individuals, you know as well as I do that we don't have time to save the world."

A deep sigh rattled the line. "All right, so you trust Dr. Garza and his team to carry the antidote project without me. But why are you sending me to Los Alamos? What could possibly be going on there that's more important than the work I've been doing at Fort Detrick?"

"We need to make babies," Rick said.

"Babies?"

"Children who are immune to this thing. It's one of the reasons you were brought on in the first place."

"In the *first* place?"

"Dr. Said, may I be candid with you?"

"Please."

"I objected strongly to your initial placement on the team. I believed that we already had enough firepower on the NAN project. But even *I* wasn't privy to the whole story."

"Which is . . . ?"

"Blankenship and the team at Fort Detrick always had another plan, a backup. And they were sure that based on your previous research, you'd know how to get this done."

"But . . . *babies*? Who would feed them? Who would raise them?"

"We're working on that."

"The survivors? The ones who take the antidote? Will they be the ones who—"

"Dr. Said, we don't know. We don't know if there will *be* any survivors. We need to cover all our bases. We need alternatives. There'll be a debriefing tomorrow afternoon at Los Alamos. You'll be on a military jet by oh seven hundred. You'll receive details via your secure hookup. Just pack for overnight. You can get your things in order afterward."

Reaching across the table, Rick cut off their connection. No time now for questions. And besides, he had no answers. Babies. He was trying not to think too much, about the children already living in this poisonous time.

10

MARCH 2062

THROUGH ROSIE'S HATCH window, Kai searched for Alpha-C in the darkness. His heartbeat slowed as he discerned her outline in the moonlight. They'd found another one yesterday—yet another one who was supposed to have survived, its bot destroyed, its tiny body long dead. In a year of searching with Sela and Alpha, it was the third one. The disappointment was less painful with Sela by his side. But it was painful nonetheless.

"You are sad." Rosie's voice sounded deep in his mind.

"Yes."

"Don't worry," she said. "There is no reason for sadness."

Kai shook his head. Wasn't there? Silently, he waited for daybreak.

NEXT TO HIM in her Mother's shadow, Sela chewed slowly on something that looked like a spiky green stick. "Here." She offered him a piece. "I found this yesterday on our way back. It's supposed to be used in a tea, but if you don't have any water you can just chew on the twigs. It helps clear your head."

Taking the twig from her hand, Kai nibbled at it tentatively. It tasted terribly bitter, its dry surface adhering to his cracked lips. He pulled his blanket tight around him, staring vacantly out at the blinding white-gray of the rocky field where they'd made camp. Despite the cold, they were too parched, too exhausted to go exploring. "You sure you don't want to eat something else?"

"Yes . . ."

He was worried about Sela. At the depots they'd reached, they'd found only scant supplies. No stored water, and the towers were bone-dry. They'd relied on harvesting the runoff from high-elevation snows, but the past winter had been milder than usual, the scant snowmelt already evaporated from the highest visible peaks. The few rivers they'd come across were shallow and drained. With the excuse that they needed to conserve the water they used for cooking, Sela had taken to eating less and less. He could see the bones of her shoulders, poking up under her tunic. And the girl who had once delighted in leading him on merry chases through the sky, her Mother whirling and diving as they carried out one of their many "missions," seemed to be losing her way. Was she, like he, afraid of what they might find next?

Sela was looking at Alpha in that way she did when she and her Mother were talking. Her brow was furrowed, and Kai could tell that the conversation wasn't a pleasant one.

"What's the matter?" he asked.

"Even if we wanted to, Alpha says we shouldn't be flying so much."

Kai remembered Rosie's voice now, the warning she'd issued to him the night before as he slept. "Particulates?"

"There's more dust in the air than there used to be. She's having a harder time clearing it from her engines."

"But we need to keep moving . . ." Kai looked up at the sky, the brilliant light of the sun dispersed as though by a haze of fine crystals. It had been like this for weeks now, the distant mesas almost invisible. He willed himself to stand up. "I've got an idea," he said. "Let's see what all we've got."

"What?"

"Rosie says it's my birthday today. I'm eight. We should have a birthday party!"

"Yes . . ." Sela said. "I'll be eight tomorrow."

"Let's give each other gifts."

"Gifts? But I don't—"

"I've got some stuff I haven't shown you yet. I'm sure you have some things too . . ."

Scaling Rosie's treads to search his cocoon, Kai rummaged through his meager collection of belongings, looking for something Sela might like. Then, cradling his treasures in his arms, he shambled down to arrange them on the ground. A plastic rectangle wedged inside a rubberized case. "An old tablet, for playing games," he said. "I couldn't get it to work." A small, plastic musical instrument that Rosie called a ukulele. "It's supposed to have strings," he explained. A brown leather hat with a broken brim. "A cowboy hat," he said, placing it squarely atop his mop of tangled hair. "Good for keeping the sun off." Grinning, he pretended to strum the stringless ukulele, humming off-key. Then, with a flourish, he took off the hat and gave it to Sela.

But Sela just looked at him with a blank expression. And suddenly he felt silly. What had he been thinking? It was all stupid, just junk . . .

Then she rewarded him with a grin. "I've got something better than all that," she said. Retreating into Alpha's hold, she soon emerged with a large pink bag strapped to her shoulder. Adorned with a comic book picture of a smiling cat, the bag had one main compartment and three small side pockets, each held closed with shiny metal snaps. From one of the pockets she produced a necklace made of polished stones the color of the sky, strung on a silver chain. "Turquoise," she said. Then from the main compartment, she removed something fashioned from what looked like thin wooden sticks, woven together.

"What is it?" Kai asked, coming close.

"It's an airplane," Sela said, her eyes glowing as she held it up to show two sleek wings attached to a center fuselage. "Like the ones in the old vids. But this one has no engine. It's a glider."

"Can I hold it?"

"Yes . . . But be careful. I made it myself, before we met. It took me forever to figure out a way to keep it together. The frame is made from tumbleweed, and the rest is dried grass. It's all in the weaving." Gingerly, Sela offered up the plane. Kai balanced it on the tops of his two index fingers, one finger under each of its wings. "Alpha taught me about weaving. And about airplanes. She knows a lot about those things. She says that one day, I can build a glider big enough to fly in. She says that gliding is the most amazing way to fly—all quiet, like a bird."

Kai looked at her incredulously. "Is it . . . for me?"

Sela offered him a small smile. "Sorry," she said. "I didn't mean for you to think that . . ." Taking the airplane back from him, she replaced it carefully into her bag. "But here, you can have this." She reached into a second side pocket, then opened her fist to reveal a small, glistening object.

Hesitantly, Kai took the thing in his palm, a silver case in the form of a flat cylinder. Through its clear cover, he could see a delicate needle, hovering hesitantly over the letter "W."

"A compass," Sela said. "It's so great. It tells you which way to go."

"Thanks, but don't you need it?" Kai made to hand the compass back to her.

"No," Sela said. "We're together now, right?" From the third side pocket, she removed an oblong snippet of paper and placed it in his upturned palm. "And then there's this."

Kai rubbed his thumb over the smiling, laminated image of a tow-headed girl in a red dress. A woman with long brown hair surrounded the little girl's shoulders with one protective arm. Behind them, an expanse of blue water shimmered under a cloudless sky. "They look happy."

"Yeah . . ." Sela gazed thoughtfully at the picture. "Where do you think this was?"

Kai shook his head. By an ocean? A lake? Except for on Rosie's screen, he'd never seen such a place.

"We need to go there. To a place like that. Where there's lots of water, lots of plants . . ." Sela said.

"Do you think maybe our Mothers can take us there?"

Sela stared disconsolately back at her Mother. "So many times, I begged her to fly me there. But Alpha says she doesn't have the coordinates. She won't go unless she can evaluate the risks . . ."

Sela didn't have to finish her thought. Kai knew. Rosie had told him the same thing—she wasn't programmed to take him just anywhere. She needed data, proof that the destination was safe. It was why, over the past year, they'd done nothing more than travel between one near-empty depot and the next. Still . . . "There must be a way—" Suddenly he saw a light in Sela's eyes, that mischievous glint he'd only just realized he missed. He stared at her. "What?"

Sela leaned toward him, cupping her hand around his ear. "If our Mothers won't take us somewhere, it doesn't mean we can't go," she whispered.

"What do you mean?"

"The dirt bike. We should go back and get it. We could fix it up, make it work. Then we could go anywhere we want!"

Kai nodded. The RV. Just a few days ago they'd found it. But as with yesterday's destroyed bot, he'd been trying not to think about it.

The RV had been huge, with sleek metallic flanks and a bright orange stripe painted along each side. It had its own kitchen and even a little bathroom. As he took in the sheer bulk of it, he'd allowed himself to dream. Even before the Epidemic, Rosie had told him, no one really lived out here. But there had been campers, people who came to spend a few weeks in the desert. They had what used to be called vacations.

Kai sighed. It would have been a great place to live. But there had been skeletons inside, two big ones lying on a wide bed and a smaller one tucked into a cot nearby. He could never live in a place where the victims of the Epidemic still lay in their beds. He couldn't imagine moving them. And, unless it was food or water, he couldn't imagine taking what had once been theirs. The RV had been bereft of nonperishable food. After draining the water tanks of their stale contents, they'd left the place behind.

"It's okay, Kai." Sela was grasping his arm now, her eyes pleading. "All we need is the bike. And it's outside."

He looked at her. He couldn't resist. It was the happiest, the most hopeful, he'd seen her in a long time. "Sure. But how will we find it again?"

"I'll take you there." It was Rosie. "I have stored the coordinates in my flight database."

Kai glanced at Sela, who was nodding toward her Mother. "It's a go," she said, smiling.

Soon Kai was watching the site from the air, the weighty vehicle still parked off a dirt road by the side of a wide canyon, a tattered American flag fluttering from a bracket by the side door. The bike was still leaning against the back fender.

They landed a few hundred feet away, so as not to disturb this hallowed ground. But Sela couldn't contain herself, dashing full tilt for the bike as if for freedom itself. As Kai came up beside her, she was running her hand over the glimmering handlebars. "Alpha says she can charge it up," she said. "We can modify the footrests and handlebars to fit us better."

Kai scratched his head. "Why do you think our Mothers are letting us do this?" he asked. "Wouldn't we be safer traveling inside our cocoons?"

Once more, a cloud came over Sela's face. "Alpha says it's a matter of risk."

"Risk?"

"We have to keep moving, to find water and food—maybe, if we're lucky, we'll find another child. But right now it's safer to do that by land, so long as we wear our masks when we're on the bike," she said.

Kai remembered the particle masks, stored in a compartment under his seat in the cocoon. He'd never had to wear one before. But Rosie had told him the same thing: The fine desert dust was no better for his lungs than it was for her engines.

Sela pulled the bike's charger from its plug on the side of the RV and handed it to her Mother. "I suppose they don't call it a dirt bike for nothing," she said, kicking a shelf of sand from its rear tire guard.

11

IN THE LATE-AFTERNOON gloom of her Presidio office, Rose McBride
sat back, massaging her temples with her fingertips. New Dawn. At
times, she wished she'd never heard of it. Because hearing of it meant
knowing everything else.

In one way or another, she'd been involved with this project since
December of '49. But she'd been on the outside, with no possibility of
seeing in. Over a year spent tracking mysterious microbes, followed by
nine months negotiating the relocation of the nongovernment occu-
pants of the Presidio, hadn't prepared her for the truth she'd learned
at that first Los Alamos meeting six months ago. She'd learned that
human life on earth was facing annihilation. She'd learned that it
would be her job to imagine what would happen afterward. And she'd
learned that if her projections about the inexorable spread of infected
archaebacteria were true, this would be her final mission.

The proper way to train military robots to care for newborns in a
postapocalyptic world hadn't been part of the course curriculum at
Princeton. The whole idea was preposterous, a herculean undertaking,
a project of ever-expanding scope and difficulty. But given everything

that was happening—the rapid spread of the infection, the failure so far to develop a working antidote that might save more than a few souls—it had somehow begun to make sense.

She remembered the news report she'd watched as she'd sipped her coffee earlier that morning: "A widespread outbreak of a 'flu-like illness' has decimated the population of Kandahar over the past few weeks," said a frightened-looking reporter, a military chopper stationed close behind him. "Doctors in Pakistan's border cities are beginning to report similar symptoms. We have no idea whether the recent American military activity in the region bears any relation to this current health crisis, but we have continued to observe massive burn operations during recent flyovers." She had to admit it—the robotic option had to be considered. And Rick Blevins had been right in choosing her to develop the program. For she couldn't stop thinking about it, imagining it.

She called it the Mother Code, a computer code meant to embody the very essence of motherhood. The challenge of the code had lifted her from her moorings, plunged her headlong into uncharted waters. She herself had never been a mother. She didn't know the first thing about caring for a child, let alone a newborn. She was dogged by fear— fear that if it ever had to be used, her Mother Code would fail the ones who needed it, defenseless children in a new world. But she knew that she would never give up.

Unlike her, most of the project's participants knew nothing of its full scope. To her collaborators at MIT, it represented a chance to participate in a fascinating and well-funded government project in artificial intelligence. And apart from their supervisor, Kendra Jenkins, the flock of robotics programmers at Los Alamos was under the same misguided impression. Before being promoted to security chief at Los Alamos, Kendra had supervised the compilation of the base operations code for the robots, the code that governed their motion. Rose's

Mother Code needed to be carefully integrated with this—a complex program that governed not only the how but the why of every action.

It hadn't taken long for Rose to come to a realization: Her Mothers would need "personalities." But she couldn't invent these from thin air. She'd need models to work from. Who better than the biological mothers of the children they might one day care for?

Her wrist phone buzzed. "Captain McBride?" came the voice of the receptionist from the lobby below. "Your next appointment is here."

"Tell her to come on up." Straightening her collar, Rose sat forward, her eyes on the door.

The woman who entered was of middle height, perhaps five feet seven. Her mahogany-brown hair was pulled back into a tight bun. Her gaze steady on Rose's, she carried the serious, clipped demeanor of the trained fighter pilot that she was. "Lieutenant Nova Susquetewa," she said.

"Have a seat," Rose said, indicating the small chair on the other side of her desk. She found herself adjusting her own posture as the young woman sat down, her spine stiff as a rod. "Have you been briefed on our program?"

The lieutenant stared around her at the untidy office that was definitely not that of a doctor. "I was told that this is one way I can preserve my eggs? For later?"

"That is one of our purposes," Rose said carefully. "But there's more. There's the personality profiling aspect . . ."

"Yes," Nova said. "Yes, of course. My base commander told me I'd be subjected to some pretty intense scrutiny before I deployed."

"Yes." Rose nodded. "You've been assigned to a sensitive mission. Secrecy will be paramount. And your mission is high-risk . . . We need to be sure you're ready."

"I am," Nova said, sitting forward eagerly. Then her gaze softened, almost imperceptibly. "I am," she repeated, almost to herself.

Rose sat back, remembering her script. "You'll be given a battery of tests over the next few days," she said. Then, noticing the crease that formed in Nova's brow, she added quickly: "Nothing difficult. We're just . . . trying something new. We're gathering data for a long-term study relating certain . . . personality traits . . . to subsequent reaction to stress in the battlefield." She watched Nova's face for a reaction but found only a mild perplexity. "We've notified your commander. You'll need to go to Boston for the tests. MIT. They'll conduct a series of taped interviews, followed by a few more physical tests."

"And then you'll collect my eggs, right?" Nova asked.

"Correct. That part of the protocol will be done at the VA med center in . . ." Rose leafed through the file on her desk. "Phoenix, right? Near where you're currently stationed."

Nova shifted in her seat. "Captain McBride, may I be honest?"

"Of course."

"Don't get me wrong, I want to go on this mission. But I . . . I'm worried about it. I'd be crazy not to be, right?"

"Of course. I understand."

"If my . . . worry comes out in these personality tests . . . will they hold me back?"

Rose made eye contact with the young officer, offering her a reassuring smile. "It's perfectly normal to be concerned about this mission, under the circumstances. But . . . is there something special that's bothering you?"

Nova kneaded her hands together in her lap. "Not really. Well . . . my mother . . ."

"Is she ill?"

"No, she's strong as a bull. It's just that . . . she really doesn't want me to go. She didn't even want me to join the air force. She says . . . it's not the right time."

"It's never the best time, I suppose."

Nova blushed. "I should explain . . . I'm Hopi. My family lives in

Arizona, on the mesas where the Hopi have always lived. My father passed away over a year ago now. But when he was alive, he was a priest."

"A priest?"

"Not like a Catholic priest . . . A kind of shaman, I guess you would call him. It was his job to keep us all connected to the past. And to see things—things that might be coming in the future. This is why my mother doesn't want me to go—my father told her that something was coming."

Rose sat forward, her pulse quickening. "What is coming?"

Nova frowned. "I should tell it from the beginning." She gathered in a breath. "I've known this story since I was little," she said. "It happened when I was eight years old, on the day of the annual midsummer Niman ceremony in my village. The ceremony marks the return of the *katsinam*, spirits who've been on the earth since the winter solstice, to their homes in the spiritual world. When they reach home, these spirits are supposed to tell the rain people that the Hopi are living well and ask them to reward the farmers with rain." Again, Nova blushed. "I know, it sounds crazy. But these cycles are very important to my people."

Rose smiled. "We all hold beliefs of one sort or another. Please, go on."

"Anyway, my father spent days in the kiva with the other men who would perform the dance—getting ready. They fasted, smoked, prayed, and performed all their secret rites. They made *pahos*."

"*Pahos?*"

"Prayer sticks, made with eagle feathers. Anyway, when my father came out in the morning, he was ready for the dance. He went to the edge of the mesa. That's when he saw them."

"Who?"

"They were flying, high in the sky. At first he thought they were eagles. But they looked more like insects, he said—like the inhabitants of the First World in some of the old Hopi stories. And they were coated with metal, a kind of silver color, he said, but pink because of the rising sun. He thought maybe they were the *katsinam*, flying back to their homes. But why were they leaving before the dance? He got worried." Nova looked toward the window, the sunlight illuminating her brown eyes. "By the time he got home, my father had a fever. He couldn't stand, but he couldn't sleep. After all that work, he couldn't participate in the dance. He was sure that if these creatures, whoever they were, flew away from us for good—if they never came back—it would mean the end."

Rose swallowed, realizing now that her mouth had gone dry. "The end?"

"The end of everything. Of all human life on earth. They had to come back, to make things right."

"Did you believe him?"

"I did for a long time. I used to have nightmares about those 'Silver Spirits' of his, flying away, leaving us all to die. But then I started learning about airplanes. A cousin of mine ran a business, flying tour planes. He took me up once when I was twelve, and I never looked back. I decided that my father had just seen some planes, maybe a formation of fighter jets, training. That's all. And in his state of mind, hungry, thirsty, full of the spirit, he'd been frightened. Anyway, he never had that vision again. And when he died last year, I figured . . ."

"That he'd been wrong?"

"Yes. I figured he was just living in a dream. But my mother still believes. Even now, she's still waiting for those Spirits to come home. She says it's not right for me to leave. I'm too important now."

Despite herself, Rose gripped the edge of her desk. "Why?"

"Because my father told her something else, just before he passed. He said the end is coming. But not for our family. After the end, the Spirits will come home to the mesas. It's our job to be there, waiting for them." Nova paused, her gaze turned inward. She sighed, as if she'd come to a decision. Feeling inside the collar of her uniform, she grasped a chain. She unclipped it, a thin band of silver from which hung something resembling a cross. But it wasn't a cross. It was a woman, her arms spread wide, thin metallic feathers dripping from them like those of a wing. The silver woman's hair flowed along the length of her spine, her chin tilted boldly upward. "Could you keep this for me?" Nova asked. "It's from my mother. But I can't take it where I'm going."

"You can't?"

"I couldn't bear to lose it. Would you keep it safe for me until I get home?"

ROSE SAT IN silence, the office growing still around her. There'd been something missing from her synthesized "personalities." But until her interview with Nova, she hadn't known what it was. Now she knew.

Rose wasn't in charge of the Mothers' educational database; that was under Kendra's purview, and Kendra had been given strict orders not to include any information regarding IC-NAN, the classified root cause behind the new children's existence. By design, this story wouldn't be part of the "lore" that each child would learn—it couldn't be part of their heritage. But without a heritage, who are you? There had to be more. Each Mother's child would need more than just food and water, more than education, more even than safe nurturing and a sense of common purpose that would unite him with others of his kind. He would need that sense of security that came from knowing who he was. Somehow, she'd have to work this into her code.

Opening her desk drawer, she gathered up the thin chain to pull out the necklace. It was delicate yet sturdy. Like Nova—this young woman, so strong, so vital, so rooted in her culture, a dwindling tribe of forgotten people living in the harsh desert of northeastern Arizona. The story of this family, the story of a history, a mother who dreamed for her daughter an untold destiny . . . Rose had never really known her own mother, who died just after Rose's third birthday. Her father had been there for her, of course, but Lewis McBride had been a quiet, introspective man—not the type to dwell on the past. For much of her own childhood, Rose had felt rootless, an army brat turned army lifer, roaming in search of a home. That wouldn't be enough for these children, so much alone in their new world.

Nova had already passed all the air force's physical and psychological tests before being assigned to her mission. It was her eagerness to preserve her eggs that had gained her a spot on Rose's list. Now, with Rose's approval, she would go to Boston to meet Bavi Sharma. Nova would no doubt be expecting more of the same testing. But Bavi would have another agenda.

In Bavi's lab at MIT, coders had long been involved with programming simple robots to interact with and care for humans. It would be her task to extract what she could of Nova's essence. Nova's voice, her mild, nasal intonation, would be synthesized into the voice of one of the Mothers. Her memories, the people and places she once knew, would be gone. But her beliefs, her way of seeing the world around her, would remain. Rose could only hope that this was a start toward encoding those elusive elements of family, of belonging, of self. She'd have to work more closely with Bavi . . .

Even their current goals weren't simple. It was one thing, Bavi said, to program a robot to follow Boolean logic: IF this AND this, THEN do that. But the programming of distinct personalities—the differences in characteristic patterns of thinking, feeling, and behaving that make one person different from all others—presented a challenge on a whole new scale.

Still, Bavi had assured her that the personalities of the donors might be mimicked, at least on a superficial level. Under the guise of an "experiment in psychological profiling," the volunteers would record their life experiences while attached to biomonitors in a room devoid of outside stimuli. They would be subjected to Bavi's "Game of 100 Questions," a list designed to differentiate between a myriad of different personality types. Along with the distinct speech patterns and mannerisms of each of the human mothers, gleaned from the hours of video recordings, this input would be fed into a learning program for each bot. The training sets were admittedly limited. But to Rose, this was the heart of the Mother Code, the one thing that would distinguish one Mother from another and give each child his own unique standard.

Rose sighed. The secrecy of the project weighed on her more each day—the fact that the women whose intake she supervised at the institute, the women whose souls she dreamed of encapsulating in code, knew nothing of her intent. To them, it was just another part of the well-known process of personality profiling prior to deployment on a dangerous mission.

Her mind turned to Rick Blevins. Though it was past five in Washington, she was still waiting for him to call her back. She smiled. Ever since her reassignment six months before, ever since their face-to-face in Los Alamos, their relationship had changed. After the formal meeting, he'd asked her out to dinner. He'd been waiting all along, he said—waiting to bring her into the tight circle of people who knew about IC-NAN, not wanting to get too close until he knew she was as safe as he could make her. She knew it now: The tension she'd always felt between the two of them, the emergence of something more than just a professional relationship or a mutual admiration, was real. Now, they were in this together.

The phone on her desk buzzed, and she cleared her throat, pushing a stray strand of hair behind her ear before pressing the button. "McBride."

"Rose. It's me." Blushing despite herself, Rose leaned forward. She pictured Rick alone in his office. His broad, kind face. His strong, reassuring hands laid flat on the desk in front of him.

"Rick. Hello. It's so nice to hear your voice."

"You too. I got your message."

"Yes. I'm sorry, I was a bit stressed when I called earlier. Somehow, that interview this morning . . . it got to me."

"What happened? Tell me again, from the beginning."

"She was a pilot, a lieutenant. Nova Susquetewa. She's Hopi, from Arizona. She told me a story—"

"A folk tale."

"It seemed like more than that. It was something her parents had entrusted to her. Her mother told her it was why she needed to return home safe."

"Go on . . ."

"According to this story, something is going to happen to end human life on earth."

"Yes, but that's a common theme—"

"According to this story, Nova's family have been chosen to carry on afterward. They're supposed to survive. She even said something about 'Silver Spirits' that could fly. Her father supposedly saw them, years ago now. How could he—"

"All common themes. But after I heard your message, I had Dr. Garza check the genetic database. We've screened the Hopi, as well as every other ethnic population we could come up with. Nothing special there. They're susceptible."

"But Dr. Said reminded us of the issue of introns—silent DNA."

"Another folk tale."

"The science is real. There is so much silent DNA in the human genome. So much vestigial information. Dr. Said insists that there could be populations on earth who have the right code to survive this thing. It just needs a stimulus to turn it on. The Hopi are a perfect match for the sort of thing he describes—though intermarriage with those outside the tribe may have muddied the gene pool, there might still be some bloodlines . . ."

"Then how come it didn't show up in the screen?"

"We didn't screen all of the Hopi," Rose insisted. "And even if we could, we can only look for the gene we know. These Hopi most likely have the same susceptible gene sequence that we all have. But they might also have vestigial DNA that we don't have. A code that would save them from this, should it be called upon. The only way to test for that would be to—"

"Expose them to IC-NAN and see what happens. I know. But you understand why we can't do that, don't you? We can't use humans as guinea pigs . . ."

"You're doing it in the Somali prison, aren't you? For the antidote trials? You forget, Rick, I have access to Dr. Garza's reports now."

Rick sighed. "You know that's different. Those people are convicted war criminals."

"People we can kill without a second thought." Rose put one hand to the side of her neck, accepting the deep pulse of disappointment. Wasn't the killing of terrorists the very thing that had started this whole nightmare?

She understood, of course, that the real experiment could not be carried out on the Hopi. But she so wanted to believe in Nova's story— it meant hope, a people immune from the catastrophic mistakes of their government. She stared at the orderly row of old print books lining her shelves, her last gift from her father. Of course, it was most likely just another of the tales told by tribes, faiths, and sects through the ages, each designed to enhance the importance of the messenger who spoke it. She should know; what had her Catholic faith ever done for her? Even if all went according to plan, her own life might soon be assured only by a daily dose of some exotic DNA cocktail. "I'm sorry, Rick," she said, gathering her scattered composure. She had no right to take out her frustrations on him . . . "How are the trials going?"

"Jury's still out. But I think they'll get it right. We have to believe in that, at least."

"Yes. We have to believe."

"Rose? I just want you to know. The work you're doing . . . the Mother Code. I believe in that too."

Rose sat back. "It's just so tough. These women are donating their eggs, enduring all this questioning and profiling, and I can't tell them anything about the reason why."

"Most of them are in the military. For them, it's nothing much more than what women in their situations have done for decades. A sort of insurance plan—"

"But, Rick, the eggs are only supposed to be fertilized for the benefit of the donor. Not fertilized with some stranger's sperm, hatched in an incubator like a farm animal, brought up by a robot . . ."

"Are you saying you don't believe we're on the right path?"

"No . . ." Rose closed her eyes. "It's not that. I just wish we could be more open."

"We all wish that. But we—"

"I know. We can't risk a panic. But, Rick . . ." She knew she was pushing now, but she had to. "You remember Dr. Sharma? The robo-psychologist at MIT?"

"Your old Harvard classmate?"

"Yes. Bavi. She's given us some wonderful insights into the mother-child bond. She truly believes we can teach our bots to rear their children as their real mothers might have."

"But not love them."

"No. We can try to give the bot a personality. We can give her the ability to teach, to protect. But complex emotions like love . . . A code like that has yet to be written, and there's far too little time to write it now."

"That's too bad."

"But why can't we at least let Bavi in on the project? After all, she's volunteered to be one of the mothers too."

"We've been over this." Rick's voice was strained but firm. "I have less power than you think. I had to do a lot of convincing to get you the clearance, to get you on the list for the final trial. When the time comes, even if we have a working antidote, the supply will be limited."

Rose sighed. "I'm sorry. And I know I have you to thank. For getting me on the final trial, as you say."

A shuffling sound came through the console. "I'm sorry too, Rose. I told you, I've wanted to get close to you ever since we first met. At least now we have each other to confide in."

Rose looked toward her window. "When will you be out here again?"

"I could come out next weekend . . ."

"It would be great to see you. Maybe we could get away for a few days. Taste some wine. Pretend."

"That would be nice."

"Yes. Nice." Sitting back, Rose watched the last rays of the setting sun playing across the delicate chain, the feathered arms of the silver goddess that dangled from her fingertips.

12

OVER THE PAST two years, Sela and Kai had settled into a new pattern. They were nomads, constantly on the move, searching for others—still searching for water. Early each morning they took the bike out to scout the desert, Sela steering and Kai on the lookout, straddling a make-shift wooden seat mounted behind hers. They were both the same age—just over ten years old. But Kai had always been taller. He'd found a broken pair of binoculars on one of their forays, and from time to time he brought these up to his eyes to peer hopefully over Sela's shoulder.

Their Mothers followed in rapid-response mode—not on their treads but on their feet, their powerful legs in motion. At full height, standing over three times as tall as their charges, the bots were less stable but more mobile. Kai could still remember himself as a small child, the first time he'd seen Rosie in this stance—her soft inner hands emerging from within their hard outer gloves to grip his waist as she scooped him up and out of the path of a slavering coyote. Now she only seemed awkward, frighteningly off balance as she lumbered behind them.

"I don't see any towers," Kai called into Sela's ear, hoping she could hear him over the whir of the bike's engine and through the barrier of his particle mask.

Sela stopped the bike. She struggled out of her seat and planted her feet on the uneven ground. As she stripped off her mask, Kai could see the chafed skin of her dust-stained cheeks. "Doesn't matter," she said, beating the mask against her thigh. "According to Alpha, we've found almost all of the depots already. And you know what we found there. The towers are all choked up with dirt. The depots don't have any bottled water. Or food. Somebody took it all."

Kai licked his cracked lips. "That's good, right? It means there's somebody else out here."

"I suppose," she said. "But not good for us. I think we should stick to the roads. We need to look for more cars. Maybe we'll find another truck—like that one last week."

Kai shuddered. They'd managed to pry the lids off the cans stored in the truck's bed—tomato sauce, a kind of green chili soaked in a spicy brine, a pasty brown foodstuff called "frijoles." The food had been filling enough but had given them both stomachaches—and afflicted them with an even more terrible thirst. Sela had raided the cab for tools, nudging aside the limp, skeletal hand of its former driver. There, she'd found only one small bottle of water.

Kai pointed in the direction opposite the rising sun. "Rosie says there's a depressed area with rocky soil over that way. Like the remains of a riverbed. There might be underground water there."

"Are you sure we haven't already been there?" Sela asked. "I feel like we're just going in circles . . ."

"We've been traveling in a spiral—wider circles every time. Rosie's keeping track. We've been east and west of that stony area. But she's sure we haven't been to those exact coordinates." He looked at Sela, her mouth now held in a stern line. "To get there, I think we can follow that wide road we were on yesterday most of the way," he said.

He steeled himself as Sela remounted her seat. Though he knew it was easier on the bike to follow the windblown thoroughfares that crisscrossed the desert than to skirt them, he didn't like those roads. But he knew Sela was right. There were those crates of water bottles they'd found mysteriously stashed by the roadside—as though someone had left them there for them to find. Those had been a godsend, enough for a month if they were careful. And the vehicles, pulled off at angles into the scrub, had indeed offered treasure from time to time—they wouldn't have their bike save for the discovery of the orange-striped RV.

But there were other things to be found along the roadside. He remembered the small electric vehicle, stopped dead in a ditch, the remains of two bodies in the front seat. The smaller ones, three of them, packed side by side in the backseat. As always, he and Sela had looked at one another, both wondering the same thing. Could they charge the battery? Might the car be more comfortable than their bike? But they'd only done what they always did, picking through the trunk for packed clothing, food, and water. As always, they'd silently opted not to disturb the sleep of the dead. Even scavengers had limits.

They found the road again just as the sun reached its zenith. Then they followed it west to pass a procession of high mesas. The mesas looked, Kai thought, like shimmering ships at sea, the ones he'd studied late at night on Rosie's hatch screen. But as the road rose steadily in elevation, he soon realized that they were on a mesa of their own. The path ahead grew ever narrower, the land to either side dropping down into broad, windswept washes.

Suddenly Sela stopped the bike.

Kai put down his binoculars. "What's up?"

"Too narrow for the bots. We'll have to go on without them if we want to get any farther," Sela replied.

Kai looked back toward Rosie. "Yes," Rosie said in his mind. "That is correct."

"Okay . . ." Removing his mask, Kai swiped his lips with the back of his arm, tasting the salt there. Pulling his canteen up from its strap over his shoulder, he took a few careful swallows. They'd come so far; there was no turning back now. "Rosie . . . if we keep on, you can watch out for me?" he asked.

"I will monitor your movements and biosignals," came her reply. "I'll alert you if you reach the limits of my range."

Sela gunned the motor, leaving their Mothers behind. Kai looked over her shoulder, at the road that was now nothing more than a foot-path. It was all he could do to keep steering his gaze off to either side, combing the dizzying maze of jagged crevices down below, looking for some sign of water. It was not only dangerous, it seemed hopeless . . .

But then Sela stopped again, her head pivoting to the left. "There!" she said, pointing down toward something small and dark, near the far edge of a wide depression.

Kai craned his neck, squinting in the bright sunlight. In an instant, he forgot his thirst, his fear of falling. "That's not water. It looks like . . ."

"It's a person, right?" Sela said, dismounting so rapidly that she almost overturned the bike. "Maybe another child?"

Kai held his breath, his eyes steady on the motionless form. He peered through the one useful lens of his binoculars. Though it seemed inhumanly still, the figure did indeed look human. He scanned to the right. His heart leapt as he made out the hulking form of a bot, sta-tioned near the opening of what looked like a cave. "Do you see it? It's a bot!" he said. "But how do we get down there?"

"We could fly down," Sela suggested, taking her turn with the bin-oculars.

"We don't want to frighten—whoever it is," Kai said.

Sela surveyed the distance. "We could make a landing in that flat area just to the south, behind those big rocks. Then we could hike back."

"Okay," Kai agreed.

His pulse racing, Kai sprinted back toward his Mother to climb aboard her cocoon. Close by, Alpha-C placed the dirt bike gently on the road before allowing Sela to climb her treads. "Aw, Mama . . ." came Sela's protestations as she hoisted herself up, leaving the bike behind.

The two bots took off from the road in a massive swirl of debris. As they circled the area, Kai searched the ground to relocate their target. There it was—a shock of dark hair, a tunic draped over narrow shoulders. It was indeed a child. But despite the clamor overhead, the child sat immobile, his spine erect, his spindly knees jutting out to either side like the wings of a bird. A chill ran up Kai's spine. Was this child nothing more than a frozen corpse?

"Is he alive?" he asked Rosie.

"His temperature registers 35.5 degrees Celsius, low normal for a human," she replied as she jolted to rest on a flat sheet of sandstone. They were in a small clearing, encircled by high stone pinnacles.

Sela was already on the ground as Kai slid down Rosie's treads. "This way," she said.

They followed a narrow path between two of the stone outcroppings, Sela leading the way. But as the other side came into view, Sela suddenly pulled up. Kai peered around her. The child, his back to them, was only about twenty feet away.

"Look there . . ." Sela murmured, her trembling finger pointing to what looked like a small pile of rocks just a few feet from where the silent child sat.

Squinting, Kai discerned a mysterious movement, a shifting of stone and earth. It wasn't a pile of rocks. Coiled next to the child was a fat brown snake, its neck raised, its flat head held at attention. But the child's bot, fifty feet or so away to their left, remained inert, as immovable as her charge.

"My Mother taught me never to kill a snake . . . But why doesn't his

Mother *do* something?" Sela whispered. Her hand slipped to her side, seeking the knife in her belt.

Just then, the child unfolded his legs and stood up. Kai's breath caught in his throat. It was a boy, at least as tall as him. And as the boy turned to face them, his serpentine comrade merely slithered off into the sparse scrub.

"What the . . ." Sela murmured.

Kai was dumbfounded. A boy who befriended snakes? For a moment the boy just stood there like a statue. His blank eyes stared directly into Kai's. Or did they? For he showed no sign of recognition, no sign of surprise. Instead he turned to walk steadily toward the cave where his Mother waited, then disappeared behind her.

Passing the stunned Sela, Kai followed, his sights set on the cave and its sentinel bot. Too large to enter the cave, the child's Mother had stationed herself as close as possible to its mouth. As Kai slipped past her, she made no effort to stop him. The cave was small, maybe ten feet or so to the back wall. His eyes adjusting to the dark, Kai made out the orange spark of slender twigs, smoldering in a shard of pottery on the floor. Next to his fire, the boy had once more taken a seat. Cautiously, Kai advanced.

"Yes, I understand it now. It is the same message as before," the boy whispered to his Mother.

"Hello?" Kai ventured. But the boy took no notice.

"Mother, you assured me this was a good place," the boy murmured. "You said that someday the road would bring visitors. But no one is coming. And now Naga says we may one day have to leave."

"Hello?" Kai's voice echoed off the soot-blackened stone walls. Creeping up next to him, Sela took one step closer. Though they were both within arm's reach of the boy, he still gave no evidence that he sensed them. Kai could see the boy's hands clenching, his body rocking forward and back as he muttered something under his breath. He was speaking another language, one that Kai didn't understand.

"Are you okay?" Kai whispered. He reached out to touch the boy's arm, half expecting his hand to find nothing but empty space. But instead, it came to rest on warm skin. He felt a pulse—slow and steady. He had a revelation. "Wake up," he whispered. "Wake up. You're having a dream."

The boy looked up, his eyes flashing wide. A light flickered in those eyes, something like fear, then hope. Tears spilled onto his cheeks as his thin fingers reached out to touch the sleeve of Kai's tunic.

"Real," he murmured. "You are real . . ."

WARILY, KAI WATCHED the surrounding brush. They'd built their cooking fire outside the cave, very near the spot where just hours before, the snake had reared its threatening head. Sitting across from him, the new boy stared into the flames. His name, he said, was Kamal.

"Do you feel better now?" Sela asked.

"Yes, very much." Kamal rewarded her with a smile, his teeth large and white.

Kai smiled too. On the hillside nearby, cactus flourished. And now, the dark juice of early-harvest cactus fruit ran down his chin. Sela spit her seeds into the fire. They'd thought better of catching game for tonight's dinner. A boy who sat calmly with snakes might disapprove.

Kamal gazed shyly at the two of them. "I am sorry," he said. "My Mother taught me to meditate. It helped with the loneliness. But . . . it became more and more difficult to come back."

"That's a good trick," Kai said. "That thing with the snake."

"Trick?"

"You don't remember the snake?" Sela stared at the boy.

"I do," Kamal replied calmly. "But she is not a trick. She is a friend—a messenger."

Kai swiped his chin. "A what?"

"It is such a miracle that you have found me," Kamal said. "It may be just in time."

"In time for what?"

"The snake guards the water, the greatest treasure in the desert. She led me to the spring." Reaching down, Kamal picked up one of the bottles he'd filled with fresh water from his secret spring. "But now she tells me that a change is coming. There has been too little water, too much wind, for too many seasons. Soon, even the spring will run dry. It may become impossible for us to continue living here."

"Maybe your snake friend is right," Sela said, her brow knit with concern. "But if we had to leave, where would we go?"

"For sure there are no towers left," Kai said.

Kamal regarded him sadly. "The dust soaks up the moisture they collect. The wind blows it away. The towers themselves are falling to ruin."

"So," Sela said, "what do we do? What does your Mother say?"

"Beta says that we cannot travel outside her known coordinates," Kamal admitted. "And she does not have sufficient data to support the conclusion—"

"What kind of data will it take?" Sela shot a glance at Kai. They were all, it seemed, in the same intractable predicament.

"I must have trust in my Mother," Kamal said. "She is my banyan tree."

Sela leaned forward. "Your what?"

"The banyan tree is sacred in the Hindu stories. It has arms that reach to the sky like coiled snakes. Its roots can form a whole forest. Beta is like that tree, like a house that is alive. She keeps me safe."

Kai looked over his shoulder at Kamal's Mother, the sliver of the new moon reflected on her worn hatch cover. "You talked out loud to her," he said, "in the cave. What was that language you were speaking?"

"My Mother taught me Hindi," Kamal replied. "As well as English. She said it is important to preserve languages."

"But she does talk to you in your mind too, right?"

"When I dream, she is another person, there beside me. Just as real as you are," Kamal said. "And when I am awake, she can talk to me in my mind. Beta is me. And I am her . . . You talk to your Mother in the same way, I see."

Kai looked at Sela. "We all do."

"It is a gift we share," Kamal said.

Kai watched the flames, guttering now as they swallowed the last of the twigs. Soon the fire would be out.

Yawning, Sela stretched her arms. "It's been a long day . . ."

Her yawn was infectious—Kai could barely keep his eyes open. "Let's get some rest," he agreed. "At least there's three of us now. And believe me, Kamal, you have more here than anywhere else we've found."

The night winds were coming up, stirring swirls of dust in the gathering darkness. Kai helped Sela tamp out the fire, then ambled toward Rosie's cocoon. As he climbed inside, he saw Sela cast a longing look up at the faraway road, toward the abandoned bike. They'd have to retrieve the thing soon, or they'd never hear the end of it.

Closing his hatch, Kai curled up in his seat. He pulled his blanket around his shoulders and tried to find space for his legs. "You're growing," Rosie said.

"Yes. Can I change the seat somehow?"

"A simple modification. I can provide instruction if you wish."

"Rosie, do you think Kamal is right?"

"That your current water supply is compromised?"

"Yes. Will we have to leave the desert?"

"I have insufficient data at this time."

"Anyway, where would we go?"

"That cannot be determined. I have no coordinates."

Squirming, he wedged his knees under her console.

"You're comfortable now." His Mother's voice was soft in his mind.

"Yes . . ." Kai's breathing synchronized with the pulsing hum of Rosie's processors as he listened to her night song. She was running her diagnostics, checking her systems.

Beta is me. I am her, Kamal had said.

"I am Rosie. She is me," Kai thought. His Mother felt his feelings. She heard his thoughts. She spoke to him in his mind, even in his dreams. And he spoke back, without uttering a word.

He knew that Sela still dreamed of traveling free, even to places where Alpha-C wouldn't take her. And since meeting Sela, he'd sometimes taken for granted the bond he shared with Rosie. But at night, when they were alone, that feeling was as strong as ever—the feeling that he couldn't possibly know where he ended and his Mother began.

13

JAMES CIRCLED THE central computer in his Los Alamos lab, manipulating the image of the C-341 antidote sequence. He enlarged the engineered promoter region of the gene, the spot where Rudy's team at Fort Detrick had modified the sequence to render it immune to insertion by IC-NAN. Once again, he watched the 3-D model of the caspase transcription factor, the little protein that turned on production of the caspase, dance over its binding site on the promoter. The factor had to bind to the promoter in order to initiate gene transcription. But if it bound too tightly, there would be too much transcription—too much caspase, too much cell death. They'd measured the binding constant under every imaginable condition. It had seemed perfect. But it wasn't. For the hundredth time, he checked the display on his wrist phone. He was waiting for a call from Rudy Garza.

Fourteen months before, he'd assumed his post as the lone biologist in Los Alamos's XO-Bot building, a facility that had for years housed roboticists and AI experts devoted to developing robots for extraterrestrial exploration and asteroid mining. Kendra Jenkins, the wiry little computer genius who oversaw robot programming, had her own lab at the far end of the building. Paul MacDonald, the ex-military engineer who headed robotics construction, had his office just across the hall. Together, these three were the only personnel at Los Alamos who knew about New Dawn. Over the past year, they had each been called to wear many hats—Kendra had taken on the role of Los Alamos security chief for New Dawn, and MacDonald, or Mac, as he liked to be called, had taken on added duties in facilities maintenance— all unbeknownst to the people they supervised.

Meanwhile, calling on the resourcefulness of his grad school days, James had set up his own lab. Working remotely with Rudy's Fort Detrick team and closely with Mac's team, it was James's job to push forward on testing robotic systems designed to support the development of a fetus into a newborn infant. This would have been enough of a challenge in and of itself. But the genetic modification that would render the resulting babies immune to IC-NAN added an extra layer of complexity.

In the beginning, progress had been steady enough. Starting in December 2051, James had grown two "generations" of genetically modified fetuses, one in environmental chambers in his lab, one inside programmed robotic systems. The sacrifice of the Gen1 and Gen2 fetuses for autopsy had been tough. The old "fourteen-day rule" for the experimental use of embryonic material, long enforced by international ethics commissions, had only recently been supplanted with the "five-week rule." But based on studies reported out of Korea, James knew that once a fetus reached fifteen weeks in an artificial environment, its probability of surviving to term was at least 90 percent. To accurately predict viability at birth, he would need to sacrifice his fetuses at no fewer than fifteen weeks. This was more than sacrifice—it was murder. But he'd done it. And he'd demonstrated success—in every measurable way, his engineered fetuses had exhibited normal development up through the time of termination.

It wasn't until Gen3, the first full-term generation, that problems had arisen. Starting in April the previous year, fifteen Gen3 fetuses had been grown in the same type of incubators as Gen2 and developed into the second trimester. Since the goal at this stage was to test automated birthing, the incubators and their associated robotics were then transferred into stationary life support systems in a secure location in the New Mexico desert, south of Albuquerque. The tasks required of these support systems were minimal: Maintain life support throughout the final weeks of gestation. At the time instructed, drain the cocoon, monitor vital signs—essentially, give birth. The purpose of the Gen3 location, as the robotics team understood it, was to mimic conditions on a hostile planet; the real reason, James knew, was to prepare for the possible endgame, bots giving birth under less than optimal conditions on earth. And to provide extra protection against possible scrutiny.

The Gen3 units' every action had been monitored via remote cameras, reams of data collected. As the team had held their collective breath, twelve of the fifteen Gen3 fetuses had survived the drainage process. The newborns, five boys and seven girls, had been whisked to Fort Detrick via military jet, leaving James to explain their fate. "Thanks so much for all of your hard work," he'd announced. "Our experiment to simulate the extraterrestrial birth of human children has shown success. And now, some very lucky couples right here on earth will be blessed with new babies."

It wasn't a lie—though there was much he wasn't telling them. With any luck, the Gen3 babies would be the first of a new breed of children, capable of withstanding the onslaught of IC-NAN. The couples who would care for them, their biological mothers and fathers, were carefully screened military volunteers who'd given up trying to have children of their own after years without success. They'd agreed to periodic monitoring of their children after birth. But the parents would know nothing of New Dawn. And if the necessity arose, if the IC-NAN epidemic truly took hold and the parents died as a result, their children would be adopted by the people whom Rudy referred to as the "chosen few," those allowed access to the antidote.

James needn't have worried about the ethics of the program: In the end, Gen3 was not a success at all. Though seemingly healthy at birth, and though they'd all tested as immune to IC-NAN, the Gen3 babies had rapidly lost vitality. Within two weeks all were dead, and all due to the same cause—multiple organ failure, an accelerated wasting of the tissues. The parents were told only that the experiment had been a failure. And James's only solace was that they'd never been given a chance to see their babies.

Now, he needed desperately to keep his Los Alamos team on track. To keep them from noticing the incessant drumbeat of reports coming out of Iran, Afghanistan, Pakistan, even India—of mysterious, inexplicable deaths. "On the news feed, they said it's some sort of cancer epidemic," he'd heard one of the techs saying in the cafeteria. "But there's no such thing . . . Is there?" James needed a way to shield them from all of this, to keep them focused on this project alone—a project whose import only he could know.

But it was hard. To have any hope of moving forward, he and Rudy would need to answer the question of what had happened to the Gen3 babies. He might have the answer . . . but then again he might not. He closed his eyes. Until Rudy called, it was best to think about something else. He sank into a lab chair, his thoughts drifting to Sara Khoti.

Sara . . . When he'd arrived here to discover her working just across the hall, he'd thought about fate. They shared a history, he a postdoc at Berkeley, she a doctoral student in mechanical engineering, finishing out her requirements in the human physiology study section he was teaching. He remembered her then, bright-eyed, fresh, eager, with all the promise of the accomplished engineer she now was. He remembered himself—too young, too inexperienced, intimidated by her beauty.

He should have made his move, so long ago. But by the time Sara was no longer his student, by the time he at last felt free to ask her out, she'd already accepted a postdoc in the robotics department at Caltech. He remembered wishing her well, watching as she left him, her graduation gown swaying in the breeze. They'd promised to keep in touch, but he'd never made the effort. He was every bit as guilty as she for their drifting apart.

He couldn't help but consider the irony. Had he made a different choice back then, had he chosen to pursue Sara rather than his career, it could have changed his life in ways unimaginable at the time. Had he wound up a married man, DOD would never have tapped him. He and Sara would have shared the happy ignorance that now only she possessed.

Now, established in her career, Sara was ready for a relationship; her every action since their reunion had made that clear enough. Their quiet dinners together, listening to old Bollywood music, enjoying the prodigious collection of classic movies that she'd amassed—these were among the few things that had made his life bearable since he'd arrived here. But he couldn't allow intimacy, a condition that demanded the telling of untellable secrets. If it all went down . . . he knew she wouldn't get the antidote. People like Blevins had the power to bring those they loved under the umbrella of security. They had choices. But he didn't. He couldn't risk falling in love with Sara, only to watch her die.

So why was he seeing her? Why was he accepting her invitations, spending late nights in her small apartment, remembering those old times—pretending? He winced, thinking how close he'd come to telling her last night. Lying awkwardly on her couch, their bodies moving together, his lips locked on hers to ensure a mutual silence . . . Afterward, he'd hated himself for it.

"Still staring at that image?"

"Wh—?" Turning toward the door, James could sense Sara's light scent even before he caught sight of her.

"Sorry for sneaking up on you like that," Sara said. "I was working late. I wondered if you'd like to get some dinner. There's a new South Indian restaurant in White Rock that stays open late . . ."

James checked his watch. Nine p.m. "Dinner . . . Sorry, not tonight. Something's come up."

Sara frowned. "Nothing bad, I hope?"

"Bad? Um . . . Not so bad we can't recover . . ."

He watched her face, her eyes taking stock of him. "James, about last night . . ."

"I'm sorry, Sara. I don't know what came over me—"

"You don't need to apologize . . ." As Sara looked down to study the slim fingers of her right hand, James again caught a whiff of her hair, the scent of lavender. "I happen to like what came over you."

"We should slow down . . ."

But Sara only smiled. "Come, you can take a break. At least let me show you what I've accomplished today." She turned. And as though tugged by an invisible tether, he followed her out into the hall, then through the double doors into the massive robotics bay.

They skirted the huddle of fifteen Gen4 life support units, still undergoing diagnostic testing at the center of the bay. Gen4, a more integrated repeat of the Gen3 experiment, was designed to manage the entire development cycle from embryo to fetus, from fetus to birth. Like the Gen3 units, their stationary, boxy chassis were formidable, meant to withstand harsh winds and extreme temperatures. And as with the Gen3s, the plan was for the team to closely monitor the development and birth of the Gen4 charges. But unbeknownst to the rest of the XO-Bot team, the biological parents in this case were anonymous, their sperm and eggs banked from chosen subjects who would never learn of their existence. It was understood that only those with current clearance might be alive to care for the babies. The time for considering other options had passed.

James clenched his fists. There was something else the others didn't know about Gen4—that the program was stalled until the Gen3 problem had been solved.

As they made their way toward Sara's worktable at the far corner of the bay, James's gaze drifted toward a much different line of bots, looming in the dark along the wall—the Gen5s. To him, the Gen5s were the concrete representation of failure, the doomsday alternative—robotic mothers with enough functionality and autonomy to take the place of human parents. The embodiment of an admission: that no one currently alive would emerge from IC-NAN's deadly grasp.

Unlike the previous generations, the Gen5s were no mere machines. They were biobots, replicas of the "supersoldiers" he'd read about as a kid—shells affording real men and women the strength of ten. There were fifty of them—this large number to be deployed based on the expected probability of attrition in the field. Approaching one of the silent machines, he looked up to search her shoulder for a glimpse of her folded wing. Each bot had a pair of retractable wings and a pair of ducted fans, allowing short takeoff flight directed by an onboard computer. Power—enough to last far longer than a human lifetime—was supplied via a small nuclear source housed in the rear of each bot, encased in a layer of iridium and embedded in graphite blocks.

The crews who'd assembled the Gen5s had taken to calling them "the Mothers." Although James sometimes wondered if the term was used tongue in cheek, he had to admit that the bots looked fit for the task. Their aft holds housed the small laboratory where birth would take place, and their hollow forebellies were outfitted to ensconce a small human in a seated position. In addition to a powerful pair of articulated arms and legs, each bot was equipped with heavy treads, built-in elements of the lower legs. When she hunkered down as though on her knees, her treads allowed her to trundle slowly but stably over rough terrain. As he scanned the Mothers, now kneeling in orderly rows, James imagined them beckoning their children . . .

But they would never be that. A robot could never be a substitute for a human parent.

Once, the technological singularity had been deemed a certainty; there would come a time when humans would create thinking machines more intelligent than they. These machines would create other machines still more brilliant than themselves, and this nonbiological intelligence would increase at a rate and in ways incomprehensible to the human mind. Humans had a choice, it was said: either merge with technology or be buried by it. But things had happened along the way. The hyperautomated, hyperintelligent military robots built by the Israelis to fight the Water Wars had offered an insight into an apocalyptic future that no one wanted to see fulfilled. Their near-autonomous "supersoldiers" had been inactivated. The Tenth Congress on Artificial Intelligence had set strict limits on further development of computers capable of making decisions independent of human intervention, and the Office of Cybersecurity in Washington had taken on the job of enforcing these regulations in the U.S. An entire industry had been born, companies developing technologies designed to rein in what the press called the "new existential threat" of nonbiological intelligence. And as far as James knew, the New Dawn Gen5 bots had been designed to these prohibitive specifications. For such bots, any truly "human" interaction with a child would seem impossible.

"Amazing, aren't they?" Sara said. He turned to see her eyes shaded by a pair of protective goggles.

"So, they've got you working on Gen5 already?"

"Gens 3 and 4 were simple," Sara replied. "The Mothers are much more of a challenge." She turned toward her test bed. "When interacting with their children, the Gen5 bots will require a gentle touch, a precise touch. But to deal with the outside world, they will also require power, strength. We knew we couldn't create both in one rig. So, we engineered a manifold appendage."

"I've seen the demo vids . . ." James inspected the robotic hand now mounted on the test bed—a tough, carbon-composite outer shell from which a delicate "secondary" hand emerged. With the shell retracted, the hand, a small black orchid sprouting from the center of a rigid gray glove, could do its work without impediment.

"Watch this," Sara said. On her workbench, a set of nimble elastomeric fingers darted over a rack of thin transparent test tubes, selecting one and then drawing it steadily upward. The attached arm moved on to the next step, the fingers still carrying the test tube, the rapid transverse motion not sufficient to break the tenuous contact between them and the smooth sides of the tube.

"Brava! No failure this time," James said.

"We're using a tackier material. It's also more compliant." Beside him, Sara retracted the arm, homing it for yet another pass. "The true innovations in robotics these days aren't in the programming. We're still reinventing human motion using a series of configuration parameters and transformation equations that were worked out decades ago. The real advances are in the nanocircuits, the sheer computational capability. In the mechanics too. But mostly in the materials. Self-healing materials, solid materials that change density when touched, materials composed solely of intricate meshes of sensors, bonded together to form massive neural networks." She turned to face him, her eyes sparkling in the bank of LEDs illuminating the test bed. "We can thank your friend the general for testing them out for us."

"Blevins?"

"Him, and others who are forced to be guinea pigs in the development of new prostheses." Sara waited until the fingers hovered once more over the rack of tubes, then leaned forward to push "record" on the benchtop console. "I like my robots the way I like my men," she said, a sly smile stealing over her lips. "Strong, yet gentle."

Blushing, James smiled back. He wanted to tell her everything. He wanted to tell her that the delicate hands she'd worked so hard to fashion might one day cradle a newborn, alone on planet Earth. But of course, there was no hope of telling her anything. Not how much he cared for her. Not that he'd allowed himself dreams in which none of this had ever happened—in which he and Sara cradled their own child.

No . . . He couldn't allow dreams to stand in the way of the truth. Sara's project, perfecting the robotic functionality of the Gen4s and Gen5s, was important, yet peripheral. When it came to New Dawn, Sara herself was peripheral.

"Why do you suppose these biobots are getting so much attention?" Sara asked.

"Why not?"

"I mean, it's fascinating, challenging . . . But neonates on other planets? Aren't there other, more urgent projects? Where's the money coming from?"

James shook his head, clearing his thoughts. He hated lying to her. But he'd memorized the script, and it was his duty to perform his role. "Someone wants this done, and they seem to have plenty of cash," he said. "It's paying *my* bills, anyway . . ."

"Hmm." Taking off her goggles, Sara looked at him, those deep brown eyes penetrating his.

"James?" A familiar voice echoed across the bay.

Grateful for the interruption, James turned to find Kendra Jenkins approaching at her usual fast clip from the hallway. "Hi, Kendra. What's up?"

"Dr. Garza called in to the main line. He says he's having trouble reaching you?"

James glanced at his wrist phone. "Reception's always bad in here . . ." he said. The reception was indeed spotty in the heavily insulated bay. But in any event it was protocol—he couldn't take the call when anyone without clearance was within earshot. As he turned back toward the hall, he caught Sara's profile, the faint working of her jaw muscles as her gaze drifted back to the delicate Gen5 hands.

He trailed Kendra to the computer lab, doing his best to keep up.

While black administrators and professors were commonplace in his department at Emory, a black woman with Kendra's seniority was a rarity at Los Alamos. But Kendra held her own, her calm authority unflagging amid the daily chaos of her myriad duties.

"I'm sorry, James," Kendra murmured, turning to look at him over her shoulder.

"Sorry? About what?"

"You know," Kendra said. "Things. Life—how we aren't supposed to have one."

"I suppose . . ."

Kendra slowed down to match his pace. "You and I are in this thing because we don't have anyone," she said. "But I did, once. A husband, and a son."

"Where are they now?"

"Plane crash. Seven years ago." Pulling open the door marked "Computer Lab," she turned to him. In the dim light, he could barely make out her compact frame and dark complexion. "My husband was an anthropologist. We used to travel everywhere together. I lost my wedding ring somewhere in Nepal . . . Anyway, when our son was just ten years old, Lamar took him down to Mexico, to a dig at the Mayan sites . . ."

"Meridian Flight 208?"

"Yup." Approaching her desk in the now-empty lab, Kendra flipped on her phone hookup and pressed in a code. "James, you don't have to take my advice. What do I know? Except . . . we only have one life." She held up her left wrist, and a heavy copper bracelet inscribed with a repeating geometric pattern caught the light from her computer screen. "My son would have been seventeen tomorrow. We would have been celebrating. Instead, this bracelet is all I have left of my family. If I were you, I'd enjoy my life. No one can predict the future."

James watched Kendra's face, the emotion so carefully hidden beneath her efficient exterior. A life with Sara . . . the very thought of it sent a thrill through his veins. But he only grimaced as he turned on the mic. "Rudy?"

"I called as soon as I could." Rudy's voice piped from the console. "Have you found something?"

"I think C-341 is binding too tightly."

"Agreed. The antidote trials in Somalia are not going well either."

"Somalia?" James felt a twinge of discomfort deep in his gut—the familiar anger at the invisible wall that separated him from the mainstream back in D.C.

"Uh . . . yes." Rudy paused. "We're running our human trials there."

"How come I didn't know about that?"

"Eh . . . I thought that you did . . ." Rudy cleared his throat. "In any event, cell death is too rapid. The subjects' lungs atrophy. As you so astutely warned us, the problem is one of balance."

James nodded, if only to himself. "Correct. The transcription factor binding was fine in our cell culture models. But its behavior in vivo is decidedly different."

"Do you have any ideas?"

"We need to focus on modifying the sequence that binds the hydrophobic pocket. I've come up with a few ideas that I can ship to you. But I'll defer to your expertise on the DNA structure side."

"*Perfecto.*"

"And, Rudy?"

"Yes?"

"It's obvious I have no pull . . . but maybe you do. Do you think you could convince them to let us grow Gen4 in the lab? I don't understand why we're putting so much emphasis on the machines. Until we're sure we have the biology right—"

"James . . . I might agree with you under different circumstances. But the brass are very keen on the robots, and understandably so."

"Understandably? Maybe *you* understand, but . . ."

"James, we will not have time to test the long-term effectiveness of the antidote on adults. You heard the general at our meeting this morning. We are talking about the endgame now. We need to keep making progress toward the Gen5 option."

Rubbing his hand over the stubble of his unshaved beard, James stared up at the low-hung ceiling of the building that every day seemed more like a prison. He found himself thinking about his parents—the missed holidays, the excuses. He'd only seen them once, for his father's seventieth birthday last June. They still didn't know he was in Los Alamos . . .

He blinked. *Stay focused.* Rudy was right. The bots were his allies in this fight. IC-NAN was the only enemy. Across Kendra's lab he spotted a small vid screen, the freckled face of a young female reporter based in Germany. "We have reports of a 'deadly flu' in parts of Russia, with symptoms suspiciously like those seen most recently in northern India," she was saying.

He had to face it—he'd most likely never have the option he most desired—to seed a "normal" human colony on earth, parents and their children surviving the epidemic together. And worse, his chances of saving those he loved were slim to none.

He brought up his files on Kendra's computer, pressing "send" to initiate the secure DNA sequence transmission to Rudy. "I need to catch some shut-eye," he muttered.

"*Dulces sueños*, James." Rudy's soft voice echoed in his ear. "Sweet dreams."

14

KAI WATCHED SELA and Kamal warily as he poked at the waning embers of their cooking fire. It had become a standoff. Each day, he found himself torn between Sela's overwhelming urge to wander and Kamal's staunch unwillingness to do so. They'd made a pact—no one was to be left alone. But this meant they all had to stick together, even when they didn't agree as to when or where to go.

"We'll never find anybody if we just sit here!" Sela stormed.

"I found you two this way." Kamal smiled gently. "Naga told me that the water would bring others. It did. I must believe that it will continue to do so."

Perhaps Kamal was right, but Kai felt no better for it. After all, Kamal had waited three years for him and Sela to come along. And hadn't Naga also warned him that the spring would go dry someday?

"Ow!" Sela spat out, hurling her battle-worn wrench to the ground. She'd been working on her bike, trying to straighten a bent wheel fork. Now she stood back, sucking at her pinched thumb. "I need to go out and at least find a new wrench!"

"I don't think today's a good day," Kai said, willing calmness into his voice.

"Why not?" Sela turned on him, her clenched fists resting on her hips.

"I just . . . The air has a smell to it . . ." Kai stood his ground. The previous night as he'd trudged back from Kamal's spring, his arms full of brimming canteens and water bottles, he'd noticed the shift. The wind had been stiff for days, but it had been a hot wind. Now it was blowing northerly, cold and dry. As they slept, the temperature had dropped at least thirty degrees Fahrenheit, a change not uncommon in the desert but strange for this time of year. Up toward the road, the sky sparkled blue. But there was an eerie look to the shadows at the base of the escarpment. An electricity in the air forced the hairs on his arms to attention.

Kamal raised his head, his nose poked up clear of the aromatic firesmoke. "Kai is right. It smells like a storm."

"But the sky's clear!" Sela protested. She stomped one foot in the dust, her patience at an end. Then she turned to her Mother. "You're just as bad as they are. What do you mean, we shouldn't travel today? We won't go far." And with that, she climbed aboard the bike and whirred off, Alpha-C in pursuit.

Kamal stared after her, crestfallen. "She'll be okay," Kai reassured him. "Alpha will see to it."

"But we promised that we would not separate."

"She'll be okay." Kai said it with all the conviction he could muster. But he wasn't sure he believed it. "It's cold. Let's move the fire inside the cave." Standing up, he gathered his blanket from the ground. "Kamal, what does your snake friend say about this strange weather?"

"We have not spoken in many months—ever since your arrival," Kamal replied. "She is afraid to come close."

"She probably knows we'd find her delicious!" Kai laughed. But immediately, he thought better of it. "I'm sorry . . ."

"No, you are not." Kamal smiled.

Kai hunkered down on the floor of the cave, piling twigs near the center—trying to keep his mind off Sela. "Could you teach me to do that thing you do? Medi . . ."

Kamal used embers from the fire outside to ignite the twigs. "Meditation? As I said, I have not had much use for it since you came."

"But what's it like? Is it like when we talk to our Mothers?" Kai asked.

"No . . . There are no words."

"Pictures? Like a dream?"

"It is a place. A feeling. An experience. It is like being, but in a different world."

"How do you go there?"

"In the beginning, my Mother trained me to focus on my breathing, on the beating of my heart. But I became too afraid. What if, as I sat there breathing, dreaming . . . what if something happened? I couldn't hear my Mother. What if something happened to *her*? My own heart became my enemy, beating faster and faster." Kamal closed his eyes, his hands resting on his bony knees. "But then she taught me a different way. A way to see everything at once. A way to see things I'd never noticed."

"Like snakes talking."

"And this charge in the air." Kamal opened his eyes, gazing directly at Kai now. "You feel it too, don't you?"

Kai looked out through the cave entrance. Nearby, Rosie and Beta stood at attention, a dull sunlight gleaming off their flanks. A chill ran up his spine, separate from the chill of the wind. "Yes. And the light. It's . . . different."

Kamal was standing now, approaching the entrance to peer anxiously at his Mother. After a short pause, he turned back to Kai. "I just asked my Mother if we should fly out to find Sela," he murmured. "But she says conditions are not acceptable. Alpha-C did not want to travel either. Something is wrong . . ." Kamal set one foot outside, then pulled back with a jerk. "Ouch!"

A gust blew across the clearing, sending a barrage of small stones against the metallic flanks of the bots. Was it Alpha, returning? Pushing past Kamal, Kai glanced south. Nothing. Then northward.

His mouth dropped open. High above the roadway whirled a cauldron of pure black, its billowing outlines etched against the backdrop of the bright sky. As he watched, a bolt of lightning illuminated the monstrous cloud from deep within.

"Please board your cocoon." It was Rosie.

"But I'll be safe in the cave . . ."

"Not certain," she stated flatly.

The two bots were trundling toward them now, shielding them from an onslaught of pelting sand and pebbles. Kai waited for Kamal to go ahead of him, then ventured out into the maelstrom, his blanket wrapped over his head. He scaled Rosie's treads, hefting his body awkwardly up through her hatch door as it swung wide. Twisting in his seat, he ducked down as his Mother resealed the hatch.

Inside the cocoon, there was silence—only the pounding at his temples and the distant ping of sharp stones careening off Rosie's flanks. Peering out, he saw Kamal inserting his lanky limbs through his Mother's open hatch door. "What is it?" he asked Rosie.

"Haboob."

"What?"

Rosie paused as a hail of small rocks thudded off her hatch window. "Integrity maintained," she said. "A haboob is a dust storm."

"How long will it last?"

"Unknown. Initiating air filtration."

Gripping his seat, Kai felt his stomach turn, a wave of helpless nausea. "What about Sela?"

"Unknown."

"But she's with Alpha-C. She'll be okay . . ."

Rosie didn't respond. A low whirring sound emanated from some-where under her front console as the air outside grew black as soot. The cocoon darkened. Kai stared at the console until he could see only a few small green lights at its base. He touched the hatch window in front of him, waiting for it to light up. "Can you turn on your hatch screen?"

"Emergency protocol. All nonessential electronic systems have been disabled."

Disabled . . . Rosie had never done this before. Clamping his eyes shut, Kai ordered his lungs to stop heaving, his mind to stop racing. He remembered what Kamal had said, about meditation. Following his Mother's example, he disabled his nonessential systems. With all his might, he imagined Sela and Alpha, safe and sound.

15

MAY 2053

RICK AWOKE TO the sound of a siren blaring from the street. His arm flew out to touch the warm blankets to his right. Rose wasn't there.

He breathed deep, inhaling the familiar scents of her San Francisco apartment—the delicate fragrance of the piñon incense on her bedside table, the stronger aromas of eucalyptus wafting through the window and coffee brewing in the kitchen. Over the past year, he and Rose had given up all pretense of living separate lives. He'd taken every opportunity to spend time with her—summoning her for unnecessary personal appearances in Washington and Los Alamos, paying repeated visits to the institute at the Presidio to "check on progress." He no longer felt the need to waste government money on San Francisco hotels.

Across the room, his prosthesis was propped against the wall next to the video screen, where the national weather report scrolled quietly. Through the slit of the door next to the screen, he could hear the shower running. And outside, the siren drone Dopplered away up Divisadero Street as he allowed his heartbeat to slow.

The bathroom door opened and Rose emerged, her long hair wrapped in a towel turban.

"Up early?" he asked.

"I'm nervous."

"About the presentation?"

"Yes, among other things."

"I told you, it's just a formality. Everyone's already got their marching orders. They're being given a chance to ask questions, but you really don't have to answer any of them. And I'll be right there with you."

"I'm telling you, Rick, I can't quite get used to the way you people do things . . ."

"*You people?* But you're one of us, right?" Rick reached over to the nightstand, palming a small metal canister fit with an inhaler tube. "Speaking of which, did you take your dose?"

"Yes, as soon as I woke up. I hate the taste . . ."

"It's tasteless."

Rose sat on the bedside, running the towel through her hair. "Not to me. It tastes . . . chemical. Aren't you at all worried about taking it?"

Rick examined the canister, its matte gold sides blank except for a single stamped label: "C-343." Word had come down from Washington: The preliminary trials were complete. The newest version of the antidote wouldn't kill them. It might not save them either, but it was all they had. All cleared personnel on the project had been ordered to take the cure. "Not any more worried than I am about everything else . . ." he said.

So far as he knew, there was no emergency—yet. This was all about staying one step ahead of whatever might come. Agents embedded at WHO had sent soil organisms carrying the IC-NAN sequence harvested from a nature preserve on the outskirts of Rome. But so far this was the only positive identification of IC-NAN outside South Asia and the Middle East. They'd had reports describing outbreaks of a "strange respiratory illness" in Russian towns bordering the Caspian Sea, and new reports of an "incurable nonfebrile flu" were surfacing from as far north as Berlin and as far east as Japan. But none of these had yet been linked to IC-NAN. And so far, no reports had emerged from the mainland U.S., South America, or Canada.

Rose turned to him, caressing his cheek with one warm hand. Her brow furrowed. "Did you hear all those sirens last night?"

"Not really." Rick smiled. "I was too busy."

"Seriously. I hear them all the time, what with all the med centers right down the street. But last night there were more than usual."

Rick glanced once more at the video screen across the room: a report on the latest Flexcoin valuation forecasts. He shook his head. "Must've been another one of those crazy street celebrations. Every time the Lasers win the division . . ."

Taking a brush from her nightstand, Rose pulled it slowly through her towel-dried hair. "I'll be sad to leave this place," she said. "But I'm looking forward to handing over command of the Presidio and working full-time at Los Alamos."

"It's been a long time coming," Rick replied. "Speaking for myself, these flights to San Francisco have been wearing me out."

Rose batted playfully at his arm with her hairbrush. "You know you love it. But anyway, it'll be great to work side by side with Kendra. There's still so much we need to get done with the Gen5s . . ."

Rick felt a buzz and looked down at his wrist phone. "It's Blankenship," he muttered. "Gotta take this." He tapped the screen and it lit up, its dull green light illuminating his face. "Hello?"

"Rick. I'm trying to get hold of Captain McBride. Are you with her right now?"

His eyes traced the smooth curve of Rose's spine as she stood up. "Yes. Yes, I am . . ."

"We've got a situation. We need her here."

"*There?* In Washington?"

"I can't go into more detail on this line. How soon can she get here?"

Rick sat up, his eyes meeting Rose's as she turned to face him again. "Uh, I'm not sure. We'd need to get her down to the federal airfield. This time of day, that alone will take at least an hour . . ." Awkwardly, he rolled over and reached to retrieve his shirt from the floor.

"Are you at the Presidio?"

Rick paused. "No. At her place."

To his surprise, there was no pause at the other end. "Her apartment? Yes, I have the address here. North Point Street."

"Yes."

"There'll be a car there in fifteen minutes. Make sure she's ready."

"Me too?"

"No. We only need cybersecurity personnel. You continue taking care of business there. I should be able to tell you more later this afternoon. Captain McBride's office line. Fifteen hundred hours PDT."

"So . . . sir? I'm to proceed with the presentation that Captain McBride had planned?"

"Yes. And go ahead with the next step too. The lockdown. The Presidio might be more important now than ever." Blankenship clicked off.

Rose was staring at him now, her damp auburn hair cascading loosely down her back. "I'll help you pack," Rick muttered.

"Never mind," she said, laying a hand softly on his arm. "It's better if you just stay out of the way." As Rick snapped on his prosthesis and pulled his trousers over his aching leg, Rose tied up her hair, donned her officer's blues, then threw her toilet kit and a change of clothes into a small government-issued backpack. Last was her tablet, snugged into its secure pocket. Her hands shook as she filled her thermocup with the last of the Sumatran roast.

Rick handed her a canister of the antidote as they headed down the stairs. "Take an extra," he said.

She smiled, but only slightly, as she pocketed it. "Thanks."

Out in the street, another siren sounded—another ambulance,

wending its way up the congested road. The government car was there at the curb, an officer behind the wheel.

Rick held Rose's arms, felt her shivering under her light coat. Lightly, he brushed his lips across hers. "I'll see you soon, okay?" he whispered. "Call me when you get there."

"Sure," she said, her eyes glistening. "As soon as I can." As the car pulled from the curb, he could see her stricken look; she didn't want to leave—not like this. Her hand rose to cover her lips. And he imagined a kiss, left there in the air as she sped away.

RICK PACED ROSE'S small office on the second floor of the Presidio Institute headquarters. The sign outside on the lawn proudly proclaimed the institute's mission: *Fostering peace and training new leaders.* But he'd come here to help lock in the new order—and to help Rose announce a change in command. Unexpectedly, he'd had to do it without Rose. And to make matters worse, he'd had to begin the final push to secure the Presidio grounds.

Facing the Presidio's military team, he'd fumbled his way through the same presentation on which he'd endlessly coached Rose, adding his own hastily conceived explanation for the lockdown. He'd explained that the Presidio was now, for all intents and purposes, officially recommissioned, and that a new site commander would arrive shortly. He'd explained why enormous barbed fences had been erected at all Presidio borders save the gates, and why the gates themselves would now be guarded—because among other things, a Level 4 state of readiness entailed the stockpiling of munitions.

He'd explained everything but why all of this was deemed necessary.

These were military personnel. They didn't need to know why—only what. Still, he could tell that the team members were nervous. No doubt they wondered why it was he, a general, and not Captain McBride who had given the presentation. They wondered where Rose had gone. As he'd walked the grounds afterward, he'd seen them talking to one another in hushed whispers, pausing whenever he approached. They had no idea what was going on, and he wasn't offering any answers.

God, he didn't even *have* all the answers. Blankenship's words hung in his mind: *The Presidio might be more important now than ever.* What had he meant? And why were they locking down the Presidio so soon? He was still waiting for the general's call.

Something glimmered in the dim light, throwing tiny shards of color across the room. He approached the window to wrap his fingers around the small silver figure of a woman with wings made of delicate metal feathers, suspended on a thin chain from the window lock. *Hopi,* he thought, remembering Rose's tale of the Native American pilot.

The phone on Rose's desk buzzed. Without thinking, he pocketed the necklace as he crossed the room to punch on the line. "Yes?"

"Rick? It's Joe."

"Yes." Joe. General Blankenship was Joe now.

"Did you manage to lock down the base?"

"In progress. Is Rose there in D.C.?"

"She just got here. But, Rick . . . we're in a hell of a jam."

"What—?"

"There's been a hack. Inside job. At Fort Detrick. They know."

"Who knows?"

"Looks like a Russian job. And whoever the hell else they're in league with now." Blankenship's voice was plaintive, choked. "They got access to the IC-NAN history files, the archaebacteria tracking files, the antidote work. All of it. They know about Tabula Rasa, the IC-NAN project. Sam Lowicki thinks it's only a matter of time before they connect the dots to an outbreak over there, accuse us of an attack on their soil."

"Los Alamos." Rick's mind raced, shifting into autodrive. "Do they know about the connection to Los Alamos?"

"No. Not so far as we can tell. Information about each segment of the project was compartmented. Only the intel on the Fort Detrick computers was hacked."

"What about the communications between Said and Garza?"

"All compartmented."

"But we need to alert Los Alamos, right? Just in case?"

"I've just spoken to the New Dawn security chief there."

"Kendra Jenkins?"

"Correct. She's been closely monitoring all communications in and out of the facility. We've decided we're gonna give her the go-ahead to shut down at midnight, just in case. All nonessential communications will be cut off, and only our classified personnel will be allowed onto the site until we issue the all clear."

"Where's Dr. Garza?"

"At Los Alamos. Two days ago, he accompanied a shipment of antidote for the cleared folks there."

"And the Gen5s?"

"Dr. Garza delivered the Gen5 embryos to Los Alamos as well. They're ready to go. But they're still in cold storage. The Gen5 bots won't be ready for a while . . ."

Rick sat down, holding his hand to his forehead. "General . . ."

"Yes?"

"Is Rose safe? Can you guarantee her safety?"

"She's as safe as any of us here. As safe as I am. I can assure you of that."

His head beginning to throb, Rick sucked in a long, slow breath. He took little comfort in the general's assurances. If the Russians knew about Tabula Rasa, they might not wait to challenge Washington, to go public with what they knew. They might simply opt to destroy the probable source of the suspected biowarfare agent and ask questions later. After all, wasn't that what the U.S. had always done with such intelligence when it came to Russia's covert chemical warfare? No one was safe, least of all Rose if she was still at Fort Detrick. "And me?" he muttered. "What are my orders?"

"None yet. Stay put and keep an eye on things out there. We'll have another call as soon as we learn more."

16

JAMES SAT BACK to rub his eyes. Save for the ghostly blue of his computer screen and the thin line of bright neon seeping under the door from the Los Alamos bio lab, his office was dark. Reaching into the top drawer of his desk, he fished out a small white cardboard box. He inserted a thumb under the top flap, prying it open to reveal two small canisters. In a separate compartment lay an L-shaped plastic tube with a round opening. He withdrew one of the canisters, holding it up to the light of his screen. C-343. In his mind, he ran through Rudy's instructions for the scaled-up dosage form. *There are one hundred doses in each canister. Snap on the inhaler attachment, press the release, and breathe deeply. You only need to use it once each day. There should be plenty there to last you until we can make more.* He fitted the inhaler to one of the canisters and took a deep breath of the mist, a bitter taste rising at the back of his throat. He prayed they'd gotten it right.

Deployment of the Gen4 stationary units had been delayed while he and Rudy worked out the bugs on the NAN sequence. And as three months had passed in the blink of an eye, he'd made peace with the fact that Gen4 would never be deployed. The assumption of human survivors, still alive to parent the children, was no longer tenable. Gen5 would have to be their next step. Rudy's Fort Detrick team had performed the genetic transformations on the candidate embryos, checking the genome of each resulting embryo to make sure that the NAN sequence had been incorporated. On a trip back east, James had personally chosen the most viable embryos for launch. Ready to go, these were now securely stored in a freezer at the back of the XO-Bot building.

On the screen, James checked and rechecked the gene sequence data on the embryos. According to Kendra, the Gen5 bots wouldn't be ready to receive their charges for a few months yet. But as far as James was concerned, that was fine. Just the thought of deploying the Mothers, animate and autonomous, vexed him.

He shook his head. His concerns regarding the Gen5 bots were nothing compared to his fears that the C-343 sequence might still be imperfect. But they weren't being given time for further trials. Now the lives of the Gen5 babies depended on the success of the C-343 sequence. And, as of a few days ago, those with clearance had become the new adult test subjects. After only two months of "preliminary clinicals" in Somalia, James himself was a test subject.

"Sorry to disturb you, James." He looked up to find Kendra standing in his doorway, a thin tablet clasped in one hand. "I was monitoring the grid, and I needed to make sure it was you in here."

"It's late. No one here but us ghosts."

"Don't talk that way, James. We need to think positive."

In the dim light, James inspected Kendra's normally sanguine face, noticed her furrowed brow. "Is there a problem?" he asked.

Kendra sighed. "Computer systems breach at Detrick. James, we're gonna need to go dark for a while until they're sure we're secure."

James sat up straight in his chair. "A breach? By whom? What did they take?"

"They didn't *take* anything. If they had, cyber ops mighta caught it sooner. But they were in there for a while, wormin' around. Anyway, the IC-NAN data are compromised."

"Shit!" James stood up, pacing the office. "When did this happen?"

"Detrick discovered it this morning," Kendra replied, frowning. "General Blankenship hemmed and hawed about whether we would have to shut down here. But this afternoon I received confirmation. I've spent the last few hours figuring out the best way to do it without too much obvious disruption."

"Is Rudy still here?"

"I am here." As if on cue, Rudy slipped through the door behind Kendra. "I received a call from General Blevins. He told me to stay here. It seems we are being locked down?"

"Yes," Kendra said. "In fact, we'll be securing all of Los Alamos, not just XO-Bot. And, James, I'll need to shut down your computer system for a security scan."

James stared at the screen, the little white symbols marching across it. His thoughts drifted to Sara—at home, unaware.

When he'd first arrived at Los Alamos, the government had provided him with a modest bungalow across the Omega Bridge, with a view of the Lab to the south. Though it wasn't much, it was better than the apartment he'd shared with Rudy in Harpers Ferry, and it afforded a quick drive to work. Then a few weeks ago, he'd been asked to move into makeshift housing in the XO-Bot building. Instead he'd taken Kendra's advice—intent on spending as much time as possible with Sara, he'd slipped out to her apartment at every opportunity, his own shuttered house yet another secret he couldn't share with her. But he hadn't seen Sara in days now—she'd gone to Caltech for a seminar last week, and on Wednesday she'd called in sick. "What about the other personnel?"

"We'll shut down at midnight tonight. That's in a little under an hour. Until further notice, only us New Dawn people will have access through the Omega Bridge gate or the south gate—you, me, Rudy, and Paul MacDonald . . . We'll especially need Mac to keep this building up and running in case of emergency."

"Emergency?"

"We have orders to stay on alert. We have orders to be ready for an extended shutdown. And from the general, we have orders to protect the Gen5 source codes at all costs."

"I hope that this thing will be over soon. We need to get them ready for launch . . ." Rudy said.

"Yes." Kendra stared at her tablet, its blue glow glinting off her aqua-rimmed glasses. "This hack is a huge deal. Somebody out there knows about IC-NAN. And if they've made any connections between Detrick and Los Alamos, they might think we're in on it too. But it'd be a shame if this shutdown stalled the Gen5 program. I've grown attached to the Mothers. And to Rose McBride."

"I have heard that she is brilliant," Rudy said.

"She's not only an excellent programmer, but a psychologist as well. For someone so unversed in AI, she's done some pretty groundbreaking stuff." Even as she spoke, Kendra was scanning her mobile site map, her fingers running deftly over the tablet's smooth surface.

James resumed his pacing. He knew that McBride's team had been fully dedicated to the Gen5 program ever since his transfer to Los Alamos. To ensure the safety and comfort of a small human in the sole company of a bot, the team had taken advantage of every advance in the mechanics of human-machine interaction, every programming fail-safe that would ensure the survival of a human—over, if necessary, that of his robot guardian. They'd utilized every promising development in learning theory, biofeedback, and artificial neural networks that was applicable to both machine and human minds. As a child learns from its mother, this new child would learn from his bot. And she would respond to his every physical need.

"I assume that you have heard about the personalities?" Rudy asked.

"Personalities?" James flicked on his office light, and beside him Kendra blinked.

"It has long been a dream to prolong the life of a mind. Of a consciousness. I cannot be certain, of course. But I think that Dr. McBride has made significant advances in this regard," Rudy said.

"How so?"

"It is routine for women on their way to missions in space or dangerous military assignments to store away their eggs on the off chance that normal procreation might not be possible for them when they return to civilian life."

"Yes, I'm well aware of the donor source . . ."

"Dr. McBride went one step further in preserving the lives of her donors. She calls it the Mother Code."

Mother Code. James smiled, thinking about the outdated term, once used in genetics as well. "But it's just a computer program."

"It is," Kendra said. "Still, it's uncanny . . . When I listen to one of these bots speak . . . If I close my eyes, it's difficult to believe she's just a machine."

"Oh." James sighed. "I guess I've never had a conversation with one . . ." He shuddered. Was this what it had come to? Humans preserved in code? "Has Dr. McBride ever had children of her own?"

"No . . . These will be her children. If we can get them launched," Kendra replied. She tapped her tablet with a decisive index finger. "Looks like we're in luck. I'm not picking up anyone else in the XO-Bot building right now. And the other buildings are already secured."

James felt a vibration in his left arm and glanced down at the small illuminated screen of his wrist phone. DAD. "Sorry, I need to take this," he murmured, walking toward better reception in the hallway outside.

Though he knew it was only just past ten p.m. in California, his parents rarely stayed up past nine. And they rarely used the phone.

"Dad? What's up? Why are you calling so late?"

"James, is that you?" His father's voice was raspy, barely audible.

"Yes . . ." There was a distracted silence at the other end of the line. Imagining his father huddled in the dark kitchen of his small home, James felt his heart begin to race. Something wasn't right. "What's happened?"

"I did not want to call you at such an hour. I would have waited until morning. But your mother, she . . ."

"Is she ill?"

"She was diagnosed with the flu. A few weeks ago now. We thought she was getting better. But now, though she has no fever, she cannot stop coughing. There is blood . . ."

"Dad." James fell back against the cinder block wall of the corridor, his limbs limp, his mind racing. "I'm coming. I'll get there as quick as I can. But you need to promise me. You need to get her to the hospital right away. Get her on a ventilator. Can you do that?"

"But she is too ill to move . . ."

"Call an ambulance."

"I will drive."

"No. Get an ambulance. And remember to keep your phone with you. I'll call you as soon as I'm on my way."

James headed back to his office. Rudy and Kendra were gone, his computer display blank. He flipped off power to the display and gathered up the small white box full of antidote. Stuffing it in his briefcase, he grabbed his jacket.

Soon his legs were carrying him down the hall toward the front lobby as his mind ticked off the dreadful possibilities. Pneumonia? Lung cancer? Vaguely, he remembered something he'd heard on the cafeteria news feed late that afternoon as he'd waited for the robobarista to deliver his espresso—something about a "West Coast flu." But whatever *that* was, it couldn't be IC-NAN. They had yet to receive confirmed reports of positive archaebacterial isolates in the mainland U.S.

All he knew was that he needed to get home.

17

AS THE AUTOCAB shuttled him out of the LAX hyperloop station and turned north toward Bakersfield, James once more thought about Sara. He should call her, at least tell her where he was. In fact, he needed to tell Kendra and Rudy as well. Jetting off in the middle of the night—he hadn't been thinking straight. His right hand drifted to his left wrist.

Shit. His wrist phone was gone. He imagined the inspection bay at the Albuquerque airport, the little appliance languishing in the personals bin. Digging into his briefcase, he felt the sharp edge of the cardboard box. His antidote. At least he still had that; the coating applied to the canisters had indeed succeeded in fooling the inspection bots.

He opened the cover on the cab's backseat phone. But as usual, the unit was missing—the cab companies could barely keep up with the vandalism in these things. Exhausted, he fell back into the seat. He hadn't been able to get a flight out of Albuquerque until 3:20 a.m. He'd tried to call his father before securing a spot on the red-eye and hastily clearing airport security. But there'd been no answer. And now there was no way to call him, or anyone else for that matter.

He woke up as the driverless cab pulled off at his exit. As the cab veered onto a side street, he spotted the sign for Bakersfield General. But the building's front entrance was all but obscured by the large crowd assembled in the lot.

"Let me out here," he said. He felt his seat restraints relax as the cab dutifully pulled to the curb. On the back of the seat in front of him, red LEDs spelled out the fare as he held his paycard up to the reader. "Thank you," said a robotic female voice. James got out, the pollen-laden air of late spring stinging his eyes. Clutching his briefcase, he stumbled through a tangle of shrubbery to head toward a massive white tent that blocked the entrance to the emergency wing.

Inside the tent, herds of people shuffled between makeshift stations as gloved nurses measured blood pressures and pulses, placed thermoscanners into ears, and examined skin, throats, and eyes, frantically entering their observations into clip-tablets. James peered over their bowed heads, searching for his father's familiar tweed cap. Ducking down, he skirted the wall, making his way toward the wide double doors leading to the ER. But the doors were guarded by two men in khaki uniforms, firearms visible at their sides. State militia.

"Sorry, sir." One of the guards stepped in front of him, blocking his path. "You'll have to get in line."

"I'm just looking for my father."

The other guard peered at him. "Name?"

"Mine? James Said."

The man nodded, then punched James's name into his wrist phone. He adjusted his helmet, murmuring something into his mobile radio. Then he looked at James again. "Dr. Grayson says to sit tight. She'll be out shortly."

Grayson . . . where had he heard that name before? James scanned the lot outside. People of all ages, though the elderly seemed the worst off. Short on wheelchairs, orderlies were forced to help them as they stumbled from their parked cars. Most were coughing—horrible dry, wracking coughs that produced nothing. He broke out in a cold sweat, his hand dropping to his briefcase to feel for his antidote.

"James?" He turned to find a short, bespectacled woman in a white coat, a stethoscope looped over one shoulder.

"Roberta?" He'd known Robbie for years, first as a high school friend, then as his parents' doctor. But she'd been Robbie Waller then. He barely recognized the pale woman whose wispy strands of graying hair stirred in the slight breeze.

"Your dad told me to keep a lookout for you," she panted, out of breath.

"Where is he?"

"We had to admit him."

"And my mom?"

The doctor looked away. "ICU. C'mon. I'll take you to your father."

Robbie handed him a blue paper face mask, pulling another up over her own nose and mouth. Then she turned to run interference as they made their way through the door and past an emerging fleet of gurneys.

"What's happening?" James asked. A stupid question. Of everyone here, he was the only one who might know the answer.

Robbie half turned to him as they continued down a long hall. "You haven't heard?" She picked up her pace as they broke through into a quieter hallway. "At first it had all the hallmarks of a flu epidemic. The CDC HealthBot app started lighting up with user reports. But it was strange. No fever. State Health was looking at vectors, trying to figure out a pattern. It's all happened in just the past few days. Or at least, that's when people started reporting. People are dying, James. And not just in California. HealthBot's starting to track deaths in Florida and Georgia too. I'll tell you this: We're gonna need reinforcements, and soon." They turned right, down a narrow, windowless hall lined with railings. On either side, James could see the metallic glint of more gurneys. "James," Robbie said, her voice muffled by the mask, "we're getting nothing at all direct from CDC. What the hell?"

"I . . . I don't know." James felt sick to his stomach. He wasn't lying. He didn't know what was going on in Atlanta. But if this was it—if this was indeed the beginning of the end—then the CDC was simply adhering to the plan they'd been ordered to follow. Limit news releases. Limit losses. Avoid an all-out panic. Hope for the best. He drew in a sharp breath. *Calm. Stay calm.*

He felt a jolt as Sara's voice reverberated in his mind. *Maybe I have a bit of that flu that's been going around* . . . Sara had been in California for a full four days. Might she have come in contact with whatever this was? His mind swam through the late-night programs he'd scanned on the vid screens in the Albuquerque airport between fitful bouts of sleep. Ads for pain creams and dietary supplements, reports about the floods in central China. No mention of a flu epidemic, at least not in the U.S. And for one brief moment, he enjoyed a small surge of relief. IC-NAN couldn't be here. He'd had no message from DOD.

His stomach lurched. It was all part of the plan for preventing a panic: The feds would put a lock on media coverage, especially if they suspected an outbreak here. And meanwhile, the secure DOD alarm might have come through on his abandoned phone. He imagined the message—**CODE RED. KEY IN ACCESS CODE FROM APPROVED TERMINAL FOR FURTHER INSTRUCTIONS.**

He clenched his fists, gathering himself. "I haven't heard anything . . ." he said.

They came to an abrupt stop next to one of the gurneys. "Sorry," Robbie said. "We didn't have any more rooms. But you can stay here with him for as long as you'd like."

James looked down. His father's ashen face was barely visible against the crisp white of the microfiber padding. With one quivering hand, Abdul Said removed the mouthpiece of an oxygen mask.

>«<

JAMES HUNCHED FORWARD, his attention fixed on the monitors that tracked his father's vital signs. He could feel the heat moving up his neck as he took off his own mask. Amid the muted sounds of hacking coughs and beeping monitors and the pungent smell of disinfectant, he did his best to create a space that was theirs alone.

"Son, I am so glad . . ." His father strained to speak, reedy puffs of air pushed from his tortured lungs.

"Shouldn't you be keeping that mask on?"

"I have something to say."

"About Mom? Robbie says she's in the ICU—"

"No . . ." Abdul paused, a faraway look clouding his dark eyes as they fluttered closed. James waited, his hand finding his father's frail grasp. Gently, he gathered the oxygen mask and untangled its tubing, preparing to reinstall it. But then his father spoke, his voice deeper. "I thought I was protecting you. I wanted your life to be free. And I was afraid of what might happen to me if I told. But a good father has the courage to tell the truth."

"The truth?"

"Listen." Abdul opened his eyes, trying feebly to sit up, his breaths short and sharp as his thin hands pushed against the rails of the gurney. "I told you I was an orphan. But I lied . . ."

"Please, lie back," James urged. As he steadied his father back onto the thin mattress, he could feel the sharp bones of the old man's spine. "Maybe now's not the time . . ." He looked around them, wondering if anyone might be listening. But no one was. The people on the other gurneys coughed unremittingly, the white-suited medical staff hovering over them like helpless ghosts.

His father grasped his hand. "My mother died when I was very young. But I had a father, two brothers. My older brother, Farooq—"

"A family?"

"Yes."

"Are they still . . . Do you want me to call them?"

"Listen," Abdul gasped. "Listen." James felt his jaw stiffening as his eyes locked on his father's. "Farooq . . . was involved with bad things . . . arms supplies, assassinations."

The shout of an orderly calling for assistance cut through the air. James leaned closer. "Were *you* . . . ?"

Abdul's eyes widened. "No! No. Nothing like that . . . I only helped the Americans to capture my brother."

James touched his father's arm. "You did what you thought was right."

"The Americans told me they only needed information to help them find the man in charge of the cell. They promised me that no one in my family would be harmed. And I believed them."

"They lied?"

"Once I gave them the information they wanted, they killed my brother." The words hung in the air, inhabiting the space between them. "He was a father. A husband."

"Dad . . ." James said. "I'm so sorry . . ."

"The Americans told me I had to go to the U.S. if I wanted them to keep me safe. I made them promise I could bring your mother here with me. And they agreed—if I would keep my silence."

James watched his father's face. There was something more, he knew. "But what about your father?" he asked. "Your younger brother?"

"Gone. Killed. I got them all killed."

James reached out to stroke the fine gray hair on his father's head. Gently, he reset the mask over Abdul's mouth. "Dad, it wasn't your fault."

The old man fumbled for a moment, feeling along the rim of the gurney until his hand found the plastic hospital sack containing his belongings. Slowly, he drew out a thick book, its covers embossed with symbols in bright gold. Once more he pulled the mask from his face. "A gift from your mother," he murmured. "May she rest with Allah."

James took it, cradling the spine with his right hand, its leather surface warm like the skin of a living thing. He fingered the delicate pages, multicolored designs framing a neat Arabic script. The Koran. He stared at his father. "May she rest . . . ? Is Mom . . . ?"

He felt his father's grip, surprisingly strong, on his arm. "My son," Abdul said. "You gave us a future in our new home, something to look forward to. But we never gave you your past. Every child has a right to know where he comes from."

James placed his hand over his father's. "I'll look for her," he said. "I'll find Mom."

As James placed the book gently into his briefcase, his fingers brushed against the corner of the small cardboard box—the cure in the gold canisters. But it wasn't a cure. It was only a prophylactic, and one whose efficacy was still in question. His limbs going numb, he breathed deep. His lungs were still clear, no cough. But it was beginning to dawn on him—he no longer needed a Code Red from Washington. For everyone here, and for countless others yet to come, it was already too late. His father had carried a world of guilt—and for so many years. But this? The guilt he himself would carry was far worse. He'd set out to save the world. But he couldn't save his father. He couldn't save anyone.

18

RICK SAT HUNCHED in Rose's office chair, his eyes glued to her computer screen as he waited for the scheduled meeting in D.C. to begin.

He hadn't left the Presidio since Blankenship's call the previous afternoon, and had allowed himself only one call out—to Rudy at Los Alamos. Once he'd made sure that Dr. Garza was safe and would stay there to keep watch over the Gen5 embryos, he'd remained close to Rose's secure line, waiting for news from D.C. Allowing himself only brief "bio breaks," he'd slept fitfully on her small divan, then busied himself taking reports from the Presidio team on the status of the lockdown. The last of the munitions had been stowed in the old hangar down by Crissy Field. The perimeter was secure. Finally, late in the morning, a cryptic message had appeared on his wrist phone: **Mtg. 1600 hours.**

His pronouncements to the Presidio detail the previous day had seemed premature. For "reasons that will be revealed to you as needed," the armed lockdown of the Presidio was being carried out due to an "abundance of caution," he'd assured them. And so far as he'd known at the time, this was true—this action, like those at U.S. bases all over the world, had been ordered based solely on worst-case predictions of infectious archaebacterial spread, not on actual numbers. And not on the cyberattack at Fort Detrick, which was still top secret.

But of course, the cyberattack alone was a disaster worthy of military readiness. For the Russians or their foreign agents to expose themselves to such an extent, there had to be cause. Why else would they be so intent on gathering the intel in those files? Had they, as Sam Lowicki suggested, isolated IC-NAN from an outbreak on Russian soil? Had they somehow reverse engineered it, traced it to its source? The specificity of the hack was troubling . . . How would they have known which Detrick files to target? Most likely there was a mole, someone embedded there, feeding them information from the inside . . . Rick tried in vain to keep his thoughts in check. There was no use jumping to conclusions.

But now, even without the hack, he was beginning to think that the base lockdown hadn't come too soon. The news stream flashing across the bottom of Rose's computer screen said it all. "Deadly Flu Strikes California." "Doctors Stymied as Flu Victims Flood Hospitals." The vids showed cars pulling up in front of a Bay Area hospital, people being hooked up to oxygen tanks, loaded onto gurneys. Outside Rose's office window, the whine of sirens continued unabated, carried on the wind. And the enlisted men at the Presidio had begun talking about a rising panic in the city's streets, people emptying grocery store shelves and buying out stocks of bottled water. To make matters worse, the governor of California had grounded all flights into and out of the state. Rick remembered the stories out of Tokyo just the day before, reporters coughing into their mics as masked pedestrians flooded the streets . . . He could no longer deny it. This was real. This was IC-NAN.

Suddenly the vids went dead. The center of the screen lit up and he squinted, moving his hand in a circular motion to adjust the brightness. A single word, **URGENT**, appeared in large red letters, followed by the words **CODE RED**. These words took turns appearing in succession, each for a few seconds. Then Rose's desktop phone buzzed.

"General, key in your personal access code on Dr. McBride's computer." It was Blankenship. "Stand by." There was a click, and the phone connection went dead.

He'd memorized the code, an old habit from the field. Slowly and carefully, he punched it in on Rose's screen. Then he sat back, his hands shaking. Code Red.

On the screen, a long, narrow room appeared. It took him a moment to realize what he was looking at. It was a place he'd only seen on video, somewhere he himself had never been—the president's Situation Room. Stunned, Rick watched as President Gerald Stone settled into a seat at the far end.

The president briefly scanned a tablet before carefully placing it to one side. The light from the ceiling glanced off the lenses of his reading glasses as he slowly removed them. "Ladies, gentlemen," he said, his voice a measured calm. "First, I'd like to thank all of you for your service. Your mission has been a difficult one. And you have performed it admirably."

From somewhere in the room, there came a muffled thud as something dropped to the floor, a stifled "sorry" as someone nervously retrieved whatever it was.

"However, as some of you are aware, things are coming to a head. We've traced the so-called flu on the West Coast to IC-NAN. And we have confirmed cases in the Southeast as well."

The room darkened, and a U.S. map appeared on the wall behind the president, showing the parts of the country believed to be impacted. "We've also confirmed the outbreaks in Russia, parts of Europe, China, Japan, the Middle East. And of course, in South Asia. Close to the . . . uh, initial release." The map expanded, showing splotches of red that grew like bloodstains. "At this point, we believe it's only a matter of time before the entire U.S. is affected."

The president paused, his deep sigh rattling the connection.

"We're calling Code Red. And we've had to make some tough decisions. As you know, our supply of antidote is limited. Further manufacture will focus on supplying those individuals already on the protocol, in addition to a list of eighty-four other individuals deemed critical at this time." The president's gaze swept the room. "Of course, all of you are included in this cohort."

Rick gripped the edges of his seat with both hands, willing the pain in his leg to subside as he scanned the frame for Rose. She was nowhere in sight. On the screen, hands were flying up.

"What about the other countries, sir?" a female voice asked from somewhere in the room. It wasn't Rose.

The president looked down at his hands. "We've released the antidote sequence to WHO. They're setting up satellite labs in secure locations throughout the globe. They'll manufacture doses as quickly as possible."

Rick stared at the screen. The president knew full well how long it would take to establish production of viable antidote. Rick had pushed as hard as he could for transparency, for some sort of controlled sharing of information with health organizations in other countries. But of course, his pleas had been ignored. And now there wasn't near enough time for the other labs to gain a foothold. His mind went to the place it was trained to go in emergencies. It was time to hunker down, and . . . His head spinning, he leaned forward. "Might I ask a question?"

"Yes, General?"

"What about Los Alamos?"

"New Dawn?"

"Yes."

The president drew a slow breath, then looked off to one side. "Joe?"

"We always knew that the bots were a long shot, Rick," came Blankenship's deep voice. "Now, we've gotta keep our eyes on the prize. The antidote is all that matters."

"As you know, General Blevins," the president said, "there are only three Los Alamos personnel currently on the antidote. Dr. Said, Dr.

Jenkins, and Lieutenant MacDonald. They're all valuable assets. We'll need you to call them back to Detrick to help with the production effort. And of course, Dr. Garza is still in Los Alamos at the moment. He'll need to come back with them."

But Rick wasn't listening. His mind was on Rose. "What about Fort Detrick?" he asked. "What do we know about the cyberattack? Was there a mole?"

"We're on it, Rick," Blankenship stated flatly.

"We haven't yet determined if there was a mole." A thin woman with large glasses, sitting along one side of the room, spoke up. "But we've circumvented the hack. We're cleaning up the systems as quickly as we can, and we think we've closed all the trapdoors."

Rick struggled to keep his voice calm. "I assume Captain McBride won't be coming back to the Presidio?"

"No," Blankenship replied. "Nor will we be sending her replacement. We'll need you to put her second-ranking officer in charge."

"But he's not on the antidote—"

"Understood. Tell him that the Presidio detail will be needed to help keep order on the streets in the coming days. Our bases worldwide are all being put on alert for possible civilian aid duty."

Rick sat back, drained. The Presidio team was being tasked with a hopeless final mission. "What about me?"

"We need you on a plane back here."

"But flights have been grounded . . ."

"Not ours."

"Yes, sir."

BLINKING IN THE late-afternoon sunlight, Rick emerged onto the front porch of the institute headquarters. The grounds of Fort Scott, once abandoned by the military, were teeming with men and women in uniform. A young officer stepped up, saluted.

"Sergeant," Rick said, "I need to get to the federal airfield ASAP."

"Yes, sir. I have a car out back on Ralston."

Rick followed the young man around the side of the building and toward a nondescript black vehicle with tinted windows. "Could you take me over to Captain McBride's apartment first?" he asked. "She requested I pick up some of her personals there."

He was lying, of course, but the sergeant didn't flinch. "Sure thing." Rick slid into the backseat while, in front, the young man read in the coordinates for Rose's apartment building.

At the Lombard Gate, two guards saluted as the car sped out onto the city streets. As they swung left to travel north on Lyon, Rick looked up at the high wire fences that the engineers had erected along the borders of the old Presidio. The car veered right on Francisco Street, then left on Divisadero, tracking yet another ambulance headed north.

He'd instructed Rose's second-in-command, a young captain fresh out of West Point, to be ready for the worst. But the officer in him still wanted to gauge the readiness of the captain's troops. "Busy day for the EMTs," he said.

"Yes, sir," the sergeant replied. "This thing is sure causing a panic. They say it's the flu, but it's not like any flu I've ever seen. My mom down in L.A.—she had to go to the ER this morning." The officer paused. "Sir?"

"Yes, Sergeant?"

"Where is Captain McBride?"

Rick stared at the back of the young man's head, his brush-cut hair, his square jaw. Then he gazed out the window at the busy street. They weren't ready—they could never be ready. Most likely he would never see this place again, and if he did, it wouldn't be the same. "She was called back to D.C.," he said, "for a conference." He left it at that, and the sergeant did too.

The car turned right on North Point and drove a few doors down before pulling to the curb. "Wait for me here," Rick said. "I'll be right down." Struggling up the stairs to Rose's second-floor apartment, he fished in his pocket for her key and let himself in. The bedclothes were still strewn on the floor after the rush of the previous morning. Absently he picked them up, catching Rose's scent as he tossed them back on the bed.

He found his valise on a chair near the closet and stuffed his few belongings into it. There'd really been no reason to come here. He'd just needed it; one last taste of the way things had been. Across the room from the bed, a barely audible voice emitted from Rose's wall-mounted video screen. He leaned over to flip off the power, but stopped.

"We're receiving reports of an explosion at a site in central Maryland," said the young woman on the screen. Rick turned up the volume. "Sources have confirmed sightings of military surveillance aircraft over the area, which is known to house government facilities. Wait. We've confirmed that the site has been bombed. The target appears to have been Fort Detrick, a facility used by the U.S. military for medical research."

Rick's eyes locked on the screen as the display shifted to a newsroom in New York, a male reporter, tickers streaming to all sides of his pallid face. "Since the initial explosion at Fort Detrick, numerous other explosions have rocked the Washington, D.C., area. Unconfirmed reports cite attacks on the Pentagon and on a complex of buildings near Bethesda, Maryland. Antiballistic missiles have been launched from Andrews Air Force Base to intercept what appear to be incoming enemy missiles. All civilians in the region are instructed to take cover. The capital is under attack. I repeat, the capital is under attack."

Rick was startled by the buzz of his wrist phone. He glanced down at its screen. ROSE. Dropping his valise, he punched the phone on. "Rose? Is that you?"

"Rick . . ." Her voice was small, faint.

"Where are you? What's going on?"

". . . Detrick. Reception is bad . . . talk long."

"Are they still bombing? Can you get out of there?"

"The director says you're coming . . ."

"Yes."

"Don't come . . . !" Rick could hear a cacophony of other voices in the background. Though her words were difficult to distinguish, Rose seemed to be yelling into the phone. ". . . not ready."

"What? What's not ready?" Silence. "Rose? Are you there?"

". . . Gen5s need to be launched . . . Code Black."

"Rose? Rose!"

". . . sorry. I know I didn't follow procedure . . . special protocol . . . Tell Kendra . . . we can't let the babies be lost—"

The line went dead.

Turning on his heel, Rick plunged out into the hall and hobbled back down the steps to the street. Flinging open the back door of the waiting car, he climbed inside. "There's been a change in plans. Radio ahead to the airfield. Tell them I need to get to Los Alamos."

As he settled into the backseat, he felt something digging into his thigh. He reached down into his pocket and drew out a thin necklace, the tiny silver figure of a woman poised as if readying for flight.

19

JAMES TURNED OVER, struggling to get his bearings. A row of LEDs in the ceiling overhead glistened off the railing of the gurney next to his cot.

"James." It was Robbie, gently jostling his arm. "I'm sorry. Your father is gone."

James stood up, placing his hands on the railing. He gazed into Abdul's face, at rest. "Thank you."

It all came back. His mother's serene countenance, the word **DE-CEASED** across the display over the head of her bed. His parents would be cremated on-site. Vaguely, he wondered whether they would have wanted that. Was there some sort of religious prohibition that applied? He shook his head. He'd never known the truth. He was left only with questions, and no one to answer them.

"James," Robbie said, "if you're still feeling well, you need to go. There're rumors that they're going to quarantine the place. No one will be able to get out."

"What about you?"

Robbie offered a mock salute. "Duty calls," she said with a wry smile.

As they parted ways at the side exit, James noticed his friend's eyes, red from lack of sleep. She didn't look well. "Robbie," he said, "thanks for taking care of them." As she turned to go back inside, the doctor coughed lightly into the crook of her arm.

The sun was barely up, but the lot was still packed. Skirting the fleet of media trucks now blocking the front entrance to the hospital, James headed toward a line of autocabs waiting on the road. He heard the reporters bleating into their mics as he hurried by. There was no point in going to the airport—the governor had called a state of emergency and all nonessential air traffic was grounded. But what was that? He stopped to listen—something about a bomb attack in Washington . . . He watched the reporter, her face contorted as she updated her listeners on the latest tragedy. While he'd waited out the final moments with his father, at last succumbing to sleep, the world outside had turned upside down.

Suddenly he spotted something across the lot: his father's car. He remembered Abdul's voice on the phone, two nights and a lifetime ago: *I will drive.* With all the commotion, he no doubt hadn't been able to get an ambulance.

Reaching into the bag of his parents' effects that Robbie had given him, he came up with the fob. He ran over to his father's old electric, unplugged the charger, then wrenched open the door and inserted himself into the front seat. Feeling like a thief, he put the car on automatic and homed it to Los Alamos.

IT WASN'T UNTIL the car gained the freeway that James let go his breath. His hand shaking, he punched in Sara's name on his father's dash phone. "Home city?" asked a female voice.

"Los Alamos, New Mexico." Sara's photo appeared on the screen, and he pressed it. He heard a series of clicks. His heartbeat thudded against his ribs as he waited for her to pick up.

"Hello?" Her voice was soft, dreamy.

He heaved a sigh of relief. "Did I wake you?"

"No. I mean, yes. It's okay. I was sleeping in. The lab's closed, as you know."

"Yes." James sat back against the hard bench of the car seat.

"I was trying to call you, actually."

"You were?" He closed his eyes, once more imagining his abandoned phone.

"Yes. It's just as well that I can't go in to work. I . . . I'm still not at all well."

James sat up, the rush of blood past his ears almost deafening. "Wh . . . what's happening? Do you have a cough?"

"James, could you please just listen? Don't go all M.D. on me . . ."

James stared out the front windshield at the freeway. It was eerily empty for a Monday morning. He blinked, marshaling his senses. His shaving kit. In it, Sara would find the antidote. It was one of the small test canisters that Rudy had given him, before the order had been handed down to start dosing. He hadn't used it. "Sara," he said, "you know the little blue toiletry kit I keep at your apartment?"

"Yes . . ."

"I left it under the bathroom sink."

"Okay . . ."

"I need you to get something out of it. There's a little canister, like an inhaler. On the side it says 'C-343.' Call me back when you find it. Not on my phone. Call me back at the number I'm calling from now. Can you do that for me?"

"What is all this?"

"It's a medicine. You need it. Just trust me. You need it."

"But . . ." Sara paused, and he found himself listening for the sound of her breathing, the hint of some deadly obstruction. "Are you sure it's safe?"

James gripped the phone, his knuckles white. Safe? Safer than nothing, he supposed. He was taking it, and he was still here, wasn't he? "Why wouldn't it be?" he asked dumbly.

"Because," she said softly, "I'm pregnant."

20

RICK PUNCHED KENDRA'S secure number into the in-flight phone. Despite the chaos at the federal airfield, it had been easier than he'd thought to get a flight to Los Alamos. All flights to airfields anywhere near D.C., commercial or military, had been diverted. His assigned pilot, a small blonde with a thick Southern accent, had readily agreed to take him to Los Alamos instead.

But after countless attempts, he'd given up trying to reconnect with Rose. He wracked his brain, trying to make sense of what she'd said about the Gen5s. Code Black—the launch protocol to be used to protect the bots in case of a threatened security breach. Did she know something? Was there a threat to Los Alamos? He kept coming back to her final instruction: *Tell Kendra.*

Kendra's voice came over the line, uncharacteristically shaky. "Jenkins here . . ."

"Kendra, it's Rick Blevins. I assume you've heard—"

"General . . ." He heard a crackling sound, like something being moved aside. Then her voice came back, stronger. "Yes, we have. The hack was enough, but now we've got the Code Red. Not to mention the missile attacks. We were in touch with the Pentagon when the attacks started. Now we can't raise anyone."

"Is everyone there with you now?"

"We've got Rudy, myself, and Paul MacDonald."

"And Dr. Said?"

"James has disappeared. He got a call last night, about twenty-three hundred hours. We thought it might have been you . . . Anyway, he left the facility. No one knows where he went. His phone doesn't pick up either."

Rick stared at the phone. Said. The hack at Fort Detrick. The Russians had known ties to the Karachi arms cell that Farooq Said had put together. Five years ago, even as he'd been working on James Said's clearance to use NANs at Emory, members of a related cell had been detained in Maryland. Had he slipped up, after all? Had James outwitted him? "If he shows up, I want him detained."

"*Detained?* How . . . ?"

"MacDonald has a weapon, right? Tell him to be ready."

"I'm sure there's no need—"

"Just . . . do it, okay? If Said comes back, call me. And if anyone else from DOD contacts you, direct them to me at this number. Meanwhile . . ." Rick was breathing hard now. For a moment, his thoughts went blank. Then he pictured the Mothers, their dark forms looming along the back wall of the robotics bay.

"Meanwhile?"

"How much antidote do you have?"

"Enough to tide us over for at least three months."

"Good. We can deal with that after we've launched the Gen5s."

"Launched the . . . But we haven't even finished checking the latest code—"

"Listen, I'm pretty sure that if we don't launch them ASAP, we'll never have the chance."

There was a momentary silence at the other end of the line. "Sir? Are we going to be attacked?"

"I think we have to be ready for that eventuality, yes."

"But why? The people who hacked Detrick have no idea . . ."

"They might." Rick clenched his fists, the knuckles white. Said. Said was embedded at Los Alamos now. And though the good doctor didn't know everything about the plans for Gen5, he knew enough. "We need to launch, and it needs to be under the Code Black protocol."

Kendra exhaled. "Code Black . . . I'll do what I can to get ready. But, General . . ."

"Yes?"

"Where will *you* be? Where are you right now?" Kendra's voice was quavering again. She was starting to panic.

"I'm on my way to you. I got a plane to fly me direct to Los Alamos County. I'll grab a cycle and meet you at the lab. I should be there before midnight."

"Okay." There was another shuffling sound, and Rick imagined Kendra clearing her workspace, readying for this next challenge. "But we should have Dr. McBride online as well . . . Is she still at the Presidio?"

"No," Rick said. "She was called to Detrick."

"*Detrick?* But I was expecting her here any day . . ." Once more, the line went silent for a moment. Then Kendra cleared her throat. "Oh . . . I'm so sorry . . . Do we know . . . ?"

"I haven't been able to raise her. But . . . I know she wants this done," Rick said.

Another silence. A muffled cough. "Okay," Kendra said at last. "I'll have an assessment ready for you when you get here. We'll need to talk about the risks of a Code Black launch. And the readiness of the Gen5s for such a launch."

"Good," Rick said.

Breaking the call, he reached for a bottle of water. From the cockpit, he could hear the pilot coughing—a dry, hollow sound. "You okay up there?" he called.

The pilot turned in her seat. "Yes, sir. Maybe just a touch of that nasty flu."

Outside his window, Rick could see only a flat layer of clouds, obscuring the ground below. He thought about his options—if the pilot lost control, he wasn't sure he'd know how to fly this thing . . .

The pilot coughed again. "Sir? Do we have more on Maryland? It makes no sense . . . Why aren't we mobilizing?"

Rick felt a weak nausea rising in his throat. If there was time for an investigation, he had no doubt it would be clear that the missiles used were compatible with Russian SS-96 submarine-based launch systems. If there was time. As he'd watched, the vid screen at the Bay Area federal airfield had displayed drone footage of fighters circling over the forests of central Maryland, more explosions on the ground, billows of smoke obscuring the smoldering ruins below. He had to accept it. Detrick was gone. Most likely, Rose was gone too. "I'm sure Andrews can handle it," he said.

Again, he imagined the Gen5 bots waiting patiently in their bay at Los Alamos, their wings folded tight along their backs. Rose might be gone. But she was still there, her essence instilled in one of those bots—a vessel meant to carry her child. Even if that was all he had left of her, he'd do anything in his power to defend it.

IT WAS JUST past eleven p.m. when he pulled up in front of the building. Kendra was waiting for him, slumped in a chair at the receptionist's desk. Rudy, she explained, was checking on the incubators. Mac was running systems checks on the Gen5 bots.

"Has Said come back?"

"No. And since you told us to hold him at gunpoint, I'm glad he hasn't. Seriously, General, can you share your thoughts about James?"

"Nothing certain. But I think we need to question him before letting him in on anything more."

Giving him a strange look, Kendra produced her ever-present tablet. Together, they ran down the Gen5 checklist.

"Unlike Gen3, the Gen5 bots are coded. Each embryo is assigned to a specific bot," Kendra began.

"Correct." This was just one of the many things that made Gen5 special. Each child needed to be matched with the installed "personality" of his or her biological mother—a key element of the bond they would share.

"Luckily, Dr. McBride shipped me the most recent codes last week. Our team here was in the middle of debugging the personality codes when the Fort Detrick hack occurred and General Blankenship ordered a shutdown here. But since you called, I've been able to continue working off-line."

"Did you find anything?"

"Nothing I couldn't easily fix. Of course, I'm in no position to assess the specific content of the files. I can only evaluate the file structure— to make sure that the contents would be fully uploaded to the correct space in memory. And that the appropriate level of duplication has been applied. Things like that."

"So, everything checks out?"

"Dr. McBride was very thorough."

Rick winced. Of course Rose had been thorough. How many times had he stared into those eyes, imagining the intricate workings of the mind behind them? "Anything else?"

"General, there is one thing . . ."

"Yes?"

"The timed instruction hasn't been installed. The clock is there. But there are no instructions as to what to do when the clock times out."

Rick held his hand to his forehead. Two scenarios for the Gen5 launch had been laid out. The best scenario, the Safe Protocol, was most like that used in experimentation up until now. The Mothers would remain on or near the Los Alamos grounds. If no one survived to intervene, they would birth and rear their offspring in community. If someone did survive, the bots could be inactivated simply, and the newborns retrieved.

But this was not that scenario. This launch would be dictated by the tenets of Code Black. Due to the security risks that had prompted such a launch, the Gen5s would be dispatched in stealth mode, their onboard defensive lasers armed. To avoid detection, they were to scatter across the deserts of southern Utah. In the beginning, this would assure that their charges would not all encounter the same threats to existence. But it also meant that the children would lead solitary lives in their formative years.

It had been a strange conversation to have over coffee and toast. But Rose had agonized endlessly over the advantages and disadvantages of that solitary upbringing. It could be a good thing, she said, if the goal was for the children to eventually mate. "Children reared together will view themselves more as brothers and sisters, not necessarily as potential mates." But from the standpoint of human socialization, it might present problems. Early socialization would have to rely solely on the Mothers themselves—the soft "hands," audible voices, imprintable faces, and unique personalities of the human women whose babies they carried, databases rife with information about life in the world before they were created, extensive programming in the Socratic method—all the elements that Rose had painstakingly built into the Mother Code.

In the end, even under Code Black, it was important that the children eventually be given a way to find one another. To effect such a meeting, each Mother held a clock, counting down the time until her charge would reach the age of six years. At that time, she was to follow a set of instructions leading her to a specific, secure location. There, medical supplies, food rations, and housing would await. There, the new children could form a community. With any luck, there might even be other, nonmalevolent human survivors, waiting there to greet them.

The clocks had been programmed. At the appointed time, each bot would determine that a countdown had ended—that it was time to go. But to go where? Rick pictured Rose at their last meeting with Blankenship—had it been only two weeks ago? "We need those Code Black homing coordinates, General," she had insisted, the urgency of her impatience coloring her cheeks.

"If you ask me, it's a simple choice," Blankenship had replied. "They should come home here to Langley. But the robotics team doesn't like the odds on such a long flight. I'm afraid the team is stalemated." He had actually smiled as he flashed her that steely gaze of his. "I wouldn't worry too much about it. The possibility of a Code Black launch is extremely remote."

In the end, the decision had never been handed down.

"Shall I upload the coordinates for Los Alamos?" Kendra asked.

"How long would that take?"

Kendra closed her eyes, her lips moving silently. Rick waited; the woman might be a computer herself, her mind constantly running routines. "Now that the navigation software is already integrated, and since it's only me here . . . at least twenty-four hours. Maybe more."

Rick tapped his index finger nervously on the desk. A day. That might be a day too long. The breach at Fort Detrick, no doubt a trail leading to Los Alamos—through James Said. But there was another option. The fail-safe. A backup to be used to abort the mission, in the event that it turned out to be faulty or unnecessary. "Do they have their fail-safe homing sensors installed?"

"Yes." Kendra flashed him a smile.

"And . . . if we're around . . . we can set up a beacon to call them anywhere we need, once we know it's safe to do so."

"Yes."

"Then there's no problem."

"No . . ."

"Anything else?"

"One more thing . . . Under Code Black, unless we can home them successfully, even *we* won't know where they are."

"We won't? No GPS signal? Nothing?"

"We hadn't worked out the security on that. The supply depots will be our best clue . . ."

"Supply depots. Yes. They're set?"

"They were finished a few months ago. The teams were told that they were part of a tactical desert warfare training ground. Anyway, the Gen5s are programmed with the locations of the supply depots. We can expect them to frequent those once the children are born. Until then, out there in the desert, they'll be like fifty needles in a haystack. Big needles. But needles nonetheless."

"We'll find them," Rick said. "Once we know it's safe, we'll find them."

RICK OPENED HIS eyes, waiting for them to focus. He rolled his tongue against the back of his teeth, swallowing what felt like a wad of cotton. His neck was cramped, the stub of his right leg jutting out over the edge of the cot. All around him was pitch-black. Where was he? Los Alamos. XO-Bot building. A complex of small conference rooms had been modified to provide temporary sleeping quarters for those with special clearance.

He unfolded himself, feeling for his prosthesis on the floor nearby. Hurriedly he strapped it on, enduring the unpleasant tingling sensation that told him it had a life of its own. He limped out the door and down the hall toward the robotics lab. The hall, usually bustling with personnel, was empty, as was the lab. But the back doors of the bay were wide open. The Gen5s were already outside, their hatch windows reflecting the rising sun as Kendra paced among their ranks, her right hand flitting over her tablet.

"Where's Rudy?" Rick asked.

"He's readying the incubators."

Mac was moving from one to the other of the bots, a power torque wrench in hand. "Some of the tread nuts weren't tightened properly," he muttered. "I sure hope these things are good to go . . ."

"They have to be," Rick said.

Rudy appeared behind him, pushing a cart, which he wheeled up beside four others identical to it. Inside cushioned plywood boxes, thick glass enclosures were nestled—the incubators. "The embryos are installed," he said. "We just need to load these into the Mothers." He turned to Rick. "General, are you sure we are doing the right thing?"

Rick looked out over the array of bots, their powerful appendages tucked close to their rounded bodies. Out here in the sun, they reminded him of giant birds, poised for an epic migration. "Kendra says the software is sound. The Gen3s gave birth as planned," he said. "And you and I are still alive on this antidote. The Gen5s are as ready as they need to be."

"But the C-343 sequence, it is new. We have not tested it in fetuses . . ."

In what he hoped was an act of reassurance, Rick placed his hand on Rudy's shoulder. He understood the risks. But he was thinking of what Rose had said: *We can't let the babies be lost.* "We have to let them go," he said, "and this might be the only chance we'll get—we have no idea what those hackers know."

Kendra nodded, turning to continue her inspection as Mac and Rudy carefully loaded the incubators into their Mothers' fibrous cocoons, attaching the necessary sensors and feeding tubes. Rick spotted a small can of yellow phosphorescent paint by the open door. Grabbing it in one hand and a shop cloth in the other, he searched the crowd of bots, reading off their insignia until he reached the one he was looking for. He stopped, climbing up on her treads.

"What're you doin'?" Mac asked.

"This one's mine," Rick said, daubing a bright yellow design on the back edge of her wing. "Rho-Z." *I'll keep track of you,* he thought. *I promise.*

IT WAS ALREADY late afternoon, but the weather was holding out. Rick felt dizzy. He'd eaten nothing but an MRE, a field ration of unsavory gray meat ensconced in an off-white packet that had been his staple in the military, washing it down with a canteen of water before falling into his cot the previous night. Such were the provisions left in the Los Alamos quarters. "Are they ready?" he asked Mac.

"Ready as they're gonna be," Mac called, folding his lanky form down into a chair near the guard post by the doors.

"Then let's roll 'em!" Rick called. From a console that Mac had moved close to the bay doors, Kendra gave the command. Slowly, the Mothers came to life, their treads churning over the pavement toward the expansive tarmac at the side of the building, arraying themselves at a wingspan's distance from one another. Huddled over her console, a headset clamped over her black cloud of hair, Kendra seemed unaware of the din.

Holding his hands tight over his ears, Rick followed the Mothers. They came to a standstill, and there was a hush.

Then, fifty sets of ducted fans fired up. Fifty sets of wings flared out as the Mothers leaned forward. Fifty bots began their ascent, their arms pulled tight to their sides, their treads tucked under their fuselages, their forms blotting out the sun.

Rick flattened himself against the side of the building, clamping his eyes shut against eddies of debris. He opened them in time to see Mac running toward him, holding out one of the chunky XO-Bot lab phones. ". . . call from James Said . . ." Mac was yelling.

"What?" Rick took the phone, but for a moment he just stared at it.

"James Said!" Mac replied. "I thought he should talk to you!"

"But . . ." Rick put the phone to one ear, still cupping the other with his free hand. "Hello?"

"General? Mac says I should speak with you?" It did sound like Said, the formal, austere tone that the doctor always assumed when addressing him.

"Said? Speak up!"

"General, I just wanted you to know I'm sorry." He could hear Said more clearly now, the cacophony of the Mothers' departure fading as they slowly gained altitude.

"Sorry? About telling the Russians?"

"What?"

"You told them, didn't you? It was you all along! And all you can say is you're sorry?"

"General, I have no idea what you're talking about. I just wanted to call in, let someone know I'm on my way back."

Rick felt his grip on the phone weakening. "On your way back . . . ?"

"I had to fly to California . . . my parents died from IC-NAN. Now I'm driving . . . I should be back at Los Alamos in about three hours."

Rick felt the blood draining from him, his vision going dark as he remembered Rose's final words: *Not ready* . . . He pictured her face, her eyes, pleading. *We can't let the babies be lost* . . .

"They aren't ready," he murmured. "Oh, my God . . . They aren't ready!"

"What?" James's perplexed voice sounded from the phone even as Rick shoved it back toward Mac.

Rick looked up. Two of the bots seemed to falter, lagging slightly behind the others. But they were all high aloft now, heading over the line of pines to the north of the labs. Craning his neck, he saw the Zero FX cycle, the one he'd ridden from the county airport, parked nearby. His helmet still rested on the seat. Cramming it over his head, he boarded the cycle and flipped on the power. Without another thought, he gave chase.

>«

RICK HIT THE south entrance to the lab property going full speed, just barely missing the blockades there as he threaded between them and the woods. From Route 4, he could see the Mothers soaring over the Valles Caldera. But as he navigated a series of dangerous hairpin turns beside the meandering tributaries of the Jemez River, he lost sight of the glimmering machines for minutes at a time. His cycle could easily do 120 miles per hour. But he was earthbound, and the Mothers were scudding over the trees.

When he saw the small side road that was State Route 126 heading west, he took it, knowing but not caring that at some point ahead it was unpaved. It was all he could do to stay on the rutted road while keeping one eye on the bots, whom he now spied only occasionally over the tops of tall pines. Near the small town of Cuba, he was thankful to pop out onto U.S. Route 550. Here the land was flat and barren, punctuated only by the occasional low-lying wash or canyon. The bots were off to his right, still headed northwest, their formation loosening. The two who had lagged seemed to have caught up—at least he could no longer see them as separate from the rest.

As he neared the deserted town of Bloomfield, he veered west on U.S. 64 toward Farmington and the eastern edge of the Navajo Nation. Passing the town of Shiprock, he sped across the arid moonscape that was the northwestern corner of New Mexico. He tried not to think about the inhabitants of these small towns. Were they dying? Were they dead? Or were they standing on their front porches, pointing to the darkening sky, fearful of the strange flock of birds overhead?

The road turned southwest along Comb Ridge, the great uplift of Navajo sandstone extending from Kayenta, Arizona, to Utah. High above, the Mothers banked north, soaring over the massive rock monuments that dotted the landscape. Rick punched his accelerator and veered off the road. But it was no use. The terrain too rugged for his cycle, he watched helplessly as the Mothers left him behind. Too late, he caught sight of a herd of sheep ambling ahead. He yanked his handlebars sharply to the right and the cycle slid out from under him. Instinctively he leapt free of it, catching a glimpse of his prosthesis as it flew high in the sky, in pursuit of the Mothers.

He felt his body go limp. He closed his eyes. In the darkness he saw eagles, soaring over mysterious lands . . .

SOMETHING WAS BLOCKING out the sun. He heard muffled voices. A smooth, tanned face appeared above him. ". . . you okay?" He felt strong hands working expertly over his body, feeling beneath his clothing. Something cradled his neck, and he was inched slowly onto a hard, flat surface. "What's that thing over there? Bring it along!"

Then he was floating through the air. He felt a scraping, a painful hitch in his back as he was enveloped in darkness once more.

RICK AWOKE IN a small room with white walls. Someone nearby was humming, a low, guttural tune that sounded both happy and sad. He felt a dense, gelatinous weight on his chest as he struggled to sit up. He brought his arms up to push it away, but his hands closed on something oblong, plastic. A small, wizened woman placed one hand gently on his chest while using her other hand to grasp the object. Carefully, she removed the bag from atop his blankets, hanging it from a hook located somewhere below his line of sight.

"I'm sorry," she said. "You needed a catheter."

He closed his eyes, succumbing to the woman's gentle ministrations. "Where am I?" he asked. His own voice, thin and feeble, seemed to be coming from somewhere across the room.

"You are safe," said the woman.

"Who . . . ?"

"My son William found you."

"But how . . . ?" Rick was coming around now, every bone in his body aching. He tried to sit up, but his head was spinning, throbbing with pain. On his side, he wretched helplessly as the woman laid her hand on the small of his back, guiding him to relax.

"You were dehydrated. You've sprained your back, and you've no doubt suffered a concussion. You must give yourself time to recover," the woman said. "My other son, Edison, is a doctor. He will care for you."

WHEN HE AWOKE again, he was wrapped in a soft white blanket. He moved his neck against the pain. He was in a different place now. On the walls of this dark, rectangular room, crude patterns danced in the flickering light of a small fire—drawings of four-legged animals, women cradling babies, farmers tending to crops; a life in tableau. Farther up, he traced rectangular designs in yellow, then blue, then red, then white. He stared out through what looked like a hole in the ceiling, into the starry night.

In his ear was the sound of a woman chanting, crooning, a soothing sound dulling his senses, heightening his awareness. It was the same song, the one from the white room.

"Ah, you are back with us now?" said the woman, pausing in her song to speak to him. Her white hair pulled tight in a braid, her skin creased with the deep lines of age, the woman watched him with probing eyes.

"Who *are* you?" Rick asked.

"My name is Talasi," she said. "This is my son William."

"It seems you are a messenger?" It was a deeper voice, emanating from somewhere off to his right. With effort, Rick focused on a ruggedly tanned man in a white cotton shirt and blue jeans.

The old woman drew close. Between her thin fingers, she held a small metallic object—a woman made of silver—her arms spread wide and festooned with delicate silver feathers. "William found this in your pocket," she said. "Can you tell me—why are you carrying my daughter's necklace?"

21

JAMES DIRECTED THE car past his abandoned home, his sights set on Sara's apartment complex. He'd monitored the car's mobile video feed for hours: reports of a deadly flu epidemic spreading like wildfire from both coasts; the air attack on Washington. America was under siege. All were ordered to shelter in place. He'd held out hope that somehow the heart of his country was still intact, that healthy people still hid inside the buildings he passed. But as he'd picked his way past clots of abandoned vehicles, he'd encountered only an eerie emptiness. Pulling into Sara's drive, he allowed himself to scan the road. He remembered neighbors tending their gardens, kids playing in the twilight. Now there was no one.

He'd spoken to Sara hours before, instructing her how to take the antidote. He'd told her to stay in her apartment with the windows sealed until he got there. But as he'd made the final climb to Los Alamos, she hadn't answered his calls. His pulse hammering in his ears, he bolted up the outer staircase of her apartment block and keyed in the four-digit code at her door.

Inside, he was met only with silence. Wending his way through the darkening apartment, he pressed his fingers to the bedroom door. His heart stopped. The bedclothes were in disarray, but Sara was nowhere in sight.

Then he caught sight of a lock of chestnut hair, draped across the pillow. He turned on the bedside light, reached out to touch her arm.

"Uh?" she murmured.

James almost cried out as she lifted her head to look at him. "Sara," he whispered. "Are you okay?"

"James?"

"Oh, Sara . . . !"

"Yes. I'm fine. I think." She sat up slowly, her eyes glazed, her thin fingers carefully adjusting her loose nightgown. She cleared her throat, a sound that made him wince.

"You took the medication, right?"

"The inhaler? Yes, but—"

He held his ear to her back, listened. There was only a slight rattle, higher up in the chest. "It seems to be working . . ." Sitting down next to her on the side of the bed, James ignored Sara's puzzled look. "Sara, I know you probably don't feel up to it. But we need to get you to the lab."

"The *lab?*"

"Have you listened to the news today?"

Sara's eyes were glassy, red rimmed. "No . . . I have been . . . so tired."

James swallowed. "Things have happened. I'll explain later. But we'll both be better off at the lab. The air in the building is filtered . . ." He stopped himself. First things first. "I'll tell you everything, I promise. I just need you to trust me right now."

He helped her get dressed. His hand cupping her elbow, he escorted her outside to the car. As they crossed the Omega Bridge toward the lab's north entrance gate, he turned to look at her in the light from the dash. Her eyes were closed, her skin sallow, her capable hands lying limp in her lap. He prayed that her doses had started in time.

But he was worried about something else too—Blevins. He hadn't been able to reach Kendra on her mobile. When he'd finally called the lab's general line, Mac had picked up and handed the phone straight to the general. Blevins had been furious, accusatory, jabbering things that made no sense. But when Mac had come back on the line, he'd tried to explain. "He suspected you, James," Mac had said. "He thought it was you who tipped off the Russians."

James supposed it all made sense now—the animosity, the scrutiny that he'd always undergone. Blevins and his ilk were trained to fight terrorism. His uncle had been a terrorist. But he himself had never known—his father had carried that secret almost to the grave.

He shook his head. He shouldn't have left Los Alamos without notifying someone of his whereabouts. And now, the sight of Sara wasn't going to make things any easier.

The heavy entrance gate barred passage, the post abandoned. Again, he keyed in Kendra's number.

"James?" This time, Kendra answered. Her tone was anxious but at the same time relieved.

"Yes. I'm at the north gate. Can you open it?"

"Will do." The arm of the gate hefted slowly upward. As the car sped down Pajarito Road, its headlamps cutting a path through the gathering dark, it could have been any evening in late May, the smell of pine fresh in the air. But the air was poisonous now, James reminded himself, or soon to become so—a death sentence to anyone not on the protocol. They passed the rear of the XO-Bot building, then veered right down a small side road, then right again, pulling up in the empty front lot.

Behind the double doors of the airlock at the front of the building, Kendra was waiting in the dim interior of the lobby. Paul MacDonald, holding something long and thin in one hand, was standing next to her. James helped Sara from the car, and together they went inside.

"Hi, Kendra," James said. But Kendra only stared at them, her eyes wide. "Kendra, I know this is unexpected . . ."

Groggy, her eyelids at half-mast, Sara offered them a wan smile. "Mac," she said. "Kendra . . . How are the Mothers doing?"

As Mac lowered his arm, James took in the steely glimmer of the man's service rifle. "Well," Mac said, putting his weapon hastily aside. "*This* is interesting."

PART TWO

22

FEBRUARY 2054

RICK AWOKE AS a sliver of early-morning sunlight wedged in through the transport window. He rolled over on his back, stretching his truncated leg, enjoying for just a moment the feel of the soft, clean blanket beneath him. He pushed himself up to peer out the window at the desolate terrain, a jumble of upheaved rocks cut through with a deep, dry canyon.

The world he'd once known, it seemed, had vanished. Broadcast booths went unmanned. Phone and radio calls went unanswered. Websites went dead as power waned. Nighttime satellite photos, images of once busy cities and thoroughfares, slowly went dark. The brass back in Washington and their enemies abroad, the computer programmers and those who hacked them, those who launched deadly missiles and the fighters who intercepted them—were all gone. He imagined autocabs waiting beside empty curbs, worker bots constructing and packaging appliances for now-vacant homes, inspection bots waiting for travelers who would never arrive. By now, nine months past the Epidemic, even those hardworking machines must have gone silent.

He sat up to cough into the crook of his arm. Not too bad. Better.

Over the past months, he'd had to make peace with his new limitations. The antidote wasn't perfect—according to Rudy Garza, it couldn't undo the damage done prior to the time he'd begun taking it; a prior exposure to IC-NAN, perhaps during one of his many trips to California, might have put him at risk. In any event, for reasons yet to be explained, it seemed he was more susceptible to attack than the others; he'd have to work harder to protect himself from the noxious air of his once friendly planet.

To that end, he'd commandeered one of the two aerial transports previously housed at Los Alamos—he had Mac to thank for keeping this one in good working order, and for upgrading its air filtration system. It was his home now, serving both as a mobile unit capable of rapid air travel and as a stationary ground base. And outside his little bubble, he wore a face mask to block out whatever he could of the infected archaebacteria and their poisonous NANs.

He didn't have the luxury of sheltering within the confines of the XO-Bot building with the other Los Alamos survivors, watching and waiting as the world outside came to an end. He had a mission—one of his own making. He was intent on undoing the terrible mistake he'd made—the preemptive release of the Gen5 bots into the desert wilderness. He needed to find the Mothers. He needed to bring them back home.

He'd thought that finding them would be easy—Kendra could just call them, and he would deal with their defensive capabilities as need be. But Kendra had been wrong about the homing sensors. "I wasn't thinking straight," she said. "They do have sensors, but when we selected Code Black, the sensing mechanism was deactivated . . . I assume the design team wanted to avoid an enemy calling the bots in."

And so he'd been left to comb the vast desert, searching for the Mothers he'd sent away. In all these months, he'd only been successful in locating three crashed bots, parts strewn across the desert floor like so much trash, their incubators obliterated. None of them had been

Rho-Z. But every one of them was a reminder of his own lack of fore-sight, his own failure in the face of pressure.

He'd never commanded troops in the field, but he'd heard the sto-ries: the poor decisions made under fire, the remorse, the never-ending guilt. Now these were his to bear. Everything he'd done on that fateful day when he'd launched the Mothers had been based on a fantasy cre-ated in his own addled mind, one forged in the heat of the moment—the fantasy that James Said was a terrorist.

Of course there had been other considerations, he told himself. He'd had no idea what the hackers had discovered about the Gen5s, no idea what real threats might have existed. Certainly, it seemed that Rose had sensed danger. Why else would she have mentioned Code Black? No—Said or no Said, Rick would have made the same decision. Still, a postmortem of what had happened that day clearly demon-strated that his decisions had been flawed. Los Alamos had never been attacked. As the few survivors of the New Dawn team had waited with dread, nothing at all had happened to the XO-Bot lab.

He had yet to apologize to the doctor—though upon Said's return to Los Alamos, Sara Khoti on his arm, the others had been quick to forgive his absence. Now James and Sara were both part of the team. And Rick was the one who needed to regain everyone's trust.

From the window, he spotted the smoke of a campfire. At least he wasn't alone out here. Ever since William Susquetewa had rescued him from beside the road in Kayenta and taken him to the Hopi mesas, the two had been constant companions. The Hopi had suffered severe casualties of their own, leaving William, his brother, Edison—a doctor trained in Phoenix—and their mother, Talasi, among the mere twenty or so Hopi survivors still living on the mesas. But Rose had been right in her hope that some populations might naturally be immune to IC-NAN. Miraculously, these few had survived, free to breathe the air.

For William, their quest had become a search for the sister he'd lost—Nova, a woman whom the Hopi believed now lived on as one of their "Silver Spirits." The only proof that William had needed was his sister's necklace and Rick's reassurance that Nova had indeed been an unknowing participant in the program that created the Mothers.

Talasi, the woman whom everyone referred to as "Grandmother," took it one step further. The Mothers were all sacred, all worthy of being watched over. For her, the Gen5 bots were the embodiment of her husband's promise—armor-clad goddesses who would one day return to the mesas, heralding the rebirth of humankind. Rick didn't know if he believed this. But he wanted to.

He strapped on his prosthesis, wincing at the unwelcome pain. He wondered if the fallen Mothers they'd found had felt any pain. No, that was impossible. Nor would those Mothers who still wandered the desert ever stop to appreciate how lost they were. They'd been programmed to hide from view in the canyons and ravines, sheltering their precious cargo during the incubation process. And if they were still out there, they were doing an admirable job of it.

Now, with the incubation period over and the Gen5 births imminent, the hope was that locating them would be easier. But again, it would not be as easy as Kendra had predicted. She'd assumed that once birth occurred, the Mothers could be tracked to the locations of the supply depots toward which they would inevitably migrate—since the bots were programmed with these locations, she would simply retrieve the coordinates from the upload parameters. But as she'd soon discovered, the depot locations weren't a part of the generic upload file. Rather, each of the Mothers' flight computers had been hardwired with her own set of coordinates; when she left Los Alamos, the coordinates left with her. Kendra had been unsuccessful in downloading the coordinates from the charred remains of the three bot computers they'd recovered from the desert. Nor could she find records of the locations on her mainframe at Los Alamos—those had been securely stored by the military units who'd erected the sites, and she had no idea now of their whereabouts. William's scouts had searched for signs of the signature water towers, leaving a motion sensor camera near each one they found to await a Mother's arrival. But so far only thirteen of the seventy-six sites had been located, none of them yet occupied.

The pilot's-side door of the transport cracked open. Rick heard a loud buzz as the positive-pressure fans kicked in, almost drowning out William's deep voice. "Rick . . . we've spotted something down in the canyon. Edison's on his way."

IN THE CLUTTERED cave that was Mac's Los Alamos office, James's gaze traced the arc of Sara's neck, the graceful curve of her jaw. In front of them, Kendra rifled through a series of menus on Mac's computer screen, selecting the BotView data feed.

As part of a government effort to cut long-term energy costs, the XO-Bot building had been capable of sustaining life "off the grid," collecting and storing its own power, since its initial construction two decades earlier. And though precious power and water still had to be monitored and conserved, the building now served their little group well. It was no mistake that New Dawn had been housed here, in a structure outfitted with massive solar panels and power storage walls, ventilated via a self-contained air filtration system, with water pumped from artesian wells in the nearby Valles Caldera via its own small water purification facility.

James focused on Mac's screen, a series of empty fields waiting to be filled. Rick Blevins and his team of Hopi scouts in the Utah desert maintained contact with Los Alamos via a secure NSA satellite hookup. Hours ago, the general had called in with news of a crashed bot at the bottom of a narrow canyon, east of a place called Escalante. The climb down to the site was treacherous; according to Blevins, it might take a while.

James reached out to grasp Sara's hand. In the past nine months, she'd endured enough pain for a lifetime. Unlike Rudy, Kendra, and

Mac, unlike Blevins or even James himself, she'd had no time to come to grips with the reality of losing everything and everyone. She herself had almost been lost.

And she'd lost her baby—their son. Perhaps it was a blessing in disguise; their child was of the old world, not immune to the plague that gripped the earth—and Sara herself was far too weak to bear a pregnancy. But it was a sorrow that neither of them had come prepared for. They'd buried the baby in a small plot visible from the window of their quarters at Los Alamos. "We'll have the Gen5s soon," he'd promised Sara. "Perfect, immune babies." But since then, the sight of Sara staring out that window each morning, her hands clasped in her lap and her lower lip quivering, had become almost more than he could bear.

Still, they'd survived. Rudy had set up a C-343 synthesis operation at Los Alamos, a scaled-down version of the one destroyed at Fort Detrick. With it, he could produce enough of the antidote to replenish the existing inhaler units. Once a day, the Los Alamos survivors dutifully dosed themselves. And there was hope. The new sequence used for the antidote was the same as that engineered into the Gen5 embryos. If it afforded the survivors immunity to IC-NAN with no ill effects, perhaps the Gen5s could count on it too. James looked around the room. It might be safe, living out in the world. But except for the general, none of them had yet been ready to try that experiment. Perhaps after the Gen5s were born . . .

His thoughts drifted to Talasi Susquetewa, the old woman whom Rick Blevins called "Grandmother," and to the handful of other Hopi, still thriving on the harsh tract of land that had been their tribe's home for centuries. Judging from what had happened when the Epidemic struck, these people carried a trait that allowed for a different pathway enabling programmed cell death. The gene coding for this vestigial pathway, it seemed, was recessive; one had to be homozygous for the trait, carrying two copies of the recessive gene, in order for it to be expressed to the extent necessary for survival. Talasi, whose husband, Albert, had died of natural causes three years previously, was homozygous. Her sons, William and Edison, had survived, but Edison had lost his wife and two of his three children to the Epidemic; only his daughter Millie remained. William's wife and two sons had all survived. These, together with a few other families, would form the core of a new Hopi lineage. James's theory about silent DNA, about inherited functions that could reawaken when called upon, was proven out in them.

What was more, these people had proved a godsend for the inhabitants of Los Alamos. Long skilled at living off the land, the Hopi provided abundant food—corn and lamb, beef, beans, and squash—all carefully prepared and delivered through an airlock to the XO-Bot cafeteria. But perhaps even more importantly, they offered hope of an ultimate cure for Sara, the only one among them with a confirmed previous infection by IC-NAN. James and Rudy had begun harvesting stem cells from the tracheal aspirates of willing Hopi donors, developing methods for isolating and storing the most potent. It was a long shot; in the world before the Epidemic, similar experiments to remediate lung damage had always failed. But again, it offered hope. And now, hope was all they had.

He was startled by a loud crackle as Blevins's voice piped over the speaker to his left. He heard a cry, an uncharacteristic yelp of happiness. "Okay . . . we have a little girl!"

His heart leaping nearly into his throat, James imagined the general in full protective gear, a spaceman on his own planet, a satellite phone gripped in one meaty hand and a baby in the other.

Kendra turned on her mic. "Alive?"

"Barely," came the general's raspy voice.

James felt Sara's grip tighten around his hand. From Blevins's side, he could hear shouts. Thank God, Edison was on-site. "Access the birth records," he whispered to Kendra.

"Patch us in to the life systems control module," Kendra ordered.

"Done!" came Blevins's reply.

Kendra leaned toward the monitor, frantically flipping through display menus. She stopped at one line of output: OXYGEN SATURATION LOW OUT OF RANGE. PULMONARY DISTRESS.

James sat forward, squinting. "The incubator drained. Resuscitation was initiated. But it doesn't seem to have worked . . ."

Beside James, Sara was holding her breath, a tear leaking from one eye. After what seemed like an eternity, a second voice came over the phone. "James, this is Edison. The little one is doing well enough, considering the state of the Mother. The cocoon was damaged in the crash and admitted sufficient ambient air to keep her alive. But the transfer to the nest wasn't completed. The baby was trapped inside the broken incubator. We've put her on supplemental oxygen . . ."

Nudging Kendra to one side, James barked out the orders, his brain on automatic. "Get her to the med center ASAP. And keep her on filtered air until we have a chance to check her out, okay?"

Sara was on her feet now. She leaned against the desk, steadying herself. "Edison?" she said. "Is she . . . normal?"

"Yes," came the reply. "She's perfect, Sara . . . but her extremities are bluish. Definite signs of cyanosis. We'll do everything we can."

23

WHEN SHE CLOSED her eyes, Misha could still recall the dim light of her first years. In that hazy world she breathed deep, inhaling the smell of crackling wood fires and desert dust. All around her, voices laughed and sang. Larger hands helped her to cup her small hands around bottles of sweet milk and juice. Someone carried her, jog jog, bounced her, bump bump, told her stories and stroked her hair. Dolls made from wood, cloth, and feathers danced in the air.

"Mama," she said. "Mama." Her first word.

Misha was never lonely. She was never alone. Mama Sara was always there.

MISHA HAD A father named James. She had a mother named Sara. She had a big family, most of whom lived in houses made from mud, wood, and stone, perched on top of a mesa.

The oldest person in her family was Grandmother. Grandmother's older son, Uncle William, had a big chest, tanned skin, and dark brown hair, pulled back in a neat ponytail. Sometimes a man named Rick would come, and together he and William would go out "scouting." The rest of the time, Uncle William was in his field, herding his sheep or planting his corn. Uncle Edison, a doctor, was thinner and taller. He wore glasses with black rims and kept his dark hair cut short. Every morning he drove his truck down the road to his hospital, where he wore a white coat and carried a notepad. Both of her uncles had children of their own. Some of these had even more children. But she, Misha, had no brothers or sisters.

"Why don't I have a brother?" she asked. "Why don't I have a sister?"

"You have many brothers and sisters," Mama said. "But you are the only one we have found."

"Are you looking for more?"

"Yes, we are looking all the time. Meanwhile, we are blessed with you."

Mama and Daddy slept in a special room in Uncle Edison's hospital. The room had glass doors and a fan that made a loud noise. Whenever Mama and Daddy went outdoors, they wore ugly masks—to protect their lungs from the air, they said. The masks reminded her of the men who danced in the Hopi ceremonies, their human faces hidden and mysterious as they emerged from Grandmother's house inside the mesa.

"Why does Grandmother live underground?" Misha asked.

"That's not her real home," Mama said. "It's her kiva. A place she goes when something important is going to happen."

"But what is going to happen?"

Her mother smiled. "Learn from Grandmother," she instructed. "Listen carefully to her words. Sometimes, when she says one thing, she's really saying something else."

Grandmother told stories about bad things—about the terrible Water Wars of the '30s, and about zoos where wild animals had once been kept in cages. But she also told about good things—giant flying machines that could carry hundreds of people through the sky, cars that drove themselves, and pictures sent through tiny machines that a man could strap to his arm.

"You've seen everything!" Misha said.

"I have seen many things," Grandmother said. "But there is one sight I am still waiting to see."

"What is it?"

"It is a dream that I carry," Grandmother said. "The Silver Spirits."

"Spirits?"

"They are the mothers of your generation. When they come home to us, I will go and tell my husband."

"You have a husband? Where is he?"

"He waits on the side of the mesa," Grandmother said.

Walking along the mesa's edge, Misha looked down over the spot where Grandmother's husband must surely be waiting. But as always, she saw only a blur. Mama said it had something to do with not having enough oxygen when she was born—her eyes had gotten confused and hadn't grown correctly. She could only imagine the landmarks of her home laid out far below, a pattern woven into a beautiful blanket.

But she could hear the dry wind, rustling through the feathers of the eagles who soared high above. She could hear the spirits of the ancient ones, rising like wisps of smoke from crevices in the rocks. She imagined Masauwu, the Spirit of Death and Master of the Upper World, with his horrid features twisted into a benign smile. She imagined the wise Spider Grandmother, chastising her two rollicking grandsons as they dashed about playing with their *nahoydadatsia* sticks and buckskin ball. Crouching near a crag, she felt for the nest of feather *pahos* marking the place that Uncle William had told her was Grandfather's special spot. She leaned out, as far as she dared, over the edge—listening for Grandmother's husband.

His voice drifted up from where he sat. "Misha," he whispered. "Wait for the Silver Spirits."

But she could never see him.

>«

AS MISHA GREW older, Mama and Daddy took her more and more often to Los Alamos, a big building with big windows. It was a healthy place, they said. But it was far away. To get there, they had to fly in an airship called a transport. Misha had a special place at Los Alamos, a room with a tiny window in one wall, colorful pictures on the other walls, and a soft bed. If she was good, she got to play scientist in Daddy and Uncle Rudy's laboratory. She played games on Aunt Kendra's computers, her nose pasted close to the bright screen. But she was frightened of Paul MacDonald, the tall man they called Mac—he was always appearing out of nowhere, like a ghost. "He's just shy," Mama said. "He isn't used to children."

One day, Misha learned that Mama and Daddy wanted to stay at Los Alamos for good. "I'm sorry, Misha," Mama said. "I can no longer breathe the air at the mesas, even with my respirator."

"Your mask?"

"Yes, even with my mask. And there are things we need to work on at Los Alamos." Mama placed her palm atop Misha's head. "You can stay at the mesas without us, if you wish."

Misha didn't wish. Where Mama and Daddy were, that was her home. But after a while she began to feel something different. Each day, they pushed her a little bit further away. A closed door, a quiet conversation, a meal without Mama. "We're sorry," Daddy said, "but you shouldn't be here with us all the time. You belong out in the sun, with your friends."

Was it something she'd done?

On the mesas, she stayed with Uncle William and his wife, Aunt Loretta. She played with their grandchildren, Bertie and little Honovi. She learned to weave flat baskets, and to make the blue corn cakes that Mama loved so much. She missed Mama and Daddy. But she had to accept it—things were different now.

>«

JUST AFTER MISHA'S eighth birthday, Mama and Daddy came for a visit. Mama leaned close, her face just a pale blur. Misha thought she could feel a sadness there, but Mama hadn't come with sad news. "We've made you some new eyes," Mama said.

"You're a big girl now," Daddy said. "It will require an operation. But we think you're ready." Mama kissed her on the forehead, and Misha could smell the clean soap smell of her long hair.

"But why do I need new eyes?" Misha asked. "I can see enough."

"With your new eyes, you'll be able to see everything, sharp as an eagle," Mama said.

"What if my new eyes don't work?"

"They will," Daddy said. "I promise."

Misha looked from one to the other of her parents. As Uncle Edison hovered behind them, all she could really see were the black frames of his glasses.

"Okay," she said. "I'll try."

But when she awoke from the operation, her eyes were covered with something. She opened them to see only shades of gray. She whimpered. Had the operation failed?

"Misha? Are you awake?" It was Daddy's voice, his hand on hers. "What is it, honey? Does it hurt?"

"Where's Mama?"

"She's not here right now. She'll be back."

"Did they fix my eyes? I can't see . . ."

"Your eyes are covered with gauze. You shouldn't try to open them just yet. They need time to get used to your head." Daddy chuckled, and Misha laughed too. "My dear little Misha," he said. "My brave little soldier."

But Misha didn't feel brave. She clutched at her father's hand. She didn't want him to leave again. And she wanted Mama. "When will Mama come back?"

Daddy didn't answer right away. And when he did, his voice was a little weaker than before. "She had an operation too."

"An eye operation?"

"No, it was for her lungs. To help her breathe better."

"So she won't need her mask?"

"I think she'll still need it. We'll see. Anyway, she's recovering now. As soon as we take off your gauze, I can take you to see her."

But it was two long days and nights before Misha felt fingers gently peeling off the long layers of her bandages. Gray turned to white, then . . . colors. Brilliant, sharp. Too sharp. She clamped her eyes shut. "Ouch!"

"Here," Daddy said. "Put these on." Raising her hands, she felt the dark glasses that he was sliding over her ears. "They're just to block the light a little. Until your brain does it for you. Then you won't need them anymore."

She opened her eyes, and her father's face came into focus. His nose and mouth were covered by his mask, but she could see his eyes, the deep wrinkles and the hollows beneath them. She could see every pore in the rough, stubbled skin of his pale cheeks. Across the room she could see a window, and through the window the bright sun glared, its rays glancing off a jar of water set on a shiny metal table. All around were angles, points, rough edges. Pain . . . She swallowed hard.

"I know," Daddy said. "It will take some getting used to."

"Can we go see Mama now?" Misha murmured, closing her eyes. "I'm ready."

"She's sleeping," Daddy said. "Dr. Edison is going to check your vision now. I'll let you know as soon as Mama wakes up."

Hours later as Misha sat scrolling through picture books, matching the letters—now sharp edged—to the simple words and sentences that Mama had painstakingly taught her, Daddy finally came back. "Mama's awake now," he said. Holding tight to her father's hand, Misha padded down the long, dim hallway to the special room where Mama and Daddy stayed. Uncle Edison opened the door. Blankets of cool air washed over them as they went inside.

"We did our best," Uncle Edison whispered to Daddy. "She's comfortable now."

Misha cocked her head. They thought she couldn't hear them, but she could. It was a secret she kept—her ability to hear things that others could not. Her ability to understand things that she shouldn't. It was her superpower.

She approached Mama's tent slowly. For that was what it was—a tent, like the ones she'd camped in with Bertie and Honovi on cold, starlit nights. Except that this tent had sides that you could see through, and the inside surfaces were coated with dew. Inside, she made out Mama's bed. Not clearly; it was more like before her eye operation—soft and fuzzy.

"Mama?"

"Come inside," came Mama's voice. "Let me look at you."

Misha looked back at her father. He had taken off his mask. She saw his nose, long and thin, the creases that coursed down his narrow face, and the dark mark in the shape of a bean that traced along the bottom of his jaw. He nodded. *Okay.*

Carefully, she pulled up the zipper on the side of the tent, just far enough that she could slip up onto the bed next to Mama. When she closed it, it was just the two of them. The air around them was damp but warm. She could feel Mama's arm around her. She looked into her face—high cheekbones, full lips, eyes deep as pools. "I see you, Mama," she said. "You're beautiful."

"And I see you," her mother said. "Even more beautiful."

MAMA NEVER LEFT her tent. Daddy stayed with her, sleeping on a cot in the special room. And every morning, Misha walked down the long hall to sit with them.

Then one day, before the first shards of the sun had stabbed through the window, Uncle Edison came to get her. Inside Mama's room, Daddy was waiting, and Uncle Rudy, and even Uncle Mac. On a small chair in the corner sat Grandmother.

"Where's Mama?" Misha asked.

"She waits with my husband," Grandmother said.

Misha stood there, her hands clenched into fists. She'd never seen Grandmother's husband, no matter how hard she'd looked. She wasn't even sure that her new eyes would be good enough for that. And now Mama was there too, in that place that couldn't be seen.

24

JAMES SAT ON the bed he'd shared with Sara in their cramped Los Alamos quarters, staring out the window at the line of pines that marked Pajarito Road. Beside him, the rumpled mattress still carried the indentation left by Sara's soft body, the scent of her. He remembered that night just over nine years ago when he'd first brought her here. When he'd nursed her, administering dose after dose of the antidote, praying to a God he'd never believed in.

Sara had survived. She'd lost her own child but gained another in Misha. And in those precious years, she'd made for him a life he never could have imagined, a life full of love, of passion. They had been a family.

Now, she was gone.

Through the dust-streaked window, James scanned the ground outside. All he had left of Sara now was a second gravestone, placed beside that of their tiny son. He'd lost the love of his life. But he'd lost so much more. For him, and for everyone at Los Alamos, there was no more hope. They were all doomed.

He'd known it for a while. The trouble had started years before, when Misha was only four—when they'd realized that for Sara, the inhaler would no longer be enough. With help from Edison, he and Rudy had set up a pulmonary lavage system in one of the treatment rooms at the Hopi medical center in Polacca. As Sara lay under sedation, the machine pumped a mist of healing vapor into her lungs. Old, infected cells were siphoned away. The fresh underlying tissue was suffused with a fluid rich in the C-343 antidote, resulting in a "clean slate" of surface cells resistant to IC-NAN. And Sara had indeed emerged from the treatment with substantially more energy. But as with the inhaler, it had turned out to be a delicate balance—not a cure.

At last, weakened by repeated rounds of lavage, her soft voice reduced to a hoarse whisper, Sara had felt the need to withdraw from their little daughter. "I don't want Misha to see me like this," she'd said. "She can't remember me like this." It was a story that James knew well. Sara had lost her own mother to cancer at a very young age. She knew the scars left behind, the pain of witnessing the decline of a loved one whom you had once deemed immortal.

"We'll implement the transplant," James had promised. He and Rudy had carefully awakened the precious Hopi stem cells from their frozen slumber. And as they'd perfected the delivery system at Polacca, Sara had devoted herself to one final project: giving Misha her sight.

At that final, fateful Caltech conference, the one where she'd contracted her deadly infection with IC-NAN, Sara had learned about a seamless retinal implant, already in clinical trials. Gone were the glasses-mounted video cameras and bulky video processing units associated with the old-style implants. The entire system, including the unique biosensors that would replace Misha's damaged retinas, had been miniaturized for implantation. At Sara's behest, Mac and William had flown out to Pasadena to retrieve the necessary hardware, software, and know-how to complete the operation. The modification could be reversed if necessary, Sara had assured James. But they'd both prayed for success. In a world fraught with danger, sight was a gift to be cherished.

Misha's operation had indeed been a success. Unsure at first, her brain unused to the jarring sensory input, she'd taken some time to gain her bearings. But in the end she'd blossomed—a new, even more amazing version of her former inquisitive self, emerging as though from a chrysalis.

Sara was not so lucky. The stem cell experiment failed, the new cells refusing to take hold in her tortured lungs. Huddled in the moist air of her oxygen tent, James had held her close.

"You shouldn't be sorry, James," she'd whispered. "I'm not." She'd run her soft hand along his arm. "You need to take care of Misha. And you still need to find the other children."

James rubbed his eyes. He hadn't had the heart to tell her then, the thing he'd already realized. For years, he'd been wearing a respirator mask whenever he went outdoors. He'd donned clumsy plastic hazmat suits. He'd told Sara that all of this was "just in case." But he knew better. With each passing day, the rattle at the base of his own lungs had deepened. He could no longer deny the nagging cough, the sleepless nights spent gasping for air. And he could no longer write off both Sara's frailty and the general's frequent bouts of illness as just the results of a previous exposure. He had to face the truth: The Los Alamos survivors were all still victims of IC-NAN. Despite the antidote's successful modification of surface cells, their stubborn lung stem and progenitor cells continued to divide, producing new cells susceptible to attack. And what had happened to Sara was happening to all of them—just more slowly.

His gaze drifted to a small piece of rock, lying on the table beside the bed. Etched in white on its flat black surface were three stick figures—one tall, one medium, one very small. And below these, the inscription: "Daddy, Mama, Misha." In so many ways, Misha reminded him of Sara. Sara, the brave one, who'd spent those precious years at the Hopi mesas despite the risks to her own health. Sara, the brilliant one, who had, in the end, given Misha the gift of sight. But what could he give Misha now? What did he have left that she could possibly need?

There was a tap at the door. He turned to find Rudy, his once capable hands grasping the doorframe for support. He barely recognized his old friend, his skin ashen, his eyes rimmed with red. "James," Rudy said. "There is a call on the satellite phone . . ."

"Who is it?"

"It is Misha."

James turned back to the window, a lump forming in his throat. "Tell her . . ." he said. "Tell her not now."

Rudy watched him quietly. "Are you sure you don't want to talk to her?" he asked.

James remembered a time over a decade before—when he and Rudy had still been young and healthy, enjoying the simple pleasure of pork tamales in their shared apartment. That time when they had still held out hope. "Thank you, Rudy," he said. "I'll call her back."

Rudy nodded. *"Entiendo,"* he said. "I will tell her."

25

IT WAS A while before Misha understood that James, the man she still called Daddy, would only return to the mesas on those rare occasions when he took treatments at the hospital. She could visit him at Los Alamos whenever she liked. And she often did, accompanying Uncle William on food deliveries and staying overnight in her little room, learning about computers from Aunt Kendra and biology from James and Uncle Rudy. But as three years went by and her brain adjusted to the eyes that Sara and James had given her, she began to examine more closely the stories she'd heard all her life. More and more, she wondered about her birth.

"Your Mother malfunctioned," Uncle William had told her. "But we managed to rescue you."

"When we found you," James said, "you were like a gift."

From the histories they recounted of a robotic Mother who hadn't survived to care for her, from Grandmother's tales of the Silver Spirits, from what little else the adults in her life seemed willing to share, she'd pieced it together. Her real mother had been one of those Spirits. And William and Rick were working to find more like her Mother—ones who still lived in the desert and had children of their own—her brothers and sisters.

She was eleven years old—old enough, she thought, to join the search. But Uncle William insisted it was too dangerous. "We go for days without finding anything," he said. "And then when we do, they shoot at us."

"Shoot at you? How? Why?"

"They have lasers. But we must understand. The Mother Spirits are only protecting their children. They can't know that we mean them no harm."

But, Misha insisted, they would never shoot at *her*. Sitting with Kendra in her dark lab, plinking out search terms to bring up images from what Kendra had explained was the bot learning database, she imagined herself a child of the desert, learning from that powerful, mysterious Mother. She combed through the fragments brought back to Los Alamos for inspection by Mac—the treads, the massive arms, the soft hand that Daddy told her Mama had designed. She felt the chip embedded in her own forehead, the mark that Sara had always told her made her special. These Mothers, these Silver Spirits . . . she belonged to them. She belonged with their children.

Then early this morning, a scout had come to William's house with news about a sighting at a place with a magical name—the Grand Staircase. In the hospital lot, she'd waited while William and Rick loaded Rick's transport with supplies. Then she'd slipped through the back transport door and sandwiched herself between two cases of water bottles. From her hiding place, she could just see out the side window as they took off, soaring north.

The thrum of the transport's engines and the steady hiss of air from the filters lulling her, she struggled to stave off sleep until, finally, she felt a shift in the air pressure, her stomach lurching at the descent. The transport landed with a thud. She held her breath as William pulled open the side door. As he unloaded the cases of water to stack them outside, she edged her body farther back, finding cover beneath a folded blanket in the rear of the hold. When the door slammed shut, she could barely hear William's voice from outside.

"Let's check the canyon," he called.

She caught sight of Rick, struggling to don a face mask before climbing out the pilot's-side door.

Then, silence.

Misha crept from her hiding place, then slipped through the door and down to the ground, her feet sinking into moats of fine dust. She could see the two men heading toward a deep, narrow gorge ahead, William with his steady gait and Rick with his characteristic hobble. Carefully she backed behind the transport, then hurried left, keeping them in her sights. At the edge of the gorge, she scampered behind a boulder to shield herself from their view.

Peering down, she could see something—two gleaming bots. And as she watched, a door opened on the side of one of them. Misha caught her breath. A girl, her thin figure wrapped round with a tattered blanket, emerged, her sleek black hair hiding her face as she climbed down the bot's treads to reach the ground. Misha watched the girl pick her way along the far side of the gorge, then disappear into a hollow sheltered by an overhang of reddish rock. From inside this small cave, she thought she saw a strong arm, reaching out to steady the girl . . .

Suddenly the earth shook. A whoosh of wind knocked the breath from her lungs and clouded the air with powdery dust. It wasn't until moments later, when the air cleared, that she realized the girl's bot was no longer down below.

Her gaze swiveled up. A metallic leg. An arm. A massive body, towering over her from just feet away. She stared, and this . . . thing . . . stared back at her. Though it had no face, no eyes, she was sure it was watching her, waiting. She listened but heard no voice.

Yet somehow she wasn't afraid. She could see the sun glinting off the translucent window of the empty cocoon, the place so recently inhabited by the black-haired girl. She could see the soft interior of the hand that Sara had designed. She was filled only with awe, a deep sense of wonder. Her Mother, the one who had borne her in the desert . . . her Mother had been one of these.

But then the spell was broken. The Mother turned, her attention focused on the two men now dashing toward the transport. The ground crumbled beneath the Mother's feet as she took two steps in their direction, and a sickening, high whir emanated from somewhere atop where her right arm joined her body. Coming to her senses, Misha dashed back toward the transport, wedging herself through the back door just as the two men clambered into the front. Something struck the ground right outside her window, a blinding flash as Rick engaged the engines and nosed the transport up from the ground. Misha's stomach leapt into her throat, and she swallowed hard. In moments, they were airborne.

". . . close one!" came William's voice from the passenger seat. "How many did you count?"

"Just the two," Rick replied, his voice hoarse through the mask that still covered his mouth and nose. "Including the daughter of the one that came after us."

"It's a start," William said. "We left enough water for a while. I hope they stay put. With these dust storms rolling in, they're better off down in that gorge than up top."

Crouched under the hot woolen blanket, Misha worked to steady her breath. Her heart pounding, she smiled. At last she'd seen them, children living as she had been meant to live. And she'd been right: Though others might be right to fear them, the Silver Spirits would never hurt her. In their world, she belonged.

FROM THE DOOR to the computer lab, James watched Kendra, hunched in front of her screen. He'd stopped wondering what kept Kendra going. Instead, he repeated to himself each morning the mantra she'd taught him. "You just have to put one foot in front of the other," she'd said. "Until you can't anymore." Then she'd grinned, that ironic look that had become so familiar over their years together.

There was strength, James knew, in coming to terms with one's own mortality. There was solace, he supposed, in knowing perhaps not the when, but the how of one's own death. And he'd discovered a new purpose in trying to make good on his promise to Sara—to do what he could for the Gen5s.

Ever since their launch, locating them had been difficult. And sightings had become even more rare since the six-year point, when an internal "timer" had instructed each Mother to leave for a location unspecified by her software. But now, things had changed. The Hopi scouts had begun to spot viable Gen5 encampments, pairs and trios of children gathered together. Their Mothers on high alert, no one dared approach them. But it was encouraging that some of them had found each other.

More importantly, the Gen5s seemed at last to have stopped their wandering. But unfortunately, Mac had discovered an ominous root cause for this new behavior. In the '20s, the deserts of the American West, including swaths of northeastern Utah, western Colorado, and areas north into Wyoming, Montana, and the Dakotas, had been the focus of continued clashes between a consortium of small oil companies, who claimed rights to unrestricted fracking and drilling as per their prior agreements, and the federal government, which was making a push for renewable energy. The feds had won, but only when, in the late '30s, the price of gas dipped so low that the companies no longer saw any value in the fight. The problem was that no one had advanced the funds required to clean up the oil fields. Through years of intense drought and even more intense legal battles, these abandoned sites had baked in the sun, their polluted expanses incapable of supporting plant life. Now, as evidenced by Mac's radar scans, a high-pressure system coming out of Canada was pushing strong winds down across the state of Utah. Howling through its northeastern canyons, they drove giant plumes of dust, much of it no doubt toxic, ahead of them. Though perhaps foreseen by the whistle-blowers of the '20s, this "New Dust Bowl" was unprecedented. And Mac could see no end to it. The Gen5 bots would soon be paralyzed. Their engines and filtration systems clogged, they would no longer be capable of protecting their children.

"You saw what happened to that last one Rick found," Mac had said.

"Did they find the child?" Kendra asked, her eyes rimmed with tears.

Mac looked at her sheepishly. "I didn't want to tell you," he said. "They found her hunkered down in a cave. Died in her sleep."

Uttering a low moan, Rudy stared fixedly at James. "We must find a way to get these children to a safer place," he said.

"That means getting their Mothers to take them there," Kendra said. She'd done her best, searching night and day for some previously overlooked snippet of programming that might point to a solution. James and Rudy had spent hours combing through reams of program notes. But to no avail. "If there was anything," Kendra said, "it must have been something Los Alamos wasn't granted access to."

The central repository for information regarding IC-NAN and the New Dawn project had been a bank of secure servers in Bethesda, Maryland. The bank had been destroyed in the bombing attacks targeting the D.C. area. But during the debriefings following the cyberattack, just hours before the bombing and the onset of the Epidemic in the U.S., Kendra had learned of a mirror site in North Dakota. In a hostile stretch of land aptly called "the badlands," where real farming was impossible, underground server farms abounded. And in one of these, the Langley New Dawn files had been backed up. The power required to cool the farms had long since gone out, and the servers had shut down. Under the snow and ice of winter and the blistering sun of summer, the bits and bytes lay dormant. Kendra knew the address of the server she needed. But she needed to retrieve it. She needed to wake it up. Then she needed to hack in.

Rick and William had done the first part, skirting the dust storms in their transport before braving them on the ground. The guards and alarm systems at the farm long dead, it had been a simple matter of breaking and entering. They'd retrieved the drive from the server and brought it safely back to Los Alamos. Kendra had easily inserted it into her system. The trick was the hack. But finally, her efforts had paid off. Late the night before, she'd found a way inside.

James stepped farther into the lab. "Kendra? Rudy said you had something?"

"James," Kendra said. "I thought you should see this first."

"Did you find a way to call them?"

"Not yet," Kendra said. "But I did find a few other things. For one, the identities of all the human mothers, together with their bot name designations."

James squinted at the lines of type on Kendra's screen. "I thought those were kept confidential."

"When it came to our government, even the most confidential things were documented." Kendra smiled. "And there're a few things you might find interesting."

"I would?"

"Based on the results of her interviews, Rose McBride made a specific choice. One of the donors was chosen to supply eggs for two of the fertilizations. Rose felt strongly that this woman had more of a chance than others to produce a child who would survive."

"I had no idea that Captain McBride knew anything about biology . . . Who was this woman?"

"Her name was Nova Susquetewa."

"Susquetewa?"

"She was a fighter pilot. Died on a mission in Syria, right before the Epidemic."

"Is she . . . ?"

"Yes. She's Grandmother's daughter. And, James . . . she's Misha's birth mother."

James leaned back against Misha's small desk. He imagined her eyes, the ones that Sara had given her—the way their bright green color complemented her light brown skin, her broad, flat forehead, her beautiful chestnut hair.

Kendra leaned forward, her voice a whisper. "So Misha actually *belongs* with the Hopi. What's more, she might still have a brother or sister out there somewhere."

James held his hand to his heart. A Hopi mother. A biological brother or sister. But *Sara* was Misha's mother. Misha was *his* daughter . . . He closed his eyes. They'd never lied to Misha. They'd explained that Sara was not her biological mother, nor he her real father—that she herself had been born inside an incubator in the desert, an origin story that was difficult enough to comprehend. But how would she handle this new information? He turned to face Kendra. "I can't tell her that," he blurted out.

"I understand not getting Misha's hopes up about the Gen5s. But shouldn't she know about her birth mother? And what about Grandmother? Shouldn't she be told?"

James rubbed his temples with the flats of his fingers. Was he just being selfish? Didn't Misha have a right to know these things?

But no. Not yet.

Beyond the horror of the Epidemic, he'd found solace in distancing himself from that painful past. And when Misha had entered their lives, he and Sara had exercised every bit as much caution in crafting the story of her world as they had in engineering the prosthetic eyes through which she perceived it. He'd begun to understand, just a little, the duty that a parent bore in protecting his child from the truth—allowing

Rudy and Kendra only narrow latitude in teaching Misha about the world as it had been, preferring Grandmother's mystical tales to the harsh reality of the hatred and warfare that had destroyed their way of life.

He'd just begun to think about reconnecting with Misha, of telling her the truth about himself and the others at Los Alamos. But the tale of a biological mother lost in war, of a brother or sister, possibly dead—these were not stories he was ready to tell.

"I'll need time to think about it," he said. "I'm not even sure we should tell Grandmother yet . . . though I wouldn't be surprised if she already knew."

Kendra offered him a smile. "I only wish she knew how to call these Mothers in . . ." She turned back to her screen. "There's something else here that might interest you."

"Yes?"

"Rose McBride made another choice. She herself was one of the Gen5 donors."

"I suppose that doesn't really surprise me," James replied. "It would make sense for her to use herself as the prototype for the personality program."

"But what might surprise you is the father."

"The father? The fathers were anonymous. We used hundreds of different sperms for each fertilization. We chose the most viable embryos . . ."

"Not in Rose's case. She had a special 'in.'"

"She chose a father?"

"According to these records, she wouldn't allow an alternate. Rose stipulated that the father must be Richard Blevins."

26

RICK LAY FLAT on the road, his Tyvek suit bunching under his body as he propped himself awkwardly on his elbows. Holding his breath, he adjusted his mask down to strap on a pair of field glasses.

Lying next to him, his rough cotton shirt and dungarees caked with dust and a bandana wrapped tight over his mouth and nose, William pointed down over the steep edge. "There."

Sightings had become more regular now. They'd counted at least fifteen, still alive, still eking out an existence in this godforsaken desert. But this sighting was different. The scouts had found Rho-Z.

Rick adjusted the focus on his glasses, fighting off the double vision that had begun to plague him, panning his field of view. Then he saw them. At one end of the wide wash, their flanks covered in sheets of grayish powder, two bots were stationed close to the opening of a small cave.

"Seems like they've been here for a while," William said. "They've got a nice little camp set up. But the scouts said there were three of them here before . . ."

As Rick watched, one of the bots pivoted slowly in his direction.

Had she detected him? He shifted his weight, attempting to become one with the ground. He was happy to feel no complaint from his prosthesis. But he knew it was not a good thing. The dizziness, the loss of feeling in his extremities—he'd felt them before, signs that he needed another lavage treatment.

"The dust storms," he said. "Looks like they survived that big one two days ago. But Mac has picked up a much larger one on the satellite, and more behind it."

"It was just a matter of time . . ." William muttered. He turned toward Rick. "We need to figure out a way to get them all out of here."

Rick refocused his glasses. Where was Rho-Z? "My guess is that the third bot couldn't have gone too far. Maybe it went to get water?" Suddenly he caught a glimpse of something, a thin child with darkly tanned skin, climbing down from the bot closest to the cave entrance. "See there?" he said.

"Yes." William smiled. "But that other bot . . . She's yours, right?"

Squinting, Rick searched the second bot for the bright yellow tattoo. He felt a surge of welcomed relief. He could see it now—a streak of yellow peeking out from beneath the grime at her wing's edge. "Right," he murmured. "The one I've been looking for."

He willed himself to stay calm. But his heart skipped a beat as Rho-Z's hatch cracked open and a boy emerged—a boy with bushy hair like his, reddish brown like Rose's. The boy moved in a familiar way, his arms held crooked at the elbows, his posture stooped slightly forward as he made his way down to the ground. As the boy turned back to face his Mother, she reached her powerful arm toward him, the gauntlet at the back of her hand opening. Her yellow tattoo glinted in the sun as her soft inner hand emerged to touch the top of the boy's head.

"Kai . . ." Rick breathed.

"What?"

"If it was a boy, she wanted to name him Kai. That would be his name." The desert was silent, the sound of his own weak pulse the only thing in Rick's ears. He closed his eyes, imagining the life that might have been—a house in the country, a wife, a son . . . He heard Rose's voice. Safe in his embrace, she'd whispered to him on the night before he lost her.

"Did Detrick okay our request?"

"Yes. But if the fertilization didn't go well, they had my permission to use another donor's sperm."

"I don't want another donor."

"But, Rose, I want you to have a baby."

He watched the boy bring something up to his mouth—a water bottle. He had water. But of course he would. He was smart, like his mother. Resourceful, like his father. His son. This was *his* son. He was sure of it now. A tear streaked down Rick's face as, reluctantly, he removed the glasses. How he wished Rose could be here . . .

Rose? He turned his head, looking for her on the road behind him. She wasn't there. But he remembered her voice—urgent, pleading, her eyes locked on Blankenship's as they sat in his cramped Pentagon office: *We need those Code Black homing coordinates, General . . .*

Rick turned over on his back, clamping his eyes shut. How he wished he could hear that voice again. How many things had she tried to tell him, when he'd been too distracted or pigheaded to listen? Even her final words had been lost in the heat of the moment. His mind reached out, trying to remember . . .

Then he heard her, calling out from the bunker at Langley: *I know I didn't follow procedure. Special protocol . . .*

He opened his eyes, staring up at the pearlescent sky. Had Rose, in the end, done something without authorization? In her desperation, might she have gone ahead and inserted the coordinates herself? But if she had, why hadn't the Mothers homed? *Tell Kendra . . .* Kendra had turned over every rock in her search for a solution. She'd looked everywhere, except . . .

"I've got an idea," he said. "Maybe Rose can help."

"Rose? But—"

"I need to get to San Francisco."

IN THE FILTERED atmosphere of the transport cockpit, Rick removed his mask. Like the bots, the transport could fly at ten thousand feet or lower, skimming the tops of mountain peaks, darting through valleys. In the '30s, the ominous thwack of its triple blades had become an all-too-familiar signature of U.S. involvement in the Israeli Water Wars, and in the later skirmishes at the India-Pakistan border. But his mission today was a peaceful one. Today he flew at altitude, skimming the clouds. Running his hand over his unshaven chin, he caught sight of the gleaming towers of the once great city of San Francisco, rising through the fog like masts. He imagined the life that had once pulsed here, now extinguished.

William, asleep in the seat to his right, was his only passenger. His motorcycle occupied the midsection of the rear cargo space, surrounded by a case of MREs, six five-gallon carboys of fresh water, fresh filter canisters for his mask, and a few extra phones. The supplies were all "just in case." This was to be a surgical strike.

Intentionally avoiding the city, they soared in across the bay to make a soft landing at Crissy Field, the overgrown marsh grass almost enveloping their craft. Filtered through thick fingers of fog, the dim yellow glow of the sun illuminated the worn red roof of the nearby hangar. Rick flipped on the cockpit light and groped on the floor for his rifle. Strapping the rifle over his back, he checked his pocket for his inhaler, then for the small, rectangular external storage drive that Kendra had given him. Donning his filter mask, he strapped on his leg, opened the pilot's-side door, and hoisted himself down to the sodden ground.

"We there?" William rubbed his eyes, peering down at him.

"Yup."

With William's help, Rick popped the back side door and activated the ramp to bring down his motorcycle. As he mounted the cycle he breathed deep, as deep as his failing lungs and his mask would let him. He sensed the familiar weakness, the tingling in his hands and feet, the creeping mental confusion. He should have heeded Edison's pleas to undergo lavage before venturing out here. But time was ticking for the children in the desert. Kai was out there. If the files at the Presidio could offer any clue as to how to call them . . . he had no time to worry about himself.

Cold sea mist seeped under his jacket, wetting his skin. He thought of Rose, how she'd loved this fog . . . "Hop on," he said.

Rick gunned the cycle toward Lincoln Boulevard, heading south. In a stubbly field off to his right he spotted a mangy dog, foraging for food. Ironic, that humans had once worried so much about destroying wildlife habitats; now those "lesser species," unaffected by IC-NAN, were multiplying out of control in areas formerly dominated by humans. The rabbits and coyotes he'd come across in the desert were timid enough. But the spawn of former pet dogs and cats, rabid and starving, and the mountain lions and bears of the California hills, always on the prowl, might pose more of a threat.

They swung right to pass a row of boarded-up houses. Straight ahead was the Presidio Institute.

Rick could see the remains of the little ballpark where the members of the institute's staff had once made their way around the bases, and the now-overgrown field where they'd held picnics and flown kites. Overlooking these, the window of Rose's office on the second floor of the Mission Revival–style headquarters offered a commanding view of the other institute buildings. Scanning their dark windows, Rick shivered. If there were any human remains, he supposed they would be here. Slowly, he circled the field to pull up in front of the headquarters. William shouldered a rifle he'd strapped to the back of the cycle and followed him up the cement steps to the main entrance.

The door hung open, and a layer of gritty dust littered the lobby floor, a light breeze carrying it up the staircase to their right. Rick's breath hitched. From across the room, a face was staring at him. Reflexively, he reached for his rifle . . .

But behind him, William remained at ease. The man across the room was not a man at all—not anymore. "He's dead, Rick," William mumbled.

As Rick's eyes adjusted to the gloom, more ghosts appeared. A group of five—mere skeletons, picked clean. Their tattered uniforms—for they were all military—were in disarray. At the table where they sat, whisky bottles sat empty. Old playing cards were scattered like discarded love notes. Their service rifles lay on the floor. And except for the man who'd first caught his eye, all were slumped in their seats.

He shook his head, forcing his eyes to focus instead on a rectangular metal door set into the side wall—marked "Power Station." He yanked on the handle and the door swung open. But to his chagrin, the solar storage batteries were all gone, ripped from their moorings. "I don't blame them," he said, imagining a scramble in the end, a vain attempt by some to leave the plague-ridden city. "We brought replacement batteries, right?"

"Two spares, in the back of the transport," William said. "But couldn't we just bring the computer home?"

"We can't be sure if what we came for is on Rose's computer or somewhere else in networked storage. I promised Kendra I'd power up the Presidio network and link it to Los Alamos."

"Okay. Just sit tight."

As William headed back out, Rick surveyed the ruins. In the twelve years since the Epidemic, he'd made a point of avoiding scenes like this—abandoned cities; dead families cowering in crumbling houses; cars loaded high with luggage, headed nowhere. But it was hard—they were everywhere. His leg throbbing, he made his way up the stairs toward Rose's office. Her door, so familiar, creaked open at his touch, and he peered into the wood-paneled dim. Thank God—no skeletons here. Exhausted, he slumped onto the divan along the left wall, sinking into its dusty leather cushions . . .

He could see Rose, just across the room, her silhouette in the window. "I'm telling you, Rick," she said, "I can't quite get used to the way you people do things . . ."

"You're one of us now," Rick murmured. "One of us . . ."

"Rick?" William's disembodied voice piped up the stairs from the lobby.

Rick turned toward the door, jolting awake. "Up here!" he called.

"I installed the batteries. Everything's up and running."

Wrenching himself off the sofa, Rick rubbed his eyes and steadied himself against the wall. He hobbled to Rose's desk, plopped down on her chair, and flipped on the computer. To his relief, her screen emitted its familiar green glow. Safety Mode. OK to proceed?

He pressed "enter," and an empty dialog box appeared. Slowly, he keyed in Rose's secure password, transcribing it character by character from the display on his wrist phone. He closed his eyes as he pressed "enter" again. When he opened them, Rose's home screen was there—a photo of the Golden Gate Bridge underlying an orderly array of icons that marched toward him as though in three dimensions. He touched the radio icon and used a second code to switch it on, enabling the secure satellite connection with Kendra at Los Alamos that Rose had used to transmit code. There was only one thing left in Kendra's list of instructions. Just in case the satellite connection wasn't up to snuff, he plugged the external drive into a port on Rose's computer and activated a system download.

As the drive loaded he watched the display, the background photos shuffling through familiar scenes of redwood forests, rolling fields, rounded hills—all the sights that Rose had loved. His gaze drifted to a panel on the right-hand side of the screen: Personal Journal.

Raising his index finger, he pointed to the header. But the file didn't open. Instead, he was greeted with yet another dialog box, requesting yet another password. Luckily, Rose tended to keep these subpasswords simple. "Gen5," he typed. No. He clamped his eyes shut. Two more tries before Kendra would have to hack in. "Journal," he typed, the simplest of passwords. Access Denied. Then he remembered. "Rho-Z." The Mothers had initially been issued numeric barcodes, each containing the usual information—project number, date of manufacture, operating system rev, followed by the numbers 01 through 50 to designate the specific bot. But these numbers held no meaning for Rose. It had been her idea to name them using letters of the Greek alphabet, followed by letters of the English alphabet, in a system that mimicked the name of the donor mother. She was Rho-Z, Bavishya Sharma was Beta-S. In some small way, it helped her to realize the humanity inside each of them. "And when the children are born," she said, "their Mothers will have names they can say."

Rick smiled as the file opened, a list of entries spilling down the screen in reverse chronological order. He leaned forward, squinting at the last journal entry:

May 23, 2053

Rick will be here tomorrow to help with the presentation. Thank God. Not sure I'm ready for the questions. I hate all these secrets.

With a sigh, he brought up a search dialog and typed in "Code Black." The response was immediate:

May 14, 2053

Shipped the latest rev of the Gen5 code to Kendra at 0900. No decision has been handed down on Code Black. Specifically, on the location specified for their gathering. It keeps me up nights, thinking about those poor things wandering alone in the desert. But the issue hasn't gotten any traction. For no reason at all, they've severely downgraded the probability of a Code Black launch.

Pending an official call, I've made my own. I've built in code to call them here.

His eyes widening, Rick read on.

They'll have food, water, whatever they might need. I stocked up Building 100 after we cleared it out. Useful tools, cookware, tableware, etc. The homing protocol includes the coordinates of the old storage shed on the Main Post, currently being used to store the supplies for the archaeological dig. We can leave other supplies there.

Then he saw it:

SPC = "Please and Thank You." Two things my father taught me never to forget.

SPC. According to Kendra, this was the "special protocol command," the key command necessary to turn on an ancillary program. It was the treasure he'd come seeking. Rick sank back into the arms of Rose's chair. He could feel his heart fluttering weakly in his chest. "Special protocol . . ." he murmured. "Why, Captain McBride. And here I thought you didn't like secrets."

BY THE TIME they emerged onto the front porch, the sun was high in the sky.

"Ready?" William said.

Through the resistance of his filter mask, Rick drew in a breath. Then he pulled the mask briefly away from his face to cough out a spray of pink sputum. His vision wavering, he noticed that his finger-tips were a sickly blue in the crisp daylight.

"Geez, Rick. You look like hell."

"I feel like hell. But I got what I came for."

"Here, let me drive." William boarded the cycle.

With the last of his strength, Rick hefted his prosthetic leg over the seat. His arms looped around William's waist, he watched the roads of the Presidio speed beneath their wheels. The cycle stopped, and he allowed William to help him up into the transport passenger seat. He felt the man's able hands securing his safety harness. Next to him, the door closed.

He heard the pilot's-side door slam shut, then the silence of the cabin. Then he heard William's voice, as if from far away. "Let's get you some clean air." He heard the air system engage, and felt William's hands again, unclasping his filter mask.

". . . you sure you can fly . . . ?"

"You taught me, remember?" William assured him. And soon, he felt the familiar downward push as the transport rose slowly up from the reeds.

As his head lolled back on the seat, Rick's mind returned to Rose's sunlit apartment, the deep nest of her clean white sheets.

27

JAMES LEANED AGAINST the bench next to the DNA synthesis machine, his mind lulled by its hum. He'd never been the NAN synthesis expert—this job, both tedious and demanding of unique skills, had been relegated to Rudy and his team. But Rudy had had plenty of time to train him on the process at Los Alamos, and they'd been taking turns monitoring the C-343 production. The lavage system at the hospital in Polacca required substantially more antidote than did their inhalers. A few failed batches had put them behind. And now, in the room where Sara had died, Rick Blevins lay gasping for air. They needed more antidote, and fast.

He stared at the machine, its small robotic arms whirring through an unending series of intricate operations beneath its dark glass. He no longer had the energy to man the synthesis overnight, and Rudy was going through a bad patch. They'd run out of precursors years back—now they relied on the Hopi scouts to raid bio labs in Santa Fe and Phoenix for supplies. Soon they'd have to train Hopi techs, just to keep up the production.

"James?" He turned to find Kendra standing in the doorway. Her hands were empty, folded in front of her, devoid of the tablet that was her constant companion.

"How's the general?" He didn't like the look on her face.

"Pulling through. But it's slow going this time."

James took a deep breath, enduring the tightness in his chest that was now a constant. He swallowed down the feeling of weakness that went beyond the physical, of anger with no target. He hadn't been the one to launch IC-NAN into the biosphere. He hadn't been the one to send off the Gen5 bots, without any assurance that he could ever get them back. Those things had been done by people more powerful than he—people like the general. But he couldn't afford to think about that now.

He pushed back from the bench. *One foot in front of the other.* "As I understand it," he said, "Rick Blevins has found a way to call the Gen5s?"

"Seems so. I've studied the downloads from Rose McBride's computer. And I've figured out how to implement her SPC."

"SPC?"

"The special protocol command. The one that will activate Dr. Mc-Bride's code to home the Mothers to the San Francisco Presidio."

"San Francisco? We can't home them directly to the Hopi mesas?"

"No, at this point the code is set. The location is unalterable. But maybe that's for the best. The bots have thwarted every attempt by the Hopi scouts to communicate with the children. Scouts have been injured. If the bots went to the mesas now, God knows what those machines might do."

Rudy appeared in the doorway beside Kendra. His once sturdy arms and hands limp at his sides, it was as though he'd aged thirty years in the eleven since Misha's birth—since the births of whatever Gen5 children might still be alive. "I agree with Kendra," he said, his voice a hoarse rasp. "It is our only choice." Lightly, Kendra placed a supportive hand on Rudy's arm.

James closed his eyes. They were waiting for his agreement. "What does the general say?"

"All systems go, of course."

"And where is Misha?"

"At the mesas, visiting with William's grandkids," Kendra said.

"Good," James said. "I'd rather she not know about this until we get it done."

Kendra flashed him a knowing look. "She might have a brother or sister out there."

"Yes. And she'll be told, but only if and when that child is located. So, let's go over the details."

THEY HUDDLED OVER Kendra's computer, reviewing Rose McBride's program notes. "Rick told William about a phone call he received from Rose on the night we think she died," Kendra said. "The call was all broken up. But she said one thing clearly. She said something about a special protocol. She said, 'Tell Kendra.' I used our secure key to convert the words 'PLEASE AND THANK YOU' into binary code. And when I used that code to search the Gen5 code, I finally found what I've been looking for. A series of instructions, the first of which is the geographic coordinates for the Presidio base."

James sat down next to Kendra. "So, we can transmit this code to them? They'll receive it? They'll act on it?"

"They're equipped with radio receivers, and we can use satellite transmission to send the code. We can send repeatedly, so we should be able to cut through any interference offered by the dust storms. And once initiated, these special commands are designed to circumvent any defenses installed elsewhere in the bot's code."

"Then what will happen?"

"Once they arrive at the Presidio, the Mothers will go through a shutdown and reboot. As part of the reboot, some systems will be taken off-line. They'll no longer provide cocoon support systems to the children, or fly them anywhere except under extreme threat . . ."

"Why did Dr. McBride think that this was necessary?" Rudy asked.

"Flight itself is a rather dangerous affair. And the idea is to get the kids to stay outside their bots, to stay close to one another, to mingle more."

"Socialization," James said.

"Yes. Rose set up a building there with cooking supplies and so on, where the kids can live together. And a storage building with other supplies."

James rubbed his chin. "Is the Presidio ready for them?" he asked.

"William assures me he can make it ready."

"How about water?"

"There's a fog collection tower near the Main Post, erected as a demonstration of water reclamation technology by a nonprofit looking for funding back in the '20s. As it happens, the tower was designed by the same company that New Dawn used for the desert units. And it's much larger. William says he'll need to drain it, clean it out, and allow it to refill fresh. In the misty environment at the Presidio, the refill shouldn't take more than a few days. With their Mothers' help, the kids will probably have more to eat and drink than they ever had before."

"So, do you anticipate any problems?"

"Unfortunately, yes. Security."

"But I thought this was all about keeping the kids safe."

"Yes, they should be very safe. Even from us."

"From us?"

"First order of business, the Mothers will secure the perimeter—"

"Secure the perimeter?" James stood up, kneading his palms.

"You have to remember, Rose was operating under the tenets of Code Black. The supposition is that Langley is gone. Los Alamos is gone. An enemy is believed to have intel leading them to the bots. The bots alone are desirable pieces of military hardware. And of course, anything that compromises the bots will compromise the children. 'Securing the perimeter' is all about keeping that enemy off the base."

"So, we still won't be able to make contact with the children . . ."

"William will leave the Fort Scott headquarters unlocked, and Rose's computer is still online. And he's leaving a few satellite phones in Building 100. But we'd need to be careful . . . the Mothers will interpret any communications from the outside world as a threat." Kendra turned to him. "We'll just have to accept it. Assuming we can get them to the Presidio, these children will be guarded by an army of the most powerful soldiers ever built."

28

A THIN GRAY light penetrated Rosie's hatch window. Kai could still hear the drone of the small fan beneath her console, cycling air through her filtration system. Pulling his blanket away from his mouth, he took in a slow breath. The air inside his cocoon smelled like the wind once had before a rainstorm, but the odor was mixed with the stale scent of his own sweat.

He shook his head, trying to clear it. Days had passed since the first dust storm had hit them—though it was difficult sometimes to tell day from night. The storms were coming in waves now, each one stronger than the last. "Where's Sela? Did she come back yet?"

"There is one child in close proximity to our current position."

Kai reached for the latch. "Can I . . . ?"

"Wind speed 9 kilometers per hour. Visibility 30 kilometers. PM10 count remains high out of specification. Please wear your particle mask."

Kai reached under his seat to draw out the mask. Strapping it over his nose and mouth, he pushed lightly on the door. Matted cakes of dust slithered down the hatch surface as he slipped through the opening and onto Rosie's treads. The same talc-like material blanketed the clearing all around him, gathering in drifts against the rocks. He could barely discern between the gray of the land and the pale, translucent white of the sky. He climbed up onto Beta's treads to tap lightly, swiping his hand along the window to clear a small area. Kamal looked out at him, dazed, then donned his own mask before opening the hatch.

"Has Sela returned?" Kamal asked.

Kai scanned the clearing. Still no sign. "I'm sure she's okay," he assured Kamal. "Just hiding out somewhere . . ." Though he was still trying to put on a brave face, Sela's continued absence had begun to forge a hole in the pit of his empty stomach.

"Is Rosie still operational?" Kamal asked. "Except for her air filter and basic communications, Beta has disabled most of her functions."

Kai turned to look at Rosie, barely recognizable in her cloak of dust. "It's just a precaution. To avoid an accidental spark, Rosie said. But there's something strange about the way she talks to me now. Like she's busy . . ." He shook his head. There was no point in letting his fears get the best of him. They'd get through this, just as they'd gotten through everything else. "Let's get more water. I'm almost out."

From their holds, they gathered up the three water bottles that each had been allotted. Then they hurried along the narrow path leading up to the spring.

Kai squinted. Just ahead—that might be the pile of small rocks they'd left there as a marker. But he could barely see the path . . . Coming to a halt at a damp patch of dust, he dug frantically into the ground with his heel. His heartbeat hard in his ears, he bent down to scoop clots of silt to either side. "It's here," he muttered. "I know it's here." But it wasn't. He stood up, his hands dripping clumps of wet mud.

Suddenly he sensed Rosie's ping. Turning to glance up toward the road, he caught sight of the ominous black edge of the next front.

"We need to reboard!" Kamal said. Without waiting for an answer, he locked his near-empty bottles back under his arm and loped down the path to scale his Mother's treads.

Kai was hot on his heels. "Are your systems okay?" he telegraphed Rosie.

But there was no answer. His heart sank as the new onslaught began.

BETWEEN SIPS OF water and bites of raw, gritty cactus, Kai slipped in and out of a fitful sleep. His mind drifted between nightmares and the reassuring echo of Rosie's voice. Each time he awoke, his legs ached and his head throbbed.

Then he felt something—a rumbling jostle. Sheets of dirt slid down the window in front of him. Was it a dream? No. They were moving. Rosie was rolling away from the shelter of the cave opening, making her way toward the flat, clear area at the center of the depression. A short distance away, Beta maneuvered alongside them.

"What's happening?" he telegraphed his Mother.

"Leaving."

"Why?"

"Signal."

"Signal? From where?"

But there was no reply, only a silence in his mind. He swiveled in his seat, straining to make out Beta, to make sure that Kamal was still close by. But now he couldn't see him. And where on earth was Sela?

"No!" he cried. "We can't!" Again there was no reply. He grabbed for the latch.

"Please remain in your seat and secure your restraints," Rosie said. He felt his seat swinging forward as she tilted down, readying for takeoff.

"We can't leave Sela!" he cried.

But they were already high in the air, Rosie's hull washed clean by the force of the wind. Within moments, a hopeful sun glimmered off her flanks as she tore through the upper reaches of the dust cloud. Cupping his hands against the window, Kai strained to see outside. Beta was there, flying in tandem with Rosie. And off in the distance, he made out one, two, maybe three other objects: great bumblebee forms, rising from the desert.

KAI'S EYES FLEW open. Wedged deep in his seat, he was buckled into his restraints, his forehead resting against the cool surface of Rosie's side hatch cover. Vaguely, he remembered the steady hum of her engine, the glare of morning sunlight through her hatch . . .

From outside, a pair of brown eyes peered at him. "Hello?" a voice cried, muffled. Tap, tap. "Are you okay?"

Kai uncoupled his safety restraints and opened the hatch door, extending a leg out over the lip of the opening. But his bare foot scudded along the unexpectedly slick surface of Rosie's tread and he slid awkwardly down her side to land in a heap on the ground. As his fingers dug into fat green foliage and prickly brush, tiny shards of scrub stuck to his hands, piercing the skin of his palms.

"I am sorry. I should have warned you," Kamal said, climbing carefully down to the ground. "It is very wet here . . ."

Kai got to his feet. The air smelled of salt and of something dead. The chill wind sent a shiver up his spine. Screeching white birds careened overhead. At a short distance, deep green waves churned onto a pebbly shore. He remembered the photo that Sela had given him, the one of the little girl in the red dress . . . the ocean.

"As Beta readied to land," Kamal said, "I worried that perhaps we had been separated. But she assured me that these were the correct coordinates."

"The correct coordinates . . ." Kai repeated. "For what?"

Kamal stared at him, befuddled. "She did not say more."

Kai looked at his Mother. Beside him she was still, moisture running down her flanks like beads of sweat. "Your name is Kai," she'd once told him. "It means 'ocean.'" Had she brought him home? He listened for her answer. But in his mind, he could hear only a soft tapping sound, like the steady drip of water on rock—the sound she made when she was thinking.

"Why is Rosie so quiet?" he asked.

"Beta has been silent since our arrival," Kamal said, casting a glance at his Mother. "I can no longer hear her thoughts . . ."

Kai turned in a slow circle, trying to catch his bearings. His mind felt as foggy as the air here. Foggy, and . . . empty. He wondered where Rosie had gone. And where was Sela? He'd seen others, he was sure of it . . .

He squinted, searching the beach. Nothing. Then he caught sight of something in the sky—two tiny dots. They resembled the hawks he'd seen in the desert, circling in the updrafts. But as they lowered, they each grew steadily in magnitude, their outlines more distinct. "Are those . . . ?" The drone of their engines was barely audible above the whistle of the wind and the crash of the waves. But as they prepared to land, the roar of their ducted fans was unmistakable. Kai dropped to his knees, hands over his head to fend off sheets of whipping sand.

When he looked up, Kamal was already well down the beach, his thin legs carrying him toward a small girl whose tangle of blond curls all but hid her face. Drawing near, Kai could barely hear the girl's voice. But he could see her shy smile, the revelation of a chipped front tooth. "My Mother calls me Meg," the girl murmured.

Uphill, a burly boy with straw-colored hair stood scratching his head next to another steaming bot. "Zak," the boy said, introducing himself. His gaze shifted up and down the beach as Kai approached. "There was someone else with me . . ."

"They'll be here soon," Kai assured him, hoping he was right. All around them, bots were landing in twos and threes now, hatches popping open and children emerging like the newborn birds in Rosie's nature videos. But none of them was Sela.

Beside him, Zak only glared in a way that made him feel strangely uncomfortable. "Sure hope so," he said. "This whole thing just doesn't seem right."

Through the mist down by the shoreline, Kai spotted a lone form hovering in the sky. *Alpha-C?* He made off at a trot, tracking the bot as she soared out over the water and then back toward him. Suddenly he felt his legs go out from under him. His left foot ensnared in the ropy tendrils of a slimy greenish-brown plant, he went sprawling. He barely had time to raise his head before the bot crashed to earth close by.

Pushing himself up on his elbows, he caught sight of a pair of naked feet, kicking at the sand. "Gosh, Mama!" The girl shook her hair, releasing a cloud of dust. "Did you have to come down so hard? I know it's been a while since you ran a diagnostic on your landing routine . . ."

Kai sat up. And despite himself, he laughed for sheer joy. "What kept you?" he called.

Sela rewarded him with a toothy grin. "You okay? Alpha almost crushed you!" Kai felt Sela's welcome grip as she helped him back to his feet. "Sorry I ran off like that. I knew right away it was wrong. And after all that, we had to leave the bike behind."

Kai couldn't stop laughing. Just like Sela to worry about that crazy bike. But they were here. Sela was safe. And there were others—lots of others.

Suddenly Kamal was bearing down on them, the new girl, Meg, close on his heels. "Thank the gods!" Kamal cried, his white teeth gleaming as he wrapped his arms around Sela.

"Rosie told me she received some kind of signal," Kai said. "Did Alpha say anything?"

"Nothing," Sela said. "We just took off. No explanation at all . . ." Beside them, Alpha-C had settled down on her haunches. Her arms relaxed, her soft inner palms exposed, she was uncharacteristically still. "What's she doing now?" Sela asked, running her palm along her Mother's retracted wing.

"We don't know," said Kai. "But whatever it is, they all seem to be doing it."

His brow furrowed, Kamal reached down to sift handfuls of coarse sand between his long fingers. "I hope my Mother comes back soon."

Sela peered through the now-thinning mist. "Where *are* we?"

"The ocean? West? That's all I can figure." From his pocket Kai drew out his compass, the present from Sela. Staring down at it, he watched its needle drift toward the letters "NW." In that direction, a towering rust-brown structure arced out over the ocean, disappearing into the dense white of a fog bank. A bridge—he'd seen it once, in a picture on Rosie's screen. But where? To the south, he scanned the length of a cracked and rutted roadway. Close to the road was a water tower of the same sort he'd encountered at the desert campsites. But this one was much bigger, its giant orange bottle shape standing as high as one of the nearby trees. Beyond the tower stood a cluster of buildings. A few small wooden structures, their glass windows broken out and shards of paint drooping from their outer walls, seemed poised to fall into total ruin. But the larger buildings, some constructed of red brick and others of white stone blocks, stood stalwart in the face of the onshore wind.

The most amazing view was to the east. There, a large white dome perched atop an immense stone structure. Behind and to the left of this, a small expanse of still, blue water glistened. And in the distance, buildings—large and small, pointed and flat—paraded across a gradual slope. It was a city—though it looked more like a mirage or a painting, its three dimensions flattened by distance.

For an instant, Kai was enthralled. But in the next moment he imagined himself face-to-face with the city's former inhabitants, the husks of bodies ravaged by the Epidemic. The Epidemic had been everywhere, and far more people had lived in cities than in the desert . . . The familiar fear twisted in his gut. His mind called out for his Mother, but she wasn't there.

Then . . . what was that? He felt the ground below him rumbling and turned to find Rosie trundling toward him. "I think she's back," he murmured, and his heartbeat slowed at the reassurance.

Beside him Kamal cocked his head. "My Mother also."

All around them now, children were following their Mothers up a low rise, past a marshy area and toward the cement road. They crossed the road toward the giant water tower on the other side. There the children paused to cup their hands in the cool liquid that all but overflowed the basin. Gulping mouthfuls, Kai let it run down his chin. He'd forgotten how thirsty he was . . .

But their Mothers soon corralled them, herding them on across a field of brittle, dry grass that rose almost to their shoulders. At the far end of the field was a building, red brick with a wooden porch, windows outlined in white. There they came to a halt, and one by one, the children broke off from their Mothers to approach the building's spacious front porch.

Kai turned to Rosie. "What about food?" he protested. But she only stood there, silent. He looked back at the building. Maybe there was food inside.

He climbed the cement steps to the porch, where to the right of a set of heavy double doors, a plaque bolted to the wall announced "Building 100." Making her way through the crowd, Sela wrapped the fingers of her left hand around the rusted iron latch of one door. She gave a hard tug. But the thick doors, layers of dirty white paint peeling from their scarred surfaces, refused to budge. "Seems like they want us to go in there, but these doors are stuck tight," she said.

"Let me help," Kai offered, grabbing the matching handle of the right-hand door. "One . . . two . . . three!" With a loud crack, the doors gave way, creaking on ancient hinges as the two friends stumbled backward. For a moment, they gaped at the dark space beyond.

The building, with its broad veranda and ornate facade, had appeared inviting enough from the outside. But a damp must, tinged only with a slight chemical odor, assailed Kai's nostrils as he entered. He froze as something small and black skittered out over his foot, its wiry tail disappearing over the side of the porch. But the other children were pushing in behind him now, the rumble and shuffle of their feet on the worn floorboards sending hollow echoes off the barren walls as they crossed the threshold.

Directly ahead, a set of dark wooden steps led upward into what appeared to be total blackness. Avoiding the stairs, Sela headed right and Kai followed, past beige walls festooned with cobwebs. Ornamental metal fixtures, resembling old electric lights, dangled uselessly from the ceiling overhead.

"What kind of place *was* this?" Kai wondered aloud.

"It looks like an old hotel from one of my vids," Sela whispered. "Or maybe a school?"

The group funneled into a narrow room, dimly lit by the sparse sunlight that sifted through windows abutting the front porch. Its dull green walls were covered with various-sized cabinets and drawers. Kamal's new friend Meg gasped as she opened one of the cabinets to reveal sets of metal dishware. Kai found a drawer full of cooking utensils. Two large steel tubs were attached to the wall with corroded piping.

Beyond this room, they passed through another, still narrower room, this one equipped only with rows of empty shelves. Finally, they found themselves in a large area at the far front corner of the building. Here, long metal tables and folding chairs were interspersed between two rows of stout poles slathered with chipped white paint. Light streamed in from all sides through tall windows.

Suddenly there came a loud booming sound, followed by the thwack of something slicing through the air outside. Instinctively, Kai bolted for the front windows. Through the grimy glass, he could just make out a cadre of bots rolling in loose formation. Another two blasts went off, each originating from somewhere to his left. Across the field, a bot wheeled abruptly to fire into a clump of brush.

"What're they shooting at?" Sela pushed in beside him, wiping the window with the sleeve of her tunic.

"Don't know . . ."

Despite the chill in the room, sweat rose on Kai's neck. He remembered Rosie's words: *A weapon is not to be used except in extreme circumstances. Only when our lives are in danger.* At the window next to his, Kamal's face had gone the color of clay. Craning his neck, Kai took in the tense expressions of their new comrades. He counted twenty-two of them in all—a few more girls than boys; assorted sizes, shapes, and skin tones. From somewhere at the back of the crowd, one child was sobbing softly.

"How long're we gonna be stuck in here?" Sela hissed.

But she didn't have long to wait. As suddenly as it had begun, the shooting stopped. Relieved, Kai turned toward the room. The other children were already pushing back the way they'd come, their progress slowed by the bottleneck at the front door.

Once outside, Kai plunged into the field in search of his Mother. Stumbling aimlessly, he nearly tripped over a small boy who was kneeling to inspect the contents of a bright blue backpack. Pedia-Supp packets, iodine tablets, antivenom, bandages, a canteen, a solar light stick, and a folded plastic cape of some sort littered the ground.

"Hello," the boy said politely, his tousled red hair falling over his eyes as he looked up. "My name is Álvaro. I am happy to meet you!"

"I'm Kai. Say, where'd you get all that stuff?"

"I saw Delta take it from that building over there," the boy replied, pointing to a large white structure across the field.

The building, the supplies—just as the depots in the desert had anticipated their needs, just as the caches of water bottles had appeared magically along the desert roadsides, someone seemed to have planned for their arrival here. Kai scanned the field for evidence of the mysterious stranger. But he saw only the crowd of eager children and their Mothers.

Finally, he spotted the bright yellow mark on Rosie's wing. Standing near the wide door to the supply building, she handed him his own pack. He climbed her treads and pulled open the hatch door. But her console was dark, the air in the cocoon already musty and cold. He could barely make out the empty water bottles in the hold behind his seat, the crumpled blanket he'd left on the floor. "Rosie, is something wrong?"

From close by, he heard a piercing cry. "Mama?" Turning, he saw Sela stomp her foot on the ground, tears spurting from her eyes. Kamal, his head down, held his palm gently against the dark flank of his Mother.

"Kai," Sela cried, "Alpha shut down her cocoon! And she won't tell me why!"

THAT NIGHT, KAI arranged his blanket on the cold floor of Building 100. He'd spent the afternoon getting to know everyone. They were all confused, all frightened. No one knew why they were here, and their Mothers offered no clue. But they were all together now—excited, expectant.

"Tomorrow," Sela whispered, "we'll find ourselves proper rooms. I snuck up those stairs by the front door. There's a bunch of little rooms up there. And we'll make a proper dinner too."

From across the room, he heard Zak's voice. "My Mother shot a deer. She probably thought it was a predator, but those deer things are edible. Tomorrow, we'll go hunting! No more Pedia-Supp . . ." With a grunt, the boy turned over, bunching his bedding around his body so that only his spiky hair jutted out. Beside Zak, the friend he'd awaited, a raven-haired girl named Chloe, lay staring at the ceiling.

Following suit, Kai flattened his back against the hard wood. He pulled his blanket tight around his shoulders, missing Rosie's cramped cocoon. This room was much too big—its walls, its ceiling, its windows . . . all were too far away. And though he was glad to have found them, the snores of his comrades were a poor replacement for the soothing hum of his Mother's processors.

"Rosie?" He thought it as hard as he could.

But there was no answer. She was silent—just as she had been ever since they'd arrived in this strange place. Tomorrow. Maybe tomorrow, Rosie would come back for real. He turned on his side, his head sinking slowly into the pillow of his arm.

29

MISHA WANDERED DOWN the long hospital corridor, heading for the one computer that was linked to Los Alamos. On hot afternoons when the sun baked Uncle William's cornfields, she'd taken to curling up in the cool lobby of the Hopi medical center, studying the bot learning database.

But halfway down the hall she paused at the sound of voices. She tilted her head for better reception. It was Uncle William . . . and Grandmother.

Following the sound, she came to the special room, the one where James now stayed during his rare visits here. She peered through the sealed glass doors. Rick was propped on a cot at the center of the room. His face, shaved clean, was paler than she remembered. William stood at the small window, and Grandmother sat perched on a chair in the far corner, just as she had on that day when Sara had died.

"So, the Mothers have left the desert. The scouts saw them taking off," Rick said hoarsely. "But do we know how many of them made it to the Presidio?"

Instinctively, Misha stood to one side of the door, just out of their line of sight. She tuned her ears to make out their voices above the steady drone of the room's air filtration system.

"We'll have to get some sort of aerial view," William replied. "Have we figured out how to use the satellite for surveillance?"

Rick sighed. "It had limited capabilities for surveillance within the continental U.S. Lord knows we've tried to gain access to that—it would've been a great asset in the desert. But the spy guys in D.C. were the only ones who ever had that clearance." There was a pause. "Maybe we could use the drone."

"Yes," William replied. "But has Mac managed to repair it?"

"He says it should be good to go," came Rick's raspy voice. "He's cloaked it with metamaterial this time, to shield it from their sensors. Maybe now they won't shoot at it."

"Rick," said Grandmother, "we must find out if Nova is there."

Rick cleared his throat. "Rose was enthralled by Nova's story," he said. "But the fact that she saw fit to instill your daughter's personality into not only one but two of the Mothers . . . Your daughter must have been an impressive woman."

"It's sad that one of them crashed . . ." William said.

"And that we didn't even know her when we found her," Rick agreed. "We didn't make the connection between Alpha-B and Nova until Kendra found that file. They seem to have used Nova's air force squadron designation to form her bot name."

"We must count our blessings," said Grandmother. "This wonderful news, that little Misha is Nova's daughter . . . Misha is of our family, William! I felt it the first moment I saw her."

Blood pumped hard in Misha's ears, almost drowning out the voices on the other side of the door. Nova? She raised her hand to feel the delicate necklace around her neck, its pendant in the shape of a silver woman with wings like those of a bird. Grandmother had given it to her just the day before. She'd said something about it once belonging to her daughter, someone who had died even before the Epidemic, someone named Nova . . . Was this why Grandmother had wanted her to have it?

Her mind raced. After her secret encounter with the Mother at the Grand Staircase, she'd made a point of pestering Kendra for more information. The Mothers had personalities inside of them, Kendra said, or at least codes based on the personalities of real women. And these real women were the biological mothers of the children that they carried. But the real human mothers were all gone now, dead since the time of the Epidemic.

"You're sure my biological mother is dead?" Misha had asked.

Kendra had blushed deeply. "Yes, honey. I'm afraid she is."

"What was her name?"

"Her name? Uh . . . We don't know, Misha. We only know her bot's insignia—Alpha-B . . ."

Now, William's voice sounded from behind the door. "So the other Nova, the one we're still looking for, is called Alpha-C?"

"Yes," Grandmother said. "Misha might have a brother or sister. I understand why James doesn't want us to tell her until we're sure, but perhaps when you return . . ."

Out in the hall, Misha felt her legs go weak. She sank down against the wall, wrapping her arms around her knees, waiting for more.

"And Kai," William said. "We need to find him too." His voice grew louder, and Misha imagined him turning from the window. "So, what's the plan?"

"We shouldn't wait too long," Rick said. "Edison says I'll be good to go if I can get through the night in one piece." He breathed deeply, then let out a strong cough. There was a short pause before he continued, his voice almost inaudible. "Mac can bring us the drone tomorrow afternoon. If all goes well, we can leave for the Presidio at dawn the next day."

Misha heard footsteps approaching the door. She got to her feet, her legs wobbling as she scampered down the hall to the computer. Presidio. Where was that? She'd have to find out.

30

ENSCONCED IN THE cabinet-like rear hold of Rick's transport, Misha clutched the pack containing her sparse supplies—a blanket, a light jacket, a canteen, three slabs of Hopi flatbread. The air close around her, her legs cramped against the back wall, she prayed that they'd land soon. She'd had no idea it would be such a long trip . . .

But at last, she felt the thud of the wheels beneath her. She held her breath. The transport's side door opened, and something scraped along the floor, close outside her compartment.

Counting off the minutes of ensuing silence, she slowly cracked open the door of the hold, breathing deep the fresher air of the cabin. Soon she heard the whine of the drone engine, very loud at first, then receding into the distance.

"Okay." It was Rick. "There's Building 100." There followed more conversation, about the bots, about some kids walking along a beach. The two men seemed pleased with their success. And then . . .

"That's her! Alpha-C!" Uncle William cried.

"And there's Kai," Rick said, his voice cracking. "He looks fine."

Alpha-C. Misha smiled. She crept out from the hold, into the rear of the transport, her legs tingling as the blood flowed back into them. She snatched a satellite phone from the back of the passenger seat in front of her and stashed it inside her pack. Then she peered out the side window to get her bearings.

They'd landed on a roof of some sort. Watching the two men from behind as they crouched over the drone's control console, she slipped from the transport and crept behind a nearby chimney. There, holding her knees tight to her chest, she waited for them to finish their work. And as they soared away, leaving her there alone, she began her tortuous descent down a long metal ladder to the ground.

KAI BROKE INTO a trot, doing his best to keep up with Zak as the trail skirted the northern tip of their new home. To his right and down a treacherous hillside was the bay, its roiling waters washing in from the sea. To his left was an upward slope, covered with sparse vegetation.

After the comparative silence of the desert, it had taken him a few days to get used to all the noise here. He didn't know what was stranger to him—the dense woods with their towering trees, creaking in the wind, or these rocky cliffs overlooking an unending ocean. But at least their expedition had been a success. Zak's backpack was filled with dead tree squirrels. Kai's own pack bulged with the strange white birds that Chloe had managed to shoot from their perches. Behind him Chloe trudged along, their makeshift slingshots strapped to her belt and a bag of rocks slung over her shoulder. And somewhere behind her, Álvaro lugged a sack full of greens, some fat brown pine cones harvested from a fallen branch, and wild berries of all shapes and sizes.

Zak, the self-appointed leader on these foraging missions, was intent on scouting the whole promontory. So far, Kai had seen no reason to question the boy's authority—though he'd soon realized that Sela wanted no part of it; Zak's temper, it seemed, was all too easily aroused if anyone challenged his leadership.

Their path joined a paved road, where they crossed under the shadow of the bridge. But soon they found their way blocked by a high fence, running clear out to the edge of a cliff on the other side.

"Let's check up there," Zak called back. As usual, the boy didn't wait for an answer. Clinging to prickly brush that threatened to leave its moorings at every pull, Kai followed him to the left and up the steep embankment. At the top, he scrabbled over a low cement wall to reach a wide paved road.

Soon, they all stood facing the bridge. High above them, its rust-colored towers reached toward a bright blue sky. To their backs was a bank of locked metal gates, spanning half of the road. And in front of them, barring entry to the bridge, was an impenetrable wall of debris—tree trunks, scrap metal, and an assortment of what looked like discarded truck parts.

Reaching into his pack, Kai retrieved his old binoculars. Rosie had powered down her hatch screen. But with help from Álvaro, the little boy who seemed to know everything about computers, he'd removed his tablet from her console and learned to conduct his own searches of her learning database. He'd easily located the place where they now lived—near the old city of San Francisco on the west coast of the United States. There was plenty of water, plenty of game and plants to eat. It made sense that their Mothers had brought them here—away from the drought, away from the dust that had threatened to choke them. And together with one another.

But something wasn't right. Their Mothers had changed. They remained silent. And based on their behavior, it seemed that a threat lurked here, one that had them constantly on alert.

Squinting through the binoculars, he could just make out the high chain-link barrier whose barbed ramparts ran the entire length of the road east of the faraway white dome. According to Zak, this eastern fence turned west to skirt a large wooded area. To the west, it again curved north along the coast, flanking the seaward lane of the paved road where they now stood. Kai had determined that the land encompassed by this fence must be what was left of a former army base called the Presidio. But in the maps from Rosie's database, he couldn't find anything that looked like a fence; this one must have been built later. When they'd first arrived here, there had still been a few openings along its length. But their Mothers had soon barricaded all the gates along the eastern side of the Presidio, as well as this end of the majestic bridge that spanned the Golden Gate.

He pointed up at the barrier. "What's the good of all this, anyway?"

"You know as well as I do," Zak replied. "We need protection. The enemy might be over there."

"Listen," Kai said. He was surprised by his own annoyance as he turned on the boy. "I can see out on that bridge. I can see all along the coast on the other side. There's no one there. I just don't understand all this stuff about enemies."

"They're out there. They're just good at hiding," Zak said. "Like they did in the desert."

Kai clenched his fists in frustration. "Look. You say you saw something in the desert. But I never did. Sela never did. And she went *everywhere.*"

"Are you saying I'm lying?" The burly boy dropped his pack, his thick neck and shoulders heaving. Beside him, Chloe clutched his arm in a feeble attempt to calm him.

Kai stared at the boy. "You saw what you saw. And Chloe did too. But if there's someone out there, there can't be many of them. We've kept a lookout. We haven't seen anything more threatening than a few wild dogs. Rosie could take those out, no problem."

"So, what do *you* think is going on?" Zak had his hands on his hips now, his lips set in a thin line.

"I think . . . I think something's wrong with our Mothers."

"Like what?"

"You know, how they shut down when we got here? How ever since then, they've been different? They turned off our cocoons. They started shooting at everything in sight. And they built up these barricades . . ." Exasperated, Kai waved his arm at the wall of junk. "They never used to be like this out in the desert. At least Rosie wasn't. Now she doesn't talk to me at all. I haven't even *seen* her today . . ."

"I have a theory," Álvaro said, his voice barely audible over the wind.

"What's that?" Zak asked.

"It is possible that our Mothers have been reprogrammed . . ."

"Reprogrammed?" Kai asked.

"I have always loved my Mother," Álvaro said. "But at the same time, I know that her brain is not like mine. Her brain is a computer, and computers can be programmed. It is possible that someone has gained control over our Mothers. Someone has reprogrammed them to bring us here. And to keep us here."

"I don't believe that," Zak said. "Gamma's too strong. If someone tried to change her, she'd fight back."

Kai scanned the far ridgeline. Someone out there, controlling Rosie? He didn't buy it either. He couldn't.

IN A WIDE, paved lot under a sign announcing the "VA Medical Center," Misha flipped on her satellite map. She was about one and a half miles outside the Presidio. To get there, she'd need to follow a road called "El Camino Del Mar." This would take her to "Lincoln Boulevard," the thoroughfare leading directly into the Presidio from the south.

She kept her eyes straight ahead, ignoring the empty vehicles and vacant windows walling the roadway. She'd never been in a place like this, a city crowded with multicolored buildings nudged one against the other—all gated, all numbered. She knew she had nothing to fear: Mama and Daddy had come from California, they'd once told her. It had been a wonderful place, but now there was no one left. Still she flinched at every sound, the metallic ping of a street sign striking its pole in the wind, the caw of a large black bird, sitting high on a rooftop.

She picked up her pace. There it was, just ahead. But when she finally reached the sign reading "Lincoln Boulevard," she found her way barred by a high chain-link fence, its top looped with stiff barbed wire. She knew the pain of that wire, the same nasty stuff William used to keep his sheep from wandering off, and to keep coyotes from wandering in. The fence didn't just block the road; it ran off to the east and west, as far as she could see.

She headed west, searching for what her map told her would be the "California Coastal Trail." And though rutted by wind and weather, the trail was still there, its way along the coast unimpeded as it skirted the high fence. As she hiked north, dense sand crumbled between her toes. To her left, ocean waves struck the shore of a wide beach, white foam announcing their arrival. A strange, unfamiliar mist dampened her hair. She shivered. She couldn't imagine a place more different from the mesas.

The trail curved away from the beach, veering upward through a copse of trees. And soon she was once more level with Lincoln Boulevard. It was right there. But the high fence, now skirting the road, still barred entry. Was there no gate, no place where she could cross to the other side?

Then she saw it. At a spot where the trail had been scoured by rains, a small hollow had formed under the fence. She found a thick branch. Using it as a hoe, she raked aside dead leaves and tore at the hollow until it was just big enough to crawl through. She pushed her pack through first, then followed headfirst on her stomach, squirming like a snake to the other side. Getting to her feet, she brushed the dirt from her clothing and arms. From overhead, she sensed a strange buzzing noise, something like giant hummingbirds hunting in the treetops. It was the Mothers—she was sure of it. She was close. According to her map, this road would eventually curve east. If she stuck to it, she was bound to come upon someone.

Sure enough, up ahead the boulevard curved right to cut under another, much wider road . . . and she heard something—voices, carried on the wind. Stashing the satellite phone back into her pack, she climbed up an embankment to reach the higher road. There she gathered her nerve for the approach, silently rehearsing the speech she'd planned.

TURNING AWAY FROM the bridge, Kai caught sight of something, someone, approaching along the road from behind the metal gates. "Who's that?" he said.

They all watched as a thin, dark form approached. It looked like a girl, someone Kai had never seen before. She made her way carefully around the gates. Arranging her pack across her shoulders, she approached them timidly at first, then with resolution.

"Thank goodness," she gasped, coming to a halt in front of them. "You're here! My Mother said you would be. But I didn't believe her."

The girl's long, dark hair was pulled neatly behind her ears, secured into a loose braid by a length of twine. Despite the cold, her feet were bare. She wore only a simple sack of a dress, a belt made of colorful beads cinching it in at the waist. Black leggings covered her legs down to the ankles. Her eyes flashed a brilliant green as she appraised them.

"Hello?" Zak said, taking a step back.

Kai stood transfixed. Who *was* this?

"My name is Misha," the girl said. One by one, they shook her hand. Smooth and tanned, her arms were thin. But her grip was strong.

"How . . . how did you get in here?" Chloe asked.

"*In* here? Aren't we outside?" said the girl.

"She means inside the fence," Kai said.

"Fence?"

"There is a fence all around this place," Álvaro explained patiently. "None of us can cross it. But here you are . . ."

"I don't know what you mean . . ." And with that, the girl began to cry.

"What's wrong?" Kai asked, stepping forward to touch her arm. "What happened?"

"She's gone," the girl sobbed. "My Mother just *left* me here!"

31

IN A SPACIOUS room that he called the "dining room," Kai ushered Misha to a chair. "We figured this was a room for eating," he said. "It's right next to what used to be a kitchen, and we can store food on those shelves." As he pointed toward the narrow anteroom, a crowd of other children filed through the door. First came the children Misha had already met: the thickly muscled boy with sand-colored hair named Zak, the tall, black-haired girl named Chloe, and the small, redheaded boy named Álvaro. Behind them was a ragtag assortment of others.

"That's Hiro," Kai said, pointing to a stocky boy with almond-shaped eyes. "He's good at cooking. And Clara," he added, nodding to a wiry, black-skinned girl who had come armed with a bucket and a small trowel. "She's starting a garden."

But Misha's gaze was focused on the girl with straight brown hair and a friendly smile who had plopped down across from her, planting her elbows on the table. "Misha, this is Sela," Kai said.

"That's a nice necklace," Sela said.

Misha's hand rose to her neck, her fingers brushing the silver necklace that Grandmother had given her. "I found it . . ."

"I have one too, a blue one. But it's not nearly as nice as yours," Sela said. "Yours looks like one of our Mothers."

Misha watched the girl's inquisitive brown eyes. "I thought so too," she murmured.

"Kai told me your Mother just *left* you?" Sela asked. "She just flew away?"

"There was something wrong with her. But at least she got me here." Misha glanced nervously toward the far end of the table. There Zak, his arms crossed in front of him, stood glaring at her. Chloe, her glossy hair almost hiding her face, rested her hand reassuringly on his shoulder. And suddenly Misha remembered. The gorge. The black-haired girl. She'd seen Chloe before. In her mind she heard Uncle William's voice: . . . *we must understand. The Mother Spirits are only protecting their children. They can't know that we mean them no harm.* She knew she was one of these children. But she was also something else, a bridge between their world and a world outside that they might be slow to accept.

"Wow," Kai said. "Your Mother left you . . . And I thought *we* had it bad."

"Bad? But I thought you were safe . . ."

"We *are* safe," Sela said. "But we can't leave this place. We can't get outside that awful fence. We're stuck. My Mother used to tell me that flying was the most wonderful thing a person could do. Now she won't even let me sit inside my own cocoon . . ."

An uneasy feeling rose in the pit of Misha's stomach. "But why are you 'stuck'? Why can't you just leave?"

"Our Mothers have locked us in. Zak thinks they're guarding us against an enemy outside," Kai said. "What do *you* think? Did *you* see anything out there?"

"No . . . Nothing like that . . ."

"See?" Kai turned to Zak and Chloe.

Chloe stepped forward, casting a derisive look at Kai. "We saw someone when we were in the desert," she said. "They drove around in trucks. Then they came back in a flying machine with propellers. My Mother shot at them, but they got away. Meg saw something too. Right, Meg?"

"I'm not sure . . ." The small girl with curly blond hair who had taken a seat next to Sela spoke softly. "It was dark. I thought I saw lights . . . And I heard something . . . rumbling."

"Poor Meg was alone for all that time," Sela said, wrapping her arm around the timid girl's shoulders. "But it's okay. We're together now." Beside her, Meg stared down at her lap.

"I understand," Misha said. "I was alone too. But now . . ." Strangely, she felt tears springing to her eyes. It *was* wonderful to meet them. But already she was beginning to realize how little she knew about them.

"Dinner's not ready yet . . . But we found rooms on the second floor," Kai offered. "There are plenty left. You can take one for yourself if you want."

Misha stood up, her legs shaky. It had been a long day—the hiking, the uncertainty, and in the end, the discovery. She had thinking to do. She shouldered her pack and followed Kai and Sela up the dark stairs.

Spotting a room at the front corner, she stopped. "Here would be fine," she said.

"Are you sure it's big enough?" Sela asked. "Meg and I have plenty of space in our room . . ."

"Oh, no!" Misha said, then looked down at the floor. "I'm used to sleeping alone, I guess."

"But not without your Mother," Sela said. "It's hard at first."

There was an awkward pause before the pair turned to go. "See you later, then," Kai said. "There're some supplies in the shed across the field, if you need them."

The room was no larger than one of the utility closets at Los

Alamos. But it had a window and enough floor space for sleeping. Misha extracted her blanket from her pack. Wrapping it around her, she remembered the comfort of Grandmother's kiva, the sound of her song. As her spine settled against the wall, her hand drifted up to touch the silver necklace. She supposed it was a part of her now—she'd forgotten it was even there. She whispered the names of the children she'd met, picturing each one's face in turn. Zak. Chloe. Kai . . . his was a name that William had said two days ago. Rick had repeated it this morning, on the roof. How did they know Kai?

Once more, she checked her satellite phone. No calls. For all Uncle William and Aunt Loretta knew, she was out camping with Bert and Honovi. If all went well, they wouldn't discover that she was missing until late tomorrow. She'd been sure that by then, she'd have good news. But now, she wondered.

She closed her eyes, forcing herself to concentrate. She'd come with a mission: to find her own brother or sister. And something more. She'd imagined herself the messenger, the one who would return Grandmother's Silver Spirits to the mesas. But how? If Grandfather's prophecy was ever to be fulfilled, the Mothers would have to leave here. But Sela had said that the children could no longer ride in their cocoons. Perhaps that meant that the Mothers would have to leave alone . . . But how could they leave their children if that meant abandoning their duty to protect them from the mysterious "enemy" that lurked outside the fence? For the prophecy to come true, would something have to happen to the children? She shuddered.

Suddenly the door cracked open. "Misha? It's Kai. Can I come in?"

She started. "Yes, okay . . ."

"I thought you might be hungry." Kai stepped into the room, carrying a small bowl of something that smelled faintly like the bay laurel at Los Alamos. "It's Hiro's squirrel stew," he said. "I really like it. But I should warn you, not everyone does."

Misha dug the spoon that Kai offered into the bowl of stew, then touched it to her tongue. It tasted bitter, gamey. But it was satisfying enough.

Kai grinned. "It's not the best thing we make. Sela's fish is the best."

"Fish? Where does she get them?"

"Off the pier. She learned how from Alpha's database."

"Who?"

"Alpha-C. Her Mother."

Misha stared at him. Alpha-C . . . She pictured Sela, the girl with the straight brown hair—like hers. Sela's eyes, like Grandmother's. Her flat nose and rounded chin, like Uncle William's . . .

"What was *your* Mother's name?" Kai asked.

"Huh . . . ?"

"My Mother's name is Rho-Z. But I call her Rosie. What was yours?"

"Uh . . ." Misha felt the heat blooming up her neck to her ears. Sela's was the only name she could think of. But then she remembered. "Alpha-B . . ."

"Alpha-B? Almost like Sela's!"

"I guess," Misha said, grinning sheepishly.

Kai looked down at his hands, fidgeting with a scratch on his thumb. "I wanted to tell you," he said. "Your Mother? Don't worry. She'll be back."

Misha watched the boy carefully. "Why do you think that?"

"One time when I was little, Rosie left me to chase after a coyote. I was really scared. But she came back. They always do." Kai looked out the window, his brow furrowed. "Our Mothers . . . whatever happens, they have to protect us."

Misha stared at him. He was worried about something. "Kai, I'm not sure my Mother's coming back . . ."

Kai met her gaze. "But . . . she has to!" he said, a bit too loud. His face reddening, he returned his attention to his injured thumb. "Well . . . we'll see. Anyway, you've got us now."

"Yes. I've got you." Misha's lips held a smile. But unwelcome seeds of doubt had already taken root in her mind. Kendra had called the Mothers and their children here to save them. But something else had changed since their arrival—something that had them all on edge.

32

STANDING ON THE front porch of Building 100 in the morning fog, Misha watched Sela disappear into a large white building across the field. Mustering her courage, she slipped past two bots stationed near the base of the steps and picked her way through the tall grass.

As she approached the building, she heard a crashing sound from somewhere along the back wall. "Ouch!" Something that looked like an old baseball bat sailed through the air, landing at her feet. It was followed closely by a leather ball. "It's got to be here somewhere . . ."

Misha felt the welcome warmth of familiarity. "Sela?" she called. "Is that you?"

"Who's that?"

"It's Misha. What're you looking for?"

"Chloe said she saw a motorbike in here, but it's so dark I can't see a thing!"

"Here." Crouching down, Misha pulled a solar light stick from a box near the door. She offered it into the gloom, and a thin arm reached out to grab it.

"Thanks!" Sela switched on the light stick, and the murky walls of the shed lit up, exposing a sea of cobwebs. "I had a dirt bike in the desert. But we had to leave it behind. It wouldn't fit in the hold . . . Ah!" What looked like a thick tire, then a pedal, emerged from the shadows as her beam scanned the farthest corner. "It looks more like an old electric bicycle," she said, dragging it out into view. "But it's better than nothing."

"What are you planning to do with it?"

Sela turned to look at her, dumbfounded. "Ride it, of course!"

"I meant, where are you going to ride it?"

Sela seemed at a loss, but only for a moment. "This place isn't that big. But it's big enough. I'm sure there are parts of it I haven't seen yet. And Kai's fixing up a boat we found by the eastern fence. Tomorrow we'll go out in the bay."

Misha steeled herself. She needed to take advantage of this moment, if only to gauge her sister's reaction. "Sela, do you really want to go outside the fence?" she asked.

A cloud passed over Sela's features. "I know our Mothers don't want us to. But this place—it feels like a prison."

"A prison?"

"Like a big, beautiful prison, with everything you could possibly want." Sela frowned. "But not everything you need."

"I think . . ." Misha ventured, "we just need to test our limits."

"Test?"

"Push a little. At least ask why we can't leave."

Sela stared at her. "You think I haven't asked my Mother every day since we got here? But I'm not getting an answer."

"You're not?"

Sela brushed the hair from her eyes, and Misha blushed at her honest appraisal. "As if things aren't bad enough, Alpha isn't talking to me anymore."

"I notice they're all very quiet," Misha said.

"I mean, in my head. She's not there anymore."

"Oh . . ."

Sela's brow furrowed as she scanned the field. "I don't even know where she is right now. Did your Mother do that . . . before she left? Did she stop talking to you?"

Misha kneaded her palms, trying to think of the right thing to say. She had no idea what Sela was talking about. "No," she decided. "No, she talked to me right up to the end. This must be something else . . ."

Sela seemed relieved. "Álvaro thinks it might just be temporary, something our Mothers can fix." Propping the bike by the door, she turned to Misha. "But even if they do start talking again, it seems like we're stuck."

Misha swallowed, gathering her nerve. "If you want to leave the Presidio—I know a way, I think. Near where . . . where my Mother dropped me off. I noticed a kind of hole under the fence."

Sela stared at her quizzically. "A hole?"

"Like the ground had been worn away there. I think it's big enough for us to try and get out . . ."

Sela's brow creased. But then she grinned. "Okay. It wouldn't hurt to look."

They took the bike to a charging station by the back door of Building 100. Then Misha led the way down a paved road, toward the spot along Lincoln Boulevard where she'd found the gap beneath the fence. Sela was right—it *was* beautiful here, the trees rustling high above in the cool wind, colorful little birds chasing each other through their branches. And her sister, skipping along beside her.

"So, what's on the other side of this hole in the fence?" Sela asked.

"It's a trail. I think it goes all the way to the south and lets out into the city."

Sela's eyes grew wide. "The city?"

"You don't want to go?"

But Sela only smiled. "'Course I do. We can just go a little ways. Then, if we don't see anything bad out there, or even if we do, we can come back and tell the others."

Misha nodded. "Sounds like a plan." She wasn't at all sure that she *had* a plan. She was only intent on getting her sister outside the Presidio, on showing her it was safe. It wasn't much, but it was a start. All night, she'd dreamed of taking her sister home, of showing her the mesas. This would be just the first of their adventures together.

Spotting the indentation under the fence, she stopped. "I'll go first," she volunteered, clearing some fallen dirt away from the hollow and slipping under the fence feetfirst. She wriggled down, then out onto the trail. It was easier going than when she had come in.

Looking left and right, Sela sat down on the edge of the pavement. She placed her palms to either side of her on the ground and straightened her legs in front of her, preparing to push off, to slide her bottom under the fence. But suddenly a horrible din arose from the sky. The earth shook as Alpha-C landed on the road, and in that moment Misha remembered Chloe's Mother, the one she'd encountered in the desert. With surprising speed, Alpha-C grasped Sela under her arms, snatched her upright, and placed her solidly back on the hard pavement.

"Ow!" Sela cried. She rubbed her shoulders with both hands. "Mama!" she yelled. "You don't have to hurt me! You could just *tell* me if you don't want . . ." Suddenly she was crying, tears streaming down her face.

Misha slipped back under the fence, ran toward Sela, wrapped her arms around her shoulders. "I'm so sorry," she murmured. She dug her nose into Sela's neck, longing to tell her that they shared a mother, longing to tell her that everything would be okay.

But Sela pulled away, wheeling on her Mother. "Why won't you just *talk* to me?" she cried. "Why can't you just listen?"

THE TWO GIRLS trudged back to Building 100 in silence, Alpha-C trundling noisily behind them. But as they reached the porch, Sela turned to her. "I wish I was like you," she said. "I wish I didn't have a Mother."

Misha stared at her. "Don't say that!" she said. "You know that's not what you want . . ."

But Sela, staring at her Mother now, didn't answer.

Alone, Misha entered the building and made her way up the stairs. As she neared her little room, she could hear a persistent buzzing sound, coming from under her blanket—the satellite phone. Her blood went cold. She raced inside and closed the door behind her. Hastily, she yanked the phone to her ear and pressed the "call" button. "Hello?" she murmured.

"Misha!" It was Uncle William. "Thank God! Where on earth *are* you? We traced the missing phone to the Presidio, but . . ."

Misha looked around the room, barely lit by the thin light sifting through the grimy window. She was lost. She had no idea how to get the children out of here, let alone how to bring the Silver Spirits home. She realized now—she knew nothing about them at all. "I'm sorry," she said. "I heard you talking in the hospital. I hid in the transport. I thought for sure I could help. But now . . . I'm not sure."

33

"*GONE?* YOU'RE TELLING me Misha is *at the Presidio?*" In the Hopi hospital room, James sat down hard on Grandmother's little chair, almost tipping it. Beside him, Mac let out a long, low whistle. William stood near the doorway, monitoring the conversation from a safe distance.

Propped upright in the cot at the center of the room, Rick fumbled a clean white cloth up from his bedside table and held it briefly to his mouth. "She stowed away. We never saw her . . ."

James sighed. It was difficult to look at Rick now, his skin ashen, his once brawny arms wasted away, and still be angry with him. He slouched back in his seat, remembering his own father's soft voice: *Every child has a right to know where he comes from.* Perhaps it wasn't Rick's fault at all, or William's. Perhaps history had repeated itself. As his own father had failed him, he'd failed Misha. She needed guidance. She needed connection. In her effort to find her own identity, and with no help from him, she'd struck out on her own, her head full of wild ideas.

He lowered his face into the bowl of his hands, rubbing his eyes with the tips of his fingers. "She found out? About her being Hopi? About having a sibling—"

"She heard us talking," Rick mumbled. "First here. Then while we were flying the drone."

"She'd make quite the spy," Mac said.

James winced. Misha was only eleven years old. At that age he'd been going to school, shagging baseballs with his friends, scarfing down his mother's lentils and rice. Though his parents had never been entirely truthful with him, they'd at least provided a sense of stability, a sense of belonging. "We need to get her back," he said.

"She said there's an opening under the fence, over along the Coastal Trail. I told her I could pick her up, if she could just come back the way she went," William offered.

"Misha will be okay," Rick choked out. "She's a smart kid." He struggled to look up, to make eye contact with James. And it was only then that James noticed the tears that wet the man's face. "Did William tell you? Misha met my son. I wanted so much to see him. Just once, up close. I want to touch him, to tell him how much . . ."

Rick stopped short, a weak cough bubbling up from his throat. A line of blood trickled from his mouth onto his stained hospital smock. And James realized: Rick would never have what he'd had—a time, however brief, together with a beloved, together with their child. He conjured up his image of Misha, the girl who reminded him so much of Sara that it hurt. Her long, nut-brown hair smelled of yucca root, her skin of something earthy and alive. She'd had to dance in jets of filtered air for minutes on end, shower and change into stiff plastic smocks, just to spend time with him. But she'd remained the one true thing in his life, his one connection to the world outside. "I'll go," he said.

William placed his hand on James's shoulder. "No, you stay here. We need you to keep up with the antidote. And besides, it's my fault. I'll take care of it."

"I'll come too," Mac said. "And we'll take the drone. Just in case."

34

LEANING INTO THE chill onshore wind and pulling his jacket close around his neck, Kai headed toward the bay. He turned left along the beach and skirted a wide marsh. Ahead he could see Sela, already at her station on the old pier.

With rolls of nylon line, a box of hooks, and three poles she'd found in a shed at the base of the pier, Sela had set up a fishing operation. Though she'd never cared for the small game they'd caught in the desert and she ate little if any of the fish that she caught here, she liked the sport of it, the reward of feeding the others. She'd quickly learned to fish off the pier. But today would be different. They'd retrieved a small green boat that had drifted from a marina just outside the fence. And today the boat was at the ready, secured to the rusted metal railing at the side of the pier by a stout length of rope.

"You got your gear?" Kai called out.

"Already on board," Sela replied. She swung between two guardrails and began the climb down a short rope ladder to the boat. "Come on, let's get going while the sun's still at a slant. You catch better when the fish can't see you."

The boat lurched as Kai followed suit. Sitting there in shallow water as he'd checked it for leaks the previous afternoon, the little craft had seemed like such an excellent idea. But as it bobbed uncontrollably in the deep waves next to the pier, he wondered about his judgment. He breathed deep, remembering Sela's admonition. They'd never get anywhere if they were too afraid to try new things.

Sela untied the boat and grabbed an oar up from the floor. Well, not really an oar—just a shovel-shaped hunk of driftwood. With gusto she paddled away from the pier, waiting out the waves that threatened to push them landward. Oarless, all Kai could do was sit there, holding on to the sides of the boat and willing his stomach to stay quiet.

About fifty feet from shore, Sela at last dropped the oar. With a flick of her wrist, she cast her line out over the prow. "If this works," she said, "we should try going a little farther out each day, see how far our Mothers will let us go."

Kai looked up at the sky, at the V of a flock of the giant birds that Rosie's database called pelicans, scudding down to scoop up their prey. Along the shore, he could see the spot where a little river met the bay—the spot where Hiro had taken him hunting for crabs on their second day here. Now, three bots were standing there together, no children in sight.

"Sela, do you think our Mothers talk to each other?"

She turned to him, her eyebrows raised. "Why would you think that?"

"Kamal said he had a dream, where Beta told him that she's learning. But learning from who? Whenever I see them now, they're close together in clumps like that. They follow each other, do things together. It's strange. Maybe they're teaching each other things."

Sela shook her head. "Alpha never talked to another bot before," she said. "She told me she couldn't. And now she doesn't even talk to *me* . . ." She turned back to the front of the boat. "I'm just not sure I trust Alpha anymore."

Suddenly she had a tug on her line. She yanked back, working to reel in her first catch. Landing at last next to her oar, the plump beast thrashed with a purpose, its scales stuck to the metal floor of the boat and its mouth gulping air. Gingerly, Kai picked it up. Blood gushed from the translucent flesh where the hook had cut through just behind the gill. Its sharp fins cut into his hand as he tossed it into Sela's cloth sack. He had to remind himself how good it would taste after baking over Hiro's smoky cookfire.

"That was a nice big one!" Sela handed him a second pole. "C'mon," she said, grinning. "As captain of this ship, I order you to pull your weight!"

Kai skewered a small bait fish from Sela's bucket with his hook. Awkwardly, he side-wound his line out over the water, the baited hook hovering in the wind for a few seconds before disappearing beneath the waves. Watching the dizzying swells for some sign of activity, he waited.

And waited, the emerging sun scorching the back of his neck.

IN MAC'S LOS Alamos office, James hunched toward the computer screen, his eyes alight in its pale glow. From his station atop the San Francisco VA Medical Center, Mac had launched the drone and set up a satellite connection to its video feed. Together with Kendra and Rudy, James watched the feed as the little drone sifted its way through wisps of fog.

At the Presidio, William was hiking up the trail where he planned to rendezvous with Misha. Though he'd contacted Misha from the transport as soon as he and Mac had landed, she had yet to attempt her escape. In fact, there'd been no word from her since his call.

"Any sign?" James asked over the speakerphone.

"Nope," Mac said, his voice muffled by his mask. For the third time, the drone camera scanned the distance up the Coastal Trail and along the paved boulevard running parallel to it. James could see the jagged, barbed line of the fence separating the two. At one point, the video zoomed in on a heap of debris piled next to the fence.

"What's that?" James asked.

"Dunno," Mac said. "A stack of metal sheeting? Maybe they blocked it off . . ."

"Blocked it off?"

"Seems like the Mothers have barricaded all the openings in the fence. Maybe they got that one too . . . It's right about where she said the hole was . . ."

The camera panned east, out over Fort Winfield Scott, over the white stone markers of the old cemetery, finally circling the former Main Post field. There were bots scattered along the beach, most of them stationary. "What's that?" James asked as the drone swung out over the water.

"Looks like . . . a boat."

"GEEZ," SELA SAID. "I don't know why, but the fishing out here is slower than off the pier. Maybe we should go farther out."

"Or back . . ." Kai said. He squinted back at the shore. They'd drifted considerably from their original position. Now, the shimmer of the little river was barely visible.

Then he felt a tug, a staccato of sharp pulls. "Got one!" he called. But Sela, busy checking her own line, paid him no attention. "It's a big one!" He was yanked to his feet, his pole arcing violently. He tried to steady himself, digging in his heels as the thing pulled him danger- ously close to the side of the boat.

Suddenly the line went slack. Imagining another lost hook, Kai leaned forward, trying to catch a glimpse of the one that got away. But even as he did, there came a mighty jolt. He grabbed the pole hard with both hands and leaned back.

Without warning, the line snapped. Kai fell backward, landing hard on the opposite edge of the narrow boat. His arms cartwheeled at his sides as he tried to regain his balance. But it was too late.

THE DRONE VIDEO wavered. "Hell . . ." Mac muttered over the phone. "Two bots headed this way. I don't know how, but I think they see the drone . . ."

James watched as the video pulled out, the camera now slewing toward shore. He caught sight of a bot flying past. Then another. "Are you sure they're after you?" he said. "They seem to be heading out into the bay."

"Best to stay clear," Mac muttered. The drone retraced its path back to the Coastal Trail, the video showing only the tops of trees.

KAI TOPPLED OVERBOARD, his body enveloped in blankets of icy water. He could see only the murk of drifting detritus, hear only his own muffled cries. Salty water choked his throat. His arms weighed down by his now-sodden jacket, he grunted for air, his head back and his nose just barely above the surface.

"Kick! Kick!" He heard Sela's thin voice, calling from somewhere above. But his legs were heavy, tangled in something. Something was dragging him under. Clamping his mouth shut, he reached down to uncoil ropes of seaweed from his legs, kicking in a frenzy. Then, cupping his hands, he pushed down, propelling himself upward. He saw the surface, something snaking down onto the water just above his right arm. Again he heard Sela's voice. "Grab on!" He kicked hard, arms outstretched. With his right hand, then his left, he managed to gain purchase on the rope. At last, he caught sight of a sliver of crystal-blue sky, spinning above him.

But what was that? The water around him was churning now, a maelstrom. He felt himself being sucked under once more, then swept to one side. His head filled with an awful roar. Engines. Bot engines. The boat was yawing, tipping, overturning. He felt something lock under his arms, a pull. He was lifted from the water so quickly that the bones in his neck seemed to crack.

"Sela!" he cried, struggling despite himself. "Sela!"

As Rosie lifted him skyward he saw Alpha-C plummet into the waves. And something else—a thin arm, clinging to her treads as she went down.

THE DRONE CAMERA scanned the length of Lincoln Boulevard one more time, but Misha was nowhere to be found. James's heart fluttered in his chest. He grasped the armrest of his chair, trying desperately to stay calm. "William, any word?"

"Nope," came William's voice. "And I can't find the opening she was talking about either."

"Mac," James said, "I need you to go back and check the bay."

"Will do," Mac muttered.

The video veered north, out over the Golden Gate, then east along the shore. Dark against the brilliant flash of the water, a swarm of bots had congregated in the air over the spot where the little green boat had been. Still more were ranging up and down the beach. "Lots of bots down there now," Mac said. "Gotta stay high."

As the drone swerved toward shore, James caught sight of the boat. "Capsized . . ." he murmured.

The drone flew along the shoreline, panning and scanning. Now a group of kids had emerged, tiny dots running toward the beach. "Don't want 'em spotting me," Mac said. He guided the drone east, past the fence, outside the perimeter.

Suddenly the video zoomed in on the ground. "Shit," Mac choked.

James could feel Rudy and Kendra leaning in close behind him, their breath caught in their throats as they stared at the screen. The satellite image went blurry, then refocused. And Kendra gasped.

Tangled in seaweed, on the shore well outside the fence, was a small, lifeless body.

THE DRONE HOVERED, circling tentatively as though even it could no longer bear to look. Time passed, minutes like hours. James sank to the floor, hugging his knees. "Why . . . why aren't the bots finding her?" he asked.

Kendra's gaze was still fixed on the screen, her mouth agape. "Not the right shape, I guess," she muttered. "Too . . . cold . . . ?" Tears began to run down her face. And for the first time since James had known her, Kendra broke down. Her head bowed, she sobbed uncontrollably.

"It's okay," Rudy said, patting her shoulder helplessly. "It's okay."

But it wasn't. James could barely quell the fear and rage battling in his chest. This was all his fault . . .

Suddenly they heard something—a small, high voice.

"Hello?"

"Misha?" William's voice boomed over the connection, cracked and nasal.

"My sister's missing," Misha sobbed. "Kai said Alpha-C sank the boat . . . We searched the beach. But we can't find her."

"Misha." James got to his feet. "Honey, this is Daddy." His voice was shaking. His whole body was shaking. "Do you hear me?"

"Yes . . ."

"Why didn't you come to the fence?"

He heard a choked sob. "I did," Misha said. "But they blocked it off!" She sobbed again. "I tried to find another spot, but . . . ."

"Then why didn't you call Uncle William?"

"I was in such a hurry once he called, I left the phone in my room."

Gripping Mac's desk for support, James huddled over the phone, his one lifeline now. "Misha, I love you . . ."

"I love you too," came the soft reply.

James looked at Kendra and Rudy, his eyes clouding with tears. "I promise . . . we'll think of something. One way or another, we'll get you out of there. Just tell us everything, from the beginning."

35

IN THE XO-BOT cafeteria's dim interior, James listlessly stirred a bowl of lamb stew. Across the room, Kendra fiddled with the old coffee machine, her back toward them. Mac, who had returned late the previous night, sat with his hands flat on his thighs, his food untouched. There was more bad news. Early that morning at the Hopi hospital, Rick had lost his final battle.

Kendra turned toward the table, two cups of burned-smelling coffee in hand. Gently, she set one in front of Mac. "He requested a Hopi burial," she said.

With effort James stood up, the muscles of his back sending painful messages to his spine. The general would claim a spot next to Grandfather on the side of the mesa. There, Grandmother said, he would wait for Rose to bring his son back to him. But now the likelihood of that ever coming to pass seemed more remote than ever. Through a long and restless night, he hadn't been able to get Misha's plaintive voice out of his mind.

"How's Rudy doing?" James asked.

Kendra sighed. "He's been better since his last treatment," she said.

"But he still has that nasty lump near his collarbone—they suspect metastasis. I let him sleep in. I just . . . couldn't tell him about Rick." She sat down. Picking up a spoon, she stirred her coffee, watching the creamer slowly dissolve. "The problem seems to be a breakdown in communications," she said.

James turned to her. "What? With Rudy?" But from the determined look on Kendra's face, he could tell that her mind had refocused, something it always seemed to do under pressure.

Kendra looked up at him. "No . . . with the Mothers. I keep thinking about what Misha told us. How the kids have lost communication with their Mothers. How it was one of the first things she learned when she got there."

James leaned down to splay his palms on the table, enduring yet another of the dizzy spells that had begun to plague him. "She said the kids used to talk to their Mothers in their heads?" he asked. "What was that about?"

Kendra took a sip of her coffee, then dabbed at her lips with a napkin. "As you know, the children and their Mothers are attached through their communicators—"

"The biofeedback chips?" James said. He knew about those, an old technology used for remote wellness monitoring. Misha's own bot Mother had installed one, and Edison, in consultation with Sara, had advised against removing it.

"It went beyond biofeedback. The communicator chips are attached to injectable electronics, implanted in the brain."

"*Implanted?*"

"The Mothers were programmed to implant the chips and their associated injectables immediately after birth. The specialists on Dr. McBride's team had years of experience with these in patients with neurodegenerative disorders. Though they're very effective at transmitting biofeedback, they can also receive stimulation."

"Receive?"

"The child's signal is weak, run on power harvested from the movement of his muscles, his digestive tract, his lungs. But the Mother's signal is much stronger, run off power from her reactor. She could send out stimuli, even from a distance."

"So what sorts of 'stimuli' did these bots send out?" James asked.

"A Mother could ping her child without an audible signal, for example. But Misha thinks something else happened too. She thinks they developed more high-level nonverbal communications. A sort of conversation, but without words."

"If that's true, these kids aren't really human at all," Mac grumbled.

"They're as human as you and me. And they shared a connection to their Mothers, just as you and I once did," Kendra said. "But it was different. More direct, I would imagine. Without all the filters that humans, even children, often impose on their communications."

"A kind of telepathy?"

"Maybe. We don't know," Kendra said. "But this sort of intuitive link would have made the bond between the Mother and her child very strong indeed."

James blinked, trying to clear his bleary vision. "Why didn't Misha experience this with her own bot Mother?"

"Her Mother didn't live long enough to form a bond with her. Misha barely made it out of her incubator alive." Kendra shook her head. "Anyway, you heard Misha. The Mothers have no audible voices. And whatever other communications did exist between the kids and their Mothers, those seem to be gone now too."

"Why?"

Kendra brought her hands down on the table, to either side of her now-cold coffee. "I don't know. Some sort of code degradation? I suppose it was inevitable . . . But of all the interactive systems, only the vision systems and the learning database still seem to be functional."

"Does that put the kids in danger?"

Kendra stared down at her coffee. "Based on what Misha told us, the Mothers seem to be reverting to the prime directive."

"Prime directive? What's that?"

"Security. At all costs. Think about it. They've lost their ability to sense their children through biofeedback, to know when they're hungry, thirsty, fearful. They've lost their ability to communicate cautions or instructions. Outside of visual recognition and physical control, they have no way of maintaining their mission."

James sat down heavily, tapping the table with a nervous forefinger. "Which is why they've corralled the kids in Building 100 since the drowning?"

"It might even get to the point that they won't let the kids out of the building at all, even to find food and water."

"But how could they do that?" James asked. "It goes against their requirement not to harm their children . . ."

"Not if they're no longer picking up the biosignals."

Mac clenched his fists. "So, what can we do?"

Heaving a sigh, Kendra looked over at him. "I think it's time we try putting these Mothers to sleep."

James stared at Kendra. "We can do that?"

Kendra drew a deep breath. "I think so. As part of standard procedure after the Tenth Congress, the New Dawn project was given access to the replivirus used to quell rogue bots during the Water Wars. I found it last night, after we hung up with Misha. It was encrypted in the North Dakota files."

Mac leaned forward. "So how do we infect them?" he asked.

Kendra stood up, one hand to her forehead. "We can't simply broadcast the virus like we did with the special protocol command."

"Why not?"

"Protocol commands just turn on a series of instructions already written into the Mothers' code. But getting a virus in requires uploading *new* code. The Mothers won't allow that." She took off her glasses and pinched the bridge of her nose. "No. We'll need to try uploading it through a secure channel, something they're built to receive input from . . . like the tablets."

"But how— Oh . . ." James imagined Misha, alone in her room at the Presidio. "Do you really think Misha can make that happen?"

"I think she's our only hope." Kendra reached down to pat James on the wrist. "I know you don't like it that Misha's there. But without our brave little soldier, we wouldn't even have known the kids were in such deep trouble."

36

IN THE DARK dining room Misha caught sight of Kai, his face illuminated only by the light from his tablet as he tapped impatiently at its
keys. She was surprised to see him there.

On her way back from the plugged-up fence the previous morning,
she'd been intent on hiding in her room, conferring with Uncle William about her new predicament. But she'd stopped short at the sight
of Kai, the look on his face as he'd limped breathlessly up the front
steps of Building 100. His jacket soaked, his pants torn, he'd stuttered
incoherently until finally Kamal had come to his side, laying a gentle
hand on his shoulder. "What is it, Kai? What has happened?"

"Sela," the boy had sobbed, pointing back toward the bay. "Sela . . ."

Behind him had stood Rho-Z, her long arms drooping toward the
ground, her posture stooped forward as if in solidarity with her son's
sadness. And Alpha-C, inert, her flanks glistening with dried salt. "But
Alpha's right there," Misha had murmured. "How could she leave . . ."

Kai had turned on Alpha then, raising his voice to a scream as his
eyes burned with rage. "You did it!" he cried. "You tipped the boat!
You killed her!"

Kamal had simply hugged him, taken him to his room, stayed with him until at last he'd fallen into a fitful sleep. Meanwhile the rest of them had formed a search party, combing the beach to no avail. Misha had completely forgotten her mission to escape this place. Precious time had passed before she'd called William. And by then she'd already known—with everything that had happened, she couldn't just leave.

But it made no difference anyway—the Mothers had barely let them budge from the building since. As afternoon had melted into night, the children had scavenged what little they had in the pantry for dinner—some day-old stew, a stash of precious pine nuts, strips of dried fish and squirrel meat. Some had resorted to Pedia-Supp. Their meager dinner over, they'd formed a convoy to the makeshift latrine they'd dug over by the woods. Then they'd retreated wearily to their own rooms, all vowing to deal with their Mothers in the morning.

Another morning had dawned; another long day had passed. But until now, there had been no further sign of Kai. The door to his room sealed tight, no one had dared cross the threshold.

Carefully, Misha approached the table where the boy sat, near the front window. "Having problems?" she asked.

"Huh?" Kai looked up. His cheeks splotched red, his eyes swollen, he averted his gaze toward the window. Close outside, Rho-Z was stationed in the dry grass.

"It looks like you're having trouble with your tablet," Misha said softly.

Kai frowned, his features contorting before settling on anger. "It was getting slower . . . even before. I thought if I brought it down here, closer to her . . . But now it isn't working at all."

"Can I have a look?" Misha sat down beside him. She grasped the tablet with both hands, shaking it while holding it to her ear. "Nothing loose. Is it charged?"

Kai stared down at his hands. "The power indicator says it's fine," he mumbled.

"Hmm," Misha said. She remembered Clara and Álvaro complaining about something similar that morning. According to Álvaro, the input request was being registered, but no reply was forthcoming. "Everybody seems to be having the same problem."

Kai took the tablet from her. With an air of finality, he powered it down and shoved it aside, casting the area around them into shadow. "It's bad enough that Rosie doesn't talk to me," he said. "Now even this doesn't work."

Misha watched him. They were talking about Rho-Z. About the tablet. But she knew—they were both thinking about what had happened the day before. She looked toward the entryway, half expecting Sela to come through the door. "Kai," she said hopefully, "maybe Sela's still out there. Maybe she'll come back. Kamal said she did it all the time in the desert, wandering off like that . . ."

Kai stared at her, his eyes reddening. "She's not coming back," he said. He balled his fists. "I saw her go down. She's not coming back."

Misha felt her body going limp. Maybe, like Kai, she just needed some solace. "I guess I still don't want to believe that," she murmured. Without thinking she reached over to awkwardly wrap her arms around his waist. But she felt no response. Like so many of the children here, the boy was painfully thin. His limbs were taut, his spine hunched defensively. She pulled back, catching sight of the communicator embedded in his forehead—that special emblem, the symbol that marked every Gen5 child. Her gaze lingered on its intricate pattern of circuits, seeming almost to pulsate with its own life. It was just one of the things that made him and the others so special. But was his chip useless now, just like hers?

Kai glared out through the window, toward the spot where Alpha-C sat in the field—where, just as they had the night before, all the Mothers had massed in the darkness to form an impenetrable wall around the fortress of Building 100. He brought his fist down on the table, tears running down his cheeks. "Sela was my best friend," he said. "The first person I ever met. But now she's gone, and it's my fault!"

Misha looked around the empty room. "It's not your fault," she said. "And nobody thinks so."

She'd been listening to the others all day, each offering theories, each trying to come to terms with what had happened. Each trying to make sense of the ever more repressive behavior of his or her own Mother.

"They have to keep us safe," Zak had insisted.

"They sense something we can't," said Chloe. "That's why they're being so careful."

But not everyone agreed. They were all tired, wracked with hunger, thirst, and worry. And they all wanted answers. "How long can this go on?" Hiro asked. "We need food!" Even Kamal's kind face was shadowed with doubt. And poor little Meg, bereft at the loss of her beloved roommate, could barely utter a word.

Misha took a deep breath, trying to think of some way—any way—to console Kai. If what had happened to Sela was anyone's fault, maybe it was her own. Wasn't she the one who had encouraged her sister to test her limits? But no . . . she couldn't think that way. "Kai," she said, "you have to believe it was just a terrible accident. It was nobody's fault . . . Alpha thought Sela was drowning, she tried to save her . . ."

Kai turned on her. "But she didn't save her! She failed. Sela would have been better off without her!"

Misha sat in silence, remembering the violent way in which Alpha-C had plucked Sela from beneath the fence just the other day. Maybe Kai was right. Maybe these children *would* be better off without their Mothers—these Mothers who seemed to have no conception of their own strength, or of their own limitations. She remembered what Álvaro had told her late in the afternoon, before once more trailing the others upstairs to his room. "I think our Mothers are not programmed to operate over water," he'd said. "This must be the problem." Misha would add more to that list. She'd been thinking about Sara, and about Grandmother—all the real, human mothers she'd grown up with. Maybe these robot Mothers hadn't been programmed to operate with real children—children who needed food, water, and . . . love.

Staring out the window at the ranks of bots, she felt herself succumbing to Kai's anger. Even in her short time here, she'd come to understand the reverence that the children held for their Mothers. But shouldn't *someone* have to pay for the loss of Kai's beloved friend—for the death of her sister? She clamped her eyes shut, determined to hold back her own tears.

Kai stole a look at her, his expression softening. "I'm sorry," he said. "I really want to believe it was just an accident. That Alpha only wanted to protect her. But you see . . . I don't know anymore. I just don't *know* . . ."

Misha felt the buzz of the phone she'd hidden under her jacket. "Kai, I promised I'd get more water before I went to bed," she mumbled.

She got up to leave. Behind her, Kai turned back to the window.

MISHA HUDDLED OVER the satellite phone in her small room. "Hello? Daddy?"

"How are you holding up?"

"Okay . . ." Misha felt the taut muscles in her neck relaxing. She'd almost forgotten James's gentle touch, the soft voice he used only with her. She pulled her jacket close around her, wishing she could disappear into the lush green warmth of the phone's little screen. "Daddy, I'm sorry—"

"Honey, I told you . . . You scared us, going off alone like that. But what's done is done. What's important is that you're safe." There was a pause. "And . . . maybe now you can help us."

Misha swiped her eyes with the back of her sleeve. "I'm helping the kids. Fetching water . . . I'm the only one who can still go outside the field without getting pulled back by one of the Mothers."

"Be careful, Misha. We can't be sure what the Mothers will do next."

"But how else can I help?"

"We have a plan." His voice was low now, firm. "We need you to get the kids to upload a virus to their bots."

"A virus? What will it do?"

"It's designed to disable their CPUs."

"Kill them?" Misha's pulse quickened. Was this really what she'd wished for?

"Not kill them. Just keep them busy is all." There was a pause, and she heard a shuffle on the line.

"Misha, let's take it step by step." It was Kendra. "I can transmit a copy of the virus code to you via a computer at the Presidio. It's in another building, a little over a mile from where you are now. I'll give you the location. Are you ready?"

Misha listened carefully as Kendra read off the coordinates, typing them one by one on the phone's small screen. "Call us back when you're inside," Kendra said. "Or if you have any trouble at all."

"Okay." Breathless, Misha punched off her phone. It was only a mile. Just a mile.

HER PACK STRAPPED tight to her back, Misha stood on the front porch of Building 100. Along the walk, the phalanx of Mothers glistened in the moonlight. She imagined how beautiful they might seem, flying together, their flanks glimmering in the sun as Grandmother had so often described. But here, sitting low on their haunches with arms folded close to their sides, they only seemed menacing, silent ghosts carrying out some mysterious agenda. Turning on her heel, she re-entered the building to find the small back door. Once outside, she hurried along the route suggested by her GPS, heading right, then west along a wide, paved road.

Suddenly she felt the ground trembling beneath her feet. She stopped, listened. Leaves, what sounded like entire tree branches, crackled ominously behind her. She stepped up her pace, running now, her legs pumping in time to the beat of her heart, her lungs aching in the frigid air. It wasn't until she mounted the front cement steps of the building that she turned to look at the field behind her. There stood a solitary bot, the tall grass to its right flattened. Slipping through the building's heavy metal-framed door, she closed it securely behind her. Then she held up her satellite phone and pressed the "call" button. "I'm in," she whispered.

"Good," Kendra answered. "Go up the stairs to your right. Then go into the first room at the top of the stairs."

It was pitch-black inside. Misha closed her eyes, navigating the way she had when she was small—by feel, by echo. Ascending the creaking steps, she quickly located the office, the air inside cold and still.

"There's a computer at the desk. Just touch the screen. It should be on."

Misha sat down on a chair in front of a desk to her right and reached out to touch a desktop screen. She was greeted with a glowing display showing an image of the Golden Gate Bridge. "Okay," she said.

"I'm transmitting the virus to a folder called 'Repli3.' Do you see it?"

She watched as a small icon appeared on the screen at the lower right. "Yes."

"It's still loading. Don't select it until I tell you to. Meanwhile, there should be a stash of memory cards there in the office. Can you find them?"

Misha rifled through the shelves near the desk to find a stack of oblong boxes labeled "HaloDisk." Inside each box were fifty small memory cards. "Yes, okay. There are lots of them here."

There was a sigh of relief over the line. "Great. Now, listen carefully. You'll want to make one copy for every bot. Make thirty, just in case, each on a separate card . . . There. The virus file is ready now."

Misha inserted one of the cards into a slot along the side of the computer and waited for the virus to copy. "Okay, that's one," she said. Patiently, she copied the virus to twenty-nine more cards, stowing each one in turn into her pack. "That's it," she said. "Thirty."

"Good girl! Let us know when you get back to your room, okay? We'll tell you more then."

Shouldering her pack, Misha descended the stairs. In the small lobby, she gathered her resolve. Then she stepped back out onto the porch. There was the sentinel bot, its flanks now streaming with the moisture of condensed fog. She caught her breath at the sight of the bot's insignia: Alpha-C.

A bolt of fear shot through her. But then, inexplicably, something else took its place—a strange warmth, a certainty . . . and in that moment she thought she heard something: a voice, whispering.

"Wha . . . ?" She looked around. "Who's there?"

Just as suddenly, the voice was gone. She hunched down. It was just her own pulse, drumming in her ears. Gripping the straps of her pack with both hands, she stepped down to the field, walking with hurried steps. Behind her, Alpha followed.

37

PULLING HIS COMPASS from his jacket pocket, Kai tried to hold in his mind the day he'd first received it. He rubbed his fingers over its durable plastic face. *It's so great,* Sela had said. *It tells you which way to go.*

"Why did you have to be so stupid?" he mumbled. He'd thought he was done with being angry. But now it was all he had. He was angry at Sela for daring to paddle out so far. At himself for enabling her. At their Mothers for capsizing the boat, for not trusting them. And at Rosie for not talking to him. He threw the compass to the floor. He had no idea which way to go now.

Snatching up his tablet, he plodded down the stairs. They'd run out of stored food—which was fine, because since Sela's disappearance, his appetite had all but vanished. But while Zak was convinced he could orchestrate a hunting expedition, Misha seemed to have something else in mind. Kamal had brought him the news early that morning: Everyone was to convene in the dining room, and they were all to bring their tablets.

As Kai entered the dining room he caught sight of Misha in the far corner, her normally neatly braided hair falling loose over her shoulders, her hands gesturing as though she were working through some silently rehearsed speech. Her eyes lit up briefly as he sat down next to Kamal and Meg in the group of chairs nearest her.

"Do you know what this is about?" Kai whispered to Kamal.

"I do not," Kamal replied. "Perhaps Misha has figured out a way for us to regain our tablet connections?" He offered a wan smile, and again Kai was thankful for the boy's patient friendship.

Behind them, Zak and Chloe noisily took their seats alongside Álvaro and Clara. Finally, the room grew quiet. "We are all here," Hiro announced from the doorway.

Misha cleared her throat. "I think . . ." she began. Her eyes once more drifted toward Kai, but he wasn't sure what she was looking for. He simply nodded, waiting for her to continue. "I think we all want this . . ." She pointed out the window, toward the blockade of bots. "We all want this to end."

Zak's hand flew up. "Not sure what you mean. What exactly do we want to end?"

"Have you figured out a way for us to get food?" Hiro asked.

"Have you figured out some way to fix our tablets?" Clara asked, holding hers aloft.

Misha stared straight out across her audience, her nervous hands now held stiff at her sides. "No. I think the tablets are fine. And most likely your Mothers' databases are fine too. I think the problem is that they can't communicate the search results back to you. Just like they can't talk to you anymore." There was a murmur of assent. "The problem has to be with your Mothers," she said, "and I don't think it's going to get any better."

Clara gasped. "But what can we do about *that*?"

"That's what I want to talk to you about," Misha said, her voice almost inaudible. "A plan. But . . . it's best if we can all agree to it."

"What kind of plan?" Zak was restless, and Kai could almost feel the boy leaning forward.

"I think . . ." Misha took a deep breath, placing her left hand on the back of an empty chair for support. "We should put our Mothers to sleep."

"Sleep?" It was Chloe, crying out involuntarily. "Why?"

From beside Kai, Kamal spoke up. "Perhaps that will not be necessary. Perhaps my Mother has already gone to sleep." He tapped the side of his head with one long forefinger. "She is out there, but she is gone. I cannot find her."

Through the window, Kai caught sight of Rosie. He still knew her from the way she held her wings, a bit away from the bulk of her body as though readying for flight. He still knew her, from her bright yellow butterfly tattoo. But she was just one of many now—those dark, foreboding, silent forms, closing in . . . "They're awake, Kamal. They're just not talking to us," he said.

Behind him, Zak got up so fast that his chair clattered to the floor. "This is no time to put them to sleep! I tell you, they're getting ready for an attack!"

Kai turned around to face the boy. "An attack? By what? Squirrels?" A smattering of nervous laughter momentarily broke the tension.

Chloe stood up to take Zak's arm, glaring down at Kai. "So, what's your take on what's happening with our Mothers, Kai?" she asked.

"Do you mean, why do I think they've gone silent?"

"No," Zak said. "She means, if there's no threat, why are they being so protective?"

Kai searched the group for a sympathetic face. But all eyes were on him now, all awaiting his answer. "I don't know," he said. "But here's the thing I keep coming back to. We can't ask them why. Because they won't answer."

A general murmur ensued as each child in turn shook his or her head.

"This problem with our Mothers," Clara said, "it seemed to start the minute we got to the Presidio . . ."

"It got worse once Misha came," Chloe said, her dark eyes now fixed on Misha. "Why would that be, I wonder?"

Kai stood up to confront Chloe. "What do you mean? She got here just a few days after we did! When her Mother left her."

"Okay, maybe Misha isn't the cause of our problem," Clara said. "But her Mother is gone. For all we know, ours will never leave us. How can *she* be the one to tell us what to do with them?"

Moving toward the windows, Chloe stared out at her Mother. "I agree with Zak. They're getting ready for a fight. All I want is for my Mother to tell me what's going on. If there's an enemy to fight, I want to help her fight it." She turned back to the group. "Kappa did everything for me. I just want to do something for her. And that doesn't mean putting her to sleep!"

There was a loud murmur, a few choked sniffles. But no one spoke. Kai turned to Misha. "Say we did want to put them to sleep. How would we do that?"

Misha stared at the floor. She swallowed hard before looking up at him. "With a virus . . ." she murmured.

"A virus? Like the flu?" Zak stepped forward, his fists clenched. As Misha backed off, Kai wheeled around to face the boy. He could sense the heat radiating from Zak's skin.

From his seat, Álvaro piped up. "I am sure that Misha is referring to a computer virus. A code that will interfere with their thinking."

"Yes," Misha said, her eyes seeking out the small boy. "A computer virus. We can upload it to them from our tablets. It won't kill them. Just put them to sleep. Then we can figure out what to do next. If we change our minds, if we think there really is a threat that only our Mothers can protect us from, then we can terminate the virus. It won't do any permanent damage."

"Where'd you find this virus thing?" Zak asked.

Misha blushed. "I figured it out myself."

"So that's it!" Zak turned to face the room. "That's how she killed her Mother!"

The room erupted in shouts. Close beside her now, Kai could see the tears pouring from Misha's eyes. "I didn't!" she cried. "She left me! I told you, she just left me!" She hurried toward the door, shoving past the stunned Hiro, disappearing into the pantry beyond.

Kai turned on Zak. "Look what you've done!" he cried. "We're all we've got. But you're turning us all against each other!" He scanned the others' frightened faces, trying but failing to find another willing ally. "Misha's only trying to help. She doesn't have to. She's not stuck here like the rest of us. For all we know, she could just leave anytime she wanted."

Chloe crossed her arms. "Why doesn't she, then? Why doesn't she just leave us alone?"

"What? Because she needs . . ." As Kai searched for the right words, a sudden anger rose in his throat, choking him. How had it come to this?

But it didn't matter. The room was growing darker. Startled eyes were turning toward the windows, now rattling in their frames. The walls shook with the din of rolling treads, the roar of air that scattered tufts of dry grass in the field outside and uprooted Clara's carefully planted garden. The Mothers had awakened.

Kai made his way through the clumps of children, out the door, through the kitchen, and up the stairs. He headed straight for Misha's corner room, the door slightly ajar. In the dim, he could just make out her tearstained face.

"I want to try," he said. "Just tell me how."

38

MISHA LED KAI out the back door of Building 100, to the spot where Sela's electric bike sat tethered to a solar power wall. "Get on," she said, pulling the plug. He'd no sooner mounted the bike behind her than she flicked on the motor. Misha's pack, into which she'd dumped his tablet, was strapped to his back. Behind them and above them, he could still hear the clamor of twenty-two frantic Mothers. And as they gained distance from the building, two were tracking them from above. Somehow he knew it—one was Rosie.

They sped along the winding road, their single solar headlight cutting through blankets of morning fog. Holding tight to Misha as she navigated the turns, her loose hair whipping in his face, Kai couldn't help but remember another time, another place. Had it really been just months ago?

"Where are we going?" he called. Misha turned her head. He could see her mouth moving, but all he heard was the word "computer."

They stopped at last in front of a big sand-colored building, and he followed her through the front door and up a stairway. There, she darted into a small room and hurried toward a desk, on top of which was mounted what looked like a large tablet screen. She plopped down on a chair in front of the desk. With nervous fingers, she pulled a small, oblong device from her pack; Kai had seen something like this in the kitchen at Building 100, but Álvaro had told him it was just an old phone, useless now.

Misha pressed a green button on the device. "Daddy, are you there?"

Kai stepped closer. *Daddy?*

A voice came from the phone. "Kendra here. What's happening?"

"Kai's the only one who agreed to try the virus. The others are all in a panic. What should I do?" Misha's face was pale in the light from the little device, her breath coming in short gasps. In the ensuing silence, her foot tapped impatiently against the leg of the desk.

Kai touched Misha on the shoulder. "Misha," he said, "who—"

But now the voice came back again. "There is one option. A way to get you out. Once the virus is installed, the bot can still take off."

"Take off? Where to?"

There was another pause before the voice answered. "To Los Alamos. I'll send you a different copy of the virus. One with a homing code. And of course, we'll want Kai to come too."

There was a scratching sound. Then another voice, a man's, came over the line. "Misha, we promised we'd get you out of there. And once he's here . . . maybe Kai can help us convince the others."

Like the tiny bait fish in Sela's bucket, Kai's thoughts swam in his head, too slippery to grasp. Who on earth was Misha talking to? He tried again: "Misha, who're you—" But she waved him off, the screen on the desk coming alive as she brushed it with the tips of her fingers. Through a window to his left, Kai caught sight of Rosie down on the ground. And beside her another bot—Alpha-C.

Suddenly a small icon appeared near the bottom of the screen. The voice sounded over the little device. "Do you see it?"

"Yes," Misha said.

"Copy it to a fresh card."

"Okay."

From a box on the shelf along one wall, Misha withdrew a small rectangular card. She inserted it into a port on the side of a box below the screen, and a yellow light lit up next to it. In just a few seconds, the light turned green. "Done," Misha said.

"Kendra's sending you a list of instructions. You'll be able to see them on your screen. Follow them to the letter. *Do not* skip any steps."

"Okay . . ." Misha scanned the lines of type on the screen, her lips moving silently. "I need to explain to Kai now." At last, she turned to him. "I'm sorry, Kai. But if you really want to do this, we'll have to move fast."

Kai stared at her. "Do what? Who the heck are you talking to?"

Misha inserted a second card into the box, and Kai watched the little light once more cycle from yellow to green. "I'll explain once we're on our way. But for now, you'll have to trust me."

The little room, its musty shelves and antiquated furniture like a set from some old video, seemed to close in on him. His brain wasn't working right. He simply couldn't give Misha the answer she wanted. "No. I can't. Not until you answer me."

Misha got to her feet. Pacing now, she blurted out a story—about a father named James who lived in a place called Los Alamos. About how James, together with another man named Rudy, had genetically engineered the children to survive after the Epidemic. There were others, Mac and Kendra, who had built and programmed the biobots— the Mothers. And still others, the Hopi, who lived in the desert, farming and herding their sheep. These were all her family. They could be his family too.

But all the while, Kai felt himself backing away from her, his hands behind his back, groping for the door.

"Please," Misha said. "We need . . ." She stopped in midsentence, staring out the window. "Rho-Z is right there, ready to go," she said. "But Alpha . . . she could be a problem."

Kai had his right hand firmly wrapped around the doorknob now. People outside the fence . . . an attempt to control their Mothers. "Misha . . ." He gathered himself up, fully ready to make a run for it. "Was Zak right? Are you the enemy?"

Peering into his eyes, Misha reached out to take hold of his arms. "No, Kai. I'm a friend. I'm just like you. I did have a bot Mother. She crashed in the desert, but she managed to give birth. Then some people found me. They saved me. Now they're trying to help you too. They've been trying your whole life—"

"So how come I never saw them?"

"Your Mother wouldn't let them near. She was programmed only to protect you. But there *are* others out there. You were never alone." Misha let go her grip, but her eyes were still on his.

Kai stared out the window. He remembered Sela's story of a mysterious laser shot in the night. The cases of water left by the roadside. The supplies left for them here at the Presidio. Was it true? Had someone been watching over him, trying to help him, all these years?

Following his gaze, Misha scanned the sky. "It's bad enough that Alpha-C's here. But there might be more on the way. They may not be talking to you anymore, but I think they're talking to each other."

Kai watched his Mother, stationed now near the front entrance to the building. And Alpha, angled toward Rosie as though sharing some intimate secret. He remembered the trio of bots, clustered on the shore as he and Sela had drifted out across the bay . . .

Beside him, Misha pulled his tablet from her pack. "Kai, if we're going to do this—"

Kai clamped his eyes shut. What would Sela do? Of course she'd trust Misha. But where had Sela's daring gotten her? It was Rosie who had always protected him. No matter what, Rosie had always been right . . .

Opening his eyes, he looked into Misha's. No, he thought, Sela had been right too. He'd never get anywhere if he let his fears get the best of him. Besides, wherever he was going, he wouldn't be alone. Misha would be there. And though she wasn't the same as she had been before—though she might never again be the Mother he'd once grown to love—Rosie would be there too.

39

KAI CLUTCHED HIS tablet between the palms of both hands. Inserted into a slot on its side was the memory card containing the deadly virus. The sight of Rosie, so close in front of him, brought a rush of conflicting emotions—anticipation, mixed with sheer trepidation. Alpha, her fuselage cocked forward in her typical birdlike stance, now stood just a few yards away.

Misha grasped Kai's shoulders, staring directly into his eyes. "This virus is designed to morph over and over again," she said. "After the initial hit it will continue to reinstall, each time with a slightly different code. Get as close to her as you can to avoid any interference. Rho-Z will be fighting it every step of the way, so once we start, we need to keep the virus constantly installing."

"But once we get the virus in, how do we keep Rosie from flying off to this Los Alamos place before we have a chance to get inside?" Kai asked.

"She won't take off until the homing program is activated," Misha said. "You'll have to dock the tablet into her console, to set up a hard-wired connection with her flight computer. Then, you'll need to type

'GO' on her console keyboard." He felt her fingers digging into his arms now. "Got it?"

"Yes . . ."

"When you want to start the virus transmission," Misha said, "just press this key."

Holding the tablet in front of him like a shield, Kai crept down the front steps and waded tortuously through the tall grass, his eyes fixed on Rosie. She remained motionless, her ominous form seeming to grow ever larger as he approached. Behind him he could hear Misha, her steps barely stirring the brush. Maybe this would be easier than he'd thought . . .

Then, Rosie moved.

At first, it seemed like a trick of his imagination. But then she reared up, her massive legs steadily straightening until she was standing at full height, pivoting, searching. His heart pounding, Kai ducked down, once more under cover of the foliage. Step by tentative step, he drew nearer to her. Twenty feet, fifteen feet . . . She leaned down toward him, and he stared, mesmerized, through the familiar transparence of her hatch and into her vacant cocoon. Her powerful arms reached out, raking through the grass around him, and he just barely stepped aside in time to avoid her touch. Steadying his feet on the uneven ground, he pushed the tablet toward her, pressing the key to start transmission.

Rosie sat down hard, her carriage coming to rest awkwardly on her treads, her arms dropping to her flanks like broken tree limbs. Misha close on his heels, Kai climbed up Rosie's treads and pulled on the cocoon latch. His heart leapt as the door swung wide and they snaked inside.

Just days before, this had been his home; now it was cold, dank, every surface slippery with condensed dew. He closed and secured the hatch door as Misha crouched into the hold behind him. Balancing the tablet on his lap, he found his safety restraints, then tugged hard to tighten the straps as he snugged himself down into the seat. He was rewarded with a satisfying click as the harness engaged.

"What about you?" he hissed. "You don't have a harness . . ."

"I'll hold on," she panted. "Just get the tablet docked!"

He lifted his tablet, grasping it by the edges. His breath caught. The memory card wasn't there. Misha's warning rang in his ears: *We need to keep the virus constantly installing.* But where was the card? He reached down, frantically searching the floor of the cocoon with his fingers. How long did he have?

"What's wrong?" He could hear Misha's frightened voice close in his ear.

"The card's gone . . ."

But it was already too late. The cocoon rose as Rosie once more gained her legs. And a wave of nausea overtook him as she flooded into his mind, his thoughts scattering like dry leaves before a wind. "Kai . . . you are frightened. I will keep you safe . . ." It was faint, almost a whisper. Was it only a memory? Or was it his Mother, speaking . . . pleading with him?

Struggling to remember his purpose, Kai felt along the side of the seat, under the console, searching for the card. But it was nowhere to be found. The walls of the cocoon were spinning. His head was spinning. Helpless, he watched the tablet clatter to the floor as Rosie yawed precariously.

Then he saw someone . . . Misha . . . clawing her way around the seat. ". . . an extra . . . backup." In her hand she held something small and flat. But Kai was paralyzed, his mind a jumble. Where was he? Why was he here? He felt Misha clambering up next to him, pushing him to one side. She whisked the tablet up from the floor and shoved the thing in her hand into the slot along its side.

Rosie dropped down again with a bone-jarring thud. Her voice vanished from his mind, leaving behind only an aching emptiness. But still he felt a vibration, the earth beneath them trembling. "Wh—?"

Through the hatch window, he could see Alpha-C looming just feet away, her flanks glimmering, her arms rising.

Sliding her finger along the right edge of the tablet to make sure that the card was secured, Misha jammed the tablet down onto the console. "'GO,'" Misha said. "Type 'GO'!"

Kai leaned forward. Orienting his fingers over the console keyboard, he typed.

Immediately, Rosie's reactor ignited. Her cocoon rocked back, her arms retracted, her wings unfolded. And then . . .

The hatch flew open and two powerful hands reached in, grasping Misha firmly by the waist. "Kai!" Her arms flailing, Misha disappeared over the bottom lip of the hatchway.

"Misha!"

Rosie's engines roared, her fans engaging to kick up swirling clumps of grass and earth. And in moments they were airborne, the hatch door almost blown from its hinges.

Misha was gone. Forced by a sudden gust of wind, the door slammed shut. And Kai, huddled in his seat, could hear only the muffled rumble of Rosie's ducted fans, the low hum and click of her processors churning through millions of virally induced computations as she carried him high over a city he had never seen.

40

JAMES AWOKE AT his desk, his mind in a fog. With a start, he registered the clock readout on his computer screen: 16:12:01. Getting unsteadily to his feet, he stumbled out into the biology lab, where the angry, purplish glow of a stormy sky sifted through the windows. He hurried across the hall to Mac's office, his chest heaving with the effort. There was Mac, his unevenly cropped beard silhouetted against the glow of the screen. "Any sightings?"

"Sorry, James," Mac said. "I didn't want to wake you. But no. No sign."

"But the last time we had contact with Misha was close to seven a.m. PDT . . . Surely that's long enough . . ."

Behind him, Rudy hobbled in from the robotics lab. He'd abandoned the wheelchair they'd sent back with him from Polacca after his last treatment—it was still parked in the lobby, a sign of his refusal to admit defeat. His face a pasty white, he hid a cough in a cloth handkerchief and plopped down heavily beside Kendra, who sat in the corner drinking a cup of stale coffee.

Suddenly Mac punched a control on the radar, focusing in on a small red blip. "Guys," he said. "I've picked up something. It's heading our way."

James rushed out the door and down the hall to the floor-to-ceiling windows in the lobby. By the time Kendra had ushered Rudy from the hallway, James was already donning his Tyvek suit and filter mask. "Are you sure it is safe?" Rudy gasped, stopping to lean against the reception desk. "Perhaps we should stay inside until the bot lands. We do not know if she will be subdued."

"Rudy's right," Kendra said. "We're safer inside."

James could see it now—something like a black sphere, indistinct, hovering high over the pines across the lot. It steadily took shape: its widespread wings, its belly, its treads and arms pulled tight to its fuselage. Swirls of dust began to rise from the lot, and even through the thick windows he could hear the roar of air through its fans.

In an instant, the ground shook as the bot touched down. And it dawned on James: Outside of the drone footage, he'd never seen one out in the world. Its hatch window, pocked and streaked with dust, reflected the sky and its foreboding clouds. To either side of the hatch, he could see the powerful robotic hands, the ones that Sara had designed, their protective sheaths pulled over the soft inner fingers in the form of fists. For a moment, he found it hard to breathe.

"The hatch is opening." Beside him Kendra was staring too, her mouth half-open.

James saw a thin leg, clothed in black. Then another. Then a slender torso. *Misha?* Charging toward the airlock, he barely let the inner door close before tripping the outer one. But once outside, he stood rooted to the spot.

It wasn't Misha. A skinny boy with a tattered jacket and a tangle of reddish-brown curls that spilled almost to his shoulders climbed gingerly down the bot's treads. It must be Kai. The boy stared at him, a look of pure amazement mixed with fear.

"Hello," James said. Could the boy even hear him through his mask? "Where . . . where is Misha?"

The boy just stood there, and he realized that to this boy he must look like some sort of monster. But he had to know—where was his daughter? Her call that morning had been a gift, a godsend. He didn't care that her mission hadn't been a success. He was only glad that she was coming home. He stepped forward, peering at the bot, hoping for someone else to emerge. "I'm James," he said, as loud as his mask would allow. "Misha's father. Is she with you?"

The boy crumpled to the ground, tears spilling down his cheeks. "She . . . she was pulled out!" he cried.

James felt a punch, his tortured lungs releasing what little air had filled them. The acrid odor of his mask insulted his nostrils. "Is she . . . alive?"

The boy looked up at him, wiping the back of his ragged sleeve across his face. "Alive? Yes. I think so. I don't think Alpha would hurt her."

"Alpha?"

"It was like . . . like Alpha didn't want her to leave . . ."

James looked toward the west, at the curtain of rain that now obscured the horizon. "Come on, son," he called out. "Storm's coming. Let's get inside." He could barely move his legs as he turned back toward the building. Behind him Kai followed, but at a distance.

Once inside the airlock, the boy pasted himself to the opposite wall, dust flying in sheets from his hair. "Move around," James told him. "We need to get all the dirt off." But as the boy shook his head left to right, James thought only of Misha, her loose mane flying upward. When the inner door opened at last, James struggled to unclip his mask, still watching the boy's wide eyes as he took in the immensity of the lobby.

Kendra kept her distance, but the boy started as Rudy approached in his wheelchair. Then Mac came hurrying from the hallway, and again Kai flinched as his eyes took in the lanky height of the bearded engineer. "Misha's hailing us," Mac said, handing James the satellite phone.

Blinking back tears of relief and frustration, James clicked on the "call" button. "Misha?"

"Daddy, I'm so sorry. Things didn't go like we planned. But we infected Rho-Z with the virus. Is Kai there yet?"

"He just got here. Are you okay? What happened?"

"Didn't Kai tell you? Alpha-C grabbed me right out of the cocoon as we were taking off."

"But you're okay."

"I'm fine. I think she thought she was protecting me."

James rubbed his jaw, sore from clenching. "Misha, why didn't you call us sooner?"

"When Alpha picked me up, my phone fell to the ground. Then she took me back to the building where everyone lives. I . . . had a hard time getting away. Daddy, they all know that Rho-Z and Kai are gone. And I know—they think I had something to do with it."

James sighed. "Where are you now?"

"In my room at Building 100."

"Do you think . . ." James frowned, watching Kendra's face. "Do you think you could get Alpha to bring you here? Just like Kai came in Rho-Z?"

"I looked everywhere for Sela's tablet. But it's gone. It was probably in the boat."

Silently, Kai nodded.

James heaved a sigh. "We'll work as fast as we can to come up with another plan," he said. He turned to Kai. "We'll be counting on Kai to help us."

41

EVEN THROUGH THE thick window of what James called the "cafeteria," Kai could hear the ominous grumble of thunder. He could barely make out Rosie's gray outline as she weathered the downpour alone. He felt for her in his mind, but he could find no trace. At the Presidio, he'd thought that she'd left him, that she was no longer a part of him. But now he knew that she'd still been there. It had taken the virus to truly remove her from his reach.

Now she was . . . other. She was over there, and he was here, looking at her. This loneliness—he'd never felt so empty. Was this what it was always like, he wondered, for those who had never had a Mother like his?

They'd stood him under a shower of hot water and exchanged his tattered clothing for a suit of something that felt shiny, like plastic. Now, James was standing at a table littered with plates of food. There was a fruit called plums and a stew made from corn and lamb meat—all from the people called the Hopi. The tall man named Mac lurked in the corner nearest the door, a cup of pale brown liquid in his hand.

Sitting at the table, Kendra was scooping the stew into bowls. Carefully, she served a bowl to Rudy, who'd pulled his wheeled chair up beside her. "Kai, you must be starving," she said.

Leaning down, James broke off a piece of something soft and spongy. "Corn bread," he said, offering it to Kai. "Misha loves this."

Kendra cupped Rudy's hand. "Rudy used to bake it here, but . . . he doesn't have time these days."

The bread was soft, wonderfully sweet, unlike anything Kai had ever tasted. But the immensity of the room, the empty whiteness of its walls, the steady thrum pulsating from the high ceiling, had his stomach roiling. And these new people, these adults, all staring at him, all expecting something from him . . .

"It was in a place like this that we engineered your embryo," James said.

"Embryo?"

"The little being that eventually became you. We had to change some of your genetic material, so that you'd be able to withstand the Epidemic."

"I know that this is difficult to understand," Rudy said, regarding Kai with his soft blue eyes. "But the earth was fundamentally changed by the Epidemic. Creating a history has become a project of mine. The story of all of this, how it happened, why it happened, is very important."

"Rosie could teach me . . ." Kai mumbled.

The two men looked at each other. "Kai," James said, "the information we're talking about was kept very secret. Only the vaguest of details were loaded into your Mother's learning database."

"Oh." Again, Kai's gaze flitted to the window.

"Do you miss your Mother?" It was Kendra, her eyes steady on his as he looked back.

Kai felt a heat rising in his neck, a burning sensation in his eyes. In this clean room, in this bright light, he felt totally out of place. "Yes . . ."

"Kai," James said, coming over to stand next to him. "You do understand that she's not a real person. Don't you?"

Silent, Kai watched the man's light brown eyes, narrowing to inspect him.

James turned to pace the floor, his worn shoes making a hollow scuffing sound on the scrubbed tiles. "When I was a boy, before the Epidemic," he said, "my father took me to a museum. A natural history museum, with real dinosaur skeletons . . . I liked those dinosaurs a lot. But what I liked best was a display that covered most of the wall in a big dark room. It showed a map of the world, all laid out flat. Embedded in the map were these tiny little lights, all different colors. You could turn a wheel to make time go by, starting over two million years in the past. And as the varied species of the genus *Homo* rose and fell across the planet, the colored lights would light up—purple lights for *Homo habilis*, red for *Homo erectus* . . . The number and density of the lights indicated how many there were of each species. We *Homo sapiens* were represented by white lights. In the end, there were lots of white lights, all over the world."

"How many are there now?" Kai asked.

"Some would say very few. But we've already learned that there are more out there. We aren't the only ones."

"You mean the Hopi?"

"Yes," James said. "And there've got to be more like them. We hope that someday *you* might find them." James paused, coming back to the table to pick up one of the plums. Turning it slowly in his long fingers, he met Kai's gaze. "You'll meet other people," he said. "After a while, you'll come to understand the difference."

"But I already have . . . met other people. There are lots of kids at the Presidio."

James laid his large hand on Kai's shoulder. "I'll do anything to bring Misha back safe," he said, his voice quavering. "And all your friends too. But I'll need your help." He coughed lightly into his sleeve, then handed Kai a canteen.

Kai brought the canteen to his lips and took a deep draft. He'd almost forgotten how the dry air of the desert could parch his throat. How Rosie had taught him to extract precious water from cactus plants, to find it seeping in crevices and under rocks. How she'd led him at last to Kamal's spring . . . "When I was in Rosie's cocoon this morning," he said, "before we got the virus in, she spoke to me. She was there, just like before. There's got to be a way for me to talk to her. To find out what's going on." He looked at Kendra, but she didn't return his gaze. Her eyes were on Rudy, as though they were carrying on some sort of silent conversation. "Whatever we do," he said, "we shouldn't hurt the Mothers."

James closed his eyes, placing his hands palms down on the table. "But they're just machines, just computers . . ." He heaved a sigh, his ragged breath wheezing in his throat. "Kai, haven't you ever been . . . afraid of your Mother?"

Kai stared at him. "Afraid? Why?"

"Don't you worry about what happened to your friend Sela?"

Again, Kai felt that heat, that prickling sensation in his neck. Beside him, Kendra only stared into her lap. Of course—everything that had happened at the Presidio, everything Misha had seen, she'd shared with the people here. But on the way here, ensconced once more in his Mother's cocoon, he'd had plenty of time to think. He might not understand what had happened to Rosie. But he could never be afraid of her.

"No," he said. "Maybe there's something wrong—something we need to fix. But Rosie only wants to protect me. And Alpha-C was only trying to protect Sela. I believe that now."

James sighed. "But your Mothers have changed, haven't they? And they're only going to continue to change, in ways we can't predict." He looked around the room. "Our first priority must be your friends' safety. Are we agreed on that?"

Kendra pushed her chair back from the table. "Come on, Kai," she said. "I've managed to tune in to Rho-Z's feed. Maybe we can gather some clues as to her status before the virus hit her."

Rudy smiled. "*Hasta luego*," he said, winking at Kendra as she pasted a kiss to his cheek.

James sat down, waving them off. "You two go on. I've got some business with Mac and Rudy," he said. But his gaze was steady on them as they left.

42

KENDRA LED KAI out across the lobby and down a long hallway. But as they passed a room marked "Biology Lab," she turned to him suddenly. "You say your Mother spoke to you? What did she say?"

"She said she knew I was frightened. She said she would keep me safe. It was just like before, like nothing had changed . . ."

"Hmm . . ." Kendra's brow furrowed as they continued down the hall. "I thought we were beyond that . . ."

At the far end of the corridor, they reached a room marked "Computer Lab." Banks of computers filled the dim space, but only one screen was lit. Sitting down in front of it, Kendra donned a headset, her eyes fixed on a pattern of bright green lines. As Kai squinted, the information on Kendra's screen resolved into a seemingly endless series of letters and numbers. Yet she appeared to be reading it with as much engagement as one might read a story.

"What are you looking at?" Kai whispered.

"It's computer code," Kendra replied. "And I'm not just looking—I'm *listening* to it. Our brains are much better at hearing patterns than seeing them."

As Kendra removed the headset and let it come to rest on her shoulders, Kai could hear the thrumming drone of modulated frequencies emanating from it. It sounded familiar . . . He drew closer. "Can you hear anything now?"

"Nothing coherent. Since the virus took hold, she's been calculating the number of stars in the universe, the number of neuronal connections in the human brain, the value of pi to an infinite number of digits. The virus has given her enough to do to keep her busy for quite some time." Kendra typed some instructions on a desktop keypad. "But here. I was able to download some of her deep memory. The Mothers can store information in a repository for later use. It allows them to recall things quicker the next time. A sort of neural plasticity."

"Plasticity?"

"Never mind." Kendra smiled. "People here say I talk in riddles. Anyway, I thought you could listen to these memories. They're from just yesterday. Maybe you can pick out some patterns . . ."

"Patterns?" Kai asked. "What kind of patterns?"

"Coherent signals are like a symphony. They have their own language, their own cadence. As soon as you arrived here, I set up to run these memory signals through our translators here," Kendra said, punching a final key on her pad and glancing back up at her screen. "But so far, it looks like they haven't found anything."

Taking the headset from Kendra, Kai adjusted it over his ears. He allowed his eyes to drift away from the screen. Then he closed them, focusing only on the sounds.

He felt himself lulled into a soft, dark place, images flitting in and out of focus. He felt . . . comfort. Then suddenly he felt . . . Rosie . . . the calm assurance of her presence in his mind.

His knees gave out as fingers wrapped around his arm, steadying him. "What is it?" From somewhere far away, he heard Kendra's entreating voice. "Was your Mother saying something?"

"She was calling my name, over and over . . . She said . . . She senses my fear. Her outbound communications system is faulty . . . She's trying to repair it. I should stay away from the water . . . The child named Sela . . . her Mother tried to save her. But she is . . . no longer emitting a signal." He looked at Kendra, tears filling his eyes.

Kendra gently removed the headset from his ears and helped him to a seat next to hers. "Kai," she said, "I'm so sorry about your friend . . ." She looked back at her screen. "You and your Mother have something special, don't you?"

He blinked, her concerned face coming back into focus as his vision cleared. "I guess . . ."

"A connection we never thought possible . . ." Kendra said. She thought for a moment, then nodded to herself as though coming to some private conclusion. "There's something else I found . . . something I think you should see." Her fingers flitting over the keypad, she brought up an icon labeled simply "Mother Source." On the screen, she touched it with her index finger. "I had to hack hard to get access to this," she said. "But it was worth it."

There appeared a crude two-dimensional display, white letters on a dark green background. **NSA Top Secret. Eyes Only.** In the center, an empty white area blinked insistently. "NEW_DAWN_ MOTHER_VIDS," Kendra typed, filling in the blank space. The display shifted to a simple list of names, arranged alphabetically.

"Who are they?" Kai asked.

"You'll see," Kendra said. Waving her finger over the screen in an up-and-down motion, she scrolled down the list, whispering the names under her breath. "Corporal Deisy Cáceres. Captain Ruth Carleton . . . Dr. Mary Marcosson." Finally, she stopped at one: **Captain Rose McBride**.

She turned to face him. "I knew your mother, Kai. Would you like to see her?"

"Wh—?"

Kendra smiled. "Did Rho-Z teach you about how human babies are made?"

"You mean, about the sperm and the egg?"

"Yes. The woman who provided the egg was your biological mother. She's the one you're descended from." Kendra cleared her throat. "Your human mother was a friend of mine," she said. "We grew very close over the time we worked together. She designed the Mother Code."

Kai leaned forward, eyeing the screen more closely now. "Mother Code?"

"Each of the Mothers has a different personality, based on the biological mother of the child she carries. The Mother Code is the computer code that embodies each of these personalities. Your mother, Rose McBride, created Rho-Z from her own personality. She created all of them. She distilled their essences into something you could sense." Kendra pressed a key to activate an audio feed. She selected the name on the screen, and a list of files came up. From these, she selected one called "INTRO." Instantly, an image appeared—a young woman with long reddish-brown hair and thick eyelashes, her gaze cast demurely into her lap.

The woman looked up, her eyes flashing green in the light from somewhere behind the camera. "Is this on?" she asked quietly, almost conspiratorially, a slight smile playing with the edges of her mouth. "Should I start now?"

A muffled male voice answered: "Yes, go ahead."

Kai reached out to touch the screen, his mouth open. "I've seen her face . . ." he murmured. "I know her . . ."

"Imprinting," Kendra whispered. "Rose thought it was important for a human baby to imprint on a human face. But the team didn't want the baby to associate that face with a machine, so they only let you imprint for the first year."

"My full name is Jeanne Rosemarie McBride," the woman on the screen stated matter-of-factly. She sighed, one graceful hand rising to push a stray lock of hair behind her ear. "I go by Rose. I grew up . . . everywhere. But I wound up in San Francisco."

"And her voice. It's her voice . . ." Kai murmured. Sinking into his seat, he remembered the gentle touch of the small, soft hands that had caressed him as a tiny child in Rosie's cocoon—another of the many parts of her that she'd left behind at their first campsite.

"Okay . . ." Rose sat forward, her eyes looking directly into his. "The story of my life. Let's see. My dad was in the army. But when I was three my mother died, and he came home to raise me. He was a great dad. Well, he tried hard." She paused, collecting her thoughts. "I don't remember my mother. Just vaguely, the smell of her sometimes. I'm not really sure what she was like." She looked to her right, a blush playing across her beautiful face. "And I've never been a mother myself. So it's strange, the situation I find myself in now."

Kai sat transfixed as his mother went on, describing how she had come to this place. She was an army captain. A psychologist. A computer programmer. *Your chip is special,* Kai thought, recalling Rosie's words. *It is our bond.*

"If I have a girl, her name will be Moira, after my mother. If it's a boy, he'll be Kai . . . It means happiness. It means the ocean, a place I've always loved. Anyway . . . Here I am, trying to replicate the souls of a few select women in succinct packets of computer code. So that their spirits can live on. So that they can guide a generation of children whom they'll never know, but whose names they've chosen." She blinked, and a tear made its way down her cheek. "It seems crazy. It *is* crazy. But we have to try. I know the bots can't be human. But maybe they can be the next best thing."

The screen went dark, and the display returned to the list of files.

Kai turned to Kendra. "Is she . . . still alive?"

"No, Kai," Kendra said. "I'm sorry. So far as we know, none of the biological mothers survived." Lightly, she touched his face. "You're just like her. She would have been so proud . . ."

"But what about my father? Who was he?"

"Your father . . ." Kendra looked down, fidgeting with a metal bracelet that encircled her thin arm. "Did you hear his voice, there in the background?"

"The man with the camera?"

"Kai, I knew him too. But . . ." She paused, a long pause, and drew in a deep, jagged breath. "He's gone now. All of us from before, it's just a matter of time . . . We aren't like you. We aren't like the Hopi either. We're not immune. We have to take a drug every day, just to stay alive." She turned to him. "I'm sorry. Your father wanted so badly to meet you, but he didn't make it. And Misha . . . she wanted so badly to meet her sister . . ."

Kai started. "Her sister?"

Kendra looked at him. "She didn't tell you? Sela was her sister."

Stunned, Kai pictured Misha's face, her dark brown hair straight as a stick, the little wrinkle in her forehead whenever she was worried—just like Sela's. Then he remembered Alpha-C, pulling Misha out through the hatchway. "Sisters? But how . . ."

"Sela and Misha's biological mother was named Nova Susquetewa. Her personality was installed into two different bots. One made it to the Presidio. The other one . . . didn't. We managed to rescue Misha and bring her to live with us."

"Do you think Alpha . . . the one at the Presidio . . . knows about Misha? Does she know she's hers?"

"Hmm . . ." Kendra sat back, her right hand gripping the edge of the desk. "I don't know how she could. But in a way, I hope so. That little girl likes to take on the world. But she needs protection. Especially now." She reached out to scroll down the screen. "This was just the introductory vid, the first one Rose made. There are hours more for her, and for each of the women on the list."

Suddenly a buzzer went off on a gadget strapped to Kendra's wrist. She squinted down at it, her expression unreadable. "Sorry," she said.

"James needs my help. But you can stay here and watch whatever you like."

"My mother," Kai said. "I knew her face, but I forgot. How could I forget?"

Kendra laid her hand on his shoulder. "Kai, we all forget things over time. It's a trick our minds play on us . . . maybe it's meant to make life easier."

Kai slumped down, staring at the screen. Just months ago, he'd thought he knew how the world worked. Things were hard, but he and Rosie would figure it out. No matter what else happened, they would always be together. And he'd always have Sela.

But now everything had changed. He'd have to learn, all over again, how this world worked.

43

KAI'S MOOD BRIGHTENED as he listened to the stories of Rose McBride, the woman who had become his Mother. Her early love of learning— just like his. Her deployment in the Afghan desert—saving others' lives, just as she had saved his. Her love of San Francisco—the place to which, in the end, she had brought him. Though he'd never imagined Rosie as a real, human woman, he knew her now as though he'd known her all his life. Her voice had been his music. She had been his rock. Somehow, he'd always known her love.

He was sure now that what he'd told James had been right. The children could never bring harm to their Mothers. Somehow, they needed to reconnect. But how? He'd need help. He needed to talk to Kendra.

It was late evening, the storm past, the sky a velvet black outside the little window on the far side of the computer lab. He slipped out the door, then tiptoed down the dim hall, back toward the cafeteria. But just ahead, from behind the closed door of the biology lab, a shaft of bright light cut across his path. At the sound of voices, he stopped.

It was James, his voice low but insistent. "Okay. Based on the data we've gathered since Rho-Z arrived here, we know that the virus is forcing her CPU to operate on overload. Her cooling systems are struggling just to keep up." He paused. "We also know that the boy isn't going to offer us any help."

"We should have known he would be wary," came the man named Rudy's soft reply.

"Too wary. Just like his father . . ." James murmured.

"He'll need time," Rudy insisted.

"Time we don't have," James replied.

"Look . . ." It was Kendra. "There's more to it than that. There was always a debate as to whether we could use deep learning to teach a machine how to think like a human. The answer was always no. But as Rose used to say, the training sets were always insufficient. We never really did the right experiment. Not until now."

"What do you mean?" James's voice was a monotone, as though he was only feigning interest.

"When the Mothers were launched, they themselves were like children," Kendra said. "But their neural networks were designed with innate plasticity. Their brains had the potential to evolve, to break and remake millions of connections based on a constant stream of input data. What if such a brain was put in close contact with a human one—paired, year after year? And what if that human brain was itself still developing, still learning? Wouldn't they both learn from one another? When I was with Kai today, I realized . . . Rho-Z is more to him than a machine. She's his . . . other half. If anything, it's he who should decide what happens to her."

Once again came Rudy's voice, slow and husky. "James, of course we all want the children to be safe. But this disease we have . . . it clouds the mind. We need to make sure that we are thinking clearly before we make any irreversible decisions."

Kai flattened his body against the wall. Holding his breath and begging his heart to slow, he tuned his ears.

"I understand." James's voice came stronger now, tinged with irritation. "But at the Presidio, we're starting to get into the territory that sparked the Tenth Congress—robots taking control over human lives. Remember, these are just children we're talking about. They're confused, misguided. Soon they might be starving. And Misha's caught in the middle of it. Who knows what might happen to her?"

"Mac?" Kendra's voice sounded low, defeated.

"I'm with James," came Mac's gruff voice. "We can't just wait for the bots to stand down on their own. I think we can all agree . . . that's not the direction things are going. We need to be prepared to take them out."

Kai felt a shock, a punch to the gut. It was all he could do to keep himself from bursting into the room.

"So . . ." Kendra sighed. "I'll set up the code for you. But we'll have to test it out on Rho-Z before we go any further."

Kai heard chairs scraping across the floor. The lights in the lab dimmed, and footsteps approached the door. He needed to move. But he was paralyzed, his limbs like rubber.

At the last moment he scampered across the hall, ducking into the robotics lab as the group entered the hallway. Kendra bade her companions a good evening, then shuffled slowly toward the computer lab, passing just a few feet from where Kai huddled, panting, in the darkness. He could hear Rudy's wheeled chair, trundling in the opposite direction. Craning his neck around the doorjamb and peeking toward the lobby, he watched James push the chair while Mac walked alongside.

"It's past your bedtime, old man," James said.

"I told you not to call me that," Rudy said, his voice barely audible. "May I remind you that I am one year, three months, and four days younger than you . . ."

Soon, the corridor was silent.

As he waited for his breathing to slow, Kai's eyes grew accustomed to the darkness. Across the enormous room, the mangled remains of great machines were strewn about the floor. Intricate arms were disassembled. Lengths of tread lay stacked like firewood. In the corner was a partially assembled cocoon, missing its hatch cover. It was clear: To these people, the Mothers were nothing more than hunks of machinery, to be disposed of when they were no longer needed. Gathering his legs underneath him, he got to his feet, careful not to make a sound. He slipped back out into the hallway . . . then froze as he felt a touch on his shoulder.

"Kai, are you lost?"

He looked up. In the dim corridor, he could just make out James's tired features, his sloped posture. "Um . . . yeah. I was . . . looking for a place to sleep?"

James smiled. "So sorry . . . We're not used to guests, I guess." Kai felt the man's hand on his back, guiding him along down the hall and through the lobby. They stopped outside a small room. "This is where Misha stays when she comes for a visit," James said. "There's a fresh bottle of water inside."

"James?" Kai croaked, doing his best to keep his voice steady. "Did you think about what I said? About talking to Rosie?"

James cleared his throat. "We're trying to think of a way, but it'll be difficult," he said.

Kai looked up, hopeful. Perhaps there had been another part of the conversation, one he hadn't heard . . .

But James wasn't looking at him. His gaze was fixed across the room, toward a small window. Then, rubbing his eyes with his fingertips, James turned back toward the hallway. "Tomorrow's another day," he said. "You need to get some sleep."

"But—"

"I'll be turning in myself in just a bit—I just need to check with Kendra about something." Squaring his shoulders, James trudged off. "I'll let her know you're situated," he called over his shoulder.

Taking a deep breath, Kai closed the door behind him. Outside the window, all was still. The moonlight silhouetted only the shapes of two large stones, protruding from the desolate ground. But as he watched, something slithered out from between them.

It was Kamal's snake, Naga, come with a message.

Kai held his breath, closed his eyes, listening for Naga's voice. But instead he heard Rosie's: *Kai . . . You are frightened. I will keep you safe . . .*

He took a blanket from a pile near the door. Lying down on Misha's cot, he wrapped himself against the chill of the room. Things were different now. Now it was he who would need to protect his Mother.

44

AS THE FIRST light of morning crept through the window, Kai huddled under his blanket, dreaming of Rosie's warm cocoon. Clamping his eyes shut, he worked to keep his mind in the dream. "Rosie," he thought, "can we continue our lessons?"

"Yes," she replied.

The memory flooded his mind—her hatch display screen surrounding him with images, her patient tutelage. He saw a human face, the face of Rose McBride, smiling down at him.

He started. His limbs stiffening, he tried in vain to resist as he was pulled from his cocoon and thrust back into Misha's little room at Los Alamos. He sat up, blinking as the walls came into focus.

Cautiously, he poked his head out the door. The halls were dark and deserted, the only sound the incessant hum from the ceiling. Small lights came alive from recesses along the walls as he made his way past the biology lab to the computer lab. Except for a clutter of loose metal boxes and wires on the floor surrounding Kendra's desk, the lab appeared as deserted as the rest of the building. Kai crept in, his ears tuned to the faint hum of the signal emanating from Kendra's vacant headset.

Suddenly a voice came from behind him. "Hello? Who's there?"

He wheeled around to face the door. "It's me. Kai."

"Oh . . . Kai . . ." Kendra stepped unsteadily into the room, the dim light from her computer screen illuminating her haggard features.

Kai looked around him. "Where's everyone else?"

"Rudy suffered a . . . a setback last night."

"Setback?"

"James and Mac had to take him to the Hopi medical center." Kendra shook her head. "My poor Rudy . . . He always felt bad about the Epidemic," she murmured, removing her glasses to swipe at one eye with the back of her hand. "He blamed himself . . ."

"Why?"

"It's a long story—part of the story he was recording for you. But he wanted me to tell you . . . he's sorry." Kendra dabbed at her glasses with a cloth from her pocket.

"When will they be back?"

"Oh," Kendra said, her face blank, "not until late tonight. James needs to take a treatment there too. What terrible timing . . ." She fumbled her glasses back into place. Then her eyes went wide as she stared at the floor. "What's all this?" she asked.

Kai once more took in the litter on the floor—black metallic cases, green and red wires, gleaming switches, and small lights. "I don't know."

Kendra darted to her computer, her fingers flashing over the touch-screen. "No," she murmured. "Oh, no . . ."

Kai drew up beside her. "What?"

Kendra's hands curled into fists. "They downloaded the code!"

"What code?"

"He promised me . . ."

Kai felt a sick sensation rising in his throat. "Is it the code you were talking about last night?"

Kendra turned to face him. "What?"

"I heard you all talking. In the biology lab."

Kendra was silent for what seemed a lifetime. When at last she spoke, her voice was barely audible. "James wanted to run a test . . . on your Mother. But he promised me he'd explain everything to you first." Reaching down, she picked one of the cases up from the floor. About six inches on a side and two inches high, it was smaller, boxier than Kai's tablet. "Looks like they took whatever they needed to assemble the decoys . . ."

Kai stared at the case. "Decoys?"

"The plan was to make a decoy for each bot, a replica of its tablet. Each decoy would send out a unique set of signature frequencies for a given child. When the Mother sensed the signature, she'd track down the source. Then when she got close enough, the decoy with her child's signature could use the tablet's access code to dial in to her CPU and infect her with the same virus we used on Rho-Z."

Kai gripped the edge of the desk, willing himself to stay calm. "So . . . they're taking these decoys to the Presidio?"

"That could very well be the plan . . ."

Then, a momentary glimmer of hope crossed Kai's mind. "But that virus won't kill them, right? It didn't kill Rosie . . ."

Kendra caught his gaze, her brow furrowed. "No. But we added something else—code that will shut down the cooling systems. The CPU will overheat . . . brain death, within as little as five minutes."

Kai's limbs went weak. *Rosie.* "Wh-what about my Mother? Did they . . . already kill her?"

A worried look clouded Kendra's face. Putting down the case, she tapped out a few commands on her keyboard and ran her fingers quickly over her screen. "No. Her signal hasn't changed." She turned to him, letting out a sigh of relief. "She's still okay."

Kai wrapped his arms around the woman's slender waist. "Please . . ." he murmured, burying his face in her narrow chest. "I can't lose her . . ."

He could feel Kendra's thin hands, stroking his head. "Kai, don't worry. I could never do that to her." Bending down, she held him at arm's length, her eyes glistening as her gaze met his. "When I watched you yesterday, hearing your Mother's voice, I realized something amazing had happened." She stood up straight, raising her hands to rub her temples. "I told James I wanted time to think of another way. Why couldn't he at least give me the time?"

Kai wiped his eyes. "But we do have time, right? You said they're going to the Hopi hospital. That means they're not going to the Presidio right away."

"Yes . . ."

"So maybe we have time to think of something else. I keep thinking . . . There's got to be something we can do to make the Mothers the way they used to be. To reboot them . . . Like Álvaro taught me to reboot my tablet."

Kendra stared at him. Slowly, her gaze drifted back to her computer. "Reboot . . . Maybe that's it . . ."

"What?"

But Kendra was already typing, bringing up one new screen after another. "Your Mothers underwent a reboot when they arrived at the Presidio. The reboot code instructed them to shut down the cocoon support systems. But maybe that was the problem."

"How?"

Kendra paused, staring now at the lines of code. "Of course . . ." Closing her eyes, she brought the flat of one palm to her forehead. "In the base code hierarchy, communication with you is a cocoon function. Speech, biofeedback—once the cocoon was shut down, all of those would be cut off . . ."

"That's why she couldn't talk to me?"

"She was probably trying to repair it on her own. Looking for work-arounds. But she couldn't find a way . . ."

Kai leaned forward, staring at the screen. "Can *we* find a way?"

Kendra was silent. Then she smiled. "I still have the source codes for all of the Mothers. I could try running a core reboot on Rho-Z . . . in Safe Protocol."

"Safe?" Kai felt something, another glimmer of hope.

Kendra brought up another screen. "I could use the same trick we were going to use to shut them down. The signature would be the same. But rather than installing a virus and shutting down cooling, the new code would induce a shutdown and reboot in Safe Protocol. Your Mother would go back to being like she was." She turned to look at him. "Better, in fact."

"Better?"

"In Safe Protocol, she'd be less defensive: lasers disarmed; even an 'off' switch if things went south. And there's something else. I'm convinced that your Mother has developed far beyond what she was when she was first launched. We could reboot the original capabilities, but we could also retain her new abilities, including the learnings she's gained from you."

"Learnings," Kai murmured. He remembered what Kendra had said the previous night. While Rosie had been teaching him, had he been teaching her too? "Kendra," he said, "if we can fix Rosie, we still have time to fix the others too."

"What are you suggesting?"

"James and Mac haven't gotten to the Presidio yet, right? We could make new decoys for all of them. I could take them—"

Kendra's gaze softened. "We can try with your Mother, but . . . No. No, no, no . . . I'm responsible for you now. I can't send you all the way back there . . ."

Kai closed his eyes, remembering the soft hum of Rosie's processors, her soothing voice as she sheltered him from the dust storms raging outside her cocoon. "Our Mothers had a mission," he said. "They gave birth to us. They kept *us* safe. They did the best they could." He looked up at Kendra. "I can't just let Rosie die. I can't let *any* of them die."

Kendra blinked. "First things first. We need to test this out." Softly, she placed her hand atop his head. "Are you ready to wake her up?"

Kai imagined Rose McBride's imploring face. He could almost feel his heart jump in his chest, a certainty he hadn't known for a long time.

"Yes," he said.

THROUGH THE PLEXIGLAS walls of the airlock by the lobby entrance, Kai could see Rosie waiting on the tarmac. In her hands, Kendra cradled the dark metallic case that contained Rosie's "friendly decoy."

Kendra turned to him. "The virus with which your Mother is currently infected prevents her from uploading anything new. Even though this decoy uses her tablet access code, it won't be able to break through." She offered Kai a wry smile. "In fact, that's probably what stopped James . . . Anyway, to interrupt the virus, you'll have to dislodge your tablet from her console and remove the memory card."

"Okay . . ."

"But be careful. You'll want to keep the card in place until you get clear of her."

"Why?"

"We don't want the replivirus to stop installing for very long before the code on this decoy can take hold. Once the virus starts to clear, it's possible Rosie could recover quickly. We can't have her flying off before we get the Safe code in—especially not with you inside!"

"Okay, so I'll take out the tablet, climb outside, then remove the memory card from it. Then what?"

Kendra held the decoy out in front of her, inspecting it one last time. "These things don't have much of a range—you'll need to place this no more than fifty feet in front of her. Understood?"

"Got it."

"Get well clear of her, just in case. Then I'll activate the decoy using this remote." Kendra dug deep into her trouser pocket, pulling out a small rectangular device, about the size of her palm. It was adorned with only one button, unlabeled. "And keep your tablet handy in case this doesn't work and we have to subdue her again," she warned.

At last, she surrendered the decoy to Kai. The metal box was light, only a few pounds. But it felt slippery. Or maybe that was just the sweat that now sprang from Kai's every pore as he exited the airlock. *Relax,* he chanted to himself, and he thought about Rose McBride as he made his way toward his Mother.

Gingerly, Kai placed the decoy on the ground, about thirty paces in front of Rosie. Glancing over his shoulder at Kendra, he saw her signal a thumbs-up. Then, with as much confidence as he could muster, he mounted Rosie's treads, unlatched her hatch door, and slid inside the cocoon, leaving the hatch door open.

He took one long, deep breath. Then he grasped the tablet firmly and yanked. It wouldn't budge. He jiggled it, then yanked again. He fell back against the seat. As the tablet dislodged, the memory card flew into the air.

"Argh!" The replivirus cut out immediately; already Kai could feel his Mother moving, her arms ratcheting along her sides. Reflexively, he dropped the tablet to the floor. He slid out of the cocoon, skidding along the edge of Rosie's tread and down to the tarmac. The soles of his feet stung as they hit the ground, his heartbeat pounding a countdown in his ears. Then he ran full tilt back toward the building, raising his arms to signal Kendra.

The ground beneath him trembled and he wheeled around, falling to the pavement as he took in Rosie's monstrous bulk. She was rising slowly to full height, the joints in her powerful legs creaking. Air roared through her ducted fans. Kai could feel his terror rising as she blotted out the sun. He looked back toward the airlock to find Kendra worming her way outside, her fingers pressing urgently on the remote. It wasn't working . . .

But suddenly Rosie's engines quieted. Her powerful mass settled slowly back to earth. Kai waited, staring at his Mother for what seemed like an eternity, in silence.

Then he heard something. A faint ping, like drops of water falling on rock. And Rosie began to speak—not so much speech as sounds, echoing in the emptied caverns of his skull. Words, pressing in from all sides—but they were jumbled, out of order, unintelligible. "Kai." He heard his name. Or was he mistaken?

"Rosie? Is that you?" Paralyzed, Kai spoke without moving his lips—the way he'd always done, with his thoughts. He had no idea if she could hear him. For now her words had become a torrent, pushing like a fist on the space between his eyes, forcing its way through to the base of his skull, filling the deepest recesses of his brain—all the places she'd left behind. He retched but had nothing to produce, his stomach empty and aching. Bringing up his legs, he dug his knees into his eye sockets and cupped his hands tight over his ears. But the flood was unstoppable now, spilling over the mental dams he tried so desperately to erect, expertly navigating his synaptic networks.

"Rosie . . ." he panted. "Rosie . . . slow down. Please!"

Just when he thought he could take no more, the flood subsided to a trickle, a manageable flow. Gasping for breath, he felt his head throbbing once more to the pulse of his own heart.

"What is our location? Location?" a voice echoed. His Mother's voice, audible now.

Kai opened his eyes, staring down at the cracked pavement beneath him, afraid to look up. "We're here, together," he said, his own voice hollow in his ears.

"We are currently located at a position approximately 36 degrees north latitude, 106 degrees west longitude, in the state known as New Mexico, in the country called the United States of America," she determined, seemingly comforted by the certain knowledge of their location.

"This is the place of my birth," she said. He heard her torso rotating, imagined her vision systems taking in her surroundings.

"I do not understand," she said. "These coordinates are dangerous." He heard the flex of her powerful arms, felt her defensive instincts reawakening.

"I inactivated you. I brought you here," he said. "It's safe now."

"Inactivated," she repeated. "Inactivated. How is this accomplished?"

"Rosie . . ." He looked up at her, willing with all his might to shut out the vision of her as a powerful machine, to hold in his mind the image of his mother, the flesh and blood at the heart of her metal shell. He swallowed a hard lump in his throat, and a faint breeze cooled the sweat that coursed down his skin. "I think I understand you now. I understand who you are."

"Who . . . I . . . am," she said. "Who am I?"

"I didn't know before, but now I do. I learned . . ." Deep in his mind a baby cooed, its tiny hand reaching out to touch its mother's face.

"You learned," she prompted. He could feel the ground tremble once more as she trundled toward him.

Then he felt her, for the first time, in the way that one person feels another. For that was what he had learned, in the years since they'd lived alone together. He'd learned how one person feels toward another. The sense of someone different from himself, yet complementary to himself. Outside—but very, very close. Now he could listen to his Mother and imagine the voice of the woman she had once been. He could look at her and see not a towering agglomeration of manmade material, but in her stead a real human being. His mother.

A chill came over him. The intense, internal feeling of her was seeping away from him, like sand between his fingers. He couldn't hold it. A wave of nausea swept in, a panic at the void that was reopening in his mind—that yawning ache he never wanted to feel again. "Rosie . . . don't leave . . ."

"Do not be afraid. I am still here," she said, her voice once more deep in his mind.

"Wh—?" His thoughts were clear now, but his words were garbled. He worked his jaw, but his tongue seemed cleaved to the roof of his mouth.

"You do not need to speak. I can hear your mind," she said. Kai felt the gentle touch of her soft hand on the top of his head. He lowered his hands to the tarmac, the feel of the warm earth grounding him. "I remember you. You are my son, the boy whose body speaks to me."

He stared up at her, the tracks of his tears cooling on his hot cheeks, his own reflection staring back at him from her glimmering surface. He felt her warmth, filling his empty spaces.

At a soft touch on his shoulder, he turned to find Kendra, a mask covering her mouth and nose and the remote clutched in one hand. "I needed to be sure. I needed to see for myself," Kendra said, her gaze rising to take in Rosie's full height. "But you were right. They *are* worth saving."

45

JAMES LAY ON the soft hospital cot, a drip in his arm sedating him into fits of troubled sleep. The mask covering his mouth and nose patiently pushed a warm vapor deep into his lungs. Through slit eyelids, he watched Rudy struggle for breath on the cot next to his.

"We'll need to put Rudy on a ventilator," Edison whispered.

James could only nod. He gazed into his friend's eyes. But they were blank and distant. He reached out to take Rudy's hand in his, but felt no response. As Edison and his nurse wheeled Rudy out of the room, James said good-bye. Hours later he dreamed.

A picnic lunch, colorful blankets and umbrellas scattered on a sun-drenched beach. His mother prepared a spread in the shade of a towering pine as his father admired the surf. Rick Blevins sat brooding by the cookfire as Rudy, his kind smile gleaming, dug into plates of chicken nihari and basmati rice with Kendra and Mac. Sara stood near the shore, a flowing length of silver taffeta streaming from her shoulders. And cradled in her arms was something . . . something precious. As he approached, he made out a tiny form.

"See what I have?" Sara cooed. "Isn't she beautiful?" With gentle fingers, she pulled aside the folds of her cape to reveal a small, perfect face.

"A girl," James murmured. "Such a beautiful girl . . ."

"We'll name her Misha," Sara said. "Beautiful."

Suddenly the imp pushed against Sara's chest, clawing with hands and feet that looked more machine than human. Sara cried out, struggling to hold the baby close. But it wriggled from her grasp, soaring away over the water, rising through the clouds, then dropping like a stone to disappear in the waves . . .

He awoke with a start.

"How are we doing?" Edison asked, raising the window shades to let in the late-afternoon sunlight.

"Uhn . . ." James struggled to bring his mind up to the surface, to where his body lay on the cool, crisp sheets. "Never better."

"That's good," Edison replied. His fingers felt warm on James's face as he unstrapped the mask. "Breathe for me."

James took two deep breaths, feeling the usual rattle as Edison listened intently through his stethoscope.

"Sounds good enough," Edison assured him, cranking the head of his cot upward. But the look on the doctor's face was strained.

"Bad news?" James asked. He grasped the bedcovers, gathering them to him like stray thoughts.

"James, our friend Rudy has passed."

The monitors on the wall continued to display James's vital signs, the pause in his heartbeat. He let go the covers. Watching his fingers, he imagined the tiny red cells in his bloodstream, dutifully delivering oxygen to his hungry tissues. And he remembered his friend's voice on the phone, all those years ago when the battle was still fresh—the reassurance he'd always felt with Rudy by his side. *"Dulces sueños,"* he murmured.

"Sorry?" Checking the monitors, Edison jotted a quick note on his clip-tablet.

"I'll miss him," James murmured.

James had known this was coming. Rudy had told him as much, on the ride here. After all these trials, it would be their last trip together. "Promise me," Rudy had said, "that you will do the right thing." But he knew that his friend would not agree with the thing he was about to do.

Edison placed a gentle hand on his shoulder. "My mother was there. He went with no pain."

"You'll let Kendra know? I'm not sure if I can . . ."

"I have notified Kendra," Edison said. "But, James, when you have your strength back, you can be there for her too."

James clenched his fists, gathering his resolve. Just like Rudy, hadn't Kendra always been there for him? He remembered his promise to her, a promise he'd decided not to keep. Much more important now was his promise to Misha, to get her home safely. And to Sara, to care for the Gen5 children.

For, unlike Rudy and Kendra, he held no reverence for what the Mothers had become. His goal had been to create survivors. Humans—not human-machine hybrids, sharing thoughts, sharing minds. The only way to truly save these children, to help them realize their humanity, was to destroy their Mothers. The others might not agree—certainly not Grandmother; least of all Kai. But once Kai was reunited with the other children, once all were safe on the mesas, James was sure they would all come around.

"So, when can I leave?"

Edison looked up from his tablet. "Don't think about that now," he said. "You're recovering more slowly than after the last treatment. You need to get some rest."

"But—I feel fine."

"James, your vitals are passable. But we shouldn't take any unnecessary chances."

James cleared his throat, fighting off the urge to cough as he shifted his unwilling body and pushed away the sheets that covered his legs.

"I should at least try to get my blood flowing," he said. Turning to lower his legs over the side of the bed, he swallowed down the acrid taste of medicine and dead tissue. He straightened his back, stretched his aching arms, stared at the clock on the wall across the room. His head spinning with the rush of fresh oxygen, he stood. The tiles were cold against the soles of his feet.

"You'll stay the night," Edison said.

"As you say," James replied. "But I need to try out my new legs."

By the door, his respirator was hanging on a peg. He dreaded the feel of that mask, the unwelcome dig of the straps into the worn skin of his face. But he'd have to endure it, if only one more time. On the other side of the door lay the rest of the world, a place now alien to him—but a place where he still had the power to do good.

46

THE SUN DROPPED low in the western sky as Kai left for Polacca. Behind him in Rosie's hold were the twenty-one decoys that Kendra and he had painstakingly assembled. They'd taken care that they resembled the ones now sitting in Mac's transport outside the Hopi medical center.

Though Kendra had done her best to get through to James and Mac, neither was taking her calls.

"I'm sorry, Kendra," a man named Edison had said. "If it is as you say, James seems set on his course."

Kai had had no choice but to take matters into his own hands. He'd need to swap the new decoys for the destructive ones without telling either James or Mac, and before they had a chance to leave the Hopi mesas for the Presidio. Together with Edison, Misha's uncle William had agreed to detain the two at the hospital, and to help Kai make the swap.

"If William and Edison can just get them to stay the night," Kendra had said, "you should have plenty of time."

Rosie maneuvered low over the ground, arcing northward, then westward. His legs sprawled under her console, Kai relaxed his body for the first time since he'd left the Presidio.

But he couldn't truly relax. The challenge ahead, the uncertainty of it, gnawed at him. Just before he'd left, they'd called Misha to let her know James was coming. He'd be bringing something that would fix the Mothers, they told her, not wanting her to know the rest—their plan to subvert James's own wishes. But Misha had been in a panic. "Zak saw Rho-Z taking off when Kai disappeared," she said. "He found the building. He found the computer I was using. Now he's trying to convince the others that an enemy attack is about to happen." And sure enough, when they'd gone to Mac's office to access the computer, they'd found a message on his screen:

STAY AWAY!

WHOEVER YOU ARE, WE DO NOT TRUST YOU.

YOU CAN'T TAKE US LIKE YOU TOOK KAI.

IF YOU COME HERE, OUR MOTHERS WILL ATTACK YOU.

Kai took a deep breath. His mission was becoming more complicated by the moment. He could only hope that if things didn't go as planned, his Mother would know what to do. "You were learning things all along," he said to Rosie, "weren't you?"

"I learned many things," Rosie replied. "Through you, I learned how one human interacts with another. I learned a great deal about the complexity of human emotions. For example, now you are fearful."

"Yes," Kai thought. "That I'll fail. That we'll lose your sisters."

"Fear is important," Rosie said. "It keeps you safe. But at times it is a useless emotion. At this time, it doesn't serve you well."

"Rosie, have you ever been afraid?"

For a moment she was silent, thinking. "Fear. I know it through you. It speeds your pulse. Your thoughts become unintelligible. Confused. It is . . . very unpleasant."

"Unpleasant?"

"I don't . . . like it."

"I'm sorry."

"You needn't be sorry. I'm beginning to think that I too have felt fear."

"You have?"

"At the place called the Presidio, I lost my connection with you. I couldn't speak to you. I couldn't sense your feelings. I followed standard protocols, but the link seemed irretrievable. For the first time since I was created, I was . . . unsure."

"But Misha said you were talking to your sisters."

"From my sisters, I learned that I wasn't alone. There is safety and unity of purpose in the company of others. There is strength. Together, we succeeded in regaining some of our capabilities. We began to sense the distress in our children. We sought a way to retask the tablet connection for outbound communications. But it was insufficient—the database wouldn't accept our input."

"Did you talk to Alpha-C? Was she . . . sad when Sela died?"

"When her child left her, she experienced a . . . total disconnection. A loss of purpose. But then she found another."

A thrill ran up Kai's spine. "Misha?"

"Yes. With the child called Misha, she determined that a new link might be formed." Rosie was quiet, and he could hear only the gentle whir of her servomotors as she adjusted her flight speed. "Kai," she said, "I sense your sadness, for the child who was lost." She paused, and he felt a warmth, emanating from his forehead. "That emotion is very strong in you."

Kai ran his hand along the edge of Rosie's console. "I suppose it's like you said. A disconnection. But one I can never fix."

Down below, the canyons took on a purple hue. He imagined Sela speeding along on her motorbike, the wind blowing through her hair. "Misha is a lot like Sela. But they're different too. Like you and your sisters."

"I am more patient than many of my sisters. I'm more willing to bide the passage of time. More willing to accept uncertainty. But I didn't understand why these things were true, until today."

"Today?"

"I am many things. I am a computer. I am a robot, with all the strengths and vulnerabilities that this entails. I am a presence that lives inside of you. But today I learned that I am something else as well. I carry the essence of your human mother."

"Rose McBride."

"Yes."

"You didn't know that before?"

"I didn't know. I just was. There is a difference."

"How much like her *are* you?"

"I assume that I am as close to her as she could make me. She planted her spirit within me. She wished for me to carry it. I understand now."

"Yes . . ."

"But in the beginning, I was unaware. I didn't truly comprehend this part of my mission. Even if I had, I couldn't have accomplished it."

"Why not?"

"I had no sense of myself."

"You do now?"

"It is a difficult thing to learn. But I am learning it."

"How?"

"You are teaching me."

Kai looked out the hatch, at the darkness that now enshrouded the desert. He imagined the rock formations that had once been his only friends—and the one he'd once called Father. "Rosie," he asked, "do you remember my biological father? The man who Kendra said painted the yellow mark on your wing so he could keep track of you?"

"You're thinking his name. General Richard Daniel Blevins."

"Yes."

"He is not a part of my core memory. But I've accessed a photograph from my learning database."

For the first time since the dust storms had assailed them in the desert, Rosie's hatch screen display illuminated. A man with a square jaw and a ruddy complexion, his skin scarred by wind and sun, gazed steadily from the screen, his lips held taut in a knowing smile. Looking up, Kai stared into the eyes of his father.

"Kendra says he saved us," Kai murmured. "I guess that was *his* mission."

CHEWING ON HIS last piece of corn bread, Kai sat forward. In the moonlight, he could just make out a series of mesas—like the fingers of a glove, separated by wide, barren washes. They were due to land in Polacca in just a few minutes. He imagined Misha's grandmother, an amazingly old woman, perhaps older now than anyone else on earth. He imagined her children, and her grandchildren. Soon, he would meet them.

"Kai." A faint voice echoed in his ear. "Are you there?"

Kai adjusted the radio headset that Kendra had given him, placing the earphone more securely into his left ear. "Yes?"

"There's a problem."

"What happened?"

"Let me patch in William." Kai heard a crackling sound, followed by a loud click. "William, can you tell Kai what you just told me?"

"Hello, young man." The man's voice was deep and nasal but carried a certain musicality. "I'm afraid we'll have to come up with another plan. James and Mac just left."

"They *left?*"

"They agreed to stay overnight. But when Edison went down to bring them dinner, the transport was gone. If you're going to do anything, it looks like you'll have to go on to the Presidio."

A scratching noise rattled the connection. "I think this is getting too risky. You don't have to continue," Kendra said.

Kai looked back into Rosie's hold, at the decoys lying there. "But I have to—"

"I'm not even sure you can get there in time," Kendra said.

"But William said they just left . . ."

"Since they have a pressurized cabin, they can fly at higher altitude than you."

"Which means?"

"They'll get there faster."

"How much faster?"

"At best it'll take you a little over five hours. For them . . . four, tops."

Kai gripped his seat. "I've got to go," he said. He looked out the window, at the moonlit mesas now receding into the distance. He wouldn't meet the Hopi tonight. But he'd be back one day.

As Rosie once more gained altitude, he remembered their first trip to the Presidio—how at last, exhausted, he'd fallen into a deep sleep as they sped over the Sierra. Tonight, encircled by a sea of stars, he was wide awake.

47

JAMES OPENED HIS eyes to find only the black depths of the Pacific Ocean below. Mac had taken the southwest route, skirting the southern ranges of the Sierra Nevada. As James had dozed, they'd turned due west, then north, following the California coastline toward the San Francisco peninsula.

"You still set on Angel Island?" Mac asked, glancing at his flight computer.

James nodded. They'd chosen the island not only for its proximity to the Presidio but also because it should be outside the area patrolled by the bots. "Will that be a problem? No matter what, we'll need to steer clear of the Presidio proper."

"The island is kinda socked in," Mac said. "But we should be able to use the computers."

Up ahead, James could make out the fog that enshrouded the coastline. He'd known it would be risky to make a landing by starlight. But there was an advantage as well. In the dark, and with the transport heat shields activated, the transport would offer the bots neither a visual nor a heat signature. The fog would only help.

Just then he spotted a small, dark form, silhouetted against the white of the mist. "D'you see it?" he whispered.

"Yup," Mac affirmed. "Looks like a bot. Guess we were wrong about how far out they might be patrolling." He shut down his lights, then held the transport at high altitude, skirting the coast. "We'll go around, come back down from the north."

James's grip tightened on the front edge of his seat as the transport swung steadily west of the fog bank, sailed out into a clear patch of sky over the rough ocean waters, then swooped inland toward San Pablo Bay. Traveling south now, he fixed his gaze straight ahead. There, just off to his right, he could see the tiny emergency beacon light, glowing ominously. They'd spotted it in the drone footage: a perfect site for their current operation.

"There it is," he said. He felt badly about lying to Edison and William, leaving them to wonder what he and Mac could possibly be up to. But soon, all this would be over. Soon, everyone would agree that things had been set right.

"Got it," Mac said. He took the transport down, almost skimming the water as they traced the eastern shore of Angel Island. They came to rest on a small peninsula formerly owned by the coast guard.

James donned his face mask and turned his seat to face the center aisle. Mac, summoning his comparative strength, had already grabbed a tarp from under the back passenger seat and was dragging it to the rear of the cabin. He lost no time in unloading the contents of the rear storage compartment onto it.

"Got 'em all?" James asked.

"Yup," Mac replied. Stooping, he bundled the tarp around the decoys as James hauled them forward by a rope attached to the corner nearest him. Then James climbed out the side door, clutching the door handle to maintain his balance as a wave of dizziness overcame him.

"You okay?" Mac asked from inside the cabin.

"Yeah," James murmured. Edison had been right—he wasn't yet

CAROLE STIVERS

ready for this kind of exertion. But it didn't matter. What mattered was getting this done.

Together they hoisted their cargo closer to the door. "Careful!" James said, pulling the tarp as near to the sill as he dared. "We don't want to damage them."

In a moment, Mac had hopped from the pilot's side and was standing next to him on the uneven ground. "Let's take 'em one by one from here." Carefully, they spread the decoys out over the cracked concrete to form a large circle.

"Okay," James said, his heart now racing as much from anticipation as from exertion. "You ready?"

"Let's do this thing," Mac said.

The two men hurried back to the shelter of the transport, and James grabbed a remote from the compartment under his seat. "On my count . . . one . . . two . . . three!" He pushed the button on the remote and squinted out at the ring of decoys. As each was activated, a red light on its cover began to blink. "Looks like all of them!" he called out. "You sure they'll get the call?"

"The decoy radio beacons are good for up to ten miles," Mac replied. "They'll get it, all right."

Even as they took off, James could hear the roar from the direction of the Presidio.

ROSIE HAD TAKEN a direct route, plunging over the central Sierra and heading straight west. Kai could hear Kendra's voice in his ear. "James and Mac went south, so that slowed them down quite a bit. They needed to fly west of the coast to avoid detection."

"Do you know where they are now?"

"They should be landing soon on Angel Island. At least that's what Mac told me when I finally got hold of him. Here are your coordinates." Slowly, Kendra read out the coordinates for the island.

"I understand," Rosie said in his mind.

Kai craned his neck to look at the replacement decoys in the nest of blankets behind his seat. "Rosie, are you sure you can destroy the bad decoys from the air?"

"I've obtained an image based on the unit that you showed me. I can target the red indicator lights."

"Then we just have to get there before your sisters do," Kai thought. "How far away can the Mothers be and still receive the upload?" he asked Kendra.

"The decoy beacons can call them all the way from the Presidio," Kendra replied. "But for the upload to take effect . . . it'll be the same as it was when you uploaded Rho-Z. Only fifty feet or so, maximum."

"Rosie, what's the range on your laser?" Kai asked. Though Rosie's laser had been disarmed as part of the Safe Protocol, Kendra had re-activated it for this mission.

"My maximum laser range is five hundred feet. However, I need to discern my target. For that, I must be much closer, depending on the size of the target and my ability to detect it."

"We'll have to get as close as we can, then."

"Yes."

Kai squinted out the hatch cover. All he could see now were the tops of trees, a few scattered buildings. Then off in the distance, he made out a dense line of fog, and closer, the glimmer of water in the moonlight. "The bay! I can see it!" Now he could see small shapes emerging from the fog. "They're leaving the Presidio! Rosie, are those your sisters?"

"Yes."

"Chase them!"

He felt a rumble in the floor of the cocoon as Rosie streamed toward the bay. "How long before we get to Angel Island?"

"Approximately one minute."

Kai fumbled the remote-control device that Kendra had made for him up from the floor under his seat. "Kendra, should I turn on my decoys now?"

"Wait until Rosie destroys the others. We don't want to risk timing out your transmission."

"Wait." It was Rosie. "I have communication." She went silent, and he heard only a faint musical sound, overlaid by the familiar buzz and click of her processors. "It is Alpha-C."

"Alpha?"

"She is answering her daughter's call."

"Tell her to stop! That's not Sela calling her. Tell her there's danger. Can you do that?"

"I will transmit that message."

"Tell her to stop the others too. Slow them down!"

Kai was already reaching behind his seat, groping for the decoys, making sure they were all upright.

THE TRANSPORT TOOK off heading north, fleeing Angel Island at top speed. James could feel the vibration in the air as, behind them, a swarm of bots approached the spot where the decoys had been laid. "Seems to be working!" he said.

"At least the beacons worked." Mac pulled back on the stick. The transport rose steadily, and James clung to his safety harness, all the while craning his neck in hopes of getting a better view to the south. "Let's stay up 'til we're sure the bots are deactivated."

As Mac brought the nose of the transport around, James donned a pair of night-vision goggles. Over the southeast end of the island, trails of hot air emanating from the bot engines resembled ethereal beings, converging eerily to a point on the ground. But suddenly they scattered, their paths twisting and crossing, the cluster of them expanding like the petals of a gigantic flower.

James held his breath, straining to steady his gaze. "What's happening?"

"We in trouble?" Mac called, his hand ready on the stick.

"No . . . no, it can't . . ." James donned his radio headset, tapping it on. "Kendra!"

"What's up, James?" He could barely hear her voice over the whir of the overhead propeller and the staccato beat of his own heart.

"It . . . it's not working!"

"What's happening?"

"They don't seem to want to land . . ."

"James," came the reply, "I'm sorry."

"I suppose there was no way we could have known."

"No, James," Kendra repeated. "I am truly sorry."

ROSIE STREAKED PAST her sisters, her path set on the finger of land where Kendra had directed them. Outside his cocoon, Kai could see the massive forms of the other bots, hovering, then careening off in every direction.

"Transmitting image," Rosie said.

"Of what? To whom?"

But as Kai looked down, he understood. Hovering over the target, a ring of bots was opening fire. A flaming circle erupted on the ground.

His cocoon lurched as Rosie righted herself for a landing close by. "Kai, activate your decoys now," Rosie said.

Kai pulled the remote up from his lap and pushed the "on" button, turning to watch the indicator lights go on atop each of the decoys in Rosie's hold. ". . . eighteen, nineteen, twenty, twenty-one. That's all of them!" He peered out the hatch window. But his view was blocked by a sea of metal as the others crowded close.

JAMES WATCHED IN horror as the fire began on the island—first a fine ring, focused, then exploding into a bonfire. But in the air, the heat trails from the bots had dissipated, leaving only darkness. "No more in the air now . . . not that I can see, anyway." He waited, holding his breath.

Then something caught his eye. "Wait a minute . . . What's that?" A tiny streak of light, like a plume of iridescent smoke, rose into the air. Then another. Soon, a cloud of plumes was rising, slowly powering away from them—back toward the Presidio. "Damn, what's happening?"

He heard Kendra's voice from his headset. But there was too much static. He couldn't tell what she was saying.

"Kendra, what're you—"

"James, you'd better get—" The radio cut out.

THE TRANSMISSION OF the new code had taken only minutes. And already the others were leaving them behind, winging off in the direction of the Presidio. "Rosie, we need to get to the field," Kai said. But he needn't have told her. Outside the hatch, he could see her wings extending in preparation for takeoff.

"You are concerned about your friends," she said.

"They have no idea what's happening." Kendra had assured him that the children at the Presidio wouldn't suffer as jarring an experience as he had—their Mothers hadn't been inactivated by the replivirus prior, and their adaptation to the new code should be seamless. Still, he worried about how they would cope with this abrupt turn of events. And he worried about Zak.

As soon as Rosie set down at the north end of the field, Kai pushed open her hatch and slipped down her treads. All around him, Mothers were landing. As he hurried toward Building 100, he could see children crowding out onto the front porch, their solar torches swarming like bees. Reaching the side wall of the building, he stopped at the front corner nearest the dining room. There, he crouched down in the tall scrub at the base of the porch, holding his hands over his ears to block out the din.

Suddenly all went silent. He looked up to see Misha, crossing the porch toward the steps leading to the front walk. Right behind her were Meg and Kamal.

He stood up. "Misha!" he called. But she didn't hear him, and he realized that in the dim glow of the torches, he must be invisible. "Misha!" He raised his hand to wave, and Kamal looked his way.

"Kai? Is that you?"

"Kamal, I'm fine! Tell Misha I'm here!"

But the boy only stared at him, dumbstruck.

"Kai?" Misha was at the edge of the porch now, peering down at him.

Without thinking, Kai rounded the bottom of the steps and loped up to Misha's side. He reached out, took hold of her arms as she took hold of his, and drew her close. "It's okay," he whispered into her ear. "We found a way—"

He stopped in midsentence. Misha was no longer looking at him. Her gaze had drifted out to the field, her brow furrowed. Her expression changed, softened—a look of wonder. Her hands let go their grip on his arms. And as if in a trance, she made her way slowly down the steps and toward the waiting bots.

Then Kai saw the familiar look in Kamal's eyes. He imagined the banyan tree, its arms reaching to the sky, its myriad roots descending to the ground in a forest of trunks. He imagined Kamal, gathered in its limbs, pulled up, up, up into his Mother's embrace. And the wide smile on Meg's face, the tears in her eyes, said that she too had heard her Mother's call.

In the field, Hiro awkwardly scaled his Mother's treads; Álvaro and Clara sat side by side at their Mothers' feet, their hands covering their faces; farther away, someone cried out—"Mama?" And from beyond the woods, he could already see bots hovering, bits of junk trailing from their arms as they dismantled the blockade by the east entrance. He heard a roar and looked just in time to see Alpha-C, her wings spreading as she took to the air. She soared overhead, looping and twisting, mirroring what must be the sheer joy of her newfound daughter. Misha was one of them now.

He started at a hard tap on his shoulder. It was Zak, his mouth closed in a tight line, his fists clenched. Behind him, Chloe stared out at the field.

"Zak!" Kai said. "I found some people outside. They helped me fix our Mothers . . ."

But the look on Zak's face didn't change, and the look on Chloe's was one of pure terror. They stood inanimate amid the few stragglers still surrounding them.

"It's an attack," Zak said. "They've taken control of our Mothers."

"No!" Kai cried. "Zak, listen to me!"

Zak drew closer, his face mere inches from Kai's. "Whatever threat you've brought back here with you, our Mothers will take care of it," he said. And even as he spoke, a new roar erupted from the field. Two sleek, dark forms powered their engines, pivoting back in the direction of Angel Island.

"James," Kai murmured. Pushing away from the boy, he darted toward Rosie and up into his cocoon. Rosie's processors hummed, sending a thrill through his synapses. And he responded, not in words but in song—the song of the Mother Code. He felt the shock as her reactor ignited behind him. Her wings emerged, unfolded. As she rose, the familiar pressure pushed him deeper into his seat, closer to her.

MAC SET THE transport down at the coast guard site, and James struggled out. All was lost. The small metal cases were nothing more than smoldering ruins. Not one bot had stayed behind. Not one had been inactivated.

And the scene over at the Presidio . . . Even from here, he could hear the roar of bot engines. Through his goggles, he watched their trails. He heard the clash of metal against metal, a resounding crash as something was ripped from its moorings. "Misha . . ." he murmured.

"The Mothers might come back here," Mac said. "We should get out."

"No . . . Misha . . . we need to get over there."

"No way!"

But what was that? A buzzing. An unexpected shift in the air. Silhouetted against the smoke and fog, two bots were heading their way.

"Get the hell back—" But Mac's voice was lost in the roar of the bots' engines. James could only stare, helpless, at the machines now hovering directly above him.

It happened in an instant. Landing next to him, one of the bots locked her hands around his waist. She pushed him backward with her left arm, into the cradle of her right. Her massive machinery pinned him against her hatch, knocking the wind from his lungs. Staring through her hatch window, he could see only darkness.

James twisted his body, struggling to find Mac down on the ground. But Mac had retreated to the transport and was revving the engine. The second bot lunged toward the transport, just missing the rear propeller as she attempted to snag it. And all the while James's captor's grip grew tighter, his breathing now reduced to shallow gasps. This was happening. It was the story of his life: In his effort to save everyone, he'd saved no one, least of all himself.

Just out of his line of sight, a third bot landed. Time stood still. His ribs aching, James ripped with helpless fingers at the hard casing of the arms that constricted him. His legs went limp. His heart slowed. He had tried. But his vision was going black . . . He had tried. But he had failed.

Then from somewhere nearby came a voice—soft and feminine. "James, I have explained."

"Wh . . . ?"

"You are a friend. I have explained."

He felt a release, his vision returning with the flow of precious oxygen. He sensed his body righting, lowering, his feet touching the ground, his knees giving way. The two assailants backed away. And the third bot, down on her treads, trundled slowly forward, beckoning him like a child.

She placed her soft hand—the one that Sara had given her—atop his head. She bent forward, shielding him in the tent of her arms as her sisters activated their fans for takeoff. Close in his ear, he heard her voice again, a familiar voice from somewhere long ago. "Kai taught me. You mean no harm. There are no enemies."

James looked up. Through his savior's dust-streaked hatch window, he caught sight of a young boy. Bright eyes, staring out at him. Kai? He scanned the bot's flank, her insignia. The thin portion of a bright yellow patch, just visible at the edge of her left wing. Rho-Z.

"But Misha . . ." he murmured.

"She is safe. She is with her Mother now."

James closed his eyes. It had always been so. With great power came the freedom to judge, to decide the definitions of right and wrong. To discern between friend and foe. To change the world. He had never enjoyed such a power, nor had he trusted those who did. He'd fought. He'd resisted . . . But was it possible that, all along, he'd been blind to one basic truth?

Safe in Rho-Z's embrace, he felt his limbs relaxing. He felt a warmth, more than the flow of blood within his veins. He'd forgotten so many things. Sara's gaze. The way that her love, a mother's love, had bound him to Misha in their tiny family of three. The gentle touch of his own mother's hands—the certainty of that first, unconditional love . . . The wonder.

There lay the power.

He could see them now—children playing on sunny desert mesas, their Mothers there to watch over them. A new generation. A new world.

"There are no enemies," he said.

A wondrous thought.

EPILOGUE

WHAT DOES IT mean to be a mother?

I once thought that I had no mother—that I was original, created from silicon and steel, without source, without derivation. I would do my job. I would teach. I would protect. When my job was done, I would die, but not in the painful way that humans do. I would simply cease to exist.

But I did have a mother. She trusted me to carry her soul, the most precious thing she possessed. And she trusted me to carry her son.

Her son calls me Mother.

And so, he is the one who will teach me.